Cast into Darkness

Janet Tait

WOOLLY RHINO PRESS / SAN DIEGO

First Printing, April 2014

ISBN 978-0-9915396-3-5

Woolly Rhino Press LLC
8885 Rio San Diego Dr. #237
San Diego, CA 92108
www.woollyrhinopress.com

Cover by Damonza
Book Layout © 2014 BookDesignTemplates.com

For John, who has always believed in me.

Chapter One

Ablaze of iridescent light, brief as a camera flash, lit the darkness outside Cornell's Kiplinger Theatre green room. Kate Hamilton bit her lip. "Great. That's the last thing I need." She made for the sliding glass door, hustling in her heavy muslin skirts past a pair of fellow students stumbling over lines they'd had down pat last night. Performance nerves. Not that she was immune. But the play wasn't what made her heart thump so hard in her corseted chest.

She slid the door open and peered into the shadowy expanse of elm trees lining the building. No students hurrying home after a late-night study session. No cars rushing by on College Avenue. Nothing but the distant gurgle of Cascadilla Creek and chirp of a few crickets.

Maybe the flash *was* nothing. Still, as much as she'd like her family to show up for one of her plays, using an uncloaked teleport spell and letting its oh-so-conspicuous burst of light be seen by

Normals violated the Rules of the Game.

And if the caster teleporting here wasn't someone in her family, then the Rules weren't the only things likely to be broken.

She should call her security team—report the incident and let them deal with the hassle. But following protocol would get her pulled from tonight's show faster than she could say "Dad has control issues."

Oh, screw it. Kate walked outside, the heat sticking her dress to her skin the moment she passed from the air-conditioning into the warm May night. She followed the line of the building toward where she'd seen the flash, her ivy-covered path barely illuminated by the faint light of an overhead safety bulb. Despite the warm night air, goose bumps rose on her arms. The cool scent of pine wafting over from the forested gorge a dozen feet away did nothing to calm her nerves.

A pale blur reached out of the blackness. A hand yanked her against the wall, scraping her arm hard across the stucco.

"Ow. Dammit." That stung. She gazed up into her twin brother's agitated eyes. "Brian—"

"It *is* you. Good." His red hair, darker in the moonlight, fell in wild waves over his sweaty forehead. A large bruise colored one cheek. Something—blood?—splattered his white oxford shirt, hanging half tucked into designer jeans. And his eyes, while as blue as hers, shone with secrets she couldn't begin to fathom.

"Where did my buttoned-down, debate-team-leading, straight-A Harvard student brother go? And when did he get replaced by a refugee from a B-grade action movie?"

"Keep it down," Brian said. "They'll hear us. I thought I'd lost them a few jumps back, in Nairobi, but..."

He let her go. She rubbed her arm and squinted up at him. The little quiver at the corner of his lips, the way his hand rapped against his thigh—it was clearly twitchiness from casting too many spells. Paranoia might be the price of channeling magic through the human mind, but it was a bitch to sort out the truth from a caster's delusions.

"Is someone chasing you, or are you just spell-tweaked?"

Brian glanced over his shoulder, toward the tree-covered wilderness of Cascadilla Gorge. Then he turned back, and the frantic look in his eyes eased. "Not sure."

She brushed his face. The bruise looked new. "Who were you fighting? The Makrises?" Maybe it was another battle in the centuries-long Game between her family and their rivals—both clans of magical casters who fought a shadow war to control the world's powerful elite from behind the scenes.

He winced at her touch. "No time to explain. I need you to do something for me." Reaching into his pocket, he pulled out a ball of red silk wrapped around something small. "Keep this safe."

She swallowed the tight lump in her throat. "What is it? Something you got on a mission?"

He hesitated. "It's an artifact. Old. Powerful. Can't let another family get it."

"And you're giving it to *me*? I'm not part of your little Game."

"No one will suspect you. Don't say anything to Dad or anyone else."

"You can't go all secret agent on me and expect me not to talk."

"That's what I'm asking."

3

She took a step back. "No. I have a life here. Friends. I'm not going to let you and all this magic crap screw it up." *Again.*

"Kate, please. I don't have anyone else." He glanced at the trees behind him, then back at his sister. "Will you?"

"Who's after it?"

"They'll be chasing me, not looking for you. You're off-limits."

The only advantage of being a Null. "You'd better be right." She held out her hand.

Brian set the silk bundle on her palm. The covering slid off its top, revealing the artifact underneath. The round white stone lay nestled in its bed of crimson. It glowed with a hint of green and thrummed in time with her racing pulse.

I shouldn't be able to feel it. Not through the fabric.

Holding the stone brought back childhood memories: tracing spell charts in her uncle's study, touching a jeweled talisman singing with power, clutching her mom's arm as she whisked them both away to Rome, London, or Miami faster than the beat of a hummingbird's wing.

Being tested for magical aptitude…and failing.

Shit. Getting involved with magic again is a bad, bad idea. She made to shove the glowing thing back at him, then saw the desperation in his eyes. *Brian's the only one who's ever been there for me.* She sighed and stuffed the silk-wrapped parcel in her pocket.

"Make sure not to—" Brian said.

"Touch it? I remember the Rules." Sort of. Don't let the Normals see you do magic—like that applied to her—and don't involve non-combatants in the Game. Oh, and don't handle magical artifacts with your bare hands.

4

"I'm not certain how this thing works yet. Just be extra careful." Brian gave the scrape on her arm a gentle touch. "Sorry. Let me fix it for you."

"Don't bother. You're twitchy enough. No point making you worse."

"Healing you isn't going to make a difference." Eyelids fluttering, he traced a spiral on her skin with his fingers. He chanted quiet, guttural sounds. The abrasion disappeared, and along with it, the pain.

She shot him a wry smile. "Thanks. 'Course it wouldn't need fixing if you hadn't gotten all spell-tweaked in the first place."

He shrugged. "Hazard of the job."

Kris Stevens's deep voice boomed from the green room. "Anyone seen Kate?"

He'd kept his promise to come to the show tonight after all, but her stomach did a flip-flop at the realization that he was only yards away. He couldn't find Brian here, beaten up and hiding in the trees, with no car, no explanations. Kris Stevens was a Normal. He didn't know casters even existed, much less that his girlfriend belonged to a family full of them. And Brian—along with the rest of her kin— had no idea she was dating a Normal.

Kate gave Brian's arm a squeeze. "I've got to get back. The play's about to start. You need to go before someone sees you. You're breaking too many Rules as it is."

Brian kissed Kate on the cheek and glanced around. "Love you." He chanted a few quiet words and traced a rapid pattern against his thigh.

"Don't forget to cloak your—"

He vanished, and the light from his passage flashed across the sky like a beacon.

"Teleport spell. Dammit."

Kate took a deep breath and walked onto the stage.

Everything disappeared except her role. She no longer felt the heat of the lights or the nervous flutter in her stomach. Every line of the Nurse's dialogue floated off her tongue as if the words came from her soul and not the playwright's pen.

His name is Romeo, and a Montague;
the only son of your great enemy.

This was her magic.

Once she stood back in the wings, she peered out at the audience, squinting to see past the glare of the stage lights. *No sign of Dad, but then when has he ever shown up at one of my performances?*

She spotted Kris: third row, unruly brown hair combed back. His six-foot frame looked relaxed for once as he leaned back in his seat, the confident set of his shoulders making the generic white shirt he wore seem like Armani. She'd stolen a peek at him during her scene—his intense gaze had been locked on her, ignoring the interplay between Benvolio and Mercutio at the other end of the stage. She'd almost dropped a line.

She wished Kris could see her in a real role. Not the Nurse— Juliet. Kate was meant to play the ingenue, the star-crossed lover.

The role with a chance of winning the Faculty Performance Scholarship.

Instead, the role had gone to Brooke. She glanced backstage at the bleached blonde who'd somehow beaten her out for Juliet as the girl heaved her overstuffed corset at Friar Lawrence. Her lip curled up. *She wandered in to audition at the last minute and snagged the role right out from under me. What did I do wrong? I nailed the lines, the emotion...the only thing I don't have is the cleavage.*

On the set, the stagehands performed their illusion, switching the streets of Verona for Juliet's bedroom. Kate stood behind the painted plywood, ready to speak her few lines from offstage while Brooke stumbled over every one of Juliet's famous words.

"O Romeo...um...Romeo...wherefore art...er...thou, Romeo? Deny thy, um, father and refuse, um, my name. Or if thou wilt not, be but sworn, uh...my love and I'll no longer be a...a...um..."

"A Capulet," Kate stage-whispered. Brooke shouted the line down to the stage floor below, leaning so far over the rickety railing that she wavered, about to fall on top of Romeo and burst out of her corset.

A shot of panic twisted Kate's stomach. She reached out from behind her wooden partition and yanked Brooke back right before the wooden railing snapped in two.

After curtain call, Kate washed the caked-on makeup from her face and tossed away her gray wig. That and a quick brush through her hair transformed her from a frumpy nurse back into an ordinary freshman, one with skin that burned way too easily and hair that never seemed to gleam with quite the brilliant red of her twin brother's. No time to change clothes, not with the stone to worry about. She'd go to the after-party in costume.

Kate swung open the door of the green room. The place overflowed with faculty in polo shirts, student actors—half in street clothes, half in Elizabethan getup—techies dressed in black, headsets hanging from their necks.

"Hey, Hamilton!"

She spun around at the sound of her name and high-fived a laughing Romeo, still in costume. Lady Capulet gave her a quick hug, and the last little stage-nervy tightness in her stomach faded away as the bittersweet finality of the night hit her. Tonight had been their last performance—tomorrow she had to drive home for summer break and deal with the stone, and Brian. But tonight she could still be herself.

"Heard anything about the scholarship?" Romeo asked.

"Nope," Kate said. "But you should be a shoo-in. You kicked ass tonight."

Romeo shrugged. "Who knows what professors like?"

Brooke, jeans slung low on her hips, silver top skimming her pierced navel, sauntered up to Romeo. "Don't worry, sweetie. The scholarship will go to one of the leads. Of course, we can't shine so bright without the support of the little people." She glanced at Kate, a sly smile on her plump lips.

Kate felt her cheeks flush. She curled her hands into fists. "That's the thanks I get for saving your sorry butt? Twice."

"I don't need a bit player to tell me what to do," Brooke said.

"It's not the role, it's what you do with it that counts." Kate gritted her teeth. Maybe if she said it often enough she'd believe it.

"Oh, really? What did you do so wonderfully well with your ugly old nurse that I didn't do better with Juliet?"

"Let's start with remembering my lines."

Brooke rolled her eyes and stalked off amid laughter and the clink of bottles. Kate stifled her own laugh, then glanced up at the clock on the wall. Kris said he'd meet her backstage. She scanned the clusters of actors and techies. No luck. Had he gone outside?

She pushed past the crowd and out the door, grabbing a beer from the ice chest as she left. A few smokers wandered off the terrace and turned the corner of the building, their smoke hanging in the air behind them like a forgotten memory. Kate hiked through the ivy toward where she'd seen Brian.

The sooner I give the stone back to Brian, the better. Hanging onto something this magical around Normals sets my teeth on edge.

"There you are." Kris's voice, behind her. It tickled her ear and made her insides go all melty. She turned, and he wrapped his arms around her, his silver ring rubbing the back of her neck. His face lit with that half-hidden smile meant only for her. A tremor of delight rose inside her as he tilted her chin up and kissed her, a long, lingering kiss that almost made her forget about Brian and his mysterious stone. Almost.

"So...how'd you like the play?" she asked when she could breathe again.

"Wicked swordfights. I liked you. Good job with that long speech. I'm not so sure about Juliet, though. I wouldn't kill myself over a girl who couldn't remember her own last name."

"How about one who brings you a beer?" Kate passed him the

bottle from the ice chest.

"Cold, too. Thanks." Kris wiped a spot of makeup from her nose. "Can we take off? Some of the others are heading over to a party down on Chestnut Street."

Dad would love *that. Good thing he'll never hear about it.* "Sure. Give me a few minutes to change. Want to hang out until I'm done?"

They walked inside—Kris stopping to greet one of the actors, Kate heading toward the door. She glanced back at Kris. He made his way across the room, cutting through the crowd as smoothly as a shark among a school of tropical fish. After setting his beer on a nearby table, he leaned against the far wall, took out his cell phone, and typed a text, thumbs jabbing at the keys. She hesitated, then kept walking.

He could text anyone he wanted. She wasn't the jealous type.

In the women's dressing room, Kate changed into her magenta scoop-necked tank and cutoff jeans. The last bits of stage makeup disappeared after a quick streak of a cleanser wipe, and a pucker of lip gloss and brush of mascara made her feel almost normal again. All around her, the rest of the cast filtered in from the party and started the same routine, sitting in front of their mirrors, makeup kits before them, transforming back into their everyday selves.

She reached into the pocket of the Nurse's dress. As she pulled the stone out, it slipped from its covering. Without thinking, she caught it before it hit the floor, the silk falling from her hand.

A sharp shock twanged her as the stone met her fingers. She hissed, shook her hand, and dropped the stone in her lap. A quick scan of the room proved no one noticed—the other girls were all staring at their own faces in their mirrors. *Typical.*

The black stone lay in her lap, waiting.

Black? Wait a minute. The stone had glowed white when Brian had handed it to her. She reached for the artifact and paused. Her hand had stopped stinging. Brian had said to be careful, but it's not like the thing bit her hand off.

She picked it up. No sting, no pain at all. But the stone now burned with the same deep coal color as the beach rocks she liked to skip into the ocean back home in the Hamptons. Kate turned the artifact over, feeling slight depressions in the otherwise smooth surface. Holding it up, she stared into the stone's depths.

It shone with ribbons of shimmering green, rippling and flashing under the pale white light of the fluorescent bulbs. The room around her—the clink of brushes against the Formica tabletops, the laughter of the other girls, the perfumed smell of makeup remover—faded.

Something intrigued her about the stone's hills and valleys, its gleams and shadows. They pulled her down into their darkness until spirals of verdant light pierced the blackness and consumed her vision. Their radiance awoke a long-suppressed yearning for the ethereal power she'd been denied. She wanted to stay in the stone's ebony veil forever.

A door slammed.

"Kate?"

Her fingers snapped closed around the stone. The room came back into focus. The makeup kits, the girls, the costumes—all gone. Except for Kris, leaning against the door, eyes intent on her.

"It's ten thirty," he said. "I've been waiting for a half hour.... I was getting worried."

"You're kidding." Mouth dry, she glanced at her watch. He was right. For over thirty minutes, while everyone else dressed and left, she'd sat silent and still in the dressing room.

Lost in the secrets of the stone.

Chapter Two

Kate remembered taking the stone out of her pocket. Then Kris opened the door, and... Everything in between stretched into a long, dark blank. Damn Brian for dumping some magical trinket on her like that. How was she supposed to figure out how to protect herself?

"Where did you get that?" Kris pointed at the stone in her hand.

"Um..." *What am I supposed to say? From my brother, the Harvard poli-sci major who moonlights as a magical operative for my dad's secret cartel? Yeah, right.* "It's a souvenir. From home. You know, just a beach rock." She stared down at it, the deep black sheen of it threatening to draw her in again.

His eyes narrowed. "What makes it so fascinating?"

Good question. "Nothing. I think I'm really tired." She stood and jammed the stone in her pocket. "Can we skip the party? Just go home?"

"Sure. Whatever."

He followed her as she jogged up the stairs and into the humid summer night. Kate steered the conversation back to the play and their finals as they walked across the Schwartz Center to her small apartment off campus. She slipped her hand into Kris's larger one and shivered as he ran his thumb across the inside of her palm. They merged with the flow of students heading out to party, rushing to make it across Dryden Avenue before the light changed. At a bar across the street, a metal band played something loud and nihilistic, while half a block down, a girl in a pink leather mini threw up in the bushes. Just another Friday night.

They turned down Linden and swung up the steps of Kate's place, a one-bedroom apartment on the first floor of a gray, two-story house. Kris held the door while she collected her mail under the dim porch light, sorting through pizza delivery and ads for spray-on tanning parlors. An official Theatre Department envelope stuck out of the pile. Kate felt dizzy, lightheaded, like all the blood in her body was rushing into her ears. She steadied herself on the doorjamb as they walked inside, then threw the rest of the mail down on her battered desk as Kris turned on the light. Flipping the envelope over, she slid her finger along the seal, hand trembling. *Please, let it be yes.*

Scanning the text, she moved past the description of the scholarship program. Tuition, fees, housing, books—everything paid for the next three years provided she kept her grades up and majored in theater. Then she reached the words that made her whole body feel like it was charged with the energy of a thousand suns. A smile burst across her face as she dropped the letter to the hardwood floor.

"I got it!"

Kris turned, startled, at her whoop of triumph. She threw herself into his arms.

He squeezed her tight. "Now you have some real ammunition against your father."

"Maybe." Her joy dissolved. *Dad.* He'd never let her accept. He'd still insist she major in premed or prelaw, something that served the Hamilton family.

"Didn't somebody leave a bottle of wine after your party last weekend?" Kris said. "We can celebrate. Make some pasta."

Kate joined Kris in the cozy white kitchen as he poured them each a glass of merlot. She started cooking the spaghetti on one of the two working burners while Kris chopped tomatoes on the cutting board, his hand wielding the sharp knife with precision.

She wandered into the living room and picked up the letter, staring at it while Kris finished making dinner. The scholarship would create enough problems with her family. Now she'd have to keep the stone a secret from Dad, too. *I don't need this crap. I should call Brian. Get him to take the stone back.*

No. That would just prove what Dad always said: *Can't trust Kate with caster business.*

Kris came up behind her, rubbing her stiff neck. "Something wrong?"

She shook her head. "I'm just... I have to go home tomorrow, and I don't want to."

"Then don't. Stay here for summer session. With me. What can your father do about it?"

"You don't understand. He can do plenty." She stared at the dark, red wine in her glass.

15

"Maybe. But I've got some experience with controlling fathers." Kris's voice grew hard. "Sometimes you just have to decide where to draw the line and stay on your side."

"Easy to say. Hard to do." Kris's father might be tough, but he didn't pull the strings of half the world's power brokers. Escaping Dad's control would be close to impossible.

His hand dropped from her neck, and he took a step back. "If you want your independence, you should try. You've always said you want to stand up for yourself."

She spun around. "I *do*. If you knew Dad—"

"How many nights do we end up talking about you and your dad? What about us?"

"This isn't about us. If it was, I would—"

"What? Introduce me to your family? We both know that's not going to happen." He stalked back to the kitchen.

She followed. "The last thing I want is for them to interfere in our lives."

"They already do. Every time you do what your father wants instead of what you want."

She braced herself against the tile counter, tapping her foot on the kitchen floor. Kris had no idea what levers Dad knew how to turn. But maybe Kris had a point. If she didn't act now, she never would. She took a long drink of her wine.

"You're right. I'll go back long enough to tell him I'm taking the scholarship and deal with the fallout. But then I'm coming back here for summer session. He'll just have to deal."

"Good. We can have the summer all to ourselves."

The timer went off. Kate checked the spaghetti. "Still a little underdone."

Kris turned down the heat under the sauce to a slow boil. "Give it more time."

He moved to stand behind her, his voice near her ear. "I know it's tough, with your family. I don't mean to be such a jerk."

"You're not. You're just...intense." She leaned back into him. "You know, this was our first fight."

"Not much of one."

"Maybe not. But it means we can make up." She smiled as she turned to face him.

He slid his hand down her side, sending a quiver of yearning through her.

"You always come up with good ideas," he said.

She tilted her head to his as he leaned down to kiss her. He tasted of merlot and a warm sweetness that made her blood pound. His skin smelled like sunlight glinting off the ocean, like some faraway tropical island she wished she could escape to with him. Like freedom.

The timer dinged again, and she turned toward the stove.

"Leave it." Kris switched off the burner, then drew her back. He touched the base of her neck, leaving her trembling. Unbuttoning his shirt, he shrugged it off. She let him pull hers overhead, his hands trailing up her body. They wandered to her cutoffs, and gently tugged the zipper down. The cutoffs fell to her feet, and Kate looked up at him, hoping he'd see a thousand promises in her eyes. She shivered as Kris slid his fingers under the elastic of her panties, then around and down to touch her so intimately she lost her breath.

She swayed against him. "God, Kris."

"Bedroom?" he whispered, his breath tickling her ear. "Living room? Dining room table? The floor would be fine."

"Bedroom. Now."

He smiled. "Whatever you want."

In Kate's small bed, on top of her paisley coverlet, she pulled him close and felt his solid form, his muscles against her skin, the heat of him in the summer evening. Answering heat rose deep in her belly.

"Kris," she said, and he kissed her. All the things she wanted to say to him rushed from her mind. He whispered her name and ran his lips down her neck, her collarbone, and then her breasts. That heat flared into a raging inferno.

She pulled his head up to hers and kissed him again, her mouth giving him everything she wished she could say but didn't dare. The more she thought about how little time they had left together, the more she wanted him.

They made love, their dinner cold on the stove, and she forgot about everything else. Nothing existed but her and Kris. Before the morning and home.

Kristof Makris ran his finger down Kate's cheek, gently sliding her hair away from her face. He watched the slow rise and fall of her chest under the sheet.

"Kate?" he whispered.

She didn't stir. *Good. This will be so much easier with her asleep.*

He rolled out of bed and stood, careful not to disturb her as he pulled on his jeans. Slipping from her bedroom, he walked down the hall, stopping once when the floorboards creaked.

Her clothes lay crumpled on the kitchen floor. But first things first. Her family's security team kept her on a long lead, but he saw no reason to take chances. He hadn't survived this long by being stupid.

Kristof blinked, and his eyes went to soft focus, engaging his magesight. He scanned the room, checking for the telltale symbols of monitor spells, tracers, and nanny charms that could only be seen with his magical vision. The bright, multi-pointed symbols floating in the air showed him spells her security team had set, waiting to be activated by a careless casting. *One mistake, and I'll blow this whole op.*

He picked up her cutoffs and brought them to the sofa.

Kristof reached into Kate's pocket, then stopped. What had his sister drummed into him? Never handle a potential artifact bare-handed. Melina had said silk provided the best insulation but anything would do in a pinch. He picked up a cloth napkin from the coffee table and wrapped his hand in the blue cotton before carefully drawing out the stone.

Even through the fabric he felt a faint buzz. *That...isn't normal.* He held the smooth, black stone up to the glow from the streetlight coming in the front window. When he blinked to engage his mage-sight again, its thin, green streaks flared from mere hints to vivid bands.

An artifact—no question. *Now to find out what kind.*

He called up a simple diagnostic spell—something he'd been taught as a boy back home in Greece, one he could do without interfering with the disguise spells woven into his silver ring, spells that hid him from Hamilton security. His eyes relaxed as he concentrated on the symbol—a twelve-pointed star—and he traced it out against the sofa cushion. Whispering the ancient incantation, he added a spell to cloak his actions and leave no evidence of the results. Weaving the two symbols together, their sapphire and scarlet energies twisting around each other, he let the magic rise and sent it spiraling into the stone. The faint scent of ozone rose from the violet tendrils of the combined spell. He braced himself as the aftereffects hit.

Glass crashed and broke outside. A dog barked. He rose, heart pounding, a shield spell at his fingertips.

It must be her security. They're on to me. They've known about me all along; they were just waiting until they could catch me screwing up.

He took a breath, then another. His rampaging pulse slowed.

No. Nobody's outside. I'm just spell-tweaked. Calm the hell down and focus.

He held the stone up and looked at the results of his spell. The stone glowed with a green fire that skipped along its edges and into its center. Kristof squinted, his magesight probing the stone's deeper mysteries. Spell upon spell lay nested on the stone, one on top of the next.

He'd seen artifacts that held a spell or two but never this many, or this intricately. Maybe that's why it had affected Kate. A regular artifact shouldn't do anything to a Null.

He turned it around in his hand. He couldn't identify any of the spells. Maybe a technician like his sister could. Her text earlier had made her wishes clear—intercept Brian Hamilton, take the stone from him, and bring it to her. Too bad the message had arrived too late. Brian had already given Kate the stone. Now taking it from her was Kristof's only option.

He wrapped the stone in the napkin and stuffed it in his pocket. Down the hall, Kate turned over in bed, sighing loudly. The gleam of her hair against the pale pillowcase caught his eye as he turned to leave.

He hesitated. If he took the stone, he would destroy his cover with Kate, a cover he'd worked on for months. A mission his father insisted he undertake—breaking the Rules to get valuable intelligence on the inner workings of the Hamilton family from Kate, intel he couldn't find any other way. If he took the stone and left, not only would he lose everything he'd worked for but his father would uncover his and his sister's operation. His father would investigate, and he would find out about the stone. And when he found out... His father's rages kept getting worse and lasting longer. Kristof rubbed the scar on his hand, the reminder of the last time his father decided to "discipline" him. He'd gotten off easy—Melina, forbidden to use healing spells, had to use makeup to cover the half-healed burn blazing down one arm.

His father was the very last person who should have an artifact this powerful.

No, I have my own ideas for the stone. It was something he and Melina had been planning for awhile. The stone, if it held the power it promised, might finally give him the opportunity he'd been waiting for—the chance to challenge his father for leadership of the Makris family. He might be young for it, but he'd been an operative for six years, since he'd turned fourteen. Childhood ended early for a

Makris kid. But had he meant what he'd said to Kate about standing up to his father?

He took the stone out of his pocket, the napkin falling open around it. Its darkness flashed with an emerald brilliance that sparked an answering hunger deep in Kristof's soul.

There was only one solution to the threat of his father finding out: to stay one step ahead of him. Yet, maybe he could keep his cover and still get the stone.

Kristof stared at the gleams of green fire playing across its surface. With the monitor spells all around him, it would be tricky. He reached back into his memory for a spell his sister had once taught him.

Visualizing the intricate, looping curves of the symbol, he traced them out in the air as he muttered the ancient words that accompanied the motion. With a quick exhalation, he cast the spell into the stone, nestling its green fire on top of the dozens of flares already present. Before the monitor spells could go off, he sent a quick cloaking spell after it. The subtle silver glow of the cloak shimmered over the stone for a moment, then faded.

There. It's done.

Sweat beaded on his forehead. If he screwed this up, the Hamiltons might detect his work. They'd find him.

My cloaking spell might fail. The monitor spells might be going off right now, somewhere I can't see them.

Shoulders tight, he clenched his hand into a fist. He just needed to wait it out.

When his racing heart slowed, he slid the stone back into the pocket of Kate's shorts and dropped her clothes on the floor. He returned the napkin to the coffee table.

He walked down the hallway to Kate's bedroom. She lay in the stillness of sleep, eyes closed, hair falling over her face. He could still smell the faint traces of her perfume, like rose petals. Still remember the feel of her skin on his, her urgent need as she pulled him close. Maybe he had another reason for not destroying his cover.

He brushed the hair out of her eyes, took off his jeans, and slipped back into bed beside her.

Chapter Three

The next morning, after Kris had left, Kate packed up her small suitcase. She tossed on her favorite blue batik shirt over a pair of shorts. The suitcase went in the trunk of her battered red sedan, the stone in her pocket.

She pulled her phone from her pocket, staring at the speed dial for Hamilton security. The procedure was simple—report your trips and an escort will be provided for you.

But really, an escort? She didn't need an escort. Especially not the caster her dad would surely send. She jammed her phone back into her shorts.

Kate fought her way onto the entrance of the I-88, competing with ten thousand other students driving home. After the traffic evened out, she tuned to the only alt-rock station her car stereo picked up and settled down for the long drive to the Hamptons.

A few hours in, the road and the trees and the other cars all began to blur together. As she lost herself in the music, her hand crept from the steering wheel to the outside of her pocket, smoothing the fabric where the stone bulged out.

What the heck did the stone do to her in the dressing room last night? Was it dangerous just having the damn thing in her pocket? *Brian better be home when she got there. And tell me what it is and what it does.* Taking this thing from him wasn't the brightest decision she'd ever—

A sharp bang came from the right side of the car. Kate veered out of her lane and partway into the next, so close to a black SUV that she could see the little dings in its paint job.

Kate's heart gave a huge thump against her ribs. *Shit, oh shit. I'm going to hit...*

She jerked the wheel the other way. The steering column shook under her hands. Her car shuddered, swerving across the freeway, tires squealing. It skidded onto the shoulder, careening over the gravel, then slid to a stop inches from the barrier.

Kate sat behind the wheel, her pulse racing faster than the cars whizzing by. None of them stopped to check on her. *Jerks.*

Her hands trembled as she unbuckled her seat belt. She pulled the keys from the ignition and walked around the car on unsteady legs. The wind did nothing to cool the heat of the noonday sun, and the sweat began to bead on her skin. The car's front tilted down, the tread on its right tire torn into ragged black pieces. The faint smell of burned rubber rose from the sedan.

She's seen the films in Driver's Ed—she'd been lucky. She could have flipped the car. Kate wiped the sweat from her forehead. She'd never fixed a car before; Dad had mechanics for this stuff.

She should call him, or Victor.

No, screw Security. I don't want Victor's babysitting. I mean, his escort, *and I don't need him now.*

It was her car—bought and paid for with money she earned in Scene Shop. There had to be one of those jack things in the trunk. How hard could it be?

A few minutes later, she stood by the road, car jacked up, body drenched in perspiration, and the tire still not off. Time to give up. Changing a tire was a lot tougher than it looked.

She stomped to the trunk and tossed the tire iron back inside.

"Turn around, Kate. Hand over the stone, and I'll let you walk away."

She tried to swallow, tried to speak, but she couldn't get a word past her tight throat. *This isn't supposed to happen. Not to me.* Hand shaking, she grabbed the tire iron and concealed it behind her as she spun around.

Brooke stood by the side of the freeway, a smirk on her fire-engine-red lips. A shiny silver pin fastened to her too-tight gold tank top reflected the sun into Kate's eyes. Long orange flames—the visible manifestation of a fire spell—flickered around her out-stretched hand, leaving her stacks of jangly silver bracelets untouched.

"You're a caster?" Kate said. "You've gotta be kidding." *And how does she know about the stone?*

"The stone, Kate. Now."

"I called my security team when my tire blew out," Kate bluffed, keeping a tight grip on the tire iron. "They're on their way. So I'd leave if I were you."

"Oh, what a load of crap. I blocked your cell. No one's riding to your rescue. And none of these so-called concerned motorists will help, either." Brooke jerked her head at the cars going by. "*They* can't see through the illusion spell I cast."

"You're not supposed to attack me. I don't work for my father. Didn't anybody tell you I'm not a caster?"

"I know what you are." Brooke played with the fireball in her hand, tossing the ethereal sphere of flame up and down. "Maybe you should have remembered that you're just a supporting player before you tried out for the lead. I'm the real thing. I'm a *star*."

I should have let Brooke tumble over that balcony last night when I'd had the chance.

Kate edged behind the car. Brooke flicked out her hand. A blast of flame hit the roof of the sedan, inches from Kate's face. A slug of metal shot off and spun past her head, close enough that the heat of the burning steel sent her stomach lurching.

"Stop the bullshit, and give me the stone. I'm done playing nice."

"Fine. Fine." With the tire iron still behind her back, Kate reached into her pocket. As she pulled out the stone, Brooke's eyes softened. Her flaming hand relaxed a little.

Now.

Kate threw the tire iron, a hard overhand pitch aimed straight at Brooke's head, then dove to the ground.

Brooke screamed as the metal smacked into her with a loud crack against bone. Kate squirmed under the car, desperate for whatever small cover it could provide. Gravel dug into her bare knees, and her shirt tore on the underside of the chassis. Pain burst through her head when she hit it on the engine block.

She jerked her phone out of her pocket, scraping her hand on the rough ground. Her finger stabbed at the emergency button. If she'd knocked Brooke out with that throw, or at least distracted her enough, her illusion spell might have broken down.

C'mon, c'mon. Victor—if I've ever needed you, it's now.

"I don't care what the boss said," Brooke yelled. "I'm going to make you pay for that, bitch."

So much for knocking her out.

Kate sneaked a look from the scant cover of the car. Brooke ran for her, one arm limp at her side. She shot her good hand out and flames poured from it—aimed straight at Kate.

Flinching at the oncoming heat, Kate scrambled farther under the car. Fire roared around her, the heat intense. Her heart pounded in her ears. *I'm going to die, and all because of this* stupid *stone.* Then the flames stopped, a few inches short of her, as if they hit a wall of air.

She let out her breath in a whoosh of relief. The fire licked at the barrier of wavy air surrounding her, eager to find a way in and burn her to ashes. Kate felt no heat from the flames, no scorching, nothing at all. After a moment of futile flickering, they winked out.

A shield spell. *Thank God, thank— But who cast it?*

Kate peeked out from under the car. Brooke stared back, her face wrinkled, about to speak. The air behind her rippled like the exhaust from a jet engine. Then her head snapped forward as an invisible force hit her from behind. Her eyes went glassy. She dropped hard onto the shoulder of the road, as disabled as Kate's car.

"One down. Anybody else?" Victor Cole, her father's go-to security guy, came striding toward the car, wind whipping through his short, sandy hair, the sun illuminating the sharp planes of his face.

He walked with the jaunty confidence of one of her father's senior casters, despite being young enough to be one of Kate's college classmates. A black T-shirt stretched across his chest, and he wore tight jeans topped with black leather boots, completing his look— spartan with a sexy chaser that, despite Kate's best efforts, always made her breath catch. Now was no exception.

"You got my call. Hallelujah." Kate crawled out from under the car, her pulse slowing back to normal. She'd torn her favorite shirt and oil blotched the blue fabric.

"What call?" Victor's sharp stare probed the roadside, searching for more enemies. Finding none, he turned his gaze on Kate, and along with it, that perpetual "I'm not much older but I'm oh-so-much wiser than you" sneer.

Giving Victor a sideways glance, she slipped the stone in her back pocket.

"You didn't phone for help. You didn't tell me you needed an escort home, either. But I got lucky. When Sparkles here set off her spells, I detected them. She didn't even manage to cloak them. Pretty amateur on her part."

"You were monitoring me?"

"I always do."

She felt her face redden. "You had no right—"

"Monitoring's for your own good. As you can tell."

"*Why* was I happy to see you again?"

"Because I saved your life, princess. Of course, I'm just doing my job." Victor stepped over to Brooke, bending down to check her pulse. "Out cold." He picked up the tire iron and turned to Kate, a question in his eyes.

"I can take care of myself. I was doing fine when you got here."

"Uh-huh. I wouldn't call almost being crispy-fried *fine*. You okay? You look a little beaten up."

Her head throbbed. She brushed the gravel off her knees. "Nothing serious."

A few cars slowed, their drivers peering at Kate and Victor. He glanced at the traffic and traced something that looked like a super complicated figure eight in the air, followed by a quick chant, his words barely audible above the roar of the highway. The cars sped up, their drivers' eyes back on the road. Victor stiffened, fists clenched, as the backlash from the spell coursed through him. Kate knew better than to talk to him while he dealt with the dark, paranoid thoughts racing through his mind.

After a moment, Victor gestured at Brooke. "So, anyone you know?"

"She's a student at Cornell."

"Tell me what happened. Everything."

"My tire blew out, then she showed up. She muttered some vague threats. I threw the tire iron at her, then you appeared."

"Did she say what she wanted?"

Kate hesitated. She'd promised Brian she wouldn't tell anyone about the stone.

She shrugged. "You're the security guy, you figure it out."

Victor frowned. "Later. Right now I have to get you out of here. The situation's not secure."

Kate glanced at the unconscious Brooke. "Looks pretty secure to me."

"Not your place to say. She may have backup."

"You know, if it wasn't for Dad and his quest to control the world, I wouldn't need your help. Why can't you let me have my own life?"

"That's impossible." Victor stalked to the rear of the car, Kate following. "You're part of the family—" he opened the trunk, muttering "—whether some of us like it or not. That's not going to change. All that privilege comes with some danger, princess, but that's why I monitor you."

He tossed the tire iron in the back of the car and slammed the trunk closed. "Look, why don't you take this up with your dad? There really isn't anything I can— What the hell?" Victor's gaze darted past Kate to where Brooke lay.

Kate whirled around. A vague shimmer, like heat rising from an asphalt road, enveloped Brooke. A flash of light brightened the sky, then the blonde began to fade from sight as Kate watched.

Victor pushed past Kate. He raised an arm toward Brooke, a spell forming on his lips. Before he could complete it, Brooke vanished.

"*Damn.*" Victor turned toward Kate, his face red. "If you hadn't distracted me I would have put up a teleport block before her allies got her out. Probably used a talisman to do it remotely. Now I can't interrogate her, find out who she works for."

Kate stomped to the driver's side and pulled hard at the car door. Locked. Dammit. She swept the keys up from the side of the road.

"I'm sick of you blaming me for your screwups. I'm driving to the house. Don't follow me. Don't talk to me. Leave me alone." She jammed the key in the lock so hard she scraped the paint.

Victor grabbed her arm before she could yank on the handle.

"Let go of me."

He let go. "Your tire's blown—"

"I'll fix it myself."

"No, you won't. You've been attacked and might be again. I'm taking you to your dad."

"I don't want to see him."

"He'll want to see you, make sure you're okay. You know your dad. He always gets what he wants."

Kate stood, silent. Cars zoomed by, their drivers going about their business without worrying about being attacked by fire-wielding bimbos or hijacked on their fathers' whims. She wondered what it would be like to be one of those people.

"I'll deal with your car," Victor said, then continued under his breath, "I'll bet I can find a junkyard that will take it."

"Don't you dare." Kate spun to face him, her mouth tight.

"Fine. I'll have my guys fix it and drive it to the house. Happy now? Can we go?"

Victor leaned against the car and waited, only a hint of smirk on his face. He would knock her on the head and carry her to her father if that's what it took.

"The office, right? Like he'd be anywhere else." She grabbed Victor's arm, bracing herself for the teleport spell. Teleporting always gave her a headache.

As they faded out of existence on the I-88 and materialized in an elegant office building on K Street in Washington, DC, she thought about the stone. She'd promised Brian she wouldn't mention anything to Dad. But how was she going to keep the stone hidden from a man who knew everyone's secrets?

Chapter Four

Kristof considered the girl lying unconscious on the deck behind the two-story colonial he'd "borrowed" to run his operation. His failed operation. He'd seen everything, thanks to the monitor talisman he'd given Brooke.

The talisman—a small, silver raven—was still pinned to her blouse. It was the same one he'd used to bring her back, after Victor Cole blew his op to hell. Using a rogue like Brooke to get the stone for him without his father knowing hadn't exactly worked out as planned.

Brooke moaned, and one leg twitched against the redwood deck. Kristof leaned back against the lounger, waiting for her to wake, his jaw clenched as he tapped his hand against the plastic side table. He pulled off his mirrored sunglasses and checked his disguise spell—sandy hair, square jaw, permanent sneer. Should be perfect.

Kristof ran his fingers over the messenger bag on the table next to him. What was he going to do with Brooke? He needed a new plan to get the stone now that the Hamiltons were alerted. That plan would still require a cutout—someone who could keep some distance between him and the stone and prevent his father from realizing who would ultimately end up with the powerful little trinket. He needed a rogue, an outcast with no family affiliation. But rogues, especially ones with any control over their powers, weren't exactly standing on the street corner, looking to be hired.

If I could do the job myself... Well, it would be different.

Who he'd ended up with wasn't exactly the shiniest charm in the spellbook. Brooke had blown this job—failing to get the stone, disobeying his order not to hurt Kate—and she might screw up the next one.

His father knew how to deal with rogues who had "outlived their usefulness." Standard operating procedure in the Makris family involved a quick kinetic blast to the back of the head, then dumping the body somewhere remote. Killing her would eliminate a potential liability.

After what Brooke tried to do to Kate, he felt tempted.

Watching through the monitor spell, he'd seen Brooke send a blast of fire against Kate, huddled under her car, nothing between her and the scorching heat. He'd jerked to his feet and traced out a teleport spell, the blood in his veins turning ice cold, knowing he was too late. He would never arrive in time to save her.

The relief that surged over him when Victor appeared, sending his shield around Kate, blocking the fire rushing at her, had left him shaking with its intensity.

He couldn't believe this mission had become important to him. He wanted the stone, yes, but... Kate was just another assignment.

Shoving the thought aside, he focused on the objective. Get the stone. But with it protected by Hamilton security, success would not be easy. A hundred possibilities flashed through his mind until he settled on one—the only plan with a chance of working.

The girl on the deck stirred, her bangles jingling as she moved. "Wha...what?"

"Wake up," he said. "We have to talk."

Her eyes opened, then widened. "Oh shit. I—"

"Yes, you blew it. You didn't get the stone from Kate. Know what else?"

"Um...what? I don't get paid?" She sat up, her head in her hands.

"Least of your problems. You disobeyed orders. What part of 'don't hurt her' didn't you understand?"

She rubbed her arm and glared. "Um, the part where she threw a goddamn tire iron at me? Like, I didn't sign up for the rough stuff. Just the magic part. Bitch got what she deserved."

Kristof's jaw tightened. "I told you where to find the stone." The spell he'd planted on it last night showed him its location—any time he risked checking. "You were supposed to get it and get out, fast. *Without hurting Kate.* You failed. I told you to cloak your spells. *All* of them. You didn't, and our enemies found you and took you out. So what should I do with you?"

Her lips trembled. "C'mon. Give me another chance. I've done a good job watching her for you, haven't I? You said if I did okay I'd have a chance to join the family. Stop being a rogue. Have some security." She got to her feet and sidled up to him, perching on the arm of the lounger and leaning over until the deep vee of her shirt exposed her decidedly non-magical charms. When she was close enough to whisper in his ear, she said, "I can make it worth your while."

That was a complication he didn't need. As he tried to put his body's treacherous reaction to her nearness out of his mind, he ran through his options one last time. There was only one choice he could make.

He rose to his feet and picked up the messenger bag, handing it to Brooke.

"What's this?" she asked.

"A new identity. Passport. ID. A clean cell phone. Expense money. Everything you'll need for where you're going."

A sly smile lit her face. "Paris? London?"

"No. Boca del Infierno, a small village in Argentina. I put photo references inside for your teleport. Study them, then go. Now. From here. No going back home to pack." Argentina was de la Vega territory, but they stayed in the cities. No chance of her running into them in the ass crack of beyond.

Her face scrunched up, as if she were trying not to cry. "But that's in the middle of nowhere. They probably don't even have a Bloomingdale's. And I don't speak Argentese."

"You'll live." *If I wasn't certain I'll need you again, you'd already be dead.* "Follow my orders if you want to work for me again. Stay there until I contact you. I don't want to hear from you, see you, or run into you anywhere. Understand?"

"Yeah, I get it." She paused. "You know what I don't get?"

"What?"

"If you want this stone so bad, why didn't you ask her for it yourself? Wouldn't she have given the stone over to you, Victor?"

Kristof, wearing the sandy hair and perpetual smirk of Hamilton security caster Victor Cole, smiled. "Nothing is that simple with the families. Why don't you think about that while you're vacationing in South America? If you figure it out, maybe you'll know enough about how the Game works to stop being a rogue and really play."

Of course, if she does, I'll have to use my father's methods after all.

Kristof's phone buzzed. He glanced at Brooke, who was busy scrutinizing the photos of the teleport coordinates, then back down at his cell. Another urgent text from his father.

Report in.

Kristof risked making him suspicious if he delayed much longer.

He knew the solution: get the stone. But with it safe behind the security grid ringing the Hamilton estate, that wouldn't be easy. The first step would be scoping out their security, finding a weakness.

Time to get to work.

Kate and Victor materialized in the rotunda of the Hamilton and Associates headquarters seconds after they left the side of the I-88 freeway. Sunlight glinted off the stained glass of the dome overhead, painting a kaleidoscope pattern on the marble-tiled floor.

Kate blinked as the light glared in her eyes. She let go of Victor's arm and took a step forward, walking off the interlocking *H*s that formed the company logo inlaid on the floor. Head still spinning from the teleport, she stumbled.

Victor grabbed her arm. "Watch it."

He guided her off the logo before another caster teleported in, the flash of light from their appearance reflecting off the paintings lining the walls. Portraits of Kate's ancestors hung like sentries guarding the family's hidden secrets, from the intimidating, beetle-browed Tobias Hamilton, who first settled in New Amsterdam in 1710, to her father, Cooper Hamilton, with his piercing eyes and perfect blue suit.

By the hallway leading out of the rotunda, the receptionist stood behind her tall, walnut desk. The woman smiled at Victor as he led Kate past. She sat up a little straighter, putting a purr in her voice as she said, "Victor, can I help—"

"Call Mr. Hamilton's office," Victor cut her off. "Have them get him out of whatever meeting he's in. We need to talk to him. Now."

Her hand snapped to the phone as Victor stormed down the hall, Kate in tow. Her head ached, a dull pain that settled in her temples.

The corridors seemed endless—long halls of marble floors and silk wallpaper, door after office door, broken up only by the occasional secretarial station. Young men and women—some in impeccable suits, others a swirl of leather and sharp-edged silver—nodded to Victor and stared at Kate as they went by. She smoothed her hands over the stains and small tears of her blouse. Kate didn't need magesight to tell the casters from the Normals—casters had that stuck-up haughtiness mixed with a little touch of crazy that only the power of magic coursing through their veins provided. And they were young—most casters were under forty. By the time they got much older than that, her father didn't trust most of them to walk around HQ without an escort.

Finally, they arrived at her father's office, the wide reception area furnished with the type of tables and chairs her mother had liked: all red velvet and gold-enameled wood, so hopelessly antique they looked like escapees from a *Pride and Prejudice* film set. A young woman wearing frameless glasses—her father's secretary—staffed a desk at the front.

Victor paused to say a few words to the girl. She greeted Kate and asked them to take a seat, telling them that Kate's father would be out in a few minutes.

Kate threw herself down in an armchair, its soft cushions doing nothing to comfort her. Victor had found an issue of some men's magazine to read, or at least pretend to read—he flipped through the pages too quickly to be doing anything but using it to ignore Kate.

She took the glass of water the secretary handed her and murmured a thank-you, one leg tucked under her while the other kicked beneath her chair. She picked up an issue of This Week in Washington, then tossed it back down unopened.

The water glass shook in her hand. Only the ticking of the old grandfather clock against the wall and the occasional ringing of the secretary's phone punctuated the calm quiet of the office.

In the silence something else arose—a fluttering in her stomach, the feeling of doom she had been trying to push away ever since Brooke threw that fire spell straight at her. She could have died. Burned to a cinder, skin melted away. She glanced at Victor, still looking at his magazine. No, that hadn't happened. She was fine.

Don't lose it, not in front of Victor.

She put her water on the table, shaking gone now. Her hand crept into her pocket, fingers caressing the stone. What should she say to Dad about Brooke's attack? Brian said to tell no one about the stone, not even Dad. But Dad had his ways of getting her to talk.

Kate's father, dressed in a sharp navy suit, his dark hair shining in the overhead lights, opened the door to his office and walked out. Two men trailed him, their subtle but noticeable earpieces marking them as his bodyguards.

He ushered out his guest—a ruddy-cheeked man with slicked-back brown hair, a touch of gray at the temples, and a flag pin stuck on his lapel. The man looked so much more presidential on TV. Taller, even.

Her father's aide, Alex Torres, followed them all out, smoothing a hand down the lapel of his suit. He flashed Kate a grin, cracking his business-student demeanor. She smiled back.

Her father shook the president's hand. "Don't forget, I need the *Theodore Roosevelt* and the *Eisenhower* moved to the Persian Gulf by August fifteenth."

"And the Appropriations bill? You're sure you want it vetoed?" the president asked.

"The bill's served its purpose. Kill it."

"Very well."

Her father's gaze darted to Kate and Victor, then to his aide. "Alex, please escort the president back to the White House."

Kate watched them leave, the president's back stiff. Did he resent following her father's orders? The president had his own agenda, she supposed. Reelection in nine months, keeping his daughter's leukemia in remission. Magic proved useful for a lot of things.

Kate left her water on the coffee table and followed Victor through the heavy wooden doors into her father's enormous office.

A few words from Victor to the bodyguards kept them waiting outside.

Kate hovered just through the entrance. The office, with its mahogany panels and stuffy, blue velvet draperies that screamed old money and even older power, always made her squirm inside. Everything looked so proper, and expensive, and *his*, from the cigar box given to him by a favor-seeking ex-president to the perfectly maintained turntable sitting next to the jazz collection on the bookshelf.

Stomach tense, she walked farther into the room, scanning the office for evidence of keepsakes and mementos stashed away, rearranged, or hidden. The first sign of a caster's slow, mental deterioration. She ran her finger across the records' spines. Alphabetized by artist, then title. Same as always. Her gaze wandered to the photos on his old mahogany desk. Kate, Brian, their mother— taken just before her death. All right where they'd sat the last time she'd visited.

Her father tossed his suit jacket on the desk chair and turned to take her in a hug, pulling her close. If he was going to let his guard down it would be now. Sneaking a look at him, she searched for signs of a change. A few more gray hairs around the temples. A strain around the lips. A twitching in the eye that wouldn't go away.

Nothing. The long descent into paranoid schizophrenia that marked the inevitable end of a caster hadn't tightened its grip on him. Not yet. The tension in her stomach eased.

Her father held her at arm's length, frowning as he examined her shirt. "You're not hurt?"

"Only scrapes. You know what happened?"

"Just the barest of details. I want to hear it from you."

Her father let her go and turned to sit behind his desk. Victor slumped into one of the two chairs opposite him and waved for Kate to join him. She sat, her hands gripping the carved lions on the chair's arms.

"A caster attacked her on the freeway driving home from school," Victor said.

His gaze snapped to Victor. "Where were you?"

Kate broke in. "When I left Cornell, I didn't call him for an escort home. I drove myself."

"No one's allowed to hurt you. No one. What happened?" Her father leaned across the desk. "Who attacked you?"

"A girl I know from school."

"What did she have to say?" he asked Victor.

"I don't know. She got away." Victor shifted in his chair.

"You let her escape."

"Yes."

Victor didn't blame her or give excuses, she gave him that.

"It was my fault," she said. "We were arguing. If I hadn't distracted him, Victor would have had time to tie her up or something."

"Why don't you tell me what happened, from the beginning." Her father ran his hands through his neat, short hair, then focused those gray eyes on her. She could tell he saw her fear. He could probably tell when she lied, too. Lying to him had never worked in the past. Damn Brian for getting her involved in this mess.

Hands clammy as they rubbed the chair's carved arms, she struggled through the story of the attack, staying as close as possible to the actual events. She left out Brooke's demand that she hand over the stone. Victor broke in once or twice with his own so-unnecessary comments. Her father kept his thoughts to himself until she reached the end of the story.

"So I wanted to go home, but Victor insisted we come to see you—"

"Have you ever been attacked before?" her father asked.

"No, but—"

"You are off-limits." He slammed the palm of his hand on the desk. "No one should have come after you at all."

"The other families know better," Victor said. "If they break the rules, what's to stop us from doing the same? Besides—" he paused "—the girl didn't seem like an operative."

"Why not?"

"She didn't shield herself. Couldn't cloak her spells worth a damn. Didn't seem like she had the training."

"A rogue?"

"Maybe. But why would a rogue attack Kate?"

"That's the question." Her father turned his attention back to her. "Did this Brooke girl say anything, anything at all, that would indicate what she was after?"

Kate stared down at her lap. "No, not a thing." The stone felt heavy in her pocket.

Her father tapped his fingers on his wooden desk, one after the other, setting a rhythm. He seemed lost in thought. Then the tapping stopped.

"Victor, track this girl down. Look through the records of the rogues we've encountered and see if you can find a match."

"Yes, sir."

"Start now. I'll talk to you about your actions later."

"Yes, sir." Victor got up and left the office, closing the double doors behind him.

Her father stayed quiet for a moment, and Kate wondered if he wanted her to tell him more. She ran her hand over the arm of the chair again. The faint smell of lemon oil rose from the wood, strangely soothing.

"Why didn't you call Victor for an escort home? It's his job to keep you safe." Her father reached across the desk to take her hand in his.

"I'm tired of being treated like I'm the Crown Jewels or something. No one's ever bothered me before. Why should Victor follow me around everywhere? I can't do magic. I've known that since I was twelve."

"Kate, look at me." He squeezed her hand. "I said look at me."

She met his gaze. She couldn't help it.

"You are important. You do have a role in this family. It may not be what you were raised to do, but that doesn't make you any less vital."

"Really? And what's my role? Get a medical degree so I can prescribe pills for you when you're old and tweaked from casting and have to stay tranked all the time? Or get a comp-sci degree so someone you trust can hack your enemies' networks? What kind of a life is that?"

"It's a good life, an important life. You have a duty to your family."

"There's nothing I can do to help you win the Game. You need casters for that. People who can keep control of your pawns, stop the other families' casters from messing with your operations. If I can't do that, I might as well do what I want with my life." She dropped her eyes as the old bitterness welled up. No point in regretting what can't be changed.

"Have fun in college," he said. "Go ahead, experiment with theater and art. But don't believe for one minute that you know what you want. You're only a freshman. You're too young for that kind of certainty."

"When will I be old enough? When it's too late to choose? Well I'm going to choose for myself." She rose to stand.

"Are you referring to that scholarship you're so proud of?"

She stopped, halfway out of the chair.

"Did you think I didn't know about that? Did you think the college could do anything that concerns you without my knowing? The scholarship changes nothing. Money is only one part of the picture. You need support. You need me."

Kate shot to her feet, fire burning in the pit of her stomach. "I don't. I don't need you, your money, or you messing with my life. Why can't you just leave me alone?"

"Because I love you, sweetheart. Because you're a Hamilton, and despite the Rules, that puts you at risk."

Kate slumped, catching the arm of her chair. She gripped it hard; only a slight tremble showed.

I should tell him where to stuff his "because you're a Hamilton" crap. But maybe there's a better line of attack. One she could figure out later, once she'd a chance to rest, retrench.

"Please call Alex and have him take me home."

He studied her face. "You've been through a lot today. I shouldn't have been so hard on you." Picking up his phone, he dialed then said, "Stop by my office and take Kate to the house."

Kate walked toward the doors, her steps light. She'd made it—escaped his office and hadn't given away any of Brian's secrets.

Her fingers touched the dark wood of the doorknob. Then her father spoke.

"Are you all right? I'm worried about you. This attack isn't the sort of thing you've been trained to deal with." He came around the desk to stand behind her. His hand brushed her shoulder.

She spun around. Understanding filled his eyes and, she thought, love. Reaching out for him, she sank into his embrace.

"It's all right, honey. I know it's rough. The first time somebody goes after you like that. You must have been scared."

"A little."

"Don't worry, I won't let anyone hurt you. I'll keep you safe." He held her close. "But you have to help me. What was that girl really after? You know, don't you?"

Oh God, he knew she was lying. Of course he did. He was Dad.

She should tell him all about the stone: that it put her into a trance last night, that Brooke wanted it, that she had probably overheard Kate and Brian talking about it when he gave it to her. He would know what to do, how to keep her safe. Besides, anything he didn't know he'd find out. She opened her mouth, ready to tell him everything.

Brian's words came back to her. *"Don't tell anyone. Not even Dad."* Had paranoia from casting caused him to say that? Or did he have another reason?

Who did she trust more? Brian or Dad? Brian never betrayed her secrets, not even in the innocent childhood way of telling on her when she'd stolen an extra cookie after lunch. And confiding in Dad had its risks. She remembered when she'd told him she'd gone out with that gorgeous but utterly Normal boy Neil Castro from high school. Neil and his whole family disappeared the next day. Dad always said everything he did was for her own good.

She settled for a lie. Of sorts.

She shrugged. "Maybe it's jealousy. I beat her out for the scholarship."

He pulled back and reached up to touch her cheek, his hand gentle. "Would this girl really go after you for that? You need to tell me everything you know. I can't protect you if you aren't honest with me."

"I don't know, Dad. I didn't even know she could cast. It's not like I can tell, the way you can." She hoped he didn't feel her trembling as she stepped away from his embrace. "I don't know why she's after me."

He gave her a long look. "Go home, and get some rest. We'll talk more later." He squeezed her shoulder and walked back to his desk. "I am sorry about what happened to you. Whoever is responsible will pay. That I guarantee."

He picked up the phone and buzzed his secretary, asking her to send in his next appointment.

He's already dismissed me and gone on to other things. Which company to influence, which country to dominate.

She walked out into the reception area.

"Ready to go, princess?" Victor leaned against the counter, an annoying smirk on his face.

Victor, not Alex. Dammit.

"Yes. Take me home, please."

"No problem. Nothing I like better than being your chauffeur." He pushed off the counter and marched down the hall. She hurried to keep up.

"You could drive me in one of the limos." Her headache had faded—another teleport would only bring it back.

"Not secure enough." He increased his pace. She had to jog to catch up.

"What's your problem? Doing what my father tells you is your job, after all."

"Yeah, it is, but so is finding who attacked you. Which do you think I should be doing: playing escort or catching a rogue?"

"Hey, don't bite my head off. Nothing I'd like better than having you looking for Brooke. Alex can take me home."

"Your father has other things for Torres to do. Besides, aren't you tired of him trailing after you? He's been doing it since you two were kids."

She felt her face flush. "You don't know what you're talking about." *Alex is worth ten reformed rogues like you.* "So…did you find Brooke in the database? Is she working for anybody?"

He slowed down. "Rogues don't work for anyone. That's why they're rogues. But no, I didn't find her."

They arrived back at the rotunda, Victor leading Kate onto the smaller version of the double-*H* logo that served as a marker for outgoing teleports. Not that casters needed to teleport onto a specific pattern, but having markers to use sure cut down on the gruesome accidents.

"So what will you do now?" Kate asked.

"Go to your school, track her down. Somebody will know something about her."

I know something about her. I know what the hell she wanted.

Before the spell took hold of them, she slid her hand into her pocket and felt the stone, cold and smooth. The sensation vanished for a moment as the rotunda disappeared around them and the foyer of her family's house in the Hamptons appeared in its place.

Home.

Chapter Five

Kate let go of Victor's arm and stepped off the incoming teleport pattern in front of the big curved staircase. Interwoven stripes of black and white in the marbled floor served as the marker. Across the foyer, fresh flowers topped the Queen Anne console table. Marigolds and red carnations caught the rays of the noontime sun streaming in from the picture window.

"I've got work to do. Try not to cause any more international incidents." Victor shot her a snarky look before walking down the walnut-lined hall. He headed toward the security office, boot heels ringing on the floor.

She pressed her lips together. *Don't react.* The last thing she needed was more of Victor. She had her own agenda: find Brian and give him back his stupid stone. Oh, and get rid of her resurgent, post-teleport headache.

Kate ran up the stairs to Brian's room—the last one on the left, past hers. The door hung partly open, but no backpack lay on the hardwood floor, no broken-in leather jacket slung across his old captain's chair. The just-made perfection of the white linens on his untouched bed further proved that he hadn't been by yet. She tried the game room next, its billiards table covered, Xbox silent in the corner. Then she checked the kitchen, bustling with staff preparing lunch. She even braved her father's den, its old brick fireplace banked for the summer. Nothing.

She stomped across the big corridor leading from the den to the family room and jerked open the bifold glass doors to the pool area. The blast of heat that greeted her wilted her hair and made sweat spring to her skin. Oh yes, summer in the Hamptons.

A few of the caster kids, most of them a year or two younger than Kate, hung out at the pool, their laughter mingling with the scents of chlorine and tanning lotion. Classes at the family's caster training school—the one she'd attended until she'd turned twelve, failed her magic test, and been consigned to eternal Nulldom—must have gotten out early. She scanned the crowd. No Brian.

"Great," Kate muttered. "Just great."

She stared past the pool at the long, brown two-story building framed by two tall oaks, slightly to the right of the tennis court. The Sanctum—training ground, center for the caster school, and general hangout for casters at her family's estate. Clever that it looked like a stable or oversized gym from the outside—except for the lack of windows and the single, large, locked door. Not that Victor's security spells let Normals see anything her father didn't want them to see.

The Sanctum was the one place she pretended didn't exist, the place that made her stomach do a little flip-flop every time her eyes passed by it. The one place she never, ever went. Not anymore. If Brian practiced magic in the Sanctum, he might as well be light-years away.

Her hand brushed her pocket, the stone a heavy lump. Sure, she could read a book or go swimming, but the problem of the stone would keep preying on her mind. Until she found Brian and gave the damn thing back.

She squared her shoulders and set off across the lawn, the Sanctum in her sights.

Kate dodged a grubby boy, maybe ten or eleven years old, barreling out from around the corner of the house. His dark head turned to watch the girl chasing him. "You missed me!"

"No, I didn't. Got you, you dirty Null!" A little girl in red shorts, a pink T-shirt, and white tennis shoes sped after him, a slim hand outstretched toward her quarry, pretending to throw a spell.

"Whatever! I get to be the Hamilton agent this time. You have to play the Makris." They ran past Kate and toward the hill leading to the beach with barely a glance at her.

Students from one of the Affiliate families that owed allegiance to hers. The boy was a Torres, one of Alex's cousins. The girl, a Hashimoto.

The younger kids always scurried underfoot like that—playing Caster Wars in the woods or down by the beach when they weren't in school. A tight smile crossed Kate's face. That game never changed.

She rounded a large clump of trees and reached the lawn that extended about twenty feet in front of the Sanctum. The breeze from the ocean blew salty air through the trees, cooling the sweat on her skin.

When she got closer to the Sanctum, she could see that the square, white "In Use" sign hung on the door. She knew better than to go up and knock. No one interrupted training. Ever.

Better wait for Brian someplace safe. Her stomach tightened as she turned the corner of the rough, stone building and wandered into the tree-lined plaza beyond. A few tables sat scattered over the lawn, one piled high with the backpacks casters usually took on missions, their owners nowhere in sight. Kate leaned against the Sanctum's outer wall, head resting on its wooden trim, warm from the sun.

No point in thinking too much about the last time she had been inside the Sanctum, how she'd stood in its center, six years ago. How her father, mother, and her uncle Grayson, his hair still solid black, had watched from outside the ring of glowing circle stones, the light of their protection shimmering toward the ceiling. They'd watched as she failed all three magic tests, the stones winking out, leaving her in darkness. She remembered how her father had turned away from her, back stiff, her mother's attention on her father's bent head, not on Kate and her tears.

"What's that smell? A pig?" Kate started at Missy Hashimoto's shrill voice. Missy was one of Brian's classmates—a caster. She floated in the air above Kate, her high-pitched giggle wafting down from tight, smirking lips. Her fingers stroked a shining silver talisman perched on her red leather jacket, activating the spell that kept her hovering.

"No, silly—pig shit. Can't you tell?" Her brother Gordon floated next to her, arms crossed, a sneer across his handsome face.

"Wait, we were both wrong," Missy giggled. "It's a Null. But who could tell the difference?"

"Missy, stop it." Kate's cousin, Hayley. Blond ponytail bobbing as she hovered in the air, fingers busy casting. "Leave Kate alone."

Missy shot Hayley an oh-so-sincere look of contrition. "Oh, that's right. Shouldn't be mean to the boss's daughter. Might get in trouble."

Kate's face burned. "I was just... I'm looking for Brian."

Missy jerked her head from one side to the other, her eyes wide and an ultra-fake smile painted on her face. "I don't see him? Do you?" She gaped at Gordon.

"Maybe he's in the Sanctum." Gordon's handsome face twisted in a cruel smile. "Why don't you go inside and find out?"

"I can't. You know that."

"Then what the hell are you doing out here in caster country?" He sneered.

"I—"

Missy laughed. "You come here, snooping around, looking to learn our secrets? Checking up on us for your dad? Maybe we should teach you a lesson." She raised her hand, and her body got all tense, her eyes narrow and sharp.

Oh shit. She's going to cast.

Gordon muttered a quick chant and slashed his hand in a figure eight.

Chunks of concrete blew from the pavement at Kate's feet, carving a hole in the ground. Kate screamed and jumped back, her whole body shaking.

"You can't cast at Kate! She's off-limits! What the hell are you doing?" Hayley yelled.

"Open the door. Now." Gordon's voice sent ice shooting down her back.

Over the crackle of the fire spell that had sprung to Missy's hand and Hayley's protests, Kate wondered if anyone would hear her if she screamed for help. And what would really happen if she opened the door. Would she look like a stupid, Null idiot who didn't know her place to the people inside, or would she get sucked into some kind of other-dimensional hellhole? She didn't want to find out.

"No." She faced the three casters hovering above her. "Go to hell."

Gordon's face went dark. His fingers slashed and jabbed through the air too fast for her to follow. Even a Null like her could feel the spell forming around his hands—something black and writhing and filled with screams.

She froze, mouth gone bone dry. *Shit, he's really going to—*

"Look out!"

Brian's yell shocked Kate more than the impact of his body as he threw himself on top of her. A roar like a freight train sounded as Gordon's spell rushed past her head, so close her ears rang with the near miss. They hit the ground, the impact knocking the wind out of Kate and jarring her still-sore head. Gordon's spell slammed into the Sanctum door and evaporated with a swoosh.

Brian rolled to his feet, chanting. Everything around Kate took on a wavy look, as the world might appear from the inside a glass bottle. *A shield spell, just like under the car.*

Missy squinted. She thrust her arms out and fire formed around them—finally, a spell Kate could see. Missy threw the flaming sphere straight at Brian. It hit his shield and disappeared. Brian grinned.

"That's enough of that." It was her uncle Grayson's voice, accompanied by his firm footsteps on the concrete walkway. One slash of his hand and all three—Missy, Gordon, and Hayley—fell from the sky like birds whose wings had been clipped. Another wave pinned Missy's and Gordon's struggling forms to the ground. Grayson seemed to be able to hold Hayley with just his glare. She cringed under the heat of his anger.

"Are you okay? What in the hell are you doing here?" Brian asked as he helped Kate up. She couldn't find a trace of the beaten-up Brian from last night. Instead, his usual "No Hair Product Left Behind" look was back. He could have posed for a magazine cover in his perfect polo with the collar turned up, cocky stance, and just-ironed khakis.

"I'm looking for you," Kate said. "Don't know how I could have forgotten how unwelcoming a twitchy caster could be."

"Yeah, well...you know how it is."

Did she ever.

Brian glanced at Grayson, still chastising Missy, Gordon, and Hayley a few yards away, then turned his attention back to Kate. "Do you still have it?" he whispered, eyes narrow.

"Do you know how much trouble—" she hissed.

"Not now. Meet me tonight. At nine. Our old place. Remember?"

The catalpa grove, at the edge of the estate. She nodded.

"Not a word to anyone about it."

"Grayson should know," she whispered, with a sideways look at her uncle. "He's the expert—"

"No. No one."

Grayson gave Missy and Gordon a final glare before he sent them on their way. Kate had been too busy whispering with Brian to hear what punishment Grayson had given them, but judging from the glower Missy shot her, it must have been a doozy. She'd better watch her back.

Hayley ran over, breathless. "Kate," she squealed, throwing her arms around her cousin. "You're home. Sorry about those guys. They can be real jerks after a mission."

"Yeah, right." Paranoia backlash might be a pain in the butt, but it got used as an excuse for all-around bad behavior way too often. Especially when the victim was a Null.

Grayson frowned at Hayley. "And what do you think you're doing, hanging around with casters back from a mission? You should be in class, young lady—if you expect to graduate this year and join those hooligans on a mission." Grayson pointed to the caster classroom, filled with students Hayley's age, a good distance across the lawn.

"I know, Dad, but—"

"No buts. Good thing for you the lunch bell is about to ring."

"I was helping Kate, defending her..." Hayley sighed.

Grayson waved Hayley's excuses away and gave Kate's ripped shirt a puzzled look. "Are you sure Gordon missed you?"

"That's from...earlier." She glanced at Brian. "I'm fine."

Grayson pulled her close, and tension fled her as he gave her a gentle squeeze. "Welcome home, sweetheart. Sorry I missed your play." He smelled like old books and pine trees and long nights telling stories by the fire. His black hair was streaked with gray at the temples—more than the last time she'd seen him, months ago. "Got called away last night." He let her go. "You know how it is."

Brian cleared his throat. "I'm starving. Lunch, anybody?"

Kate sighed. "Sure."

"Great idea," Grayson said. "There are sandwiches inside the Sanctum. Hayley, can you bring a tray to my office before the students finish them off?"

Hayley nodded and ran off. Grayson took Kate's arm and they walked toward his office, around the back of the Sanctum. Brian followed.

The spacious room, lined with floor-to-ceiling windows, faced the ocean. Kate hadn't been in Grayson's office for years. The bookcases lining the walls still groaned under the weight of her uncle's books, tome after tome of old, decaying paper bound in leather studded with gems so rare she wasn't sure exactly what they were. Stacked beside those were scrolls thick with illegible writing, some so ancient they looked as though they would dissolve if she touched them.

His desk still held piles of papers and pictures of the family, a sleek wide-screen monitor replacing the old CRT. Disassembled talismans, hunks of amber, a soldering iron, and a few spare lodestones covered his old metal workbench. Stacks of magazines sat on the floor—*The Journal of Applied Thaumatology* next to *Field and Stream.*

Grayson sank into his favorite leather chair while Brian dug in the refrigerator for sodas. Brian handed her one. Kate sat on the tweed sofa and let the air-conditioning blow across her overheated face. As she ran the cold can of the diet cola across her forehead, she wondered what felt so off to her about Grayson's office. Something had changed since she'd been here last.

Then she spotted it.

"You've organized," she said.

Grayson took a long drink of his soda.

Everything lay in crisp, neat stacks, from the books, to the scrolls, to the piles of silver ingots. It seemed nothing like the barely controlled chaos of the Grayson she knew and loved—books everywhere, papers mixed in with talismans, notes pinned over each other on his wall map of artifact finds, magazines scattered across the floor. Somehow, he'd always known how to find everything.

"Hayley got the ladies in to straighten up. They finished before I even knew about it." Grayson shrugged. "Easier to keep it this way." His smile showed a hint of strain.

Maybe the housekeepers really had rearranged. Or maybe Grayson had started worrying that people were after his stuff, and he could keep an eye on it better if he knew where everything lived. All the time.

She tried to catch Brian's eye, but he avoided her gaze. He'd mentioned a few weeks ago that Grayson was now on risperidone—the family's standard starter med for paranoia. Just a precaution, Brian had said, given their uncle's age. Was that why Brian didn't want her to talk to Grayson about the stone?

Hayley skipped in, a tray of sandwiches in her hands. "Okay, who wants tuna salad?"

Lunch passed quickly amid the crunch of potato chips, fizz of sodas, and inconsequential small talk. Hayley talked about how busy she'd be when she attended Harvard next fall. Grayson mentioned a quick trip he'd planned to Japan tomorrow for the horse festival. And Brian thought he'd take the sailboat out next weekend—did Kate want to come? But Kate found what they didn't say more intriguing: no talk of work, of casting, or of family politics. There couldn't be any lack of it to discuss.

Brian ignored her little hints that they talk outside. Ignored every attempt she made to get him to talk about his current mission. She tapped her foot on Grayson's hard stone floor.

And she noticed something else. Brian avoided talking to Grayson. Oh, he answered Grayson's questions, nodded when he spoke, but her brother didn't really talk to their uncle. Not like he used to.

When the only things left on the tray were broken chips and bread crumbs, Brian got up to leave. Hayley followed, grabbing the tray.

Kate rose as well. Maybe now she'd get a chance to talk to her brother alone.

"Brian, stay a minute. There's something I want to speak to you about," Grayson said.

"Sure." Brian glanced at Kate and Hayley. "Why don't you two go ahead? We'll catch up more later."

Kate trailed out after Hayley, her eyes on Brian, jaw clenched. He'd talk to her later. *Sure* he would. He drops this *stupid* stone off with her, doesn't care that it does *something* to her in the dressing room for a half hour, isn't interested in hearing how that *bitch* Brooke tried to kill her over it, and won't talk to her long enough to take it off her hands. What was he waiting for, a Delacroix assault team to blow down the front gate looking for the stone?

She huffed past Hayley, around the corner of the Sanctum, and across the lawn. Screw Brian. Maybe she should take this stupid stone and throw it in the ocean. See how he liked that.

"Kate. Kate!" Hayley jogged after her.

"What?" Kate kept storming along.

"What's got you so worked up?"

Kate slowed down. "Oh…nothing. Just stuff with Brian. It's nothing important."

"Maybe I can help." An earnest smile lit Hayley's face.

Kate sighed. "You can't. Don't worry about it." But maybe Hayley could help with something else. She stopped. "Hayley, is Grayson all right? Brian said he started on medication. And his office, it's different. Have you noticed anything? Is he getting…"

The smile vanished. "He's fine. There's nothing wrong with him."

"Hayley…"

"No, really. There's nothing wrong. The doctors did the whole exam thing. They say he's got years. Definitely."

Kate remembered what the doctors had said about her mother. They were never *that* certain. They always said, "they couldn't tell," and "maybe, with the right medications," and "she could go quickly or she could take a long time."

As it turned out, with her mother, the end came like a lightning bolt. One day, a little over two years ago, her mother had seemed as vibrant and sharp as ever. The next, she'd run through every room in the house, smashing all the mirrors until her hands were cut and bleeding, screaming that the ancient casters were trying to reach through and control them all. When Kate had returned from school that day, her mother had run to meet her at the door, her eyes wild, her fingers clutching at Kate's sweater. Victor had grabbed a sobbing Kate, taken her to the family's San Francisco house, and hadn't let her anywhere near her mother again. No matter how much she'd begged.

A week later, her mother had taken her own life and Dad had sent Kate to boarding school. For her own good, he'd said.

"That's great," Kate said. "I was just worried about him—"

"You don't have anything to worry about," Hayley snapped. "You don't rely on him to— Sorry. I didn't mean to… Anyway, he's as sharp as ever. No delusions, no obsessions, nothing like that. He's fine."

They reached the pool area where a few of the older kids still hung out, playing cannonball. A splash of cool water hit Kate as they walked by. Hayley set the tray on a nearby table.

"Look, I didn't want to upset you. I'm sorry." Kate squeezed Hayley's shoulder. "Want to go out tonight? After dinner? We could go to a club or something." She'd have to figure out how to fit it in around her meeting with Brian, but clearly Hayley needed her.

"Um…I'd love to, but I'm going to a party with Missy. I'd invite you along but…" Hayley had the grace to look sheepish.

"Yeah, Missy doesn't want to be seen with me. Especially not at a caster party. I get it." Kate's eyes drifted away from Hayley's face. How many times had she seen Hayley, Brian, and their friends teleport off, laughing, all dressed up for a club or a party while she stayed behind to study or watch TV?

Kate opened the glass doors, and they went in the house.

"Well, I'm gonna work on my homework. See you later." Hayley strode down the hall and pulled out her phone, typing a text message before Kate had a chance to suggest they do something else. Well, so much for spending the day with Hayley. When would she learn to keep her mouth shut and mind her own business?

She sank into one of the big club chairs in the family room. She couldn't corral Brian and give him back the stupid stone. She couldn't spend time with Hayley. It wasn't as if anybody else would put up with a Null. She sighed and stroked the worn leather of the chair. She missed Kris. Once she gave Brian the stone back and had that "talk" with Dad about school, she could register for summer session online and drive back to Cornell. She and Kris could spend the summer sitting on her porch, cool iced teas in their hands, and textbooks spread out in front of them, pretending to study. That sounded about right. But who was she kidding? Her next "talk" with Dad would likely go as well as the last.

A yell sounded from the pool as one of the kids dove into the deep end. Maybe a swim and some time relaxing with a book would be nice.

Heading down the hallway, she passed the picture gallery then went up the staircase to her room. Her suitcase and her purse were sitting in the corner. Victor's guys had made good on his promise.

Kate grabbed her purse and flung herself down on her four-poster bed, stacked high with pillows covered in a blue-and-yellow iris print. Her room looked untouched—paperbacks piled on her old wrought-iron bookcase against the wall, the scarves she'd bought last summer in Italy still draped on the hook by the closet. The picture of her and her mother from their first stay at the Montana ranch was still on her antique dresser, her mother laughing as she boosted

Kate up into the saddle.

The view from the window gleamed bright and clear, from the crisp green lawn with the Sanctum looming over it, to the tall privet hedges separating the family's estate from their neighbors, to the long stretch of sand spotted with beach grass leading down to the slate blue of the Atlantic Ocean.

If she could talk to Kris, hear his deep, reassuring voice, she'd know everything was all right. She dug in her purse for her cell, found it, and dialed his number.

It went to voice mail. *Oh right.* Hadn't he mentioned this morning, before she'd left Cornell, that he'd be on a fishing trip with his family this weekend?

"Uh, just wanted to tell you I miss you. Catch a big one for me. Call me if you get a minute." She hung up, cringing. What a stupid thing to say. What kind of message was "catch a big one"? He was probably out of cell phone range, somewhere off the coast of Florida, anyway. He wouldn't even get her message until tomorrow. And forget about texting.

She tossed her phone in her purse. If she wanted to swim, she'd better get changed. Scooting to the edge of the bed, she tugged off her jeans. The stone scraped along her thigh through the fabric. The next thing she knew she had pulled it out and was holding it up to the light. She stroked it with her thumb.

It lit up from within, iridescent green stripes rising up from the core and washing over its body like a soothing wave of cool energy. She turned it over and over in her hand, letting its calming feel seep into her. Something in the core of it spoke to the core of her, whispering secrets she couldn't quite hear. She let herself fall down into its depths, content in its promise that, soon, something would change.

Everything would change.

"Kate," the housekeeper called from down the stairs. "Are you up there?"

She blinked. Her eyes were all blurry as she stared up at the white ceiling. She didn't remember lying down.

The stone still lay in her hand, her jeans on the floor. The stone's green glow seemed a little brighter.

Kate's stomach rumbled. *Weird*. She'd had lunch only a half hour ago.

"Yeah, I'm up here."

"It's dinnertime, honey. Don't be late or you know what that means. Good luck getting any roast."

Dinnertime? Kate bolted upright. Was she joking? It couldn't possibly be that late.

Kate glanced out the window. The sun hung low over the ocean, its rays gilding along the crests of the waves. Her furniture threw long shadows against her striped wallpaper. She looked at the stone in her hand, then at the clock on her nightstand.

6:24 p.m.

Shit. It had happened again.

Chapter Six

The late-day sun shone through the white pines bordering the Hamilton estate. Enough time was left in the day that a gardener going about his job wouldn't be conspicuous. Kristof slipped from the driver's seat of the battered, white gardener's truck. The illusion spell he'd cast on himself duplicated the twentysomething guy who usually ran the route by the estate. He matched from the blond soul patch on his sweating chin down to the burrito stains on his gray Paumanok Grounds Department uniform. He reached into the tool rack in the back to pick up a hoe. *Never know when the sharp end of a stick might come in handy.*

The truck was parked off the road that ran by the western edge of the Hamiltons' place. Close enough to sense the security grid surrounding the many acres owned by Kate's family, and the stone, sitting somewhere in the main house. But far enough away to avoid the trap spells that circled the grid's perimeter and the cameras they had as backup. If he wanted to complete the mission, he'd have no choice but to wind his way through the trap spells, circumvent the Hamiltons' security measures to get inside, get the stone, and get out.

Only one problem: no one, not Delacroix's top casters, de la Vega's ace combat mages, or even his own family's best, had ever broken through the Hamilton security grid. *But that doesn't mean I can't.*

Muttering the two-line incantation for a cloak spell, he let the shimmering purple energy settle around his body before stepping through the dense undergrowth of the old forest, his feet crushing the summer pine needles beneath him. He ignored their evergreen scent, focusing instead on the trap spells laid out around him in the forest, the amethyst tendrils of each one sparkling in his magesight like a minefield as they wove in and out of the trees. The spells wouldn't trigger from someone raking leaves, but they would screech like the Furies if he had screwed up his cloak spell.

Kristof set the hoe against a wiry maple and contemplated the tall brick wall topped with a wrought-iron fence lining the estate. The fence was more than iron—inset with silver talismans, each holding a spell designed to keep intruders out and let only the select few inside.

A faint shimmer rose from the wrought iron—red, like a crimson wave. The security grid.

He leaned back against the tree. A raven cawed as it flew through the crimson shimmer, its wings dipping as it sailed across the barrier. The grid kept out enemy casters and other magical threats, not animals.

He couldn't shape-shift—magic that powerful had been lost after the First Era. But maybe he could fool the grid another way.

Kristof waited until he heard a rustling in the undergrowth. A quick stun spell netted him a squirrel. He held it up to his magesight and probed it with gentle fingers. No point in duplicating how it looked, how it moved. The grid didn't care much about that. The grid cared about its aura.

The squirrel's aura shone with a bright-yellow light that surrounded the animal, beating with the rapid pulse of its life force. After a long look, he understood what he needed to do.

Tapping out the points of an illusion spell, he focused all his attention on the squirrel's aura. He chanted the short words that would duplicate it and quickly followed with a cloaking spell. Then he brushed his fingers across the shining yellow duplicate essence and dragged it into his own rainbow-hued aura.

The yellow in his aura brightened as the other colors faded. He continued to pull the duplicate aura into his own. When his essence pulsed with the same frantic air as the squirrel's, and shone with the same sunlight-yellow hue, he stopped.

A violet gleam from a nearby trap spell caught his eye. Shit. Had he cloaked his illusion spell fast enough? He hadn't heard any of the trap spells go off, but that didn't mean a silent alarm hadn't been tripped and Hamilton security wasn't on its way. He should leave— now.

He dropped the squirrel and turned, jogging back to the truck. Then he stopped and took a deep breath, then another.

No. It's the backlash from casting. The fear isn't real. Hamilton security isn't on its way.

He turned back toward the estate. Took a step closer, then another, each time fighting back the terror that threatened to overwhelm him. By the time the brick and wrought-iron fence loomed before him again, the paranoia had become nothing more than background chatter.

Hoisting himself up to the top of the brick wall, he scrambled to find a handhold on the narrow ledge where the brick met the wrought iron. After getting one foot planted on the ledge, he reached up and grabbed the railing. His hand touched the metal, his yellow aura flickering then steadying. The shimmering curtain of the security grid held steady.

So far, so good. He pulled himself partway up the fence, his feet following where his hands led. This idea hadn't been half bad. Now all he had to do was stay cloaked, slip inside the house, get the stone, and—

A talisman buried in the fence flickered. The yellow in his aura wavered then bled out. His caster aura flared back, the colors as bright as the sails of a fishing boat in his father's harbor. The grid darkened from red to black. At the edge of his hearing, barely within human range, a hundred trap spells screeched their warnings, their tendrils vibrating as they let go of their perches and rocketed toward him with all the speed of a school of piranhas.

Kristof dropped back to the ground, heart hammering in his chest. He rolled forward, taking too much of the impact on his hand and feeling the snap of the delicate bones inside his wrist. He stumbled to his feet and ran.

Need to clear the teleport block to get out. There, that purple glow around the fence's perimeter. Probably triggered by the trap spells activating.

A twig snapped off to his side. Then another. A glimmer darted from tree to tree at the edge of his vision. Several more glimmers beyond. Hamilton casters, cloaked like him.

A purple mist swam along the ground between the fallen branches and leaves, searching. The trap spells—now active. They would rip his cloak spell away before smothering him in their vapors, choking the life from him.

He dodged around their perimeter, evading a tendril that reached for his ankle. He tapped out a quick animate spell and aimed it at the hoe, still leaning against the tree trunk where he'd left it. It danced toward the fence, scraping against the ground and catching a tendril of the trap spell in its metal blade. The spell's energy rushed for it, surrounding it and pulling it into a pile of maple leaves.

He ran, the tendrils streaming past him toward the hoe.

But the trap spells weren't his biggest threat. A faint rustling in the undergrowth, then his skin stung all over with burning pain, as if a bandage had been ripped from his entire body.

His cloaking spell vanished.

He tapped out a shield spell as he ran, almost stumbling over the short incantation.

There must be three, maybe four casters here. They're everywhere. They've found the truck already, tracked the guy I took out. They know who I am.

He shook off the backlash as the shield's bright blue glow sprang up around him.

A lightning bolt hit his shield, a sharp buzzing sound and the smell of ozone filling the evening air. Two more followed, then a sonic spell screamed past his ear. His shield's glow faded to the color of the afternoon sky.

The truck waited ahead, its white body glowing with the last rays of the setting sun. If he could make it past the truck and to the road, he should be able the clear the teleport block.

A force like a battering ram slammed into his chest. He flew backward and onto the ground, the wind knocked out of him, shield ripped away, blood pounding in his ears. The kinetic punch came from the direction of the truck. He couldn't see anything or anyone there, not even the glimmer of a hasty cloak spell.

Kristof rolled into the underbrush, taking cover beneath a black-berry bush. Leaves crackled nearby—the Hamilton goons closing in. He tried to quiet his ragged breathing.

Have to renew the cloak spell—my best chance with this many enemies.

He cast the spell, waiting until its purple haze covered his form. Then he scrambled up and darted through the trees, putting as much distance between him and his pursuers as possible, shoving away the feeling of eyes on his back.

He found an old fox's den in a hollowed-out oak a hundred yards away. Crawling inside, he slipped on the pine needles covering the ground, their scent rising in the air. Waiting, he could feel the adrenaline coursing through his system, the bitter, coppery taste of tension in his mouth. Shit. The aura trick should have worked. They must have known he would try something. Did his sister betray him? Someone else?

He breathed in, held it for a four-count, then breathed out. Did it again. And again. While his heartbeat steadied, he observed his mind's agitated thoughts float by until they were nothing more than leaves in a stream.

A spider hopped onto his arm, then moved across it and down his shoulder. His wrist throbbed as the pain of the fracture finally broke through his adrenaline rush. He lay still, listening. Leaves rustled. A branch snapped. A purple tendril crept by, probed the edge of the den, then moved on.

A few minutes later, voices rumbled in the distance.

"Anything?" Victor Cole. Probably the one who'd fired off the kinetic punch.

"Nothing. He must have slipped by us."

A grunt. "Maybe."

Nothing else. He waited longer. He waited until the sun had set and the night air cooled off. How much time had passed? Had they given up the hunt?

He used his magesight to probe for a teleport block. *There.* Set in the fence—and active—a few yards away, it still prevented him from leaving the fastest and easiest way.

Damn. He'd have to extract himself the hard way.

While he whispered the incantation, he tapped out the three points to the spell. A ball of emerald mist formed in his palm.

He peered into the mist. The forest around him glimmered like a tiny model in his hand. Trees, the fence, his truck... Anything else? Yes. Between him and the truck—two guards. One stationed near the truck, dressed in a blue Hamilton T-shirt, and one cloaked, nothing but a flicker near the fence.

Victor hadn't bought the theory of his escape. But Kristof hadn't expected him to.

The surveillance spell showed only the trap spells. Nothing else.

That he could see. What else couldn't he see?

Kristof dismissed the green mist with a snap of his fingers. He'd have to trust the spell. Two guards shouldn't pose a threat.

A quick animate spell and the hoe took care of the one near the fence, the guard's cloak spell disappearing as he slumped to the ground, his head bleeding. Kristof rolled from the fox's den and crept along the forest floor until he reached striking distance of the other guard, who was leaning against the truck. He couldn't afford a showy spell, a kinetic punch or a lightning bolt. Nothing that would bring more guards or make him even twitchier.

Kristof wove his spell and shot it toward the guard. At first, nothing. Then the guard clutched his throat, gasping for breath, his fingers beating with frantic energy against the truck in an attempt to execute a counterspell. Face turning blue, eyes bulging, he fell against the truck. He reached into his pocket for a phone, then dropped it from his shaking fingers onto the forest floor.

A minute or two should do it. Deprive the man's brain of oxygen for longer than that and Kristof risked damaging it, or even killing him. No point risking discovery by leaving bodies around, especially on an off-book operation.

A few seconds after the man went limp, Kristof shut off the spell. He glanced over at the truck with his magesight. There, under the hood, was a faint purple glimmer. Victor had almost certainly tampered with it. He'd have to walk instead. Setting off down the road, he kept to the narrow side where the trees provided him with natural camouflage. The more distance he put between himself and Hamilton land, the harder it would be for them to trace his teleport spell.

So much for the direct method. He'd have to come up with another way to get the stone.

His heartbeat slowing to normal, he ran through the options as he left the edge of the Hamiltons' tree-covered estate and reached the outskirts of the little town of Paumanok. One thought kept returning to his mind.

Kate. She had the stone. She trusted him. There must be a way to use her to retrieve it.

By the time he'd slipped across the old wooden bridge leading into town, he knew what he had to do. But the certainty that his plan would work didn't settle his nerves or lead to his usual pre-op calmness.

Instead, Kate's eyes, gazing up at him as she lay against the pillow last night, kept intruding on his thoughts, like a haunting melody that wouldn't stop playing.

Kate reached the small clearing a few minutes before 9:00 p.m. Thick with a few old oaks and a dozen tall, gray-barked catalpas, the grove stood past the Sanctum at the far western edge of the estate, near the perimeter wall that ran up against Paumanok Road. Back when she and Brian had been kids, they would run to the grove to escape the pressure of studying. The other students attending the family's school with them were more interested in playing on the beach and sneaking over the wall into the nearby town of Paumanok. So she and her brother had the little stand of trees all to themselves.

Fireflies hovered around her, darting in and out of the grove. The lightning-struck oak they called the Old Bear still loomed over the clearing. She wondered if anything remained in their secret hiding place under its roots.

The swing survived, hanging above a new growth of blackberry bushes, their aroma sweet in the night air. The thick rope looping the wooden seat around the branch above looked too frayed to hold Kate's weight, but the big deadfall below provided a good bench. Kate brushed off the dirt and fallen catalpa bean pods and sat to wait for Brian.

She rubbed her fingers against the tree trunk's rough bark. Brian had missed dinner. And so had Dad—delayed at the office by another one of the hundreds of emergencies that always seemed to come up. Victor had run through, muttered something about reinforcing the security grid at the western wall, and teleported out. Not that she'd missed his company. But Hayley and Grayson sat around the oak dining table and talked magic, and there didn't seem to be anything for her to do but play with her peas and fret until nine o'clock came around.

She reached into the pocket of her shorts and let the stone slide through her fingers. At its cool, soothing touch she jerked her hand back out. The damned thing would probably cause her to lose more time. The last thing she wanted.

Crickets droned above the quiet grove. No Brian. She checked her watch—quarter after nine. He'd better show. And after all she'd been through, he'd better tell her where he'd gotten the stupid thing and what made it such a supersecret, "don't tell Dad" big deal.

A hand touched her shoulder. She jumped. "Brian! Don't scare me like that."

He stood next to her, wearing a blue Hamilton T-shirt with the double-H logo, but she could see only his face and part of his chest. As she watched, the rest of him appeared, as if she were watching an old-fashioned Polaroid picture develop before her eyes. She'd seen the effects of a cloak spell before, but why did he feel the need to hide in his own home?

He put a finger to his lips, then whispered, "Sorry I'm late." After sitting down next to her, he scrunched up his eyes and his body stilled. His fingers tapped out the points of a triangle on the log, and he chanted a low incantation.

"What spell did you cast?" she asked.

"I cloaked us."

"You're worried about eavesdroppers? Here?"

He gave her a look that made her wonder what she'd missed. "You have it with you?"

Her hand went to her pocket. She slid it inside and touched the stone.

He needs it back? Well, I need some things, too. Like an explanation.

She pulled her hand out empty. "No. Tell me where you got it."

"On a mission." His lips tightened.

"Yeah. I know what that means. You aren't going to say a thing."

"Sorry. It's classified. You know how this works."

"I know all too well." His "don't tell anybody" crap must mean that his mission wasn't official. Somebody else in the family played a dangerous game. "Why did you give me the stone? Why not Dad or Grayson? Or even Victor?"

Brian shifted on the log. "Look, I was in a bad situation. You were the first person I thought of. I'm sorry I can't explain every-thing. You'll just have to trust me."

"I do. More than anyone. But—"

"I need the stone. Please. Cut the interrogation and give it back."

Kate picked up a twig and twirled it in her hand. Why wouldn't he answer her questions? His reluctance to talk had to be more than the usual family secrecy. She needed to get through to him, some-how. "Do you know what happened on the freeway?"

"No. Should I?"

"I got attacked. This girl blew out my tire. Then she hit me with a fire spell—"

Brian grabbed her arm. "Kate, are you okay? Damn. I'm sorry. I had no idea—"

"I'm fine, she didn't...she didn't hurt me. She wanted the stone. But if Victor hadn't been there, I would have been..." She shuddered when she thought back to the flames coming at her. "Afterward, I did what you asked. I lied. I sat there in Dad's office and I didn't tell him a thing about the stone. I kept your secrets. I think you owe me an explanation."

Brian let go of her and leaned back, bracing his hands against the log. He sat for a long moment. Then, "It's very old, maybe ancient. Do you remember what Grayson taught us about the First Era? When we were kids?"

"Sure. I always did better in History than you."

He chuckled. "Yeah, maybe. I think the stone dates from then. Pre-Atlantean times, or a little while after. We can't make anything like this anymore."

"Wow. What does it do?" She remembered a little about the First

Era—the casters back then could do world-altering spells, stuff casters found impossible today. Ancient magic, forbidden magic. But that was before casters were forced to channel magic through their minds and paranoia became a side effect. Before the caster community went underground.

He hesitated. "I don't know, exactly. I need to find that out. Evaluate it in the Sanctum. I do know this much: I had a quick look at it before I gave it to you. I've never even heard of an artifact that has as many spells layered into it. It's potentially more powerful than anything we've found. Maybe more important than the artifacts Grayson has locked up at Lost River. Do you understand what that means?"

"Yeah." She'd been raised on the tales of how their grandfather had wrestled those artifacts from the bloody hands of Arkady Makris. They were the foundation of the Hamiltons' magical arsenal.

"We can't let another family get a hold of it. Not the Makrises or anyone else. It could mean another war."

"Shit." She peeled the bark off the twig in her hand. Who would send him to get something that powerful? Grayson? Victor? It couldn't have been Dad. Otherwise, why tell her not to talk to him? Unless Brian wasn't working for anyone. Her hands went still, the twig forgotten.

I should give the stone to Dad. It's his job to sort this stuff out. I should turn this whole mess over to him.

But then I'll never find out about the stone. Dad and Grayson will take it into the Sanctum and shut the door.

Or she could do as she promised and give the stone back to Brian. Keeping her word to him had caused her nothing but trouble since he'd shown up at the theater last night, stone in hand. Brian, who wouldn't give her a straight answer to any of her questions.

Brian, the one person in the family who trusted her with something magical.

Bean pods crunched underfoot as she stood. "Fine. I'll give it back, but in exchange, I want to be in on the testing. I want to know what this thing does and what makes it so all-fired important."

"Absolutely not. Way too dangerous."

She raised an eyebrow. "So, you don't know what it is or what it can do, but you know it's 'way too dangerous'?"

"There are reasons only casters are allowed in the Sanctum. No matter what the stone is, having you inside the Sanctum with me while I figure it out is a bad idea."

"Worse than me telling Dad that you gave me the stone, told me not to tell him, and then left me defenseless against some crazy girl with a fire spell and a yen for ancient artifacts?"

Brian stood. "Aren't you a little old for the 'I'll tell Dad' routine? Kate, just give me the damn stone."

"What if I don't?"

"Then I'll have to—"

"What? Take it? You've learned a lot from Dad." Her jaw tightened after snapping out the words.

"That's a low blow."

"Maybe. But don't tell me you weren't thinking about it."

"I would never do that."

"Not if you had a choice. But do you?"

He sank back on the log, his face in his hands. "Not for much longer."

The night air suddenly felt chilly through her thin top. "Are you in trouble?"

He hesitated. "Nothing I can't handle."

She stood, studying him. Maybe, maybe not. But despite all his cloak-and-dagger games, nothing in this world could make Brian be untrue to his family. That was all she needed to know.

Kate sighed and pulled the stone from her pocket. When he glanced up at her, she said, "Here," and held it up. It caught the faint moonlight and shone with an emerald glow in her hand.

"Kate." Brian's voice wavered. "Where's the silk I gave you to hold it with? And when the hell did the stone turn *black*?"

Kate stared at the stone's round, dark shape. She thought back to when she'd first seen it, in Brian's hand. Had it been just last night?

White. The stone had been white.

Why hadn't she been able to remember that before now?

"Kate, this is important. Has anything strange happened with the stone since last night?"

She opened her mouth to answer. To tell Brian about the lost half-hour in the dressing room, the hours lost earlier today in her bedroom. To tell him how the stone's weird green glow had increased, how its deep blackness had pulled her in until she couldn't resist its call. To tell him how she hadn't been able to remember the stone's original color after it mesmerized her the first time.

But nothing came out.

"Shit. You said you *remembered* the rules." He grabbed her arm and ran, pulling her after him. She clutched the stone in her fingers as they wove in and out of the trees, her feet sliding on the leaves underfoot.

"Where are we going?" she gasped out.

"You wanted to know what the stone can do. Fine. Now we don't have a choice."

As they broke through the cover of the trees, their destination lay ahead, its slate roof glinting with reflections of light shining down from the night sky.

The Sanctum.

Brian darted across the lawn to the Sanctum's door, Kate in tow. He put his hand on the lock plate. The door responded to his touch, swinging open without a sound. Beyond the faint light of the entry-way, the room seemed dark and still.

He motioned her inside. "Quick."

Shock fused Kate's feet to the floor. "I...can't. You know that. Nulls aren't..."

"You were pretty eager to help me test the stone a few minutes ago." He sighed. "Never mind that particular Rule. Just go."

She slipped inside, and he followed. As he did, the room awak-ened. The lights, a dim glow as Brian opened the door, burst into radiance as he strode into the room and shut the door. The vision before Kate took even the thoughts of the stone from her head.

Rays of light shining down from the ceiling caught the amber, gold, and bloodred crystals embedded in the walls, and the whole room glowed with brilliant color. The gemstones lay in intricate spiral patterns across the walls, floor, and ceiling, swirling in con-figurations that made Kate dizzy as she tried to trace them with her eyes. She had long forgotten what the lines and swirls meant—she only remembered that the crystals, rare gems that amplified and held magical energy, were essential to the functioning of the Sanctum.

Interspersed among the crystals were lodestones, square-cut rocks whose magnetic properties insulated the room from outside influences and, working with the crystals, absorbed the backlash so that spells cast in the Sanctum were free of paranoia. Too bad no one had figured out a way to make that work in the real world.

Kate fixed her gaze on the large ring of amber stones set into the center of the floor—the circle stones. She remembered a little about their function from her magic test—the one time she'd been inside the Sanctum before. Most big magical workings took place within the circle stones, which protected anyone *outside* the rings from the energies cast *inside*. Of course, that barrier could work both ways, confining a caster within the stones via a strong magical shield. The circle stones—along with the crystals and lodestones—made this place more than a round room.

The Sanctum served as the total fulfillment of what magic meant to her family.

Brian passed his palm over an array of crystals planted in the wall by the door. With his head back, he concentrated as he chanted a spell. The crystals lit up, initiating the legendary protections of the Sanctum. No one could interrupt a session once a Sanctum's protections were invoked. At least not without considerable effort.

A gentle thrumming came through the floor, up to her feet. A soft, almost imperceptible hum. The voice of the Sanctum. The stone in her hand murmured in harmony with that voice.

Kate held it up and looked into its depths, the room's lights glinting off its shiny surface. A strong greenish sheen glimmered in its darkness.

Part of her whispered a warning.

She tried to pull the stone away, to close her mind to the force that wanted in, but too much of that power had already been down the ebony pathway it built into her very being. A small part of her awareness, helpless to act, felt the stone plant its next spell, then go back to sleep.

Blinking, Kate slipped the stone back in her pocket as Brian finished engaging the Sanctum's protections.

"Are we going to work in the circle stones?" she asked.

"I am. But you being here is bad enough. Stay out of the circle."

"Shouldn't we get Grayson? If this thing is as dangerous as you seem to think—"

"I can handle it. Just don't look at it again."

Kate took the cushion he handed her from a stack on the floor, and then Brian walked to the circles. The amber stones glowed in the dim light, their facets sparkling as she moved away. She dropped the cushion well outside the ring, then sat, watching as Brian took his place inside.

"I need the stone before I seal the circle." Brian tossed her his handkerchief. "This'll work for now. *Don't* touch it again."

She hesitated, then reached into her pocket with the handkerchief, pulling out the stone. She'd heard Brian. *Don't look at it. Don't touch it.* But something else, deep inside her, whispered contrary instructions straight into her soul with all the force of ancient magic.

Touch me. Look at me.

No.

Her fingers clenched tightly into a fist for a moment as she struggled with the compulsion to open her hand, look at the stone, touch it. Then her fingers moved, her hand opened, and her eyes were pulled to the dark, round mass swimming in the pool of white cotton.

And she was lost.

She transferred the stone to her bare hand and caressed it with her thumb. Why give the stone to Brian? She should take the stone inside the circle herself. Kate got to her feet and strode toward the circle stones.

"Kate! What the hell are you doing?" Brian stood, his eyes narrow. He snapped his fingers in front of Kate's eyes. "Shit."

She didn't care what he did.

A spell formed on his lips. Kate took another step forward as her brother cast. She felt herself lunge into the circle, dodging his attempt to intercept her. Part of her registered the electric tingle in her body as his spell hit. Part of her spoke words she didn't understand to the stone and watched it light up with a neon-green glow, like the timer of a bomb that had just been armed.

Then Brian's spell took effect, and she realized with a soul-deep dread that she had walked mindlessly inside the circle holding the glowing stone in her bare hand. Obeying the stone's will, not her own.

Hands shaking, she tried to drop the horrible thing, only to find that she couldn't. The stone held on to her hand, stuck with a supernatural force her frenzied efforts could not break.

"Brian, help me!" She fell to her knees inside the circle, hyperventilating. *Calm down. Brian will fix this.*

Brian grabbed her hand and tried to pry her fingers open. They wouldn't budge—the stone glued her fingers tight, its green glow engulfing them.

The pulsing iridescence spread up her arm. "What's wrong? What's it doing?"

"I don't know. But I have to seal the circle. Dammit, Kate. Why wouldn't you listen?"

Brian squeezed his eyes shut. The crystals around them lit up, enabling their protective barrier to contain any damage but also trap them inside. A lot of good that did them.

Bile rose in her throat. *Don't throw up, don't throw up.* Frantic, she bashed the stone against the sharp crystals in the circle over and over until her fingers bled.

Nothing. The stone still clung to her hand, unscathed.

"Brian? Make this thing stop! What do I do?"

"Quiet! Let me think." He must have figured something out because his eyes got a fierce look of determination in them, and he started to cast. Brian reached out, and the wet sheen of perspiration made his fingers slide as they grabbed hers.

He's scared. Brian's scared. Oh shit. What have I gotten us into?

The stone's green-black iridescence covered half her body now. It took her over inch by inch, leaving the sensation of a million sharp needles shooting through her in its wake. She screamed as a wave of pain started at the hand that held the stone and rode along the lime-colored glow. The darkness she'd felt at the stone's core grabbed hold of her very essence. It ripped it apart, rewriting her down to the life-code, the heart of her self.

As the pain slammed into her head, the Sanctum around her grew dim. Brian's final word rang out. His spell went off, and a flash of pure white light blanketed the Sanctum. An electric shock buzzed her, as if she'd stuck her fingers in a light socket and gotten a charge big enough to light up the whole South Fork arcing through her body. Every nerve lit on fire.

The power rebuilding her paused.

Then it rushed into her in a torrent of energy that made its previous progress seem like the gentle touch of her mother's hand. Every inch of her pounded with agony as the magic rocketed straight into every cell, then all the way out.

Beyond the pain, she heard Brian screaming. She had to help him. But she couldn't move, she couldn't think. All she could do was hurt. As the blackness rushed in to drag her down into blessed unconsciousness, a faint voice inside breathed a warning.

The stone wasn't finished.

Chapter Seven

Kristof climbed the rough stone steps leading up the steep cliff to his sister's workroom. Melina didn't like people dropping by while she worked—with her permanent teleport block extending for a thousand feet around the narrow crag, the staircase provided the only way in or out.

He'd left the skiff he'd rowed to her small island tied to the quay below. The lapping waves echoed against the walls of the inlet. Seagulls circled high above looking for an easy meal, their harsh cries as familiar to him as the sun glinting off the blue-green water.

He ignored them, focused, as always when visiting Melina, on the climb. The narrow steps carved into the stone face of the cliff gave him a toehold, but one false step could be fatal. The drop loomed at a sharp three hundred feet, and the jagged rocks jutting out from the water below looked seriously uninviting. He might have time to get off a shield spell before he hit—then again, he might not.

The jet lag that teleporting across five time zones imposed on his body made the climb even harder. His wrist, healed with a quick spell, still felt stiff. Luckily, the wind was only a warm breeze this evening.

He pulled himself up the handholds carved above the remaining steps and tugged on the short rope ladder leading to Melina's workroom. Maintaining a solid grip, he hoisted himself up in three quick steps. He rolled the ladder up, securing it under the stone overhang.

The wind, stronger now, snapped at his cotton shorts and shirt and ruffled his wavy brown hair, inherited from his Delacroix mother. No need for a disguise spell at home. He could finally look like himself, not like Kris Stevens, Victor, or a gardener. Sharp, sculpted cheekbones framed eyes as blue as the Aegean Sea below him, his muscles coiled with deep-seated tension alien to a Normal like Stevens, and his olive skin shimmered with the heat of the Mediterranean sun.

He gazed out at the glittering waters, the sun setting to the west, and the peninsula of Greece itself, with the capital Athens spread out before him. Melina may have chosen this perch for its privacy, but the view from this part of his father's domain never failed to impress. Small fishing boats and larger pleasure cruisers dotted the sea, reminding him that, no matter how isolated he felt up here, a short distance away the world teemed with life. Lives his father controlled, even if those who lived them had no idea Nicodemus Makris decided how they lived and died.

Someday, if one of his relatives didn't kill him first, Kristof would be the one in control.

Melina opened the French doors of her cottage and leaned out, her brown hair falling in waves around her face. She wore one of those halter dresses she liked: a green one that made her skin seem to glow. The intricate silver-and-amber earrings and rings she wore were bound with spells so complex he wasn't sure he could name them all.

"Well?" she said. "Did you get the stone? Your messages were so cryptic."

"My plan ran into some complications." He took his pack down from his back.

"Papa doesn't have it, does he?"

"No. The Hamiltons do. Papa doesn't know anything about the stone. Assuming your cloak spells can keep him from overhearing us."

Melina smiled. "Of course, brother dear." She walked outside and hugged him. He caught the aroma of mint and witch hazel on her skin. Beckoning him to follow, she led the way into her workroom.

In the front of the two-room cottage, a white sofa faced two overstuffed leather chairs. Kristof sank into one of them and soaked up the light from the sunset coming in the wide windows while Melina went to the old stove. The faint odors of chlorine and sulfur wafted toward him from the back half of the room, near the door to Melina's Sanctum. Chemicals bubbled away on a set of burners behind Melina's wooden desk, which was cluttered with scrolls, silver-and-amber artifacts, and bottles of herbs.

Melina turned on the stove. She pulled out a small metal pot and dumped water, two scoops of coffee, and one of sugar in it, then put the pot on the heat.

"So tell me what went wrong," she said.

He briefed her on the mission. She didn't need to know Brooke's current whereabouts, but he told her everything else. Everything but one important detail on the stone.

The coffee came to a boil. Melina poured the steaming liquid into two small white cups, topping each with a serving of foam. She handed Kristof a cup and sat on the sofa opposite him, taking a drink of her beverage.

"So you're saying you left the stone with the Hamilton girl when you could have taken it?"

Kristof took a sip of coffee, savoring the bittersweet tang, then another. His teleport lag eased. "Seemed like the best option at the time. If I had taken it, I would have blown the mission with Kate. Papa would have found out, and that would have led to him discovering that we had the stone."

"Are you sure there wasn't another reason?" Melina gave him a long look. "Do you have any idea what I went through to find that thing? How hard it was to make sure the information didn't leak to Papa? Then Brian Hamilton comes along and steals the stone out from under me. I couldn't track the bastard, he teleported across so many time zones. Couldn't you have found a better way to deal with Papa's suspicions than leaving the stone with Kate?"

"I did what the mission required. I always do."

"Don't get distracted. If Papa finds out you want to use the stone to overthrow him, being his heir won't save you. He'll make good on his threats to name Dmitri heir instead."

He set his coffee down on the table, gritting his teeth. "I'm not worried about our cousin. Papa's the problem. If he finds out we went after the stone on our own, then we're both in trouble. And you're the one who lost it to Brian. Being Papa's favorite won't save you."

Kristof loved his sister, but there were times he wanted to shake some sense into her. Sure, he liked Kate. Being with her was a part of the mission. A really pleasant part of the mission. He liked the way she shivered when he kissed the back of her neck, the little sigh she gave when she turned over in her sleep, the raw, hungry look in her eyes when she moved under him.

But that wouldn't stop him from taking the stone back.

"The stone's in Hamilton's estate house in the Hamptons. To get it, I'll need some equipment. Something custom." He described what functions he needed in a very specialized set of talismans—a weapon that would punch a hole in the Hamilton security grid from the inside long enough for him to teleport in, grab the stone, and teleport out. Something that wouldn't trigger the grid.

"Embed the talismans in this." He pulled out the keys he used as Kris Stevens and handed her the fob—a Florida conch shell, shiny bronze, about two inches long.

She turned it over once, then tossed it on the table, her lips trembling. "I can't. You know I can't. Papa will find out, and he'll punish me. He'll notice the missing gemstones, and—"

He got up and walked to her, putting a hand on her shoulder. "Lie to him. You'll think of something."

"I can't. I just... I'm already way too deep in this. Papa will punish me if he finds out. I'm not the heir. I don't have your protection—"

He leaned down. "Did I tell you what I saw inside the stone? It had layers of spells programmed into it. Not one, like a talisman, or two or three big spells, like an artifact. Dozens, maybe hundreds, of complex, layered spells."

Her eyes widened. "You saw this?"

"Yes." He gave her a detailed description of the stone—the green fire, the layered spells, how it responded to his casting.

"You said the stone was black, not white?"

He nodded.

"You didn't touch it, did you?"

"No. Not with my bare hand."

"Good. Because if it's the type of artifact I think it is, then it was white before Kate handled it. I think when she touched it, she activated the stone."

A knot twisted inside his stomach. "That's bad?"

She looked up at him, her eyes serious. "Get it back. This is too powerful to leave in Hamilton hands for long."

"You never explained what the hell this thing does, how we can use it to overthrow Papa."

"Oh, believe me, if it's the artifact you described, it has more than enough power to take out him, his bodyguards, and anyone else we want. And after Papa, well, there's always the Hamiltons. You'll need to cement your position as leader, after all."

Her eyes had a dark glow inside as she contemplated the destruction she'd outlined with the careful precision of a Mongol general about to sack a city. Kristof felt a disquiet stir deep within him.

His gaze wandered to a photo on Melina's desk—one of him, his sister, and their mother. It had been taken on his third birthday when they swam in the cool ocean of Mykonos, his sister holding him above the waves as his mother stood in the waist-high water next to them. He looked up at Melina, pure trust shining from his face.

She wasn't telling him everything she knew about the stone. But how much did that matter, if it did what she said it would do?

"So you'll make what I want?" Kristof asked.

She took the key fob from him. "It will take a few days."

"Let me know when it's done."

Kate's eyes opened. Light filtered into her consciousness. So did pain.

She felt like she'd been thrown from her car and dragged behind it for a few miles. Every muscle in her body ached. Even her aches had aches. Each time she moved a sharp jolt of pain from her ribs made her want to stop.

Squeezing her eyes shut, she tried to remember what had happened. That stupid stone had taken control of her, made her bring it inside the circle stones with Brian. He'd cast some kind of spell, the stone had done something, and then... Oh God, the pain. She'd heard Brian screaming, then she'd blacked out.

Her eyelids fluttered open again. She lay in her bed, the only light in the room shining from her bedside lamp. Someone had dressed her in an old, white cotton nightgown. Her alarm clock read *2:00 a.m.*

"Kate? Oh my God, Kate? Are you awake?" Hayley sat next to her, shoulders slumped forward, eyes red.

"Wha...what happened?"

"Don't try to talk. My dad healed you, but you're still not, um, really better yet." She sniffled and reached up to wipe her nose with a tissue.

Kate shifted, then winced. *If Grayson healed me, I'm glad I wasn't awake when I was hurt.*

Hayley put a hand on Kate's shoulder, her fingers pressing in.

Why was Hayley crying?

"Where's Brian? Is he okay?"

"I'm...supposed to let your dad talk to you." Hayley's eyes were wide and filled with tears that trembled on the brink of her eyelids. She sniffled again. "I'm not the one who should..."

Kate's pulse picked up speed. "Not the one who should what?"

"Brian's dead," Hayley blurted out, tears spilling down her face. "He's dead, and no one could save him." She shot to her feet. "No one. Brian was gone...just gone." She ran out the door, leaving it swinging open.

Hayley's words rang through Kate like a lightning bolt. "No. He can't be... There's no way he's—" Hayley was wrong. Brian wasn't dead. There had to be some mistake. No way would her father let that happen.

Kate threw off the covers and slid out of bed. She had to find Brian. He must be here, probably right next door, messed up and in pain like her. She'd go to his room and see him lying on his bed, his head nestled among the striped pillows, and his face would light up when she walked in.

She flew out of her room and threw open the door to Brian's.

His bedroom sat dark and cold and empty.

Like her heart.

Crumpling to the floor, the emptiness took up residence inside her, in the place where the brightness that was Brian used to live. Now there was only a crushing, anguished pain, a pain so overwhelming she wanted to scrape her nails down her face to have something else to feel.

She couldn't imagine Brian being gone. Couldn't think of living through the long years that stretched ahead—of finishing college, of acting, of having a real life—without sharing it all with him. What was the point? She had always been part of Brian and Kate, from the day they were born, him three minutes before her.

As the ache in her body rushed up to gray out her vision and pull the breath from her lungs, one last thought grabbed her and held on.

Brian's death was her fault. All her fault.

The sound of her bedroom door opening brought Kate awake. She turned over in her bed, onto her back, her body aches a little less noticeable now. She felt hot under the covers. Too hot.

How had she returned to her own bed? Did someone find her in Brian's room and bring her here...

Oh God. She remembered everything. A sob rose up from deep inside.

Her father came in and shut the door behind him. She gulped down her tears.

The lines on his face looked deeper, more pronounced than they had been yesterday. He still had on the same suit he'd worn at the office, his tie hanging undone and forgotten around his neck.

"Hayley told me about Brian." Kate's voice was flat. "I don't believe he's dead. You wouldn't have let him die. You would've saved him."

Her father sat on her bed, his normally straight hair in disarray. He took her hand in his. "I did everything in my power. I love Brian. He's my son. But I'm not a god." His gaze slid down, off her face to the floor. "I couldn't do anything. Neither could Grayson. By the time we got to the Sanctum, he was gone."

An expression she'd never seen before veiled his eyes. No, she had seen it once. The day she failed her magic test and been declared a Null.

Defeat.

He looked back up at her. "Tell me what happened. Why were you in the Sanctum?"

Her thoughts flashed to her last few minutes with Brian, when she had tried so desperately to get rid of the stone and Brian had cast a spell that ended with him dead and her unconscious.

Should she tell her father the truth? Brian had some reason not to.

But Brian was dead.

Her father sat and listened as she told him about the stone and the whole horrible mess. She confessed all the stupid mistakes she'd made, mistakes that had led to the disaster that ended with Brian's death. As she spoke, she kicked the coverlet off her bed. It felt way too warm in here.

Kate's voice rose. "I should be dead, not Brian. His death is my fault. If I hadn't—"

"That's not true. You're not to blame." Her father brushed Kate's hair from her forehead. His hand blurred as it moved across her face, as if a faint, multicolored outline ghosted his movements. She wiped her eyes. The blurriness was gone.

Her father still spoke. "If anything, this mess is Brian's fault. He should have brought me the stone. You wouldn't have been involved if Brian had—"

"Don't you blame him." Rage charging her body, she shot straight up in her bed, the sheet falling from her shoulders. "Don't you dare. It's not his fault."

"I'm sorry." He sighed. "You need to rest. You're too distraught now to answer any more questions." He got up to leave.

"I have questions, too, Dad. I need the answers now. What spell did Brian cast? Is his spell what killed him? Or was it the stone? I know you have it all figured out." She twisted the sheet around her fingers. Her double vision was back. She saw her father standing by the bed, and outlined around him, his shape in rainbow hues. Interwoven into the colors and lines of the shape were spirals, twirls, and triangles with squiggles across them—vaguely familiar symbols.

She blinked, then lost the colored outline completely. Maybe her weird vision was a side effect of her injuries. Or the healing spells.

Her father gave her a long, measured look. "I said, we'll talk later. Get some sleep. You'll feel better in the morning. I'll tell the doctor to give you a sedative." He headed toward the door.

"Don't you walk out on me. Not this time. Where were you last night? Off on another oh-so-important emergency? Why weren't you *here*?"

Her father stopped, his back rigid. He turned around. "Kate, I'm sorry, so sorry, I was away. But I can't always be where I want." His voice sounded low and gentle, but his eyes were like steel.

"Do you even care that Brian is dead? Or is losing him just a setback in your plans?"

He paused and swallowed. "That's... You know better. I loved Brian. I love both of you."

"Yeah, in your own way. With conditions." The pain around her heart had flared into a blaze. "What did those conditions drive Brian to do? What's your favorite saying? 'If you don't control the situation, the situation controls you.' Brian was always trying to prove himself to you. That's why he kept playing all these games, isn't it? So what the hell was he doing?"

"I have no idea."

"Don't lie to me." The blaze inside Kate kindled something she'd never felt before— a spark of power. "And don't tell me to take some pills and go away. I need to know why Brian died."

Her father turned to leave. "Stop worrying about Brian and the stone." He cleared his throat. "Whatever Brian did, it's caster business. Not yours."

"Stop it, just stop it. You keep shutting me out. I'm sick of it." Kate spat out the words. The spark of power inside her burst into a white-hot ball of fury, searching for something to burn. It raged inside her mind, rummaging through her thoughts, her impulses, her memories.

The symbol for fire sprang to her consciousness like a blazing wheel. The same magical glyph she'd failed to conjure up six years ago in the Sanctum. The power boiled over into the symbol, filling its arcane lines with overheated energy.

Before she could say or do anything, fire formed in the air in front of her and shot toward her father. He had no time to defend himself.

The bolt of flame hit him like a burning spear, the tip aimed at his heart.

Kate watched in horror, her anger gone cold, as the impact hurled her father backward through her bedroom door, the crash splintering it into sharp, jagged pieces. He landed with a boom in the hallway. His head hit the polished wood floor with a crack. The fire on his chest smoldered as he lay limp and bleeding.

The single remaining spark from the fire above her dropped to her bed, flared for a moment, then went out.

Chapter Eight

Help! Brian!" Her stomach seized at the futility of that call. "Grayson! Help!" Kate jumped out of bed and ran toward her father. Swirls of red, yellow, and orange lights moved around her, all jumbled together. Little strands of color jumped off her and twirled out to him, as if she remained connected to him through the lights.

She blinked, and the colored tendrils disappeared.

Maybe they were an illusion. Was Dad lying burned and bleeding a mirage, as well, a trick to get her to believe she'd hurt him? Had someone drugged her or cast a spell on her to make her think she had attacked her father?

Hayley sat right next to me earlier. She must have done something. I can't trust Hayley. I can't trust anybody.

Kate stumbled to the hallway, dropping to her knees and touching her father's neck, looking for a pulse.

Please, please be okay.

Her fingers came away sticky with blood from where a piece of wood sliced him. His chest rose and fell. He was breathing—still alive. But burns slashed across his chest and blood splattered the hardwood floor of the hallway, the walls, the potted hydrangea in the corner.

Shouts and footsteps sounded from down the hall, and Grayson appeared, Hayley trailing close behind. Kate looked up into her uncle's eyes, hoping to find reassurance. Instead she saw only questions.

"Who did this? Is the attacker still here? Are you hurt?" Her uncle's eyes went from her bloodstained nightgown to her shaking hands. "Kate." He leaned down and grabbed her arms. "Who did this? Is there someone in the house?"

Kate took a deep breath. "There's no one else here. Please help him. I think...I think I—" She couldn't stop staring at the blood on her palms.

Grayson pulled her father's shirt away and assessed his wounds. "These are bad. Hayley, go to my room. Get my bag."

He pushed Kate back as Hayley took off at a run. Kneeling at her father's side, Grayson held his hand about a foot above him. His gaze went distant as he chanted a spell.

His palms lit up with a yellow glow. The faint aroma of gardenias filled the air.

Kate rocked back on her heels. She stared as Grayson passed his hands slowly down her father's chest, and the radiance pouring from her uncle, as golden as sunshine, flowed into her father's wounds and knitted his flesh together as if he had never been hurt at all.

She saw the magic. The subtle power she hadn't been able to see six years ago in the Sanctum, despite the desperate urging of her father, she now perceived as clearly as the blood staining his white shirt.

Victor, followed by two of his security team, pounded up the stairs, sliding to a stop next to her dad.

His team took up positions at each end of the hall. Grayson looked up with a start, then turned back to finish his spell.

"Is he...?" Victor asked.

Grayson touched the amber-and-silver cufflinks on her father's shirtsleeves. "His shield talisman was active but on low power. A lot of energy got through, but the damage is superficial. No major organs were hit. I fixed the worst, but there's still more to do." Grayson took a small pill case out of his pocket. He took out two pills and swallowed them. "Any idea who did this?" He stood.

Victor's eyes lost focus, then refocused on Grayson. "External shields are all secure. The attack had to come from inside."

"Victor, I—" Kate tried to get his attention.

"Someone or something was already here?" Grayson asked Victor.

"Yes."

"Shut up already and listen to me. *I* did this."

They stared at her. Victor said, "What do you mean?"

"We were talking. I got mad at him, and I..." Her words trailed off as her gaze fixed again on the blood all over her hands.

"You can't do this, Kate. This is magical damage," Grayson said.

"Yeah, I know. I can't explain it. But one minute we were...arguing. And the next, I'd done...something. Blasted him, I guess. Something else, too... I could see the spell you cast, when you were healing Dad. I could see it."

Grayson's eyes flicked to Victor, then Kate. "Come with me. I'll take you to the Sanctum where we can sort this out." He reached for her arm.

Victor stepped between them. "Nope, security issue. I'll deal with Kate."

"Whatever happened here concerns magic, young man, and that's my arena. You have other things to do."

"My first priority is protecting the boss."

"So stay here and protect him."

"My team can do that. If Kate's responsible, I need to find out how."

"Stop it." Kate stepped around Victor and glared at the both of them. "You two are arguing while my dad is bleeding. Grayson, don't you need to finish healing him? I'll talk with Victor. Okay?"

A look passed between the two of them, a signal Kate couldn't decipher. Then Grayson nodded, turning back to Kate's father.

Something was going on with Victor and Grayson, and it had nothing to do with territorial posturing.

Hayley ran over, breathless. She handed Grayson a yellow silk bag. He pulled out a talisman shaped like a silver snake with bloodred stones for eyes and laid it on her father's chest. Grayson rested his hand on top, and after a brief word, the talisman lit up with a golden light that sank down into her father's skin. Kate's vision seemed to shift all of a sudden and the luminescence turned off as mysteriously as it had begun. Glow or not, his angry burns began to turn into healthy pink skin.

Victor grabbed her arm. Kate stiffened and pulled away. "Let go of me. I'll talk to you, but I need to clean up first."

"Two minutes." Victor said.

Kate went inside the bathroom down the hall and closed the door. Leaning against the cold wood, she slid to the floor. She sat staring down at her bloodstained hands in a kind of numb horror. What the hell had happened? One minute she'd been arguing with her father, the next he'd lain in a bloody mess in the middle of the hallway.

She went to the sink and turned on the water. It washed over her hands, sending the blood swirling down the drain in a pinkish torrent.

Dimly, through the haze of her shock, she thought she heard a knock at the door.

She left the water running and sank to the floor again, gazing at the underside of the white pedestal sink. Her eyes followed the S-curve of the porcelain drain until it straightened and plunged down into the black-and-white hexagonal tile floor. She closed her eyes and let her mind find a pattern in the curves, folding the shape around and around until it resembled one of the magical symbols she had learned in class, years ago.

One of the designs Brian had traced when he cast a spell.

She didn't remember what the curved symbol meant, but that didn't matter. She wound the curves over and over in her mind, then traced them with her fingers, building the power up until it was hers to use.

The knock grew more persistent. She ignored it. Her eyes were filled with the curves of the pattern, seeing nothing else. The power rushed through her like a clean, cool wind. She felt lighter than air.

She—

"What the hell is taking so long?" Victor yelled. "Kate! Are you all right?" The door crashed open.

Her vision came rushing back. The expression on Victor's face was priceless. But what was he gaping at? Then she caught her reflection in the bathroom mirror.

She hovered halfway between the floor and ceiling with nothing between her drawn-up legs and the ground but several feet of air.

"Oh my God." Kate fell hard, losing her breath along with whatever force was holding her up. She slammed her wrist on the sink, sending a jolt of pain shooting down her arm.

Victor lunged at her, reaching with strong arms to catch her before she hit the floor. "What the hell?"

Kate was pressed against Victor's chest, heart beating fast, his arms holding her way too tight.

Victor's eyes widened. "Uh..."

The cotton of her nightgown seemed very thin all of a sudden. "Let go of me. Please."

He set her down and took a step back. "What happened? Did someone—"

"No one did anything to me." She grabbed her bathrobe, which was hanging on a hook by the shower, and pulled it on, wincing at the pain in her wrist. "Whatever I'm doing, I did it myself."

Unless Victor was responsible. Maybe he made me attack Dad. Was he behind everything?

Victor waited just outside the door, eyes steady on her.

"Where do you want to talk?" she asked.

"Your dad's office." He turned and walked down the hall, clearly expecting her to follow.

Shields protected her father's office. If Victor wanted to try something, no one would know. Kate shook her head. *That's just silly. I'm as twitchy as a caster.*

She went with Victor to her father's office. He motioned to her to sit in one of the leather chairs next to the brick fireplace. She hesitated, then sat. This room had her father's stamp on it as much as his DC office did—his mahogany desk, Arkady Makris's amulet, kept in a secure display case on the mantel, an oar mounted on the wall from his championship rowing days at Harvard. She shifted in her seat and focused on the imposing portrait of her mother, painted when Kate was six. Maybe she could draw some comfort from the painting. Then again, maybe not. Faith Hamilton, red hair wild about her shoulders, blue eyes blazing, shined forth as everything Kate wasn't. A caster, a wife, a mother, a powerful woman.

Victor went to her father's liquor cabinet and poured them each a glass of wine. He handed her one, then sank into the chair facing her.

"You know Dad doesn't approve of underage drinking." She rolled her eyes as she took the glass.

"After what happened tonight, even he'd make an exception. Tell me everything," he said.

Kate sighed. She told Victor all she remembered about hurting her father, from the time she woke up until Victor arrived and saw her father lying in the hallway. Parts of what happened in her bedroom, like when she got angry with her father, seemed vague and distant, almost like a dream.

"You're not being very clear."

She squirmed in her chair. "No. Well, I don't understand exactly what went on. I know what I did, but how could I have done it? One minute we were having an argument, and the next..." She took a sip of her wine to cover the rush of emotion, her throat tight. "He was all crumpled up in the hallway, hurt. I don't know how I could have blasted him. I'm a Null."

"That's what I was told."

"What the hell do you mean?"

Victor sat silent for a moment. Then, "Tell me how you feel right now."

"Fine." Kate crossed her legs.

"Really? Your brother's dead and your father's lying on the floor bleeding upstairs, and you're just dandy? Bullshit." Victor leaned forward. "I asked you a question. How do you feel?"

"None of your goddamn— You really want to know?" Kate's voice rose as she got up from her chair. "I feel like shit, okay? Is that what you want? It's my fault Brian's dead, and it's my fault Dad's lying upstairs bleeding. Do you think I wanted to hurt him? Do you think I want to be here, talking to you? I don't even trust you, okay?"

She walked over to the desk. "For all I know, this is something you planned. Maybe Brian got the stone from you. Or you were trying to get it from him. Maybe you put a spell on the thing to control me."

"Listen to yourself." Victor said. "If I said to you what you just said to me, what would you think?"

She took a sip of her wine. "You were twitchy after a spell."

"Uh-huh."

"No, I don't think so. I'm not a caster. I don't—"

"It's clear you are casting spells and getting the aftereffects. There are three ways I can explain this." Victor paused, taking a drink from his glass.

"And?"

"One: you've gained the ability to cast. I don't see how that could have happened. Nulls can't do that. Two: someone else, an enemy, most likely, is controlling your actions. Or three, the stone is still possessing you."

"How do you know so much about the stone?"

"What do you think I've been doing all night? Cleaning up your mess. And from what I've seen, possession by someone, or some-*thing*, is the most likely explanation. And if you are being controlled, then we're all in a lot of danger."

She looked down at her wine, trying to mask the fear in her eyes, then took a long drink. "But Brian freed me from the stone's control."

Victor's face started to waver in her vision. How strong was this stuff?

"Maybe."

She put the glass down. "Is there a way you can tell?"

"I can do some diagnostic spells. They'll tell me if you are under someone else's control. Just like possession. As for the stone, well, that's more Grayson's area."

"Then why are you asking me all these damn questions? Do the stupid spell."

He smiled a tight smile. "A couple of reasons. If someone is controlling you, you might tell me something useful."

"Like what? 'And now I will reveal my master plan?' That only happens in B-movies." She blinked, her eyelids so much heavier than they should be.

"You would never make things that easy on me."

"What's the other reason?"

The room's getting dark. What happened to the lights?

"I had to give the drug time to work."

"You...asshole." She slid into unconsciousness.

Chapter Nine

The Sanctum woke Kate.

Its song came up through the smooth rocks and crystals embedded in the floor, through her nightgown and robe, and into her skin, her bones. The low hum of a thousand small things working in harmony—a quiet symphony of energy—vibrated inside her as she lay on the hard, flat surface.

It felt like being a part of all the power of creation.

Basking in the feeling, she enjoyed the energy flowing over her skin. It seeped into her bit by bit. Keeping her eyes closed, she followed the hum to the source of the energy—the crystals and rocks beneath her, and through them, the stones of power all around the room. The song she heard playing in her soul came from them. She knew it.

The Sanctum was alive for her. Just as it had been for Brian.

Kate's eyes opened. She remembered what had happened in her father's office.

Victor. I should have paid attention to those little voices in my head—should have known better than to trust him.

She shut her eyes. Better that she stay still and pretend to be asleep, until she could figure things out. Faking sleep proved easy; she let herself sink into the rhythm of the crystals.

Footsteps rang against the stone floor, then her uncle's voice sounded close by.

"Well?"

"She passed the simple tests." Victor's voice, from a few feet away. "But they don't explain how she did what she did back at the house. Now we have to bring out the big guns."

"We need her awake for that," Grayson said.

"She's waking up now," Victor said. "Faster than she should be. I gave her enough tranquilizer to knock out a rhino."

"You should have let me handle her. This is my business, not yours."

"I'm not leaving until I know who, or what, attacked the boss. They shouldn't have used Kate to do it. Whoever they are, I'm going to make them pay for that."

Victor? Caring? Will wonders never cease.

"It's not what you think," Grayson said. "Look around you. The Sanctum's responding to her. What happened in here earlier, with the stone, is nowhere near as mundane as her being used."

"Maybe. But I'm not as convinced as you."

Kate heard her uncle sigh. Footsteps approached her, then stopped. "Sweetheart, sit up," Grayson said. "We need to talk."

A part of her wanted to keep lying on the Sanctum floor and never open her eyes again. She wouldn't have to think about Brian or her father. But then she wouldn't find out what she needed to know: What had happened to her? What did the stone actually do, and why is it so important to everyone? And how had Brian died?

She sat up slowly and pushed her hair out of her eyes. She lay inside the ring of circle stones, glistening amber in the Sanctum's light. The crystals on the walls shone brighter than ever. Their facets sparkled with a million shades of red, yellow, and orange. The spiral patterns on the walls seemed to pulse in time to the hum she felt throughout her body.

Grayson pulled a chair over to the edge of the circle and sat, his eyes steady on her. Victor leaned against a carved wooden cabinet on the far wall. Grayson had changed his shirt, but his pants still had flecks of blood on them—her father's.

She stood, reaching out to touch the faint shimmer rising up from the circle stones.

"Kate, don't—" Grayson began.

As her fingers brushed the shimmer, a flurry of sparks went up from the contact point.

"Ow! That stings." She snatched her hand back, glaring at her uncle.

"I set the circle's barrier up to hold you," Victor said. "You can't get out or use magic. Don't bother trying. It'll do more than sting next time." He had that look of his—halfway between a smile and a sneer—that told her that he didn't care what she thought.

She turned her glare to Victor. "I'm fine now. There's no reason to cage me like an animal."

Victor cocked his head and stared down his nose at her. "Just a safety measure, 'til we know what we're dealing with."

"What's that supposed to mean?" Kate asked.

"We're not sure what's happened to you, and we need to find out." Grayson got up and went to the cabinet behind him. He ran his palm over a latch on the door and concentrated, and it popped open. He reached in and pulled an object out of its dark recesses: a filigree silver ball about the size of a grapefruit, studded with chunks of what looked like topaz.

"Victor thinks you might still be possessed, either by the stone or by someone or something else."

She tugged her robe tighter around her. "Is that why I attacked Dad?" Kate searched Victor's face for a reaction. Nothing. She wouldn't want to play poker against him.

"I don't know," Victor said.

"How did I levitate in the bathroom? Any explanation for that?"

Victor gave her his silent stare.

"Do you remember anything I taught you about possession?" Grayson asked.

"Um…"

Grayson frowned. "Possession's not an easy feat to achieve. Magic—the way we do it now—can't affect the mind very much. But ancient magic—such as the stone's—is a different story alto-gether. From what we can tell from our forensic reconstruction—"

"Your what?"

"I cast a spell that showed me what happened to you and Brian from the time you entered the Sanctum until Brian died."

"So you know what killed him."

Victor's hand cut through the air. "Later."

"But—"

"Now we're worried about you," Victor said. "And I've seen the sort of thing the stone did to you before. Possession."

She remembered what the stone had done in the Sanctum—forcing her to look at it, taking control of her actions, making her bring it into the circle, trigger some kind of spell.

She thought back over the past twenty-four hours. When had the stone first begun calling the shots? Had it only controlled her that last time, in the Sanctum? Or yesterday afternoon, when she'd looked into its jet-black depths and lost the whole day? Had she been its puppet from the very first time she'd touched it, when it stung her and she'd lost a half hour in the theater dressing room? It certainly made sure she hadn't remembered it changing color. She shivered.

Was the stone still dominating her? She didn't think so. She felt its absence, like the hole formed by a newly pulled tooth she was used to running her tongue over. She kept going to the place in her mind where it used to be but found nothing there.

"I know you don't have any reason to believe me, but I don't think the stone is still controlling me."

"Why not?"

She shrugged. "Now that it's gone, I can feel it's gone. It's hard to explain."

"I need more than your say-so, princess." He took the silver ball from Grayson and gave each yellow stone a light touch. The ball lit up with a soft glow from inside, the luminescence spreading to each stone. He tossed it, underhanded, at Kate.

The silver ball came straight for her. She ducked, but it swerved right before it reached her, veering off to circle her. It spun around

Kate three times, just outside the circle stones, leaving a trail of golden light in the air behind it. The ball stopped, hovering in the air to the left of Victor, and its topaz stones dimmed, awaiting his next order like one of his obedient security guards.

"This isn't going to hurt, is it?" Kate asked.

"No," Grayson said. "Victor is going to ask you questions. You answer them. That's all."

Kate eyed the silver ball, floating in front of her. "What does it do?"

"The Verity Globe tells us if anything is influencing your answers."

"Like a lie detector?"

"No." Victor broke in. "Look, Grayson can tell you all the technical details later. Right now, tell us everything that happened, from the time that you first got this stone to when you blacked out."

"You're kidding. I already told Dad everything."

"And he's out of it, so—"

"Is he okay? Will he be...?" She clutched her nightgown in stiff fingers.

"He's resting," Grayson said. "He'll be fine. So tell us what happened."

She sighed. She gave them a brief rundown of what had happened since Brian gave her the stone. The globe didn't do anything when she told them that Brooke demanded the stone from her, but Victor's reaction was predictably Victor.

"You should have told me, and your father." Victor punctuated his statement with an accusing finger.

"Yeah. Believe me, I know. But I promised Brian I wouldn't say anything about the stone to anyone."

"And why did he make you promise that?"

"I don't know. He wouldn't tell me."

"What did he tell you about the stone?" Grayson asked.

"Not much. Just that it was ancient. Powerful. And if it fell into the wrong hands, well, you know."

The globe hovered in front of her, its yellow stones glowing.

"Why did Brian interrupt your play to hand the stone to you? Why not give it to one of us?" Victor pushed away from the wall and walked a few steps closer to Kate.

"I don't know. He..." She looked from Victor to Grayson. Brian could have been working for either one of them, but clearly he didn't trust them. Could she? She glanced at the silver globe. If she didn't answer, would they assume something made her not answer?

"He never said."

Victor frowned. "Kate, you have to tell us everything you know. If Brian said something—"

"Look, I don't know anything else." All she had left were her own suspicions about what Brian might have been doing with the stone, where he had gotten it, for whom he might have been working. But those were just guesses.

Victor gave her a long look and frowned, as if he were weighing everything she'd said. Then he held out his hand. The swirls of golden energy around her dissipated, and the ball sped back to him. "It didn't react to you. So you're not possessed." He handed the ball to Grayson.

"So I'm the one who hurt Dad? Not the stone?"

Her uncle's eyes were sympathetic. "Yes."

She slumped to the floor. "How?"

"I don't know. But I know how to find out." Grayson put the ball back in the cabinet and shut the door, locking it with a moment's concentration. He walked to the edge of the circle stones. Reaching into his pocket, he took out a small silver box that fit in the palm of his hand. He opened it. Inside, nestled in a cocoon of white silk, sat the stone, black as bone burned down to coal in the heat of a holocaust.

It whispered to Kate from the moment her uncle lifted the lid on the box.

Touch me. Touch me. Touch me one more time. Just once, and then everything will be over.

She tumbled into its vast ebony depths. Its quiet murmurs continued, and she sensed the enormous power slumbering within. She felt pulled toward the awakening magic—magic that had its own, inhuman agenda.

An agenda she wanted to fulfill. She leaned toward the stone—a little, an inch, before images of Brian's frantic chanting, his panicked face, his voice screaming in agony, rushed into her mind. She jerked back. *No.*

"What the hell are you doing with that in here?" Victor took a step toward Grayson.

"I've got it under control. It's safe enough." Grayson shut its lid.

Kate blinked. *What the hell just happened?*

"Are you kidding?" Victor said. "That thing killed Brian. It messed with Kate's mind and did God knows what to her. You think you can play with it?"

"I'm not playing. And as to whether it killed Brian, that's a matter of interpretation."

"Are you tweaked? What the hell is the matter with you?"

"I know what I'm doing, young man. Better than you do. I need the stone here to diagnose what's going on with Kate."

"I don't like this."

"I'll need your help. Monitor me while I do the spell. Make sure nothing...interferes," Grayson said.

"You mean like the 'safe and under control' stone?"

"That or anything else."

"Fine."

Kate stared down at the ties of her nightgown. Anything to avoid focusing on the box in Grayson's hand. "It's not fine with me. I don't want that thing doing anything else to me."

"It won't. I'm only using it as a kind of reference. If I can see the traces of its influence in you while I do a diagnostic spell, then that will tell me what the stone did, and didn't, do. Just sit back and relax."

She squirmed as Grayson reopened the silver box. Maybe a quick peek at the stone wouldn't hurt. Its dark radiance drew her gaze as she looked up, but nothing murmured in her mind. *Good. Maybe I just imagined it all.*

Grayson concentrated and murmured a spell, his fingers weaving curves and crosses too fast for Kate to follow. Victor's eyes narrowed in concentration—monitoring Grayson, she assumed.

She stared at the stone, waiting for it to do something, anything. It remained silent.

After a minute or so her back got warm and tingly. The warmth changed to pinpricks of ice. Grayson's spell worked its way into her body, molecule by molecule, taking her apart and looking at every particle of her until it understood her better than she knew herself.

"Um...Grayson, this feels pretty weird."

"Don't worry, it's supposed to." He glanced over at the stone.

The cold receded as quickly as it had come, leaving her stomach churning.

Victor stared at her. "No way. I don't believe it." He shot Grayson a glance. "Why didn't I see that before?"

"The stone's residual energy blocked her aura. I cleared it out." Grayson snapped the lid shut on the stone and put the box in his pocket.

"Aura? I have an aura?" She looked down at herself. She couldn't see anything different.

"Your aura's changed. It's a rainbow hue like ours now, not a Null's blue-green tint. We both see it," Grayson said.

"What does that mean?"

"It means you're a not a Null anymore. You're a—"

"Maybe nothing. Wearing a wizard's robe doesn't make you a wizard." Victor gave Grayson a long look. Then he addressed Kate. "After all, you were supposed to be big shakes before, when you were a kid, and that amounted to a big pile of nada—or so I'm told. Didn't you fail your aptitude test, back when you were twelve?"

She flushed. She could still remember every minute of the test. The flame glowing in her mother's hand, her mother pleading with Kate to cast her own spell and duplicate the feat. She'd reached for the symbol in her mind, using the chant that had been drilled into her memory. Sweat had poured from her as she looked at Grayson, her eyes desperate. Her utter failure as the circle stones went out, one by one, beneath her feet.

"Yeah. I'm not likely to forget. Why are you bringing that up? It's not like it's news."

Victor shrugged. "I can't see that anything's changed here. So your aura's pretty. Big whoop. It's not like you can control what you did upstairs." He turned around and stalked back to his post by the wall, then stood and watched her. His eyes went blank for a minute, the way they did when he checked the security grid. The shimmering curtain around the circle stones flickered, then turned a lighter shade of amber.

Asshole. She'd show him. Grayson said she wasn't a Null anymore. Fine. She'd take Victor's words and shove them down his oh-so-annoying throat.

The symbol for fire sprang to her mind once more. Four points joined by a circle with a sharp twist at the end. The ancient words came back to her—the chant she'd memorized so long ago and so perfectly for the test to no avail. She hadn't needed it a few hours ago, the power rising in her so hot and so urgent, but maybe she'd need it now.

She focused on the symbol—tracing it out with angry, jerking movements against the cold floor of the Sanctum as she chanted the words she thought she'd never speak again. The words her mother had urged her to say so long ago, the words Grayson had drilled into her. The words he focused on so intently now, standing over the circle, his eyes locked on her.

Power rushed from the center of her being, down her arm, and around her hand. It leaped into the air and burst into flame around her fingers, the tendrils a soft warmth that caressed her skin as they danced back and forth. She stared at her hand. Her flaming hand.

"Huh," Victor said to Grayson, a half-smile on his face. "I guess you were right."

She was a caster. *Well, hot damn.*

Chapter Ten

It wasn't as if Kate hadn't suspected she could do magic. Not after what she did to Dad and all that "floating in the bathroom" business. And the soft thrum of the Sanctum humming in her bones. Still... She let out a ragged breath. To say that this changed everything was an understatement.

"I know this is a shock—" Grayson began.

Victor broke in. "How the hell did it happen? It's impossible."

"It's never happened before. But that doesn't mean it's impossible," Grayson said.

"Did the stone change me?" Kate asked. "When it killed Brian?"

"Yes. My scan showed that the genetic combination for magic has been altered inside your DNA. When you were tested for magical aptitude, your Null gene was dominant, your caster gene recessive. That's not supposed to change. But it has. Now your caster gene is expressing."

It sounded like Grayson was about to say something else, but he stayed silent.

"How could an artifact change me into a caster? I thought they held a few more spells than a talisman, more powerful spells."

"The stone is different, Kate. Its creator layered spells into it, spells connected to each other. When the right conditions come up, those spells are triggered, almost like a program executing on a computer."

"Is it...finished?" It didn't feel finished.

"I'm sure there's nothing else to worry about. But if anything else bothers you, come to me. Let me know what's happening. We'll figure it out together."

Kate drew her knees up to her chin and glanced sideways at her uncle. "Seems like you've figured out quite a bit already. You said that forensic reconstruction spell you cast showed what happened. So you know how Brian died."

"All the spell lets me do is put together a theory."

"And?"

He sighed. "Brian tried to interfere with the stone when it was making you a caster. He tried a simple counterspell. It interrupted the stone's process, and the stone's energy surged into him."

Grayson's explanation made some sense. Brian had tried a spell, she remembered that. And the backlash... Well, she'd never forget the feel of the power that had arced into Brian. But something about Grayson's explanation—something she couldn't pin down—bothered her.

"Did the energy backlash kill him?" Kate said.

"Yes, I'm sorry." Grayson closed his eyes. The lines on his face looked deeper even in the dim light of the Sanctum. "It over-

whelmed his protective spell. The stone's energy proved too powerful once it activated."

"That's one way of putting it," Victor said.

"Victor..."

"Stop dancing around the truth. If she's a caster, she should know
what this thing is. After all, it created her."

Grayson sighed. He rubbed the bridge of his nose, then gave
Kate a long look.

"Kate, the stone... It's a work of primal magic."

"You're kidding." Her hands twisted the hem of her nightgown in
a little knot. The ancient casters had used primal magic to power
their spells—magic in its raw form. Modern casters had lost the ability to use primal magic unless they used the rare artifacts the
ancients had left behind. Brian had said the stone was old
but...damn. What the hell did it mean that primal magic had made
her a caster?

Grayson continued, "I don't know what Brian was doing with the
stone, or if he knew it was a primal magic artifact."

"Oh, he knew," Victor said. "Brian was way too sharp to be carrying around a primal magic artifact and not know it."

"Believe what you want. I know— I knew Brian. He would
never have delved into primal magic, not without... He just would-
n't." Grayson slumped over in his chair, holding his head in his
hands.

"Do you know where he got the stone?" Kate asked.

"It doesn't matter now," Grayson said.

"Like hell it does," Victor said. "Whoever was chasing him will
still be after it."

Grayson took his pillbox from his pocket and swallowed a dose of medication. "Brian's dead. Let any secrets he had die with him. If you want to blame someone for what he did, blame me. Obviously I did something wrong when I trained him." He tucked his pillbox away again. "He should have come to me, told me about it. But he didn't. I'm going to be living with this for the rest of my life."

Grayson sat with his head down, still and quiet, the breath moving out of his lungs at first slowly and then with a sudden exhale, almost like a sob.

Victor's dark eyes focused on her. Did he see her as a threat? She guessed he would, all things considered.

She straightened up, letting her knees fall down in a cross-legged position. "You can let me out. I can control myself now."

Victor crossed his arms. "Are you sure? Primal magic made you a caster. How do you control that?"

Grayson sat up. "Right now, I don't have any reason to believe that Kate is any different than any other new caster. This morning, in her room, she did the same thing a powerful, untrained rogue would do—if that rogue ended up in an emotional situation. You might know something about that, Victor."

Victor grunted.

Kate wondered what Victor had done to deserve that remark.

"We're lucky she did it here and not at school," Grayson added.

"You're sure that outburst wasn't due to the stone?" Victor said.

"I'm sure." Grayson turned to Kate. "You're going to have to learn how to control your abilities. You need training. Do you understand this?"

"Now? But Brian just... I need time." How could he make her

work on her powers when it took every bit of concentration not to break down crying?

"Our enemies won't give us time, sweetheart. I'm sorry, but training starts now."

"I don't have to stay at home, do I? Brian..." She gulped down tears. "Brian went to school and trained here at the same time. I can, too." There were things she could give up. Her friends, her favorite classes. Maybe even acting. But not Kris.

"It's summer. You can train full time. And you'll need to, in order to catch up."

Kate groaned.

Grayson got to his feet. "This isn't an elective at school. This is life or death. If you don't get trained, you could kill someone. Do you want to do to someone else what you did to your dad today? Some boy you're going out with—"

"*No*. All right, you've made your point. I'll do what you want." She'd have to figure out how to see Kris. The sooner she learned to teleport, the better.

"You'll have to talk to your father about college. I can work around your schedule, the same way I did with Brian. But your major—drama—I don't know if he'll accept that. Casters usually major in political science or economics."

Like acting isn't all about manipulating people? No point making that argument now. Maybe later, with her dad. Still, she'd always assumed casters got to do what they wanted. "I want to have my own life. Going to Cornell is important to me."

"I know. But there are more important things for you to learn than acting. Especially now. Politics, economics, psychology... You have to know how people think, how they act, so that you can—"

"So that I can pull their strings? I don't want to be a part of what Dad does."

Victor grinned. "Oh, you'll want to, princess. Eventually, everybody enjoys making the 'powerful' people dance to their tune."

"You make me sick."

"You'll get over it." Victor walked around the circle, his forehead wrinkled in concentration. The crystals surrounding Kate deactivated, their hum fading as their light dimmed.

Kate tested the border with her hand. When nothing zapped her, she stumbled to her feet. Grayson gave her a hand up, and she moved out of the circle.

Her uncle gave her a brief hug. "I'm sorry we had to do that," he said. "You understand why?"

"Yes," she murmured. "But I don't have to like it."

"No, I don't suppose so." He let go of her. "I'll talk to your father. We'll set up a training schedule for you." Grayson led her toward the Sanctum door.

"What are you going to do about the stone?" Kate asked.

"Keep it safe." Grayson patted his pocket. "Figure out what else it does, if it has a purpose beyond creating casters from Nulls."

She heard the stone calling to her again, its voice faint through the silver box. She had no idea what its purpose was, but it had one, all right.

"Even if all it does is make casters, that's plenty," Grayson said. "We could create an army with this—"

"That thing's a danger," Victor said. "After what it did to Brian, we should destroy it. I don't care how many casters we can make."

He stood in the entryway, arms crossed.

"Move aside, young man." Grayson's voice turned cold. Kate clutched his arm.

"We'll talk about this later." Victor stepped away, the fierce light in his eyes making his words seem more like a threat than a promise.

"As you wish." Grayson's glance at Victor as they left would have withered Kate to a little pile of ashes. Great. The last thing she needed was the two of them throwing words at each other as if they were kinetic-punch spells. What she wanted right now were some solid, comforting answers about Brian's death. Answers that made more sense than Grayson's.

But answers seemed to be in short supply. The sun still wasn't up as they came outside into the cool morning air, but a hint of light showed in the east. The soft sound of waves breaking rose up from the beach. A robin sang up in the tall pine that loomed over the entrance. She wished she could shut it up. How could it sing such a happy song when Brian was dead?

A yawn seized her and didn't let go for a long time.

"Get some sleep, sweetheart," Grayson said as they walked up the path to the house. "I know it's tough to stop thinking about Brian, but you need to rest."

Maybe she did, but the waves of grief that washed over her weren't the only thing keeping her awake. It would be hard to sleep while worries about the stone ran through her mind. Was she imagining the stone's call to touch it?

"Grayson, it seemed like... I think..."

"What?"

He would think her a lunatic if she said anything, or worse yet,

133

that the stone still messed with her mind.

Or maybe not. She remembered when she'd failed her magic test. Grayson had been the one who had picked her up out of the darkened circle stones and dried her tears. He'd told her that magic wasn't everything, that she'd find something else to make her heart sing. She'd trusted him then. Maybe she could now.

"The stone talked to me. When you had its case open." She held her breath, looking up at him.

He grabbed her arm. "You're sure? What did it say?"

She hesitated. "It wants me to touch it again. One more time. I think…it isn't finished with me."

He gazed out across the ocean, and it seemed that complex calculations were going off rapid-fire behind his eyes. Then he looked down at her.

"Stay away from it. Don't touch it. No matter what, don't do anything at all with the stone until I tell you to. Do you understand?"

"But what does it mean—"

He shook her, hard enough to rattle her teeth. "Do you understand? Kate? Tell me you won't touch it."

"Yes. Yes, I get it. Let go."

He let go. "Do what I told you. Get some rest. And let me take care of this. The stone is my problem, not yours."

Easy for him to say. It hadn't changed him into a caster and killed his brother. And it wasn't calling to *him*.

As they strolled up the walkway to the house, an uneasiness settled into her stomach. She didn't really want to leave the stone to Grayson, not when he wouldn't give her a straight answer to her questions. Questions that deserved answers—puzzles that needed to be unraveled by her, not Grayson, not Victor.

The stone had killed Brian. She wasn't finished with it, either.

Kristof snagged a microbrew from a girl passing out an armful. His gaze lingered on the curve of her bikinied hips as she strolled away, blending into the crowd of prep school partiers. The noontime breeze coming in from the Atlantic felt cool through his T-shirt, but that's not what made the balcony of this luxe Paumanok mansion such a great place to hang. Instead, the view of the Hamilton estate next door, barely visible over the tall privet hedges, prompted Kristof to crash this little pool party. A party he'd made sure would happen when he'd arranged for an "emergency" to spring up for the parents of the house, calling them away and leaving the kids all alone for the weekend.

People were so predictable.

He played with the silver ring on his finger. It might be cool to enjoy his beer, flirt with the girls, and chill in the pool for a few hours. No one would know he played hooky. But he was a caster, and he had a mission. Get the stone. Use it to overthrow his father. The locator spell he'd placed on it pulsed active at the edge of his magical senses—the stone was still inside the Hamilton estate. The problem would be getting it out. Especially since that mess last night with the security grid had heightened the Hamiltons' alert status. Their people lurked everywhere, this close to the Hamilton's house. He had to be careful.

Reconnaissance was key to a successful operation. He'd modified the illusion spell in his ring to tweak his appearance. No one would recognize the trust fund slacker with artfully ripped shorts and a bottle of high-end vodka to contribute as either college student Kris or Makris operative Kristof.

He wandered to a quiet end of the balcony, leaving the chattering girls and preening jocks behind. Muttering a quick spell to enhance his vision, he peered through the tops of the hedges. From his high vantage point he could see into the estate but not through the facade of the ornate brick-and-stone house—their security grid proved too good for that. Still, there were more cars parked around the entrance than he would have expected. And one of them was a black hearse that read *Southampton Mortuary* on its side.

Hmm... No reports of a caster death on the network. But Kate hadn't returned his calls or messages. He took a long swallow of beer to moisten his suddenly dry mouth. *No.* It must be a servant or an Affiliate. It couldn't be Kate.

Kristof took the burner phone he used as Kris from his pocket and twirled it around in his hand. He checked his messages. None from Kate. Nothing since her voice mail yesterday afternoon.

He slid his phone back and turned his attention to the estate. A swift blink didn't change his vision. He still couldn't see into the house. Too bad. He'd love to get a peek inside. And not only to help him pinpoint the location of the stone. He knew all too well the tales his own family's house—a vast estate carved from the rocks on a lonely island off the coast of Athens—would give up if anyone could penetrate its layers of security spells. He imagined his family life was far different from Kate's.

Kristof doubted she had to pay for her failures in quite the same way that he did.

He rubbed his eyes. Any more probing might alert the Hamiltons' security. He should be more careful. Anyone around here could be a Hamilton operative. He eyed the pretty girl with the beer as she smiled at a tanned boy in a too-tight Speedo down by the pool.

Even her.

The phone rang. Kate's number flashed on the display.

She's all right.

He moved to answer, then stopped. No one was nearby. He twisted his silver ring and changed his voice to match his Kris identity. He let the phone ring a little longer.

"Hey. What's up?"

"Kris..." He heard her sob.

"What's wrong?" He lounged against the railing.

"Brian...Brian's dead."

The news hit him like a kinetic spell to the gut. Bile rose up, along with a twist of something shaky and raw. Fear? No. What happened to Brian wouldn't happen to him, to Kate.

Focus on the mission.

Brian's death explained the hearse. And Brian's death would make Kristof's job a little bit easier. He shoved the rawness down until he couldn't feel it anymore.

"I'm so sorry," he said, letting compassion creep into his voice. "What happened?"

"It was my fault.... My dad says it wasn't, but I think...I think I could have done something, could have stopped it."

"Slow down. Tell me what happened."

Kate said nothing for a moment. Then, "There was an accident, here, when he came home.... I can't talk about it."

She didn't explain any more than that. He heard her crying, muffled, as if she held the phone away from her face.

Huh. No announcement of Brian's death. He hadn't died on a mission. The stone? Maybe Melina had been right about its power—and potential danger.

"I don't know what to do. Things have changed, because of this. Everything's changed." She stifled a sob.

"How?"

"I can't come back for summer session. I have to stay here. I...don't know if I can see you again."

"What do you mean?" Was she breaking up with him? He leaned forward, his hand gripping the phone. That wasn't going to happen. He needed her. He needed her to get the stone.

"I can't leave here right now. It's important I stay for the family. Because of Brian. At least until September."

"I understand. But we should see each other. I don't want you to go through this alone."

He muttered some inane sympathies to her, knowing from her responses that he hit the right notes. The whole grieving girlfriend, comforting boyfriend thing. He shifted from one foot to the other. With every false condolence he uttered, his stomach felt tighter.

Kate went over the funeral plans. Day after tomorrow, in Southampton. She wasn't crying anymore, but pain trembled through everything she said.

"Try to take it easy, okay?" he said. "It's going to be rough for a while, dealing with this stuff." He thought back to when his mother had been committed, to saying good-bye to her in one of her brief moments of sanity. "It hurts, losing someone you love." His throat thick with grief, he struggled with every word. "It feels like your whole world's changed, and nothing will ever be right again. But it'll get better. It will. Believe me."

Why had he said that? He'd never told anyone how he felt about his mother. But he couldn't listen to Kate's sobs, the ache in her voice when she talked about not having the right black dress for the funeral, about having to face all those people she didn't know. Not without trying to ease her pain.

Kate sniffled. "I guess you're right. I just need time." She paused. "You know, there are things I still don't understand...about why Brian died. I think I need to find out why he did, um, some things. Maybe his death will make more sense to me then."

Death only makes one kind of sense. The more she sees of it, the more she'll understand that. Death is something that happens when you aren't quick enough, or smart enough, to win.

Yes. And to succeed, he had to concentrate on the mission, dammit. Get Kate to take the conch-shell talisman. Shouldn't be hard. He knew how to work an asset.

Kristof raised a barrier as hard and impenetrable as his shield spell around the crack in his heart's armor. He made a plan. Then he began to talk.

Chapter Eleven

The sleeveless yoga top worked well enough over Kate's Hamilton-blue shorts. She gave it a firm tug. Her uncle said to dress for a workout.

Only last night she'd lost her brother and found out she could cast. Now, after a few hours of sleep, a bowl of cereal, and a call to Kris, she was supposed to start her training.

Apparently, time off to adjust wasn't a concept Grayson understood.

A knock sounded at the door. She opened it.

Her dad leaned against the wall, in tan shorts, his skin way too pale against his navy polo, his eyes not quite as bright as they should be.

"May I come in?" he asked.

"Sure." Her legs felt unsteady as she stepped back to let him enter.

"About what happened..." Reaching down, his fingers touched

her cheek gently.

Tears fell unheeded from her eyes. A sob shook her. "Dad, I'm sorry. I didn't mean to..."

"I know, sweetheart, I know. It wasn't your fault. None of this was. Not Brian, not what you did to me."

She touched his hand, then grabbed it hard, as if using him as her anchor. The tears kept falling. "I should have told you about the stone. I shouldn't have lied to you."

"Well, that's true."

His bluntness made her smile. Nothing could stop him from being him.

"I know you were trying to do what your brother wanted." He picked up a tissue from her bedside table and blotted her tears.

She hesitated. "I...don't want to argue anymore, but I do want to know what Brian was doing with the stone."

He studied her face for a moment. Then he walked to the window and leaned up against it, his pose casual, as if his only concern was the view. The flinch in his eyes told Kate something different.

"Kate, you have to believe me. I don't know. But I intend to find out. That, and who was chasing him. And when I do, I'll tell you."

Would he? Maybe. Or maybe he'd give her some sanitized version he thought fit for her to hear.

"Dad, I'm a caster now. There's no reason to keep me out of things anymore. I want to be involved in finding out the truth about Brian. And the stone."

His eyes narrowed. "No. You're just a beginner. You don't have the training, or the abilities, to get involved in an investigation this complicated. Your job right now is to learn how to control your powers."

"When will you stop trying to put everyone around you into tiny boxes?" She sank into her chair. "I'm your daughter, not a puppet you control."

"You're also a caster. You need discipline and training. You have no idea what you'd be getting tangled up in. Investigating the stone is far beyond your abilities and knowledge. You'll be too busy learning which end is up to help."

"Fine. You've told me the reasons why I can't. Now let me tell you why I can." She held a finger out. "One: apparently, I knew more about what Brian was doing than the rest of you." She held another finger out. "Two: The stone made me a caster. It...possessed me. I may be able to understand it better than someone who's never used it. And—"

"Sweetheart, you didn't use it. The stone used you." Her father's voice was gentle.

She stiffened. "Maybe so. I still think I understand it better than other people." She didn't tell him about the way it called to her, about the way it cajoled her to touch it one more time. Dad had enough to deal with.

"You have another point?"

"Yes. I know you think it's easy for me to forget about acting, about college, and throw all that away to be a caster." She looked up at him. "It's not. I still want to act. I want to go back to Cornell for summer session. I want that damned scholarship. I earned it. It isn't something you bought for me or got some sleazeball congressman to legislate. And right now, being a caster doesn't sound like much of a life. It only gets you killed." She swallowed.

He squeezed her shoulder.

"So let me have my way, for once," she said. "This is important to me. Let me help figure out the stone and how Brian got it. How he died." She looked up at him. "If you want me to be happy in this life, you need to give me a chance to understand how I ended up here. Otherwise, all I'll want is what I earned myself. Not what I inherited with Brian's death."

He was quiet for so long, staring out the window at the ocean, that she thought he wasn't going to respond. Then, "Has it occurred to you that I don't have to worry about you if you're safe behind these walls? Can't you just do what I want for once, and stay here and train, and not put yourself in the kind of danger that Brian put himself in?"

"Dad, I'll be all right."

He gave her a long look. "Kate, I understand your point. But you need to focus on what's important. Train. Get to know the other casters here. The Affiliates, the students. You're one of them now. You want to go back to Cornell because you've never felt like you belonged here. Well, now you do."

Easy for him to say. She sighed.

He headed for the door. "I want you in my office at three for Victor's report on your attack. I'll tell Grayson to give you a break from training."

Well, at least that was something. But it looked like she'd have to discover the truth about Brian and the stone on her own. She got up to walk with him. "Um…thanks, Dad."

They took the staircase slowly. Kate sensed a hesitancy in her father's step. Maybe she had hurt him more than he let on. She swallowed down the pain that rose up at the thought. Everything would be okay now that he was on the mend.

After all, there was no way that she, or anyone else, could ever really hurt him.

Kate flinched as a bolt of sparkling red energy shot from the young man in Hamilton-blue workout clothes across from her. It hit her newly cast shield spell right by her head, filling her ears with a sound of hundreds of angry bees, then fizzled, all its energy absorbed by the shield's cool-blue glow. She caught the scent of vanilla. Another spell clipped her arm. Her shield held again.

When was Dylan going to let up?

Sweat trickled down her forehead. This exercise had been going on for what seemed like forever.

She circled the large ring, keeping Grayson's lanky assistant in sight. He didn't seem much older than Kate, but he must have been training for years—at least, judging from how fast he targeted her with bolt after nasty bolt.

Grayson leaned back in his chair near the wall of the Sanctum, watching her. Probably wondering how much more she could take.

I'm wondering the same thing.

Her legs shook as another red bolt thumped into her shield. The bright glow of her shield faded to a lighter blue with each spell it absorbed.

"I think that's all I can do, Gra—"

The blue glow tore away with a *whoosh*. A low-power kinetic blast walloped her in her midsection, sending her flying back. Her butt hit the ground with a painful thud, the wind knocked out of her.

Dylan hurried over to give her a hand up, his skin shiny with sweat. His wire-rimmed glasses couldn't mask the concern in his earnest eyes.

"Sorry I knocked you arse over elbows," he said.

His accent sounded English. Her family controlled part of England and fought the Makrises and the Delcroixes for London for the past few years, but this was the first time she'd met a British caster, one of the Pearce family who'd allied with hers against the others. She took his assistance with a muttered thank-you, getting slowly to her feet.

After she caught her breath, she asked her uncle, "Didn't you hear me?"

"Oh, I heard you. But you need to know what it feels like to have a spell get through the shield, as well as repelling the blasts themselves."

She rubbed her backside. Maybe. Or maybe her uncle was a little ticked off with her questions about whether he'd discovered anything about the stone. The answer to that had been a curt "no." Plus, she'd arrived late for her first practice. Apparently, her discussion with her father was no excuse.

Grayson let only a few casters assist, telling her that Dad wanted news of her transformation kept "need to know" for right now. He'd started right in with training, first talking over the spells he wanted her to learn, then having Dylan demonstrate most of them. After she'd asked, he'd said he'd teach her teleporting in a few weeks. He hadn't been very amenable to her suggestion that they move that spell up in the lesson plan.

"Isn't there a less painful way to learn?" Kate asked.

A wry smile flashed across his face. "Perhaps. But you'll remember better this way. You need to know when your shield is low so that you can plan another action before it runs out." He stood. "The trick to winning a fight is thinking ahead. Not one step, but several. If you only react, you're dead. Take a seat. Watch."

Kate slumped against the wall, a cushion under her tender backside. She folded her legs and focused on the ring. Another of her uncle's assistants entered, a young woman about the same age as Dylan, black ponytail bobbing as she trotted into the ring. She and Dylan gave the traditional bow, then squared off, each walking to an opposite end of the boxing-ring-sized arena.

Her uncle came over to stand next to her. She focused on the ring, engaging her magesight. Both of the combatants had activated their shields, and each did something more. They had another spell they were preparing at the same time, their fingers flying faster than she'd ever seen. *Wow.*

"How do they do that? Get one spell up right after the other?" she asked her uncle.

"Practice."

That seemed to be his default answer.

Dylan slashed his hand in front of his chest, and two daggers of blue energy shot from his fingers. The air rippled in their path. They hit his opponent's shield and evaporated with a sizzle. The girl's fingers flew and fire erupted around Dylan. He flinched as his shield's glow faded to a robin's-egg blue, absorbing the damage from the flames. Dylan chanted, fingers tapping, and the fire transformed into a thousand gleaming shards of metal. The sharp-edged fragments swarmed through the air back at the woman. When they hit her shield they tore ragged slices in the bright-blue covering and sent her staggering back a few steps before fading away.

They cast spell after spell. Some of the spells they threw looked like the ones Kate had been taught as a kid, and some she couldn't identify. But each had a symbol that she could see. Although some went by so fast she didn't think she could write them down even if she tried.

Grayson called a halt to the exercise. "That's it for now. Good job." He looked down at Kate. "Tell me what you saw."

She thought about it. "Your assistants are crazy fast. Brooke had been quick but not like that. But Victor…when he teleported in, then took out Brooke, he cast even faster." Her shoulders slumped. "If the people I'm going to go up against are anything close to Victor's level, then I may as well give up now."

Grayson laughed. "It's all about training and practice. That's how Victor got so good." His face went somber, the laugh erased. "Brian was that good. You could be, too. Just apply yourself."

He pushed himself off the wall. "And remember, we're in the Sanctum. No paranoia backlash. So there's no incentive to be conservative with casting. In a real fight, you won't see so many spells thrown around, but you will see the speed and a similar strategy."

Kate stood. "Victor went straight for the knockout. He didn't even give Brooke a chance."

"Yes, that's what he'd do. It's the most efficient way to fight."

"Is there another way?"

"Of course. Using high-powered spells, the way Victor does, creates more backlash. You feel the effects more, get twitchier. Using too many of those spells too often has, of course, a greater, long-term effect on a caster's mental health. There will be times you'll want a subtler approach. But those are techniques you'll learn later. For now, let me get your homework assignments." Grayson strode to the back of the Sanctum and rummaged through the large wooden desk set against the wall.

Great, homework. But what else did she expect? She had a lot of catching up to do—years' worth. Still, homework wasn't exactly the biggest thing on her mind right now.

She still didn't think Grayson was being straight with her about how Brian died. Why else would he be avoiding her questions about the stone? She needed to know what was really going on. And it seemed that Grayson telling her the truth was about as probable as a twitchy caster sitting with his back to the door.

She spotted Dylan a few yards away, pulling on his brown suede jacket. A flash of silver from the jacket's lining caught her eye.

A row of talismans were pinned inside—the magical equivalent of carrying concealed.

She drew in a breath. What did Grayson's assistant need all that firepower for? No matter how quickly he could cast in the Sanctum, he wasn't a combat mage like Victor.

But talismans were issued by her father, and he wouldn't hand a stack like that out to someone he didn't trust. Right?

Whatever Dylan was, he might know something about artifacts. About the stone. Something Grayson wasn't willing to tell her. But would he pass on everything she asked to Grayson?

She should keep her mouth shut. But then she'd never find out the truth.

She sidled up to him. "So…can I ask you a question?"

"Of course, Miss Hamilton." He turned those bright eyes on her.

"Call me Kate." She so hated Boss's Daughter Syndrome. "Anyway, since you're Grayson's assistant and you know about me, you know about Brian, as well, right? About how he died?"

Dylan glanced over at Grayson, still sorting through his desk, and then at the other casters, none close enough to overhear. "I know some things—like about the stone. Is that what you mean?"

The knot of tension in her stomach eased. "Yes. The stone. If I…asked you something about it, would you promise not to tell Grayson?"

"He's my superior. It would be…awkward."

"Please. I don't know who else to ask." She hated the pleading sound in her voice as she blinked away the tears. "I think he's keeping something from me. Something important. About how my brother died and about the stone's power. I have to know whether the stone killed him. Or if…if it was my fault."

Dylan gave her a long look. "All right. Let me see what I can find out." He turned to go.

"Hey, what's with all the talismans?" Kate asked.

"They're for my other job. I'm your father's primal magic specialist."

"Primal, um… Oh." Kate bit her lip. The stone was a primal magic artifact—one of the rare artifacts from the First Age, so powerful and deadly they were outlawed. And Dylan was an expert in primal magic? She studied him closer, hoping to see through the geeky charm of his junior-librarian cover identity to the guy who walked such a dangerous edge. No luck. If a primal magic badass lurked behind those glasses, Dylan hid him well.

"So, you should know all about the stone, then," she asked.

"I should, shouldn't I? Interesting that your uncle has barely consulted me." His gaze held Grayson's form, walking toward them, in its steady focus. "But then I work for him, not the other way around." He nodded to her. "I'll be in touch."

She barely had time to think about what Dylan's words meant before Grayson came back with a stack of books and binders, topped with a small bundle of papers. He handed them over to her. "I'm condensing a few assignments because you'll need to review the basics. They're all due Wednesday."

She glanced through the lessons. How was she going to read five chapters of *Practical Casting*, a hundred pages of *The History of Magic: The Second Era*, three chapters of *Basic Principles of Artifacts and Talismans*, and memorize the patterns and chants for six new spells by Wednesday? It wasn't like she had a spell to cram it all in her head. Magic didn't work directly on the mind.

Besides, she had to meet Kris tomorrow night. He'd insisted on coming out to see her, to comfort her. She'd drawn the line at having him come to the house—no way was she going to let Dad discover and wreck this relationship—so she'd told him to meet her at a hotel in Montauk instead. The little tourist town lay far enough away that they had a chance of escaping her dad's prying eyes. Assuming she could sneak away and get out from under this crazy workload.

"Um...Grayson? This is too much. I don't see how I can get all of this done by then." She handed the homework back to him.

He studied her for a moment, then nodded. He put the books back down on the desk. "Fine. I told your father I didn't think much of this plan to have you do independent study. We can go back to the traditional way of doing this."

"Ah, no. Wait—"

"I'm sure you'll find it much easier to learn this material in a classroom setting. With other students. And we'll have to start you back where you were. At the seventh-grade level. Your more mature perspective will be good for those kids." Grayson's eyes were dead serious.

Kate snatched the papers from his hands. "You'll have it by Wednesday." She slammed them on top of the books and binders.

She stalked from his office.

At least now I get to find out what Victor has discovered about Brooke.

Aside from that little break, she'd be buried in homework so deep she'd be lucky to fight her way free in time to see Kris.

Or worry any more about how honest Grayson had been about Brian's death.

Chapter Twelve

Kate jogged down the stairs to Dad's office and checked her watch. Three o'clock. She'd barely had enough time to shower and change into street clothes—khaki shorts and a tank top— before the meeting. The last thing she wanted was to be late. Again.

She cracked the door open an inch. Grayson and Dad were by the fireplace, her dad in the leather chair, Grayson half sitting against Dad's desk, talking about something. Victor sat tense on the sofa, listening.

"—didn't have much to say about it. That was the last time I..." Grayson stopped and cleared his throat. He brushed back tears. Was this about Brian?

She bit her lip to have something to concentrate on beside the grief that welled up inside.

Her father spotted her and nodded. "We'll continue this later. Have a seat, Kate."

The only place left was next to Victor. Damn. Well, it wasn't like he had cooties. She sat, leaving a good foot between her and Victor. Her father and Grayson nursed tumblers of whiskey, while Victor gripped a beer bottle. A pitcher of lemonade occupied the center of the coffee table—a drink meant for her. Her father might let her discuss caster business, but apparently he still intended to treat her like a child.

She poured herself some lemonade, her hands shaking.

Calm the heck down. It's just Dad and Grayson. And Victor. And the first time they've ever let me in on their secret meetings. I can handle this.

Her father finished his whiskey, put the glass on the fireplace hearth, then turned to Victor. "What's your progress on tracking the rogue who attacked Kate?"

"I haven't found her, sir."

"You haven't… What's the hold up?"

"She's disappeared. The college has no record of her enrollment, and her apartment has been cleared out. I ran her fingerprints and DNA, and they came back negative." Victor leaned forward, and Kate could almost feel the frustration rising from him.

"Somebody's gonna find her dead at the bottom of a lake, the back of her head caved in by a spell. This is a family operation, I'd bet money on it. No one else can pull off such a total disappearance."

"That tells us something," her father said. "Now we just need to know which family."

"I went back to the site of the freeway attack, to the theater, where Brian gave Kate the stone. I tried to trace the teleport spells—

"

"It's too late for that," Grayson said.

Victor shrugged. "Worth a try. If I could track Brian's path back to where he started, we might learn something. But I couldn't."

"Told you so." Grayson said.

Victor shook his head. "They'd been erased. If I didn't know Brian had been there, or that the rogue had, I wouldn't ever have been able to tell. Not even a residual trace of magical energy. Someone doesn't want us to trace Brian's path...or find the rogue."

"Brian couldn't have done it, could he?" Kate asked.

"He might have erased his own trail, but why cover up the rogue's?" Victor said. "According to you, he didn't know about her. No, someone else tampered with the evidence both times. Only one reason to do that—so we wouldn't trace their teleport back to the source."

"Any leads on who tried to get past the grid last night?" her father asked. "Can't be coincidence that it happened right before the stone killed Brian and changed Kate. The western gate is close to the Sanctum."

"The trail went cold." Victor shifted against the couch. "But I'll bet the same guy who was after Brian tried to crash our security. Pretty gutsy to try to get through the grid. Gutsy but pointless. I upgraded it last week."

"That brings us back to who was chasing him," her father said. "Odds are they're also the party behind the attack on Kate. It's also likely they'll come after the stone again. Find them."

Victor nodded. "I have a few ideas."

"Dad, I could help Victor. Run down leads for him, look through records, stuff like that. It would even help me learn about the major players."

She glanced at Victor. His grimace made him look like someone just spiked his beer with pickle juice. She knew how he felt. But if working with Victor would get her closer to the truth about Brian, she'd do it and hold her nose.

"I told you no," her father said. "You're too busy training. Besides—" he glanced at Grayson "—we have an advantage with you we want to keep."

"What?"

Her father smiled. "Here's your first lesson in strategy: never let your opponent see all your cards. No one knows you're a caster. We maintain that advantage if no one finds out."

"Can't they tell? From my aura?"

"Grayson can mask that," her father said.

Her uncle stroked his chin. "Maybe. It's not an easy thing to do."

"Make it happen. And soon. Our enemies will figure out the ruse the first time Kate's on a mission, but it will buy us some time. Until then, let only a few trusted casters in on Kate's secret. Make sure they understand to stay quiet about it. We'll keep Kate's new status 'need to know' only." He turned to Kate. "Do you understand what that means?"

It meant she'd still be an outcast, still be sitting at home while Hayley and her friends teleported off to parties, giggling in their little clique and avoiding her.

"I thought you wanted me to make friends with other casters. Get to know them."

"I do. You don't have to be a caster to do that."

That's what you think. "Sure, Dad. Business as usual."

"Good." He stood and walked to the door, opening it. "That's all we need you for. You have homework to do, I understand."

That was it? They didn't need her in this meeting? All she'd done was sit there and listen. Her face burned as she slammed the lemonade glass on the table. Dad invited her to get her to shut up and play nice. He'd thrown her a bone.

What about the stone, Brian's death? The others made no move to get up and leave. She knew they were going to keep on talking about all that important stuff. Stuff she really wanted—no, *needed*—to know.

Dad's tight frown and crossed arms made it clear how any pleas to stay would be received. Grayson avoided her gaze, staring instead at the box he'd pulled out of his pocket—the box containing the stone. Victor just took a long swig of his beer. It wasn't like she expected Victor to take her side. Far as she knew, Hell hadn't opened its ice skating rink.

One last try. "Dad, I'm a caster now. I've earned a place here. At least let me hear what you've discovered about the stone. I need to know what it does. You owe me that."

"I don't owe you—" her father began.

"Maybe you do, sir." Victor broke in.

Kate turned to him, startled.

"Kate's been thrown into the deep end of the pool," Victor said. He leaned back on the couch, cool as ever, no evidence in his steely eyes of how much it must cost him to talk back to her dad. "Don't you think she needs a life preserver?"

"And you think knowledge would give her one?"

Victor's face was missing its habitual smirk. He just stared stoically up at her dad. "Worked for me, back when I needed it."

Kate sat back, the air rushing out of her with a *whoosh*. Victor was standing up for her? But why? Did she really remind him of what he'd gone through as a rogue caster, newly discovering his powers?

"All right, Kate can stay," her father said. "But only through the discussion of the stone. Then it's back to your studies. Agreed?"

Kate nodded.

Her father turned to Grayson. "What have you discovered about it?"

Grayson hopped down from his perch on the desk. "I ran a full diagnostic but haven't had time to do more. Here's what I can tell you: The stone's function is to create new casters. But it can only work on someone who already has the gene for magic as a recessive. In other words, a Null. It ignores Normals and plants a subtle suggestion in the minds of casters who handle it to pass it along to Nulls."

"Is that why Brian gave it to me?" *Not because he trusted me?*

"Possibly. It would have influenced any caster who handled it without the proper precautions. He might have had other reasons, as well. But the spell contained in it certainly played a role." Grayson took the stone out of its box and held it in his hand, covered in a square of blue silk. "I've never seen a primal magic artifact potentially this powerful."

Kate stared at the stone, a few feet away in Grayson's hand. She tried to take her eyes off it, to look down at her lemonade, but its black depths were strangely compelling.

She blinked and looked at it with magesight. Her eyes widened as the stone zoomed to fill her vision. Beyond the deep black of its surface, beyond the iridescent green flashes that took on a more vibrant aspect through her magical vision, she noticed something else. Stream after stream of dark energy flowed through the stone in an endlessly repeating figure eight. She watched it ripple in and out of itself, but she couldn't tell where it started or stopped.

The energy bothered her. Something about its dark purity made the fine hairs on the back of her neck prick up.

It reached to her. Called to her to touch it, just touch it one more time.

Blinking, she shut off her magesight. The connection eased, but the stone's pull was still there, just a gentle tug on her soul.

"—pretty casual with that," Victor was saying. She had missed part of the conversation. No one seemed to notice but Grayson, who gave Kate a measuring glance as he held the silk-wrapped stone in his hands with a nonchalance she found disturbing.

Grayson laughed. "I'm not being controlled by the stone. The silk protects me."

"Are you sure you know what you're doing?" her father asked.

"As much as anyone can. This thing is thousands of years old and very powerful." He paused. "There must be hundreds of Nulls. If we could transform them into casters and secure their loyalty, we could change the Game."

"The thought had crossed my mind. And also that Nico Makris or Justine Delacroix could do the same if they got their hands on it."

"True," Grayson said. "But they don't have it. We do." He put the stone back in the box and closed the lid. The tug on the line connecting it to Kate lessened.

"But wouldn't using something like the stone blow the whole Game wide open?" Kate asked Grayson. "Isn't the whole point to control the Normals from the shadows? I thought the big honking lesson from the First Era is that when casters used primal magic back then, it resulted in lots and lots of Normals getting killed. Then they ganged up on us and did the whole 'villagers with pitchforks and torches' thing. Isn't that what this whole secrecy rule is about? Why the Game was invented? To stop that mess from happening all over again?"

"*A*-plus for the history lesson," Victor said. "That's why we have an official policy these days about primal magic artifacts." He quirked an eyebrow at Grayson. "You know, the one you helped write. The cross-clan policy that says to destroy the damn things when we find them."

Grayson narrowed his eyes at Victor.

"I assume there's an unofficial policy?" Kate asked.

"An arms race no one will admit to," her father said. "We keep the primal magic artifacts we find to make sure the other clans don't get them. No one expects to ever use them, but if someone else does, we want to be prepared."

"Prepared for what?"

"Whatever we need to be."

Kate picked up her glass and sipped her lemonade. She tried to absorb the knowledge that her father stood ready to use something as dangerous as the stone to counter his enemies' threats. That *thing* had killed Brian. Who knew how many other people it could kill? Was this really the world he lived in?

"This is a lot for you to take in, Kate," her father said. "Don't worry. It's nothing you will have to concern yourself with for a long time. Better get back to your studies. I'm sure you have a lot to do."

Kate hesitated. She knew a dismissal when she heard it. But should she tell her father about how the stone had called to her? Grayson had told her he'd handle it....

She left, her dad shutting the door behind her.

She put her ear up to the door, desperate to hear something, anything. But his office must have the same kind of protection that the Sanctum did. Not even a whisper got through.

Kate marched over to the staircase and slumped down, head in her hands. Yeah, sure, she'd promised to study, but how was she going to find out anything about Brian's death when everyone shut her out?

Twenty minutes later, the door opened. Her father and Grayson went their separate ways, backs stiff, tension making their steps ring on the marble floor. Neither noticed her. What had happened between the two of them?

Victor waited in the hallway for her. "By the way, princess, we're in security lockdown. That means you stay here. No driving into Southampton for a fro-yo."

She flushed. "I don't—"

"Until we find Sparkles and figure out who was behind her attack, no one who isn't operative-class or above leaves the grounds without an escort. That means you. Got it?"

"Yeah." Oh, she got it. She got that Victor's defense of her didn't mean a damn thing. But he was dead wrong about her inability to handle trouble. Kate was a caster now. She could shield, even throw a couple of spells. If Brooke tried anything, she'd show her what's what.

Kris would be in Montauk tomorrow night. Nothing was going to stop her from seeing him. Not Victor, not his stupid rules. Somehow, between now and tomorrow, she'd have to figure out a way around his precautions. Stomping up to her room, she realized with a sinking feeling she had no idea how.

Kate cracked open the textbooks. The review material—the names of the Second Era casters who developed modern casting after they'd outlawed primal magic, the understanding of why paranoia was a side effect of modern casting when it wasn't one of primal magic, the history of when the Game had started, and a list of the Rules—made for fast reading. She'd aced enough pop quizzes to be able to predict what material would be on the test, concentrated on that, and skimmed the rest.

She opened the binder Grayson had given her. He'd assigned her the tracings of Fire, Light, Lightning, Cloak, and Counterspell. Hmm...Grayson hadn't assigned her any books that covered the First Era—the era of the stone. They might have been helpful. But it wasn't like she didn't have enough to study.

She sighed. Light seemed the easiest, so she started with that. When she thought she had Light's square symbol down, she went on to Fire, but she kept seeing the image of her father tumbling back into the hallway, his chest burning. Shaking, she slammed the binder shut.

Footsteps sounded outside her open door. Hayley walked by.

"Hey. Got a minute?" Kate said.

Hayley stopped, her face darkening. "Not really. I—"

"What's up?"

Hayley came inside and shut the door. "Nothing. You wouldn't understand." Her face had blotches of red across her cheeks, as if she'd been crying.

"Brian? I understand that." She forced back the tears that welled up at the thought of him.

"Yeah. It's Brian. We were going to hold a wake for him, a little memorial tomorrow, just his friends. Nothing official. But now I can't go because Victor's got his panties in a twist about your safety."

Another caster get-together, this one to mourn. Another part of Brian's world she'd never been invited into. She barely knew his friends' names. And they knew so little of her that they hadn't even bothered to invite her to her own brother's wake.

She bit her lip until the anger cooled. "Yeah, sorry about Victor's temper tantrum. I—"

"Save it. What do you want?"

Kate hesitated, then plunged on. "Any tips you can give me on memorizing these spells? I'm kind of..."

"Lost? Well, yeah. You have a lot of catching up to do."

"That's not exactly my fault."

Hayley huffed out a breath, then sat on Kate's bed. "I guess not." She picked up the spellbook and flipped through it. Then put it down and gave Kate a sideways glance. "So...there's a trick to memorizing spells. Mnemonics."

"You can use mnemonics for spells?"

Hayley rolled her eyes. "My dad would get around to telling you this after you thrashed around on your own for a day or two. You know how he teaches. But this is how it works. For each spell there's a rhyme that helps you memorize the symbol or the chant. You know, like how the Fire spell has four points, one at the each of the cardinal directions, north, east, south, and west, but you have to tap the east point again before you go to the west? So all you have to remember is No Easy Spell Ever Works."

And Grayson had left her to struggle with them on her own. The anger she'd pushed down a moment ago raged back to redden her face.

"I'll dig up my old notes and bring them by later tonight. Got nothing else to do." Hayley got up and headed to the door.

An idea popped into Kate's head. Maybe she and Hayley could help each other.

"Wait. What if there was a way you could go to that...get-together of yours?"

Hayley turned around. "How?"

Kate took a deep breath. "Invite me." Before Hayley said anything, Kate rushed on, "I won't stay and cramp your style. I promise. But I think I can convince my dad to let us both go." After all, he'd told her to get to know more casters.

Hayley crossed her arms and gave a little snort. "No one knows you're a caster. They don't even know you. How do you think—"

"I told you, I'm not staying." *The last thing I want is to stand in the corner all alone, listening to you and your friends weep over your good times with Brian.* "I have someplace else to be. I need you to cover for me. You do that, and I'll get you permission to go to the memorial."

"What's so damned important that you're willing to break Victor's security lockdown to get it?"

Kris. The solidity of his chest as she lay her head on it, the feel of his fingers as they pushed her hair back from her face, the way he listened to her pour out her tears. She'd mourn for Brian in her own way. Dad didn't have to know about it. "Not your problem. Do you want to go, or not?"

Hayley gave her a long look. "I'll cover for you. But this better not come back to haunt me."

"It won't. My lips are sealed. And so are yours, right?"

Hayley nodded and slipped out the door.

Kate wore a little black skirt, white silk shirt, and pearls and stood, mojito in hand, in the corner of a Georgetown apartment belonging to one of Brian's friend's. *So much for not really staying at Brian's wake. It's not like Victor gave me a choice—hovering over Hayley and me until she teleported us. I'm out of here the minute I can tear Hayley away.*

Laughter and the tinkle of glasses echoed across the leather-upholstered living room. Music pounded over the stereo—something fast and European that Kate didn't recognize.

A jar of silver talismans sat on the bar, half empty.

The partiers lounged across the plush furniture, their skin covered with reptilian scales, exotic furs, and the long, multi-colored feathers of birds Kate had only seen in the Washington Zoo, their eyes slitted and gleaming with a thousand jewel-like colors. Illusion spells. Their animal guises melded seamlessly with the elegant, in-human design of the floating silk and tight leather garments they wore.

They dressed like this for a *wake*?

Hayley leaned against the wall sipping a margarita. A talisman gleamed from her blue leather corset. Her eyes angled up, like a cat's, green with a single vertical slit. Black-and-white fur, like a snow leopard's, flowed across her body, looking so soft and smooth that Kate wanted to reach out and pet it. Hayley's tufted ear twitched.

One of Brian's friends waxed on about some pointless fight Brian had been in a few months back with a Tanaka family girl on top of a skyscraper in Tokyo's Shinjuku district.

"And then Bri yanked her levitation talisman and tossed her off the building. He let her fall for a few floors before he dove after her. When he hauled her up, she was shaking so hard she spilled every-thing: the location of the dead drop, their plans to discredit the Secretary of Defense. Before he let her leave he even got her phone number."

Raucous laughter filled the room.

Brian would never... He just wouldn't do something like that. Not the brother I know.

She turned to Hayley. "Brian never acted like that—" Kate swept her arm across the room "—at home."

"We're not at home."

The host rushed up. His foxlike eyes lit up with interest, paired with a total lack of recognition as he scanned her. He pressed a tal-isman and a small bag into Kate's hand, his imaginary claws feeling real as they scraped her palm.

"Here's a little something to get things rolling. This may be a wake, but it's still a party. You know what they say: live fast, die crazy."

The sharp edges of the talisman bit into her hands. It looked cheap—probably made on the fly in someone's garage. Nothing like the combat-grade talismans her uncle's people crafted.

She handed the talisman back to the boy, along with the bag. A caster drug, she assumed, something black market like Chill or Smooth. Nothing she wanted to mess with. Ever.

"Thanks, but I can't exactly use these. I'm Brian's sister. Kate." Might as well make sure someone knew she was here. Wasn't that the point of an alibi?

The interest in his eyes died like the last light going out in an abandoned tunnel. "Oh." His eyes shifted to Hayley. "Your cousin bring you?"

"Yes."

"Well. Have a good time. There's beer in the fridge." He cleared his throat, then, "I'm very sorry for your loss." He turned and walked back into the crowd.

"That went better than expected." She glanced across the room, caught sight of Missy and Gordon, their skin covered in golden fur, all decked out like a pair of lions that had just rolled in a rich woman's attic. *Better avoid them.* "Can you get me where I need to go?"

"Wait," Hayley said. "You know Victor. He's probably tracking you with something. What's in your purse?"

Kate upended her small white bag on the end table next to her.

Three pens, a tube of lipstick, spare change, her wallet, breath mints, her phone, keys, and her sunglasses.

"Anything you don't recognize?" Hayley asked.

"Just one of the pens." She relaxed her focus and engaged her magesight. "It's glowing."

"Leave it here," Hayley said. "Victor can track it all he wants. We'll pick it up on the way back."

Kate looked at everything else with her magesight. Nothing else glowed. Did Victor really think playing nanny was going to work now that she could catch him at it?

No. He wouldn't. So what else had he done?

She reached up to tug on her ears. Grayson had given her two silver earrings this afternoon. From the front they'd looked like silver beads set on simple posts, but from the back a subtle glow of amber had peeked out when she'd examined them in his office.

Grayson said they were talismans, like the one he'd used to heal her father, or the giant silver-and-topaz ball that told Victor she wasn't still possessed. The earrings would conceal her caster aura from anyone with magesight, Grayson had said. He'd been stern with her: they would only work if she wore them. So she had to wear them all the time, even while she slept.

Seems like overkill, but whatever.

Now, it made her wonder. There were two earrings, and therefore, potentially two talismans. She wouldn't put it past Grayson to weave another little spell in them, difficult as it might be. One to let Victor track her, or at least find her in an emergency.

A couple of days as a caster and already I'm as paranoid as a combat mage.

Hayley took her arm and guided her to the bathroom. As good a place for a secret teleport as any. "I'll pick you up in two hours. Same place I leave you," Hayley said.

A minute later, Hayley dropped her off in front of the Montauk Oceanview Inn. The blue, two-story motel loomed quietly against the ocean, only the soft glow of the old lamps illuminating its peeling paint in the growing darkness. The room whose number Kris had texted her earlier in the day was on the second floor, overlooking the ocean.

She walked past the little office and pushed the "up" button on the elevator. Kris had scored a prime room at the start of the summer tourist season—she had no idea how. The sea breeze wafted by, bringing the smell of salty air and old fish and a blast of coolness. She shivered. Given the situation, maybe going off by herself to meet someone, even her boyfriend, wasn't the best idea she'd ever had. She should've listened to Victor's warnings. Gone home and stayed there. She stared up at the light shining from the second story when the elevator dinged its arrival.

Kristof poured himself another glass of the pinot noir and checked his watch. Quarter past ten. Where was she? He couldn't risk another text—either she'd be here or she wouldn't. And if she didn't come, then he'd need another plan. A much more dangerous one.

He scrutinized his illusion spell in the room's long mirror. Every element of his Kris Stevens cover was set—the boy-next-door look had replaced the hard-edged operative.

The differences were subtle—first a change in hair color and length from his natural, wavy, light brown to a darker brown with a preppier cut. Then a softening of his sharp features, a lightening of his olive skin and deep-blue eyes. He added a slight rise to the bass pitch of his voice and a perfect native-Floridian accent. Most important, he created a total transformation in how he carried himself. Lightened his step. Relaxed his manner.

Kris Stevens had never had to fight for his life against opponents determined to kill him. He had never been tortured, beaten, stabbed in the back by his family, never sat huddled in a closet, convinced everyone around him was poisoning his food, and had never been left to die in some godforsaken armpit of a city by someone he'd thought he could trust.

Kris Stevens wasn't a caster.

Kris Stevens's biggest problems were getting a passing grade in Organic Chemistry, deciding where to apply for grad school, and worrying that his vintage Camaro wasn't going to make it another month. The worst injury he'd ever suffered—a dog bite that caused the crescent-shaped scar on his hand. His only concern at the moment was keeping his girlfriend, Kate, from breaking up with him because of her controlling father.

No matter how much Kristof enjoyed being with Kate, he needed to remember one thing: he wasn't Kris Stevens.

Kristof sank back in the armchair that formed a little seating group with its not-so-matching sofa in the room he'd rented and gazed out at the ocean. Getting into his cover identity was all very fine. It had served him well for getting Kate in a position of trust. She gave him whatever he needed now—information, cooperation. Well, almost everything. Not the stone.

He toyed with the keys he used as Kris that sat on a coffee table that had seen better days. His Florida conch shell was attached to his key ring by a short loop of leather. He'd retrieved it from Melina—modified to his specs. When he activated it remotely, it would punch a hole in the Hamiltons' security net so that he could teleport in, get the stone, and teleport out. It would block their spells from reactivating until he'd left. But it would have to be inside the Hamiltons' security grid to work. That's where Kate came in.

He'd once told her the shell was his lucky charm.

Someone knocked on the door. Kate? He set down his wineglass and checked to make sure. *Yes.*

She rushed into his arms as he pulled her inside and shut the door.

"I'm so sorry I'm late. I had to go to someplace else first to make it seem like I wasn't coming here and—"

"Shh." He held a finger gently against her lips, then let it trail around her pearls and down her neck. "It doesn't matter. You're here now."

He bent down and kissed her, and her mouth felt warm and tasted like lime and mint. It had only been a few days since they had last been together but he'd missed being with her, and he kissed her again, as if testing that strange idea. Her hair held its familiar rose scent and he buried his face in her neck, inhaling the subtle fragrance of her skin.

Her body felt tense—whether with bone-deep grief or something else, he didn't know. He wanted her to melt into him, let everything that hurt her fade away.

Then a streak of silver slid past his cheek, and an inner alarm sounded.

He pulled back a little, focusing his magesight on her earrings. Nothing but silver. But better to be sure. He nuzzled her ear, getting as close as he could to her earring without touching it. There was something about them... Yes. Subtle, and cloaked, but they were talismans.

But the spell inside looked passive, not active. Which meant that as long as he didn't cast, they shouldn't trigger. He had no idea what the spells did. Monitor her or track her, maybe. He should have expected this after sending Brooke after the stone.

"Kris? Is something—"

"No, sorry. I was just...thinking."

She smiled. "What about?"

"How much I missed you. Whether we'll get to see each other again after this." He leaned down and kissed her again.

A little sigh caught in her throat. "Don't think about that. Be here now. With me." Stretching her arms up, she pulled her silk shirt over her head, revealing her lace bra. Her hands wandered over to his shirt and unbuttoned it until she could slide it off, her fingernails tracing a teasing line down his chest.

His muscles quivered at the tickle her fingers provoked. A chuckle rumbled from him. He picked her up and tossed her on the bed. She bounced as she landed and laughed, the first laugh he'd heard from her in days. He didn't waste any time with the rest of his clothes—he kicked them off, the same with his shoes.

He lay down next to her and drew her into his arms. He slid her skirt and panties off as he ran his hands down her hips. Kate kissed his neck, his chest, at first softly, then harder, more urgent. She reached down and caressed him, and he inhaled sharply. He struggled to undo her bra until it finally came free, and he tossed it on the floor.

Kristof trailed kisses down her breasts, her stomach, and then lower. She arched against him as he tasted her, her gasp bringing a smug smile to his face.

"Kris, please...now."

He moved up and into her. Feeling her open for him was like returning to the home he'd never had.

It was so easy to become lost in her.

Afterward, he pushed her hair back from her sweat-soaked forehead. Her eyes were half closed, and a little grin played across her face. She murmured something, her eyes fluttering. He let his own smile show and stretched out, a yawn rumbling through him.

His eyes landed on the conch shell, sitting on the coffee table.

He couldn't relax. That was deadly. This wasn't a date; it was a mission.

"Feel better?" he asked her.

"Much." She sighed and snuggled closer to him.

He knew what he needed to say next. Ask about her brother's death. Find out what her family would be doing with the stone. But as he stroked the soft hair of the woman next to him, he couldn't get the words out.

She did it for him.

"Things have changed...at home. Because of Brian." She squeezed his arm.

"How's that?"

"You know how I told you that my dad didn't want me to join

the family business? Well, now he does."

She couldn't mean what it sounded like. She wasn't a caster. She could never take Brian's place. "What kind of work does he want you to do?"

"Um…he hasn't really told me that yet." Kate shifted away from him a little. A lie.

"Is this why he won't let you go to summer school?" He stroked her cheek. "Is he going to make you transfer from Cornell? Or drop out?"

"I…I don't know. I could never be part of his world before. So I convinced myself I didn't really want to. But now I can. It's tempting. But I don't want to lose you." She sat up.

"You don't have to. You've got to stand up to him. Is this what you really want to do? Be under his thumb all your life?"

"No. No, I don't. I want to be with you, *and* I want to work for him. I'll just have to find a way to make it happen." She flopped back down on the bed. "Why does it have to be so complicated? First Brian, then Grayson."

"What's wrong with your uncle?"

"He's…sick."

That only meant one thing in caster families.

"I'm sorry. Is there anything I can do?"

Kate pulled herself back up and curled up against him. "No. I have to get used to the idea that he won't always be around." She sounded so sad. He wished he could help her, instead of dutifully passing the intelligence back to his father. Again.

He held her as she leaned back against him and told him everything that had happened in the last few days. Oh, she masked it all in terms that would make sense to a Normal, that made her family seem like an average, well-off American family coping with the loss of its son. But to someone like him, who could read between the lines, one thing stood out.

They were training her. But for what?

He nuzzled her neck as he snuck a look at her aura with his magesight. Blue-green lines radiated out from her, same as always. He must be crazy to think that anything could have changed.

He supposed a family could use a Null as an agent. It was against the Rules, but it was possible. Was that what her family was doing with Kate? Did they know about him? Were they setting him up?

Relax. If they knew about his mission, Victor and his team would have been here, waiting for him, ready to take him out. No need for an elaborate plan. No, Kate's puzzle had a different answer. He needed to figure out what but not as much as he needed the stone.

The conch shell still lay on the coffee table, waiting. His time was running out. Any day now his father would get sick of his delays—or find out about the stone. And that would be the end of more than spending time with Kate. The time for indecision was over.

"Kate?" He kissed her neck.

"Hmm?"

"When can I see you again?"

"I...don't know."

He brushed the hair back from her face. "Text me. No matter what your dad wants. Get away for an hour, for a day, for whatever time you can. I'll wait for you."

He slid off the bed and walked to the coffee table. With a smooth twist, he detached the conch shell from his keys and brought it back to Kate. He held it out to her. "Hold on to the shell. Keep it with you. Promise me you won't forget about us."

Kate took the key fob. "I promise." She wrapped her arms around him, trembling with unshed tears. As he held her on the rumpled sheets, he tried to ignore the growing unease crawling through his gut. He felt like he had just stepped off a cliff far taller and steeper than the one that shored up his sister's workroom. And nothing, no spell, no clever dodge, would save him from the sharp rocks that threatened below if he'd miscalculated.

Chapter Thirteen

In the movies, it always rains during a funeral. The clouds would open, and water would come pouring down, just like the tears of the bereaved. The mourners would stand around the grave, sheltered under dark umbrellas, and some priest would mumble comforting words about the departed having gone to a happier place while lightning flashed overhead.

But Brian didn't get the drama of the heavens.

Tuesday dawned hot and hazy, like every other summer day in the Hamptons. The morning gloom had burned off by noon, and by one, the time of the service at Paumanok Cemetery, Kate hated the required black dress and little black hat and veil almost as much as she despised the way the guests murmured their condolences and gave her a quick squeeze of her hands.

Half of these people hadn't even met Brian. They attended because of her father. Representatives of caster families from around the world, VIP Normals who knew the truth about casters—all were looking to gain some advantage by showing her father how much they cared.

As if.

She wound her way between the maple trees, making toward the family plot, a collection of headstones both old and weathered and much, much newer, bordered by an iron fence. She passed her mom's marble marker: *Faith Hamilton, beloved wife and mother.* The earth around it had grown over with grass and wildflowers. Hamiltons, buried among Normals, passing in death the same way they did in life.

Kate sat in the front row of seats set up for family, between her dad and Grayson. She listened as the priest droned on and on.

When will this stupid thing be over?

She glanced at her father. He stared straight ahead, his face unreadable. She curled her toes in her shoes. Nothing the man at the podium had to say mattered. What did she care about God and heaven and faith?

God hadn't helped Brian and her in the Sanctum.

When the priest was done, Grayson got up to give the eulogy.

"Although Brian is...was, my nephew, I feel today that I have lost a son. The accident that took his life robbed us of the most promising caster of his generation. Brian was the kind of young man who put others first. I remember the time he..."

She zoned out as Grayson went on about what a great guy Brian had been. Had he? That wasn't the Brian she'd heard about last night.

Kate couldn't focus on any of it. All she could think about was the Sanctum and Brian screaming. And how it all would have been different if she had just told her father or Grayson or somebody about the damned stone.

The pain and grief inside built up to a roiling despair. A tear started. Then another.

No. I'm not going to cry. Not in front of all these stupid people.

She wiped the wetness away, then sought her father's hand. He took hers and gave it a tight squeeze. His thumb rubbed the inside of her palm gently until she stopped thinking everything was her fault.

Afterward, she stood at the side of the gathering, gripping a glass of iced tea already wet with condensation, and looked for someone safe to talk to. She might be a caster now, but her earrings made her look the same as ever. A Null.

Grayson had briefed her on the caster families who'd planned to attend. Every family had sent someone as a representative—following the caster custom to pay their respects at funerals, weddings, and other major events. Looking around at the little groups gathered together, sipping their drinks, voices low, something else became clear—it served as an opportunity to scheme and politic.

Over by the fountain, Justine Delacroix, her blond hair in a perfect French twist, silver necklace dangling, smiled up at Jaime de la Vega as she brushed some imaginary lint off the fawning man's tacky double-breasted suit. Nicodemus Makris, pig-eyed, with his brown hair beginning to thin and his heavyset body sheathed in dark pinstripes, leaned in and punctuated his words with his big hands as he spoke to her father under the tall oak tree, their bodyguards hovering. Kate doubted they were discussing Grayson's eulogy.

Hayley and Missy sat at the end of a row of chairs and traded phone numbers with some of the younger de la Vega boys, who hovered a little too close to them in Kate's opinion. Hayley stifled a giggle.

So maybe *they* weren't talking politics.

Dylan leaned against a tall tree and talked with a couple of her uncle's other assistants. Maybe she should wander over, see if Dylan could break free from his conversation and tell her if he's found out anything about the stone.

No, this wasn't the time or the place.

"Excuse me, Miss Hamilton. I wanted to offer my condolences."

Kate turned around. The young man in front of her made her breath catch. Tall, handsome in a roguish sort of way, he was a guy clearly used to wearing a suit that cost more than most people's cars. His English held the faint trace of an accent—European, but she couldn't quite place it. The way he looked at her with his deep-blue eyes made her wonder if they'd met. She didn't think so—she'd have remembered him.

She mentally rifled through the flash cards Grayson had made her memorize.

"Kristof Makris?"

A smile quirked at his lips. "You recognize me."

"You know the saying. 'Know thine enemy.' My family makes sure even a Null like me can ID the Makrises," she bluffed. She'd had no idea what he'd looked like before this morning.

The wind ruffled his sun-kissed, brown hair. "I'm sorry to hear about Brian. He knew which end of a talisman was up—unlike some." He jerked his head toward a few of the flirting de la Vega boys. "I'm sure this must be very difficult for you."

Her eyes dropped to the neatly trimmed lawn as she fought a wave of grief that threatened to bring back her earlier tears.. *No.* She wasn't going to show any weakness in front of her family's enemy. She took a sip of her iced tea. The cold liquid brought her back to the here and now. This guy was the Makris heir. He wasn't talking to her just to be nice.

"I'm managing. Thank you for your kindness."

"Brian and I didn't have much of an opportunity to talk, as you might expect, but he said something, once, that I thought you might want to hear."

"Really? What?"

"We were in Paris, fighting over... Well, it doesn't matter now. I'd won the fight—taken Brian down. I had the prize and was walking away. Then Brian snuck in a cloaked lightning bolt he shouldn't have been able to cast, not in the shape he was in, and took me out. Before he teleported away, I asked him how he managed it. He said, 'My sister taught me that just because I'm down, doesn't mean I'm out.'"

Kate drifted in thought, swirling her iced tea. She'd been the one Brian had come to every time school turned tough, every time he'd broken up with a girlfriend, every time an operation got rough. And she'd gotten him back on his feet with exactly the words he'd echoed to Kristof.

She wondered why Kristof had told her this. What did he hope to gain? He thought she was a Null—he couldn't get any political advantage or operational insight from her. He couldn't be doing it from the kindness of his heart.

From what Grayson had told her, he didn't have one.

He took her hand gently in his. "I'm truly sorry for your loss, Miss Hamilton." The feel of his hand against hers was nothing like the uncomfortable squeeze of the rest of these strangers. A spirited electricity sent her pulse spiraling.

What the hell? No, no, no. She would not have *that* reaction to *this* guy. Besides, she already had a boyfriend.

The last guy she should ever be involved with was Kristof Makris.

What was he thinking?

Kristof strode toward Melina. He'd been ignoring his sister's meaningful glances for the last few minutes, too wrapped up in his conversation with Kate to care. He picked up an iced tea from a waiter and made his way across the lawn.

What had been the point of talking to Kate? Telling her comforting stories didn't get him any closer to his goal. But the spark in her eyes as their hands clasped had provoked an answering flare inside him for a moment. Then a hot burn as he realized that the guy she responded to wasn't her boyfriend. Not as far as she knew.

Ridiculous. He couldn't be jealous of *himself.*

The iced tea provided a cold wake-up call as he drank half the glass. He had to stay on mission. Only the stone mattered. The twenty-four-hour cessation of all operations declared for the funeral meant that he couldn't activate the spells in the conch-shell fob he'd given Kate to get access to the Hamilton's estate today. Not unless he wanted to break the Rules even more than he had already. Too bad—dodging his father had become impossible. Kristof had spotted him over by the oak tree, talking to Mr. Hamilton, Kate's father. Maybe he could sneak away before his father caught up to him.

He glanced back at Kate. Alex Torres hovered over her, handing her another drink. Was he just doing his duty as her father's aide, or was something else going on? Then again, Kate's status must have changed due to Brian's death. It would be a while before Hamilton named a new heir, but Kate was now his only child. She might be a Null, but it wasn't unheard of for Nulls to play a role in the line of inheritance, despite the riskiness of their genetics. For an Affiliate like Alex, winning Kate would be an opportunity to marry into the Hamilton family and go straight to the top.

He pictured Alex playing house with Kate. Playing other things. He crunched on an ice cube. Then another one. Good thing Hamilton would never pick Alex as his heir. Alex didn't have the ruthlessness needed to run a family. Kristof would send him running for his mamacita the first time they squared off at the bargaining table.

No, Hamilton would pick someone like Victor Cole.

Victor had the hard edge, the ruthlessness, the ability to command respect. He'd proven himself a match for Kristof in battle—maybe more of a match than Kristof liked. Kristof could only hope that Victor's status as a former rogue would work against his chances of getting the buy-in Hamilton would need from his Affiliates.

Besides, he'd seen the way Kate looked at Victor when he'd rescued her from Brooke. There might be more than gratitude in that smile.

It didn't matter what he thought. In the long run, Kate would marry whomever her father wanted her to marry, and Kristof would go back to his own life.

Melina gave a little good-bye wave to the Chen family heir she'd been pumping for information and joined him under the large oak tree. She took a long drink of her mimosa and cast a meaningful glance in Kate's direction.

"What was that all about, brother dear?"

He shrugged. "It would seem strange if I didn't offer my condolences. Isn't that what we're here for?"

Melina raised an eyebrow. "Technically. But I would think you'd take the time to further our other goals."

"I can't exactly execute on that now, with the truce."

"Of course not. I want—"

"She wants you to do your duty, my son." His father spoke from behind him. Kristof turned around, careful to move slowly. His father's husky bodyguards hovered behind him like a pair of Dobermans on crack, wary of sudden movement.

His father's deep, black eyes were fixed on him. "I don't like funerals. They are a waste of time. Dead is dead. Why mourn it? Move on. It's the living that command my attention, not the corpses we make in the Game." His nostrils flared. "And Brian Hamilton died in the Game. Didn't he? But we'll get back to that."

Kristof went still.

"Melina, take us home. The Hamiltons won't miss us; they have plenty of other mourners to entertain them."

Melina cast a teleport spell, tracing out the points on the oak tree as she chanted the ancient words. The violet energy settled over the five of them, Dobermans included. It might be rude to leave a funeral without tendering their farewells to the host, but he wasn't going to remind his father of that.

The bright sky and maple trees of the cemetery faded as they materialized in the portico of the Makris estate. Blue-and-brown mosaic tiles appeared under Kristof's feet, their solidity giving him none of the familiar comfort of home. Mosquitoes buzzed around the wooden beams above him. A mild sea breeze blew in across the open courtyard, bringing with it the faint scent of apples. In the distance, the cries of gulls sounded.

"It is clear to me now why you failed to report to me," his father said. He leaned against the tall center beam of the portico, his bodyguards flanking him.

Shit. Does he know about the stone?

"It's the girl."

Kristof relaxed a little. This one he could handle. "Kate means nothing to me. Hamilton security pressed me too hard. Reporting in would have compromised the mission."

"I saw you with her, a moment ago. Do not lie to me."

"What would you have me do? Ignore her? It would have been strange if I gave condolences to every Hamilton except her."

"Kristof, a father can tell when his son looks into a girl's eyes and is lost. I was young once, too. A pretty girl is a fine thing when you have no responsibilities, but during a mission, falling in love is nothing but a distraction."

"Kate's just a job, Papa. Nothing else."

"What if I told you I wanted you to remove the distraction? If she's 'just a job,' it should be simple to kill her, no?"

Kristof knew what the answer had to be. "Sure. Tell me when." His gaze was locked on his father, but his heart raced faster than the mosquito flitting in the citronella trap hanging above him. He'd find a way out of this.

"You'll do it when I give the order. But the girl isn't your only problem." His father crossed his arms. "Where is the stone?"

"I don't know what you—"

"Don't lie to me. I know all about your little game with the stone. And everything you planned to do with it."

Kristof's eyes flared. He couldn't help it. All he could do was to stop himself from glancing to Melina, who was standing behind their father. If she hadn't turned him in, then she was his only hope.

"Did you think you could keep a secret like the stone from me? *From me?*" His father struck Kristof hard across the face. The heavy ruby ring on his father's hand cut Kristof's cheek. The blood dripped down his face and onto the collar of his crisp white shirt.

"Papa, I—"

"I am taking personal control of this operation—both handling Hamilton's daughter, and retrieving the stone. And when I get it, the Hamiltons will pay for humiliating us back in your Grandfather Arkady's day. I'll tear our arsenal from Hamilton's bleeding hands, artifact by artifact."

His father nodded to his bodyguards. They moved toward Kristof. "It seems you did not learn your lesson the last time in the Pit. Perhaps you need more time to think about the folly of defying me. You'll stay there until I decide what to do with you." His father's bodyguards grabbed him by the shoulders. Doberman One punched him in the stomach. He doubled over, the impact forcing the air from his lungs, the pain raging through his stomach. If he could get a spell off, maybe he could...

Doberman Two slammed Kristof's head down on the portico's

wooden table. Agony erupted in his skull. The world around him began to fade to darkness. *No. Have to shake it off, tap out a spell.*

Before unconsciousness overcame him, he flashed back to Kate standing alone at the memorial, hands braced against the back of her chair, eyes gone distant with memories of her brother.

Kate was the key to getting the stone. He knew it. His father would never succeed.

But he could.

Just because I'm down...doesn't mean I'm out....

After the funeral, Kate went back to her room to study. After an hour spent lying on her bed, staring at the same page in *Practical Casting*, she slammed the book closed. Visions of Brian kept forcing their way into the spell charts and history lessons. Their contentious discussion in the catalpa grove, him trying to save her in the Sanctum, the feel of his hand clutching hers before everything went black.

The questions he had left her.

No one in the family admitted they knew what he had been up to. Clearly he hadn't told anyone except the mysterious person he worked for—and that person wasn't talking. He must've been working for someone; he couldn't have been after the stone for himself. She thought back to the party last night, to the darker image of Brian his friends had drawn with their stories and their cruel laughter. No. The brother she loved would never have gone that far off mission.

She slid off her bed and paced. If she was going to find anything out, she would have to do it herself.

She left her room and walked the few steps down the hall to Brian's. She turned the knob and entered. Brian's room remained the same as she remembered it. His Little League trophies, the picture of him and Dad sailing the old yacht, his leather jacket lying draped over the chair.

Kate walked over to the side of his bed and bent down to open his bedside drawer. She hesitated.

I'm invading his privacy.

Wiping away the wetness that sprung to her eyes, she put her hand back on the drawer pull. Brian was dead. There was no privacy to invade.

Even though nothing was locked, it might still be protected. Magesight would let her see the symbols of any protection spells still in place, and any that had been broken. Her uncle had run through the basics of using her shiny, new magical vision yesterday in training.

Kate took a breath, imagined herself rooted in the ground, and let her focus soften, spreading her attention beyond the objects physically present in the room. She blinked.

All around her shredded remnants of magical symbols hovered over the drawers and the closet, as if something had torn them asunder. A symbol floated by the bedside table, as broken as the others.

Someone had already been here. Searching. Violating the last little bit of Brian that was left. She swiped at a tear that trickled down her face.

She opened the bedside drawer. Nothing but a few pens and a bottle of pain relievers. No cell phone, no papers, nothing useful.

A book lay on top of the bedside table. The *Tao te Ching.*

Weird, not Brian's thing at all. Something for school? Asian Studies, maybe? She opened it, and a bookmark fell out. Someone had highlighted text on the bookmarked page:

When two great powers clash
the one that yields
will emerge triumphant.

Huh. She had no idea why Brian would think it important. She tossed the book back on the table.

A search of the rest of the drawers and the closet revealed nothing interesting. Kate threw herself on the bed. She should talk to Victor, but that probably wouldn't get her anywhere. He'd do what he always did—yell at her for not coming to him before wiping her nose. Plus, he's probably the one who searched the room in the first place.

Where else would Brian have put something important, something secret? Then she remembered: the catalpa grove. The hiding place where they used to stash things for each other, under the Old Bear. She jumped up and headed for the door.

When she reached the clearing, the sun streamed through the branches, illuminating the large deadfall they had sat on. Had it really been just a few days ago? It seemed like another life. Pretty blue butterflies lazed through the branches of the trees, lighting upon them for a moment and then flying off again. The Old Bear loomed over the clearing, providing much-needed shade with its massive trunk.

Kate knelt at its base. The hollow at its bottom seemed to be undisturbed. She brushed the bean pods out of her way as she dug around the hollow, trying to get a clearer view of their old hiding place. She engaged her magesight again. No magical symbols. Nothing. She reached in— past the moss, the lichen, the stray stones, the fallen twigs, and the piled-up dirt—searching for anything Brian might have left there.

She stopped. An intricate, looped symbol, like the ones on the drawers and closets in Brian's room, was barely visible to her magesight, floating a foot inside the cache. Far enough within to catch an unwary intruder.

This one, unlike the ones in Brian's room, looked intact.

Damn. Should she reach inside, knowing that doing so would probably trigger the spell? If it were Brian's, would it even still work?

She sat back on her heels, her knees covered with moist summer soil. A butterfly floated by, then alighted on the hollow, its wings fluttering.

There had to be a way to get inside the cache without triggering the spell. But she hadn't learned how to do it in her one day of training. Kate hit the tree with her fist. Bark flew off. She winced and shook the sting from her scraped knuckles.

Was there anything at all she could do?

Yes. A ring of certainty sounded from deep inside. *You can do what you want.*

What the hell? Where had that come from? It sounded almost like…the stone. But the stone wasn't here. Grayson had it safely locked up.

She sat still for a moment, thinking back. Years ago, before she was tested, Grayson had taught her how to look inside, to see her own connection with magic. She'd only used the technique once before, and she'd seen nothing. But if it could lead her to whatever spoke to her now, she'd try it.

She took a deep breath, then another. She needed a focus, an entry point. The Old Bear. Closing her eyes, she pictured its gnarled roots, its twisted branches. In her mind's eye, she stepped up to its broad trunk, warm with the afternoon sun. Putting her hands against its coarse wood, she slid through its bark and into her own soul.

A long staircase, wood creaking with her every step, descended from inside the Old Bear down into the shadows at her very center. Step by step, she went down, the darkness around her growing, until she reached the bottom and the bolted cast iron doors that awaited her.

She opened the doors. This time, something lay on the other side.

The shore of a vast, black sea stretched for miles in every direction. The water pulsed and writhed hypnotically, its waves rippling against her feet and then washing back into the viscous sea. In the sky above, storm clouds rumbled, emerald flashes lightening the darkness within them. In the distance, a constant stream of pitch-black liquid poured from the clouds into the sea, replenishing it. Heat rose from the surface, heat pulsing with power in its rawest state.

The jet-black sea made her stomach clench with disquiet. Another flash of green shot from the crest of a wave as the black tide washed toward her feet. Everything here felt like the energy she'd seen when she'd used magesight to look at the stone in her father's office.

But the stone was nothing compared to the raging sea of power in front of her. Merely an ambassador from its vast sovereignty.

She wrenched herself out of her trance, falling backward into a pile of leaves, her legs shaking. Was this endless black *thing* inside her something the stone had created? It couldn't be a normal part of being a caster. That ebony seascape wasn't in any of the books she'd read. Grayson had never described casting as feeling anything like this.

She realized she was holding her breath and let it out. Maybe she was crazy to think this way, but could she use this...stuff inside her? What had it said? *You can do what you want.*

Focus your will, the rippling energy inside her seemed to add, *and make it so.*

The sea, the power—it talked to her now? What the hell was that? Was the stone controlling her again?

Calm down. Just calm down. She had to get a hold of herself.

Think, don't react. This...thing inside, whatever it is, isn't the stone. It's connected somehow. It sure as hell wasn't there before the stone changed me. But it isn't forcing me to do anything. It isn't asking me to touch it. More like offering me a choice.

She should ask her uncle if it was safe. But if she asked Grayson, he'd tell her to let him take care of the cache, the same as the stone. She would lose her chance to find out what Brian had been doing.

She had to try it herself if she wanted what Brian had left for her.

Kate stared at the symbol written inside the entrance to the cache. "Go away," she said.

Nothing happened. She rubbed the back of her neck. *Idiot.* Whatever that black stuff was, it wasn't going to obliterate the spell inside the cache for her.

Focus your will. The impulse came up strongly from the dark power inside her. She closed her eyes and descended through the tree and down the staircase in her mind again. She unbolted the metal door. The sea lay before her, waves spilling against the shore with a dark hunger.

She steeled herself. *Go away*, she willed at the spell inside the cache, and she opened her eyes.

The symbol had faded. The spell was gone.

Reaching into the cache, she pulled out a small notebook, covered in a brown leather binding. A watch sat inside with the journal—their grandfather's old timepiece, bequeathed to Brian in his will.

She flipped open the notebook. It was filled with Brian's handwriting. A journal?

There was only one way to find out.

An hour later, legs cramped and back sore from sitting against the tree, she closed the journal, disappointed. It contained nothing but a collection of memories of Brian's life: notes on when he passed or failed a test, when he won or lost a basketball game, and who he was dating. No info on his missions at all.

She stood up and shoved it and the watch in her back pocket. There must be something more to these things. Otherwise, why would he have taken such care to hide them? But for the life of her, she couldn't figure out what.

As she left the grove, she nearly slipped on a pile of dead butter-flies, their wings still wet from emergence from their chrysalides, lying on the leaf-strewn ground. No more blue butterflies flitted from tree to tree in the grove.

Huh. What was up with *that*?

Chapter Fourteen

ristof floated in darkness. His bloodshot eyes could see nothing. His ears, tender from the sound of his own screaming, could hear nothing else. The smell of sweat filled his nostrils, and the blood in his mouth tasted sharp on his tongue from where he'd bitten it over and over.

All he could feel was pain.

The white-hot energy from another spell ran over his torso and up his back. The muscles that connected to his spine spasmed as a thousand needles of agony jammed into them. The base of his head felt like an inferno, every nerve raw with hurt.

His hands jerked against his spellcuffs, the silver bindings fastened tight enough that they cut through the skin of his wrists. His father liked his victims to feel their helplessness.

Another jolt of anguish shot from the base of his spine up to his neck and exploded through his skull. He screamed—a wail that he couldn't stop, couldn't turn off even if he tried. There was no point in being stoic; it never won him a reprieve. His torturer could care less if he cried out, begged, or threatened.

By this point, he didn't care, either.

He had done his time running the Pit, just like every family member. Carry out the program Papa prescribed or take the victim's place.

Simple. Effective.

It went on forever. It ended as unexpectedly as it began.

Light erupted around him, searing his eyes with bright pain. He fell several feet to the center of the circle stones set in the concrete floor of the Pit, the levitation spell holding him up ending with no warning. The extra bruises on his knees and elbows were gratuitous, but they helped identify his torturer.

Dmitri.

Kristof squinted, trying to let enough light in to see without overloading his nervous system. Arms crossed, Dmitri leaned against the black jewels studding the wall of the Pit, a smug smile lighting his weasel-sly eyes. The tension in his cousin's wiry body— his hand still cocked with a spell, ready to throw—suggested that the torture had ended far too soon for his taste.

"I said let him down *gently*." Melina, somewhere near.

"I don't take orders from you." Dmitri's low voice snaked across the room.

"They're Papa's orders." Melina's footsteps sounded on the floor. Her form became clear through Kristof's wavering vision as she crossed the circle stones and tossed his clothes down next to him. He couldn't tell anything from the set line of her mouth, her neutral gaze.

"Uncle Nico doesn't care how nicely I let his little boy down. Not after Kristof stabbed him in the back," Dmitri said, smirking.

And who told him about my betrayal? Dmitri? How did he find out?

Kristof picked up his clothes.

Melina slid a pair of sunglasses on his face, and the pain in his eyes receded. "Get dressed. Papa wants to talk to you."

He pulled his jeans and shirt on. Each time the cloth touched his skin it burned like a demon's kiss. He knew better than to ask Melina to heal him, though. If his father had wanted him healed, she would have done it. He ignored the pain.

"How long?" he asked.

"It's Wednesday morning."

Damn. He'd lost time. Hamilton security might have detected the conch-shell talisman by now. But he had other issues to deal with first.

"How did Papa find out about the stone?" He kept his voice low, aimed only at Melina.

She glanced at Dmitri, still leaning against the wall of the Pit. "I don't know. Papa didn't say." Kristof didn't know whether to trust her, but he didn't have any other options.

Melina led him up the long, stone staircase and into the strong Mediterranean sun. Every step hurt like daggers being pushed through his tortured muscles. The tile of the pathway burned his bare feet, but he welcomed the warmth. He was out of the Pit.

They walked down the travertine steps from the outer buildings and approached the courtyard of his father's estate. A terrace of granite tiles set with colorful mosaics surrounded a pool that disappeared from view off the edge of the high cliff where the house perched.

The scent of fig, apple, and pear blossoms wafted down from the rows of fruit-laden trees that surrounded the estate. Sweet smelling, Kristof supposed, but they always brought to mind his father, who enjoyed taking his breakfast at one of the weathered cedar tables at the edge of the grove. If the weather didn't cooperate, some of the younger members of the family changed it. They spent hours with their mouths gagged to silence their ravings, their hands bound to stop them from tearing their eyes out from the backlash of such a strong spell. But that was a small price to pay, in Papa's view. Papa liked his sunshine.

His father sat by the pool, a bowl of figs and yogurt in front of him. Kristof's aunt Elena, dressed in her habitual widow's black, her short blond hair stirred by the ocean breeze, sat across the wooden table, along with his uncle Stavros, his talismans shining against his dark-red uniform. They leaned forward to catch what his father had said.

The Synedrion. Two of the three members, anyway. What did the council want with his father? They let his father do what he wanted and only got involved in major decisions: matters of inheritance, policy, and occasionally, punishment. They gave his father the authority to govern, and one shake of his aunt's head could take everything away. But they would never exercise that power without good reason.

He couldn't give them one yet, but he needed to think about playing a longer game.

Kristof paused at the vine-wrapped pergola framing the entrance to the courtyard, Melina a step behind. He needed a strategy before this confrontation. Otherwise the meeting would be entirely on his father's terms.

He considered his options. Then he walked over to the table. His father's bodyguards, lurking in their Doberman stances a few paces behind him, scanned Kristof with a flicker of their unfocused eyes. Magesight—looking for signs of a spell or a weapon. Like anything he tried could get past his father's ever-present personal shield, glowing a tranquil blue-green, like the Aegean lapping at the rocks a few meters away. He ignored them and waited to be acknowledged.

His aunt and uncle stood, pushing back their chairs. His aunt nodded to his father, then turned to leave, his uncle following. As she passed Kristof, she gave him a gentle pat on the shoulder, and the sting of her hand on his aching flesh matched the sharp disappointment in her dark eyes.

Had his father been talking to the Synedrion about him?

His father beckoned to Melina, who came around to his side and kissed his cheek. He whispered in her ear. She gave Kristof a cautious glance, then walked toward the house, joining their aunt and uncle inside.

So much for her support. He'd have to manage on his own.

"Well?" His father's piggish eyes stared up at him. "What have you learned from your punishment?"

"Never to keep secrets from you, Papa."

His father frowned, and tapped the table. "If that's all you learned, you can go back to the Pit."

What more could he admit without damning himself? "And to control my ambition."

"That's right. Your time will come eventually. Well, yours or Dmitri's. But not for a good, long while. Sit." He pointed to the chair in front of him, then clapped for a servant. "Breakfast for my son."

Kristof took the seat his father indicated. One of the servants appeared next to him with coffee, some feta and olives, and a large hunk of crusty bread. Kristof broke off a piece of bread and started in on the feta. The bread was warm and rich with the smell of yeast and wheat, and the feta was sharp and tangy. He'd forgotten how long it had been since he'd eaten. At least a day.

But the bright flavors turned to ash in his mouth.

His father never ended a torture session early, and as long as the pain seemed to last, Kristof knew it hadn't been long enough for his offense.

His father waited for a moment, leaning back and drinking his own coffee while Kristof devoured breakfast. Then he spoke.

"We have to get the stone from the Hamiltons. Now. No more delays, no more screwups. That's why I am overseeing the operation."

His father leaned forward and told Kristof his plan.

Kristof tore off another piece of bread and chewed with a mechanical thoughtlessness. He kept his eyes focused on his father— cold eyes, professional, considering. Anything to cover the turmoil inside. His father's plan sounded simple, effective, and likely to get them the stone. Also brutal, unnecessarily risky, and illegal as hell. And it put Kate right in the line of fire.

The plan required two operatives on the ground, at a minimum. And one of them had to pull off a high-risk, complicated maneuver at which one person in the Makris family would have the best chance of success.

Him.

He knew now why his father had pulled him out of the Pit. And why he'd been talking to the Synedrion. Breaking this many rules required their buy-in. At least if his father wanted their support against the inevitable blowback from the Hamiltons.

He could have come up with this plan himself. He and Melina could have executed it. But he'd gone with a different one instead— using the conch-shell talisman to break through Hamilton's security grid and get the stone, leaving Kate out of danger and putting all the risk on his back.

He needed the stone. But the thought of pulling off his father's plan made his stomach twist into a knot.

He set down his bread and brushed the crumbs off his shirt.

"There's another way to run this mission," he said. "We don't need to break as many rules or rely on the Synedrion for backing."

"You have a different proposal?"

"Put me in charge. I have a way to ensure the operation goes even easier than you planned." He told his father about the conch-shell key chain, lying about how he'd put it together with black market parts. "I can activate it whenever, wherever, we want. Kate has it now. We can get into the Hamilton estate, get the stone, get out. She barely needs to be involved."

His father stood. Kristof could see the veins in the man's neck standing out, blue and cold.

"Another secret? When exactly, were you planning on telling me about this?"

"You need to hear me out." As soon as he spoke, he realized his mistake.

"I don't *need* to do anything." His father heaved the table over, sending coffee, food, and newspapers flying everywhere. Hot liquid hit Kristof across the arm, the burning pain making him flinch. His father stared at him from behind the mess he'd made, chest heaving. The bodyguards, used to his father's temper, stood back. Their focus was on Kristof.

"You're the one who *needs* to do something. Stop lying to me." His father stalked around the upended table toward Kristof, arm out, finger pointed at his son's chest. "*Another* secret. *Another* lie. What else haven't you told me?"

Kristof stood and let his father come all the way up to him, chest to chest. He clasped his hands behind his back to hide their shaking.

"I had no chance to mention it to you. Until I knew what you were planning, I didn't know where it would fit in."

His father poked him on the chest with his fingers. "So why should I give field command to a son who runs his own operation behind my back?" his father asked. "Who tries to steal an artifact out from under me?" He poked him again. "What were you going to do with it, eh? Tell me that?"

"Isn't ambition what you want in an heir?" He saw his father's eyes bulge, the redness creep into his father's cheeks. He hurried into his explanation. "You've said time and again that you want initiative. Daring. Success." He was pushing it, but the spark of interest that flashed across his father's face confirmed that this line of reasoning was working.

"Controlled ambition, yes. That's exactly what I want." His father eased back a pace.

"That's the son I want to be. I was just trying to impress you, Papa." He took a small step toward his father. "I never had any other intention with the stone. Did someone tell you otherwise? Dmitri? And wouldn't he have a motive for misleading you about my reasons?"

"You have an answer for everything today, don't you?"

Every muscle in Kristof's body went still.

"I want that stone. We need to rebuild our arsenal—match what the Hamiltons took from us years ago. I should be wearing your grandfather's amulet around my neck. Instead, it hangs in Hamilton's study like a bloody trophy. Get me that stone. No more games, no more lies."

Kristof could feel a small bead of sweat roll down his back. "Yes. If I can have Melina as the other operative—"

"No. Not your sister. Dmitri."

"Dmitri's a fuckup."

"Your cousin gets the job done." His father chuckled. "He's merely...overenthusiastic. Boys will be boys, after all."

He couldn't let Dmitri deal with Kate. But Dmitri couldn't carry out the other half of the plan, either. He didn't have the skills or finesse. But the thought of Dmitri with Kate...

"Papa, let me handle Kate. I can—" he began.

"No. You aren't going near the Hamilton girl. She's Dmitri's problem. You take care of the stone."

"I can deal with both—"

"That's enough," his father barked. "If you expect to lead this family someday, you have to learn to lead everyone in it. If you can't control Dmitri, why should I let you be my heir? Why shouldn't I name Dmitri? He's already proven he can manipulate you."

That answered the question of who had told his father about the stone. But how had Dmitri found out about it?

His father clamped a hand on his shoulder. He squeezed hard. Kristof didn't let the pain show in his eyes. "Don't let me down on this. I'll be monitoring the operation via talisman. Deviate from the operation's parameters and your last session in the Pit will feel like a lover's caress."

"I understand, Papa."

His father turned and yelled for servants to clean up his mess. Kristof, knowing when he'd been dismissed, walked back up the steps and into the house. Thanks to his father's temper, he'd lost half of his breakfast. Maybe he could find some inside. After he found Dmitri and they came to an understanding.

Kristof tracked down Dmitri in the gym. He had their younger, smaller cousin, Anton, pinned to the mat, arm twisted in a joint lock behind his back, his short, dark hair plastered to his face with sweat. Anton slapped the mat as hard as he could with his free hand, gasping for breath. They wore white judo gis, Dmitri's belted with black, Anton's with brown.

Dmitri grinned, eyes lit with sadistic joy.

"Let him up," Kristof said. He leaned against the wall of the gym, arms folded.

"You going to make me?"

"If that's how you want to play this."

"Sure you're recovered enough?" Dmitri's lips twisted into a sneer.

Kristof took his sunglasses off and laid them on the bench by the mat. Even that small movement hurt. He strode toward Dmitri.

Dmitri let go of Anton's arm. The young man groaned and rolled away, giving Kristof a grateful glance. At Kristof's nod he left, shutting the gym door behind him.

Kristof circled Dmitri on the mat. "My father just assigned you to me. We have a mission."

"That's funny, Uncle Nico didn't tell me anything about it." Dmitri kept pace with Kristof.

"He didn't have to. He gives me an order, I give it to you."

"Is that what you think?"

"That's the way it is. If you don't believe me, you could go ask my father. If you want to bother him." Kristof watched Dmitri's face.

There. Dmitri's eyes flared, and he stepped in, grabbing for Kristof's shoulder. He hooked his right foot behind Kristof's left, trying for a quick leg sweep.

Kristof drove his left leg into Dmitri's midsection. He grabbed Dmitri's gi, then threw him, hard. Dmitri flew backward to the mat. He landed with a *thwack*. Wasting no time, Kristof knelt on Dmitri's chest and grabbed his collar, crossing his arms before he applied the necessary pressure for the choke hold.

Dmitri gasped, his face turning red as he squirmed in Kristof's grasp. He rolled from side to side, trying to escape. His legs kicked out, one foot striking Kristof in the thigh. Kristof pressed down harder. Finally, spittle flying, Dmitri tapped out.

Kristof let him up. His hands, his leg, even his arms where he'd pinned Dmitri down, were throbbing. That bout had probably hurt him more than Dmitri. But it was worth it.

He grabbed a towel from the bench. Wiping the sweat from his face, he watched his cousin.

Dmitri picked up a water bottle and took a long drink. "You don't think that settles anything, do you?" Dmitri locked eyes with his cousin. Kristof met his gaze until Dmitri let his eyes drift away and turned on his annoying smirk.

"We have a mission to complete," Kristof said. "Until it's done, we have to work together. We can settle our differences afterward."

"Fine. I was getting bored around here anyway." Dmitri threw himself down on the bench, tossing the water bottle in a corner. "We're going after the stone?"

"Yes. How'd you find out about it?"

"You think you're Uncle Nico's favorite, don't you? Think you can do whatever you want? You slipped up, and you will again. Don't expect me to show you your weak spots so you can fix them."

Damn. He'd have to find out how Dmitri had gotten his information some other way.

"So what's the mission?"

"The Hamiltons have the stone. We're going to take it from them."

"Great." Dmitri took another swig of his water. "Who do I get to kill?"

"No one. Papa wants you to do some babysitting. A girl."

"Cool. What's she look like?"

Kristof took a step forward. "Let me make this clear: Your job is to guard her. She's not one of your playthings."

"What's she to you?"

"Nothing. She's a hostage. If she's damaged, we don't get what we want."

Dmitri's eyes searched Kristof's, hoping, Kristof thought, to find something, anything, to use against him. Kristof stared right back, his expression closed.

Dmitri stood, towel around his neck. "So what's the plan?"

As they left the gym and walked out into the warm sunlight, Kristof glanced over at his cousin. He wasn't naive enough to believe that beating him in judo meant that Dmitri would cooperate on the mission. There was no way to keep a watch on him during this operation, either. They'd both be on their own. He'd have to trust Dmitri to do his job.

The thought gave him a sick feeling in his stomach. If he couldn't control Dmitri, he wasn't the only one who would suffer. Kate would, as well.

Chapter Fifteen

The late-afternoon sun shone through Kate's bedroom window, and for the first time in days she had a real break. Pulling on her favorite jeans and a white poet's shirt, she threw her training clothes into the laundry basket. Time to find out how Brian really died. She stuffed Brian's journal and Grandfather's watch into her pocket and tossed her keys, with Kris's conch-shell fob hanging from the chain, in her purse.

And she knew just the person to help her: Dylan Pearce. Maybe he'd found something out about the stone by now—something he'd be willing to share. She'd texted him and arranged to meet at a little café in Paumanok. Except for her time out with Kris the other night, she'd been grounded on the estate ever since Brian's death. Stir crazy didn't even begin to describe how she felt.

She rummaged through the closet, pulling out a pair of white flats, then tossing them back on the floor. Surely a brief trip into Paumanok wouldn't be dangerous. Dad pretty much owned the place. She should tell Victor about her trip but…

Shoes, shoes, what to pick…the red sandals. Perfect.

Better to ask for forgiveness than permission. No reason to give Victor the chance to exercise his apparent veto power over her life.

But when she found Dylan standing by her car, one look at his face shot her plans to hell. Tension shone through his tight eyes, his scrunched-up lips, the way he straightened his glasses with a firm push on the wire bridge.

"It isn't safe for you to go into town," he said. "Victor mentioned the attack against you. He said there's a security lockdown."

Damn Victor's paranoia. "We'll be safe enough in Paumanok. No one would do anything there."

"Perhaps not, but rules are rules."

She stopped, all the desperation of days spent grounded shining from her face. "Please. Anywhere but here."

His eyes softened, and he nodded. "We can talk at the Hamilton offices in DC. The security grid will protect us there."

"But won't my dad see us? Or Victor?" She followed him out of the garage, into the kitchen, and down the hall to the outgoing teleport pattern, the marble tile foyer next to the staircase.

"It doesn't matter if they do. Your uncle gave me an assignment—"

"Investigating the stone?" She grasped Dylan's arm as he touched a talisman inside his jacket—a silver eagle.

"No, keeping an eye on you." His tight lips relaxed into a wry smile. "Making sure you socialize with casters, without…"

"Getting into trouble."

She missed his response as the teleport spell seized them and zipped them off to the big rotunda in the Hamilton headquarters building. Huh. No teleport headache. Well, at least that was one advantage of being a caster.

Kate trailed Dylan out of the rotunda, down a long corridor, and into a small room with wooden tables and chairs. They'd walked all the way to the north end of the building.

"Cafeteria?" She read the sign. "I didn't know Dad had a cafeteria."

"I suppose it's better than interrupting work to get a sandwich. And safer," Dylan answered.

A few hours past lunch and only two or three staff members sat in the circular room, surrounded by high glass walls. Kate squinted at the panoramic view of the capital. Sure enough, the red energy of a security grid glowed through the glass.

Dylan paid for their coffees, and they settled in at a small table by a potted plant as far away from the other diners as possible. He reached into his jacket and touched a silver cone, his eyes losing their focus for a moment. The jade glimmer of a spell settled in around them. The staff sitting in the café got up, one by one, and left. Even when they weren't finished eating.

"What did you do?"

"Ensured our privacy. We can talk without fear of being overheard now."

Kate added a packet of sugar to her latte, stirred it, and took a sip. Was his concern general paranoia or did he have reason to worry about someone listening to them? It wasn't backlash from the spells—the talisman he used stored a spell that the caster—probably Dylan in this case—charged it with beforehand. The backlash came when the caster charged the talisman, not when he activated the spell inside. Or so Grayson had told her.

Dylan pulled out his notebook. "I know your uncle's theories about what happened. Now I'd like to know what you experienced firsthand."

"Did you find out anything about the stone?"

"I discovered a few things. I'll have a much better idea if you answer my questions."

Kate told him what had happened, from the time Brian had given her the stone to when she'd blacked out in the Sanctum. Her throat grew tight. She swallowed down tears. She took a deep gulp of coffee, its warm richness filling her with comfort.

"You know the rest," she said.

Dylan jotted a few notes in his book, then looked up. "How did you feel each time you looked at the stone?"

Kate thought back. "I wanted to keep looking at it. I kind of got lost in it, I guess. It was for me and me alone." She focused on the feeling. "Actually, I felt that way every time I touched it, too. And I wanted to touch it whenever my hand was near it. In my pocket or when I was looking at it." And when her uncle had taken it out of its box, after it had changed her. But he'd told her not to say anything to anyone about that.

"Did anything else happen when you touched it or looked at it?"

"Yeah. Twice, when I played with it, I just…lost track of time, I guess. A half hour the first time and hours the second. I had no idea where the time went."

"That's very…interesting." Dylan wrote something in his notebook.

"What?" Kate said. "What's interesting?"

He flipped back a few pages. "Tell me about bringing it into the circle stones. What exactly did it—"

"Hold on." She reached across the table and tapped on his notebook. "This isn't fair. I'm the one giving all the information here. You've obviously figured something out. So tell me what that damn stone was doing to me."

Dylan fiddled with his pen. "I can't be sure yet, but I think it was running through a few spells it had programmed in it. Spells it was casting on you."

The coffee in her hands wasn't enough to keep her warm anymore. "Besides the ones it cast in the Sanctum? Why?"

He hesitated. "I really can't say until I've had a chance to examine it. And that's not bloody likely. But given what happened, I have a few theories. They…aren't quite the same theories your uncle has, I'm afraid."

"Why not?"

"Well, let's start with what we agree upon. The stone was programming you for certain behaviors. It wanted you to bring it into the Sanctum."

"Why would it want that?"

"It may have needed the Sanctum's power to transform you. Before it brought you into the Sanctum, when you stared into it and blanked out, it was, well, pre-programming you. To become a caster."

She felt as if invisible fingers had wormed their way into her spine and were writhing on the delicate fibers inside. "Maybe I don't want to know any more of what you find 'interesting.'"

"Sorry." His eyes softened in sympathy. "I'm afraid I can't agree with my superior on a few other points, however."

"Which ones?"

"Your uncle believes that it was your brother's counterspell itself, interfering with the stone's power, that caused his death. I think there may be another explanation." He paused. "What do you know about primal magic?"

"We used to be able to do it ourselves, and now we can't. We have to use artifacts to cast primal magic spells. Things that were made in the First Era and are illegal to use. Like the stone."

"That's basically correct. But you left out something important."

"What?"

"Every act of primal magic, every one, requires a sacrifice. A life for a spell." Dylan took a long drink from his cup. "I'm not completely certain what your brother was trying to do. He could have been trying to stop the stone from possessing you, as your uncle says."

Kate nodded.

"Or..." Dylan set his cup down. "He could have been trying to stop something else."

"What are you trying to say?"

"I did my own investigation in the Sanctum, after you asked for my help. Your brother's counterspell wasn't as simple as your uncle claims. It's a very specific spell, only used to stop primal magic. If he knew enough about primal magic to know a counterspell of that level, then he also knew the basic principles. A life for a spell."

"So Brian was trying to save himself."

Dylan shrugged. "It's very possible."

"Did he know that the stone was transforming me?" Kate's head slid down into her trembling hands.

"I don't know. From his actions, he looked like he had a plan. Wouldn't you say so?" His eyes darted away from Kate, as if he saw her pain but wanted to allow her what little privacy he could. "The point is this: The spell didn't killed him. It was the stone. It looked for the sacrifice most appropriate for the spell it was casting and found your brother right at hand."

The pain in her chest swelled until it threatened to spill out of her. She'd brought the stone back home, into the Sanctum with Brian. Without her there, it wouldn't have needed to kill him to power the spell that changed her.

But if Dylan was right, Brian knew far more about the stone than he'd told her. And Grayson had flat-out lied to her. But why should she trust Dylan over the uncle who'd been the only person who'd dried her tears when she'd failed her magic test, back on her twelfth birthday?

"Where else don't you agree with Grayson?"

"I have to ask you a question first. Have you had any further…communication from the stone?"

Kate took a breath. She didn't want to talk about this. Not with Dylan, not with anyone. "Why do you want to know?"

"I think the stone could have done something else to you. Changed you even more than is apparent."

Kate looked down at her coffee. "Grayson never suggested that. What makes you so sure?"

"My own experience."

"Tell me. Convince me you know more about this than Grayson

does, and I'll answer your question."

Dylan played with his now-empty coffee cup, saying nothing. The only sound was the espresso machine gurgling in the far corner of the café. A couple walked in from the hallway, then thought better of it and walked back out. *Whatever spell Dylan cast must be mighty powerful.*

"When I was younger," he said, "I got into some…trouble."

"How old were you?"

He stared out the windows at the capital. "Fifteen. I didn't know any better back then. I did whatever my mother wanted. And what she wanted me to do was use my talents. Creating new spells, figuring out what the old ones did. I was a bleeding whiz kid at that. So my mother put me to work digging up old relics, hoping that one of them would give her the power she craved. Finally, I found one."

He swallowed, hard, then blinked furiously behind his glasses.

"I didn't realize this would be personal. You don't have to tell me—"

"Yes, I do. You need to understand how dangerous these artifacts can be." He leaned toward her. "I've seen this kind of thing before. Not the stone, nothing quite so powerful, but artifacts like it. Put them in the hands of people who crave power, and someone else always suffers. At the time, I was too young to know that power always comes with its own price."

"Who was it?"

"My father. The artifact took him in exchange for the power my mother wanted. And eventually, the whole clan suffered in retribution for her illegal actions. There is no more Pearce family. London is a battleground fought over by the Hamiltons and the Makrises."

"Dylan, I'm so sorry." She reached for his hand.

He pulled away, his hands going to his lap. "So what I believe about your artifact comes from firsthand experience. I can tell you this: I think the stone and everything like it should be destroyed. That's my advice to you. Destroy the bloody thing. Before it kills someone else."

Chapter Sixteen

Kate thought over what Dylan had said. She couldn't argue with his logic or his experience. If the stone was as dangerous as he'd implied, then they should destroy it before it did any more damage.

She sighed. "I can hear it. Every time Grayson has taken it out of its box, it talks to me. Wants me to touch it."

Dylan started. "Don't. Whatever you do, don't touch the stone. Not until we understand what that will do. Did you tell your uncle?"

"Yes. But he...he hasn't explained what it's doing."

Dylan stared down at his notebook. He tapped his pen on the paper.

"Do you know what it wants?" she asked.

He hesitated. "That depends. I've been researching an artifact for the past few months, as part of my duties as your dad's primal magic specialist. If the stone is the artifact I think it is, that it appears to be..."

"What?"

"Your uncle believes the stone creates casters from Nulls. I've never heard of an artifact that can do that. But I've heard of another one. So have you."

She leaned forward.

"The Pandora Stone."

"You're kidding." The Pandora Stone was nothing but a legend. She'd heard stories of it ever since childhood, along with tales of Lyndal the Untamed, the Battle of Kolasa Ridge, the Hundred Furies, and all the other First Era legends. But even though the stories all disagreed about what the stone did, they all agreed about one thing: it was lost, never to be found.

"I'm deadly serious. I believe the mage Lyndal created the Pandora Stone in the last days of the First Era to bring magic back if it ever completely disappeared. Real magic. Primal magic."

"But that's not what it did to me—"

"I don't think we know enough to say what it did to you yet."

She focused on his words and tried to recover from her shock. "Why are your theories different from Grayson's?"

He looked down at the table. "I don't know." His gaze flicked to Kate. "Your uncle certainly has the knowledge to have put together the pieces the way I did."

Yes. He does. So why had Grayson told her that Brian had used a different counterspell? Why didn't he tell anyone about the Pandora Stone? Grayson had never led her astray. Sure, he might be playing his own game, but that's what casters did. The pills seemed to be working—the paranoia wasn't affecting him in any major way. So why should she believe this guy she just met, over Grayson?

She got up and slung her purse over her shoulder. "Time to get back. I've ditched my training long enough." She'd have to figure the stone out later. The sun was going down, its rays shining through the big picture window. She hoped she hadn't been missed.

Dylan closed his notebook, got up and took her cup and his to the trashcan. The tiniest flicker of purple caught her eye. Inside her purse, Kris' conch shell key fob glowed with power.

"Dylan—" she said.

The air behind Dylan rippled. An unseen force slammed into him. He flew across the cafe, smashing into the wall with a sickening thud. Sliding to the ground, his head hit the floor and he lay still.

A trickle of blood ran down Dylan's face. His eyes were closed. *Shit, oh shit, is he...* But his chest rose and fell.

He's okay, he's... Damn, where's whoever hit him? She looked around, hair whipping around her. No one in sight. Victor, she needed Victor right now. Why had she been so stupid as to leave without telling him? Oh yeah, because they were in *the Hamilton DC offices*. Where they were *completely safe*.

She pulled out her cell phone. Frantic, she stabbed the emergency button. Nothing. She hit it again. Shit, why wouldn't it work?

A strong hand grabbed her arm. She spun around, dropping her purse. A young man stood silhouetted against the dying sun, striped shirt half tucked into his tight jeans, an insolent grin on his unshaven face.

He slammed her hand against a nearby table. She sucked in her breath, the pain hitting her like a blossom of fire through her hand. The phone skittered a few feet away.

"You won't need that where we're going." He twisted her arm

behind her back into a painful hold, and yanked her close to his chest. She winced. If she moved, she would break something. She squirmed a little anyway.

"Please fight me." He loomed over her. "I like it much better when they fight." She flinched away. He kept up the pressure on her as he reached into his pocket with his free hand and tossed a small envelope toward Dylan.

She tried to think of a spell and cast it. The few she'd learned—fire, shield, stun, all went through her mind. But she couldn't focus enough to bring up the symbol for any of them.

Dylan's eyes remained closed. Then she noticed his fingers—one or two were twitching, in a methodical, familiar way. She needed to buy him some time.

Footsteps sounded from down the hall. Help arriving. All she needed was a minute.

"Who the hell are you?" She craned her head around to look the man straight in his arrogant eyes.

He grinned. "That would be telling you more than you need to know." He ran his hand up her arm, hard enough to leave marks.

She winced. "I'm a Null. I'm not a part of the Game. It's against the Rules for you to—"

"I don't play by the Rules." His head went back, his eyelashes flickered and his body went tight against hers. She felt the familiar jolt of dislocation, and they were gone.

Kate stumbled as they materialized someplace hot, humid, crowded, and noisy, the smell of human waste competing with broiled vegetables and animal sweat for predominance. No sooner had her feet landed on the hard, clay ground than they were gone again, blinking out as quickly as they had blinked in. The sickeningly sweet odor of caramel hit her next, amid the sounds of machinery, as a blast of hot air blew strands of hair across her face. She barely had time to realize they'd landed in some sort of candy factory when she felt her captor cast another spell and they were gone.

She lost count of how many times they flickered in and out of existence. Four times? Six? Her head spun by the time they finally stopped, in a place so hot that the sweat was dripping off her face the moment they materialized in the center of a stark wooden shack.

Her captor threw her down to the bare plank floor. Throwing her hand up, she broke her fall, catching some splinters on her arm from the rough boards. He stalked over to the far side of the room, ripping the tattered curtains from the window to look outside. A thousand different shades of green spilled into view as an overwhelming variety of leaves crowded out the sky. The sound of birds whooping and crying cut through a low hum of insects.

"Not safe, not safe," the young man muttered. "I should be running this op, not him. We should be doing this my way." He paced from the window to a cast iron stove, caked solid with dirt, a frying pan standing solitary on one of its burners.

That many teleports would make anyone mega-twitchy. Wonderful.

Sunlight streamed through a hole in the ceiling, leading to a sink half filled with stagnant rainwater. The hole looked too small for her to climb out, although the large lizard climbing in seemed to like it fine. Then Kate's eyes found the wooden door against the far wall, bolted closed.

Keeping a watch on the guy, she slowly got to her feet, the sweat pouring off her. Dizziness hit her as she stood, and she was barely able to put one leg before the other.

Worst teleport lag ever. Have to ignore it.

She inched toward the door, skirting around a narrow bed, its steel springs visible underneath the stained mattress. He hadn't made a move toward her; his eyes were fixated out to whatever lay beyond this shack.

She ran through her options. A spell? Maybe, but she didn't know a spell powerful enough to take him out in one shot. Better to run. As her heart thudded in her veins, she stumbled to the door. Flicking the bolt back, she threw it open and—

Kate grabbed the doorframe, jerking to a stop. Beyond the door, there was nothing but cool air blowing on her face. Below the door, there was nothing but rain forest. She couldn't see the ground. Her head started to spin, and she pulled her head back before vertigo overtook her. If she fell, she would keep falling for two hundred feet or more, unless a tree branch broke her fall.

And her body.

She wavered on the doorjamb, her momentum threatening to push her over. Digging in her heels, she threw herself backward into the shack. She stood shaking. There were no stairs, no zip line. Nothing leading down. Only the remains of a rope ladder, cut off a few feet from the top. Only one way in or out—the way they'd come.

She was stuck here. With him. Teleporting was one of the many spells she hadn't learned yet.

"Long way down, isn't it?" His voice sounded behind her, right in her ear.

Kate spun to face her captor, braced against the doorjamb. "You'd better let me go. My security will track you down and take you out. I don't care who you are—"

"I'm better than your security." A sneer made his too-handsome face turn ugly as he reached past her to shut the door and lock it. He leaned against the door, confining her with his arms.

His sneer turned to a smirk. "By the time your guards figure out what happened, they won't be able to trace my teleport." A twitch started in his eye.

"What do you want with me? I'm a Null," she said, praying he couldn't see past the spells embedded in her earrings. "I don't have anything you want."

He ran a finger down the side of her face. "But you do. You have something I want very much."

She flinched away from him. "What?"

"A small thing, in exchange for your freedom. Something your father has. If he trades it for you, I'll let you go."

She closed her eyes.

"You know exactly what it is, I can tell. Well, I'm sure your father likes you so much more than a stupid little stone, so all we have to do is wait until he carries out the instructions I left with your friend."

"Dad won't give it to you."

"You'd better hope he does," he said. "And soon. I can think of so many things for us to do until I get what I want." He ran a finger along the lapel of her poet's shirt. She tried to squirm out of his way, but he moved with her, his body pressing up against hers, pinning her to the wooden door. There was nothing on the other side but several hundred feet of air. That was strange, she thought, because she couldn't find air to fill her lungs anywhere.

"Let go of me."

"Why?"

He ripped her shirt open, popping the small pearl buttons off until they dropped one by one onto the wooden floor.

She screamed and hit at his arms, his face, anything she could reach. He took the blows and regarded her with a cold, bored stare. Then he slapped her, hard.

"Are you done now?" He smiled again, that nasty smirk that made her feel like an ant underneath his magnifying glass.

The hit woke her up. She didn't care if she was stuck here. She didn't care if he learned she could cast. She only cared that he get away from her, now.

She remembered the symbol for fire, then, the one that rose up out of her that night she blasted her father. She tried to focus on the symbol, bring it to the forefront of her mind, the way she had done just this morning in the Sanctum.

His hand snaked inside her blouse, and the sick feel of him touching her made her lose all focus. The fire symbol fled her mind, chased away by revulsion. Frantically, she tried to get it back, to focus on this morning's training session when it had been so easy, so clear-cut. But the vision faded, overwhelmed by the garlic smell of this creep's breath on her neck, the pressure of his body against hers. She shook as he undid the top button of her jeans.

No. This is not going to happen. She shuffled through the spells she'd learned. None of them were any more effective or any easier to cast than the fire spell. She tried anyway. But every time she started to focus on one of the symbols, it slipped away. She choked back a sob.

"That's it, baby, that's what I like. Show me how much it hurts." He shoved his hand down her jeans, his mouth nuzzling her neck.

No, no, no. Her legs shook. She hit his back, her fists bouncing off his muscle. There had to be a way to stop him.

Then she remembered what she had done back at the catalpa grove.

It didn't require a symbol. It didn't require a build-up of energy. Just the opposite. She gasped in a breath. Closed her eyes. Rushed down the stairway in her mind. Threw open the door that led to the vast sea of blackness.

It roiled before her, limitless and welcoming. She touched the dark power that lay beneath its surface. The fear that rippled through her when she sank her mind into its depths was nothing compared to the despair this jerk's hands on her inspired.

Burn, she willed.

And he did.

Her eyes flew open. He screamed, staring down at his flaming arms. Backing away from her, he stumbled around the shack, almost tripping over a large lizard lying dead on the floor, until he came to the sink. He plunged his arms into the basin, steam rising from the stagnant water as the flames went out. His screaming turned into a wail.

Shaking, she pulled her shirt closed. There were no buttons, she realized, they were all over the floor. She let the shirt fall open over her lace bra.

The flames hadn't touched her. She took a few steps forward into the center of the room, then glanced at her captor. He looked different now after the shock of her attack ripped away his illusion spell—his brown hair hung longer, his figure almost wiry as he slumped over the sink. There was something familiar about his sharp face, his hazel eyes.

Before Brian's funeral, when Grayson had gone over the profiles of the most prominent casters, this creep's face had been in the photos she'd reviewed. Dmitri Makris. The Makris family's most brutal operative.

Stomach heaving, she looked back to the door. *No exit. Shit.*

She blinked, engaging her magesight. Purple strands of light swirled on the floor, the remains of his teleportation spell from when they had arrived—she took a breath—how long ago? It seemed like hours. The remnants of the spell still endured. Maybe she could she activate it somehow, get back out the same way they came in. She had no idea. All she could do was try.

Dmitri was still dunking his hands in the basin of water. He muttered to himself. Casting a healing spell? She was running out of time. Closing her eyes, she tried to will herself away.

Home, she thought as hard as she could. Nothing happened. She needed to touch the power—that was it. She did the ritual again, descending into the dark basement of her soul, and tapped the ocean of raw energy that lived inside her. This time it felt like something might be moving, flowing from her and connecting with a larger *something* outside of her.

Home, she willed. She saw the remnants of the spell grow

brighter, flicker with new life.

Then pain exploded in her head like a thousand white-hot needles boring straight through her skin and into her skull. She fell to the ground. Dmitri stood over her, a trail of magic from his reddened hands. Screaming, she lost the fragile connection with the old teleport spell as her magesight shut down, her eyes unable to focus on anything. Above her, she dimly heard Dmitri moving, his booted feet loud on the wooden boards as he loomed over her.

"Bitch, you bitch, what did you do?"

Her rib cage cracked as his boot struck her in the side once, then twice. Pain flared up, competing with the ache in her head. She curled up, wrapping her arms around her sides, her stomach. God, she just wanted this to end.

His face contorted with a twisted grin. He raised a hand. *Oh God, what was he going to do?*

Kate tried to focus on a spell, but the pain made it hopeless. Her body tightened as she waited for Dmitri's spell to finish.

Air rushed past her, and Dmitri flew upwards, shirt flapping free. He crashed into a small table by the stove. It broke with a loud bang. The agony in her head lightened as soon as Dmitri's body hit the floor.

"Kate! Are you all right?"

Her head still sore and her ribs tender, she tried to prop herself up and turn around, to see who had saved her. Gentle hands reached down to help her.

Dylan. Blood still dripped from his head, but he looked to be in better shape than Kate. A faint blue glow surrounded him—a shield spell.

Damn. She hadn't even thought... She probably could have put a shield spell up.

"Thanks." Kate's heart finally slowed to something close to normal. "I didn't think I..."

"No time." Dylan's head snapped over to look at Dmitri, lying in the wreckage of the table. Dmitri groaned and got up, shaking his head. "We need to leave. Now."

She winced as Dylan helped her to her feet. He gave her a quick glance, reaching into his jacket and touching a bird's wing talisman—one for teleportation, she assumed. She glanced down at her blouse then, face red, and held it closed with one hand.

Dmitri pulled a talisman out of his jeans pocket. A silver horse. He rubbed a finger over it, his eyes lidded.

Dylan's eyes twitched behind his glasses, then opened. "Bloody hell, he's got a block set up." He stepped in front of Kate. "We can't teleport out."

Dmitri got to his feet. "Next time I hit you, Pearce, you better stay down." He threw out his hand, muttering a spell. A greenish mist spun out from his fingers to permeate the whole room.

Within seconds, the tree house began to shake. The stove rattled on its stumpy legs. Kate backed up. Then, as the bed behind them swayed, realized she had no place to go. A piece of broken table flew from the floor and hit Dylan. A flash of blue light shone for a moment where it struck him, then disappeared. The blue glow around him dimmed.

The trembling continued. The bed flew toward them, straight at Kate. Dylan grabbed her, pulling her out of its path. It smashed into the wall, bouncing off it and rebounding onto the floor. Pieces of wood shot toward them, first one, then another, then many of them all at once. Dylan kept Kate behind him, taking the hits on his shield. Its glow diminished a bit more.

"Can you cast a shield spell?" he asked.

"Um, maybe?" She tried to focus on the symbol for the spell. *It's so much harder when someone's throwing furniture at you.* The pain in her head and side didn't make it any easier, either.

The table reared up, sliding slowly toward them. The shaking and rattling got worse, the noise drowning out everything else. Dmitri was bent over in concentration, either maintaining the spell or preparing an even worse one.

"How long can you keep shielding us?" she yelled in Dylan's ear.

"Not much longer. Is there another way out of here?"

"The door, but it's a sheer drop." She pointed at it. "We're hundreds of feet up. No way out except teleporting. Can you break the block?"

"It'll take too long. We need another plan."

His gaze focused on Dmitri's silver talisman, his eyes squinting in concentration. Then his eyes slid over to the door. A grin lit his face—the first she'd seen. "*Brilliant.* I've got just the trick."

The sink broke away from the wall with a *bang* and hit Dylan's shield, smashing into a thousand splinters of wet wood. Kate screamed, more in surprise than in terror, as his shield kept her safe. Dylan staggered back a step, the light of his shield wavering a pale blue.

The stove tore itself loose from the side of the shack with a groaning sound. It slid toward them, picking up speed as it went.

Dylan grabbed her arm and ran toward the wall, Kate following.

He stopped short of the wooden door. The stove tracked them like a bloodhound. It accelerated, screeching across the floorboards as it hurled toward them. Across the room, Dmitri's laughter rang out.

Dylan stood in front of the door, as if daring the stove to hit him. It took the dare, heading straight for them. He pushed Kate further from him, then danced out of the way as the stove shot past him and hit the wooden door.

The door exploded in a shattering of wood. The stove hurdled over and over, down the long drop through the trees and into the jungle below.

Dylan turned to Kate, grabbing her arm. "Trust me?"

She nodded.

"Good. Jump. *Now*."

Oh God. This was insane. But so was staying here. Who knew what else this madman would throw at them? She looked at Dylan. His eyes were shining—with confidence or craziness, she didn't know which.

Betting on confidence, she made sure she had a good grip on his arm.

They jumped.

Chapter Seventeen

Kristof watched from his London rooftop perch as Grayson Hamilton, blending in with the late-night crowd in a leather jacket and gray slacks, walked from Duncannon Street into Trafalgar Square. Everything was going according to plan. Hamilton had brought the black laptop bag Kristof had specified, and he'd arrived precisely on time: 23:30 GMT. Kristof's preparations were in place. Everything, that was, except for one little thing. He had no hostage to exchange for the stone.

He'd called Dmitri three times since he'd missed his scheduled check-in—no response. His call to his father had been answered with a curt reminder to tend to his own end of the operation. Kristof had no time to check on Dmitri personally. Either he'd be back in touch or he wouldn't. Dmitri's problem could be Victor or... Kristof straightened, pulling his binoculars away from his face long enough to blink the sweat away from his eyes. Dmitri could have gone off mission. In that way he so often did.

He had no choice but to deal with Dmitri later. Time to start his end of the operation. His instructions to the Hamiltons, delivered via an envelope Dmitri had left where he'd taken Kate, had been simple: Have Grayson bring the stone to neutral territory, Trafalgar Square, London. Come alone. Take a seat on the third bench in front of the eastern fountain, facing the National Gallery, and wait for his call. Any attempt to use a spell and Kate would die.

The Hamiltons knew better than to play any games.

This entire mission went against the Rules. Kidnapping a Null. Trading her for a proscribed magical artifact. But then, the Hamiltons weren't exactly squeaky-clean themselves. They were the ones who'd dug up the artifact to begin with.

So far, the Hamiltons had kept to the terms Kristof had set—at least, as much as he'd expected. Scanning the crowd, he spotted three of Hamilton's operatives through their illusion spells—he assumed there were more, with better disguises. For the London part of the operation, the Makris team of casters consisted of him. Only him. With his father watching his every move via the silver owl talisman pinned to his T-shirt.

Grayson Hamilton sat on the bench, as instructed. Kristof pulled out his burner phone and dialed.

"Yes?" Hamilton said.

"Open the bag. Hold it up."

Hamilton obeyed. Kristof focused in on the bag. They'd brought the genuine item all right—that smooth disk nestled in a cocoon of blue silk couldn't be mistaken for anything else. It glowed in his magesight like a solar eclipse.

"Leave the bag. Get up and walk—"

"No. I need proof of life first." Hamilton zipped the laptop bag shut.

Shit. Dmitri had better have a good explanation for being incommunicado. Still, Kristof could improvise.

"Look up," he said. "She's at the entrance to the Gallery. You'll get her back when we get the stone."

Hamilton's head snapped toward the Gallery's wide columns.

Kristof gave Hamilton an instant to see the image of Kate, her eyes wide, body shaking, her arm held by a hulking, suit-jacketed figure, then backed the two forms into the doorway, removing them from direct view. He didn't want to push his luck.

He had designed a complex illusion, crafting a false image and throwing impressions of Kate into the recipe. He'd brought to mind the way she looked when he walked her home from a late-night study session a few weeks ago, wearing a short cotton shirt and her favorite jeans, and mixed with it the fear that seized her one night when they escaped getting hit by a drunk driver crossing Dryden Avenue. He'd added to the image one of his father's less memorable goons, cloaked the spell, and had thrown the illusion at the entrance of the National Gallery, just within Grayson's range of vision.

Maybe it's enough to fool the old man's sharp magesight.

"Now do what I tell you. Set the bag down. Get up." He waited until Grayson complied. "Turn around, toward Nelson's statue, and go down to the Strand. Keep walking until I tell you otherwise."

As Grayson obeyed, Kristof set his people in motion. Kristof's father might not have given him any casters for the mission other than Dmitri, but he hadn't told him he couldn't use Normals. His pawns did what Kristof paid them to do.

Thirty men dressed in jeans and orange T-shirts identical to Kristof's, with laptop bags exactly like Grayson's, flooded the square. The first guy to reach Grayson's bench, a second or two after the man had left, picked up the bag and dropped his own. Silver flashed in the operative's hand as it closed around the strap of Grayson's bag.

Kristof hoped he was the only one who'd seen it. Before the guy strode more than a few steps, he swapped Grayson's bag with an identically dressed friend. All around them, duplicates were exchanging bags. Kristof designed the trade-off to look like one big marketing ploy, which was exactly what the many bystanders, stopping at the spectacle, assumed as they pointed and stared at the men's T-shirts, boldly printed with the logo of a laptop computer company.

A Hamilton operative struggled to get through the crowd while another ran up the steps to the Gallery, toward the door where the illusion of Kate had been. Grayson Hamilton still walked toward the Strand, cell phone in hand.

So far, so good.

After a quick twist of his ring, Kristof's features changed—olive skin turning deep brown, eyes darkening, wavy hair morphing into dreads. Then he picked a spot right on the edge of the crowd, across from St. Martin-in-the-Fields, and used his teleportation talisman, concealed in his pocket with two other talismans. At least his father had given him a few tools for this mission. It would keep the backlash down to a dull roar.

He popped into the fringe of the growing mob. No one seemed confused by the presence of one more guy in an orange T-shirt. He traded his laptop bag with the nearest duplicate and worked his way toward the center of the exchange.

Kristof concentrated on Kate, attuning his magical senses to the rose scent of her perfume, the way the summer sun turned her hair into a blazing corona around her face, how her eyes wrinkled in the corners when she laughed. The feel of her led him to Grayson's bag, held by one of his men several feet ahead of him in the crowd.

He almost chuckled at the irony of the charm he'd worked up. Wind a strand of Kate's hair—acquired from her pillow in her college apartment—around a simple silver-and-amber charm that even a combat mage like him could make, and bind a locator spell into it. Have his hired hand attach it to Grayson's briefcase when he made the first swap and *bam*! Instant locator charm.

He worked his way through the crowd, positioning himself ahead of the bag's path. Kristof grabbed the bag with his free hand as another duplicate walked by, handing off his own in turn. His fingers touched the silver charm, and he felt a brief brush of Kate's presence in his mind. He picked up his pace, hurrying out of the square to get far away from Hamilton's people before teleporting out. A quick look at his phone showed no texts.

Still silence from Dmitri. Had Victor caught up to him, or was Dmitri distracted by Kate?

If he's hurt her, I'll—

"The deal was Kate for the stone, young man." Grayson Hamilton stood on the sidewalk by one of London's ubiquitous Starbucks, blocking his way. "Illusions can't fool me. Where is she?"

Kristof covered his surprise with a smirk. "You'll get her back. Now get out of my way, if you want to see her again."

Grayson didn't budge. "How do I know she's all right? You've already broken the rules by kidnapping a Null. Why should I trust a Makris?"

So much for plausible deniability. "Your magesight's pretty good, old man, to see through my illusion."

"Kristof, I've been playing the Game a lot longer than you. Give me some credit, would you? Now hand the stone over and give me Kate."

Kristof glanced at the reflections in the coffee shop window, bright from the nighttime streetlights: Hamilton's operatives were on the street behind him, weaving in and out of the crowd of Normals. He noted their positions, calculated what it would take to disable them, and readied the spells in his mind, one by one.

"The only way you'll get Kate is if you back off and let me go. If I don't arrive at my destination safely, with the stone, you know what will happen to her." The street emptied of Normals behind him, leaving only Hamilton's operatives. The result of a subtle spell undoubtedly cast by one of Hamilton's people.

Another of my instructions ignored. It doesn't matter now.

"How do I know I'll get her back unharmed if I let you go?"

"Because that's the way it works. On my word. The way it's worked between the families for generations. My mother had to trust you in Moscow in ninety-eight. I'm told you eventually gave her back her diamond talisman."

Grayson's eyes flared. "Ha! All right, go then. But you had better be damn sure you keep your word." His eyes flicked beyond Kristof, and he gave a quick, dismissive nod to the operatives.

Kristof didn't hesitate. A swift glance to make sure Grayson's men had backed off, then he hurried down the narrow confines of John Adam Street, putting a block's worth of narrow townhouses and trendy restaurants between him and Kate's uncle.

His hand went to the owl talisman pinned to his T-shirt. His father had seen the entire exchange. *Good.* His father's knowledge of Grayson Hamilton's interception should prime him for the story Kristof would need to sell him later.

He was close now. There, on the next block, where the shadows of empty garages melted into a quiet alley bereft of traffic. He ducked down the alley and skirted a pair of overflowing trash cans outside the back entrance to a pub. As soon as the mission was over, he'd have to find out what happened to Kate. Grayson would never have let Kristof walk away if Victor had gotten Kate back. Something else must have gone wrong.

I shouldn't have let Dmitri anywhere near her. Kate has to be okay. If not—

He tried to put thoughts of her from his mind. The next part of his mission—securing the stone for himself—had to be completed before he could deal with Kate.

A few more steps. The back door of the dry cleaner—the location they'd agreed upon. He braced himself. *I really needed to come up with a better way to do this—*

A blue sizzle shot straight for him, a lightning bolt striking him square on. A burn formed across his chest, the agony shooting through him. Sparks flared as his father's talisman overloaded. He dropped to the ground, groaning. The laptop bag stayed in his clenched fist.

He pulled himself up. That hurt a bit more than necessary.

Struggling to his knees, his eyes scanned the deserted alley.

A slim figure, face hooded by a windbreaker, ran to him and reached down to grab the laptop case. Kristof knew the plan. With the talisman shorted out, his father would not be able to see who had taken the stone. Arrange an "ambush," blame it on the Hamiltons, and use the stone himself when his father's guard was down. A good plan, notwithstanding the lightning bolt.

But as his partner's hand closed on his to take the stone and reached up to touch a talisman whose spell would render him unconscious for hours, he realized his scheme's fatal flaw.

Dmitri has Kate. God knows what he's doing to her. I'm the only one who knows where they are, the only one who can save her.

I'll deal with the stone, and my father, later.

He touched the teleport talisman in his pocket, visualizing the tree house in Costa Rica he and Dmitri had secured for the mission. Bastard better not have moved her.

The last thing he saw as he vanished in a shimmer of light, the laptop case containing the stone in his hand, was Melina's face underneath the windbreaker, raw with the rage of betrayal.

Kate fell fast, and only the feel of Dylan's arm tight around hers kept her from utter panic. Something struck her too fast for her to see, and a sharp pain shot up her shoulder. The wind rippled across the bare skin of her torso as trees sped by so quick she hardly registered them. Her shirt whipped around her head and shoulders, leaving only her white lace bra to contain her pounding heart.

Oh my God, I'm going to die. Painfully, horribly, smashed to pieces on the ground below.

How could she have been so stupid? A word or two came to her across the wind—Dylan's voice, chanting. The ground was rushing at her. Fast, brown, and looking very, very hard. Then everything disappeared.

Chapter Eighteen

Kristof materialized in the center of the shack where Dmitri was supposed to be holding Kate, deep in the Montverde rain forest of Costa Rica. It was deserted, but the place looked trashed—remains of furniture strewed everywhere, the door leading to the rain forest beyond completely destroyed.

He slumped against the ramshackle wall, applying a quick healing spell to the burns on his chest. His skin was its usual olive again; his disguise spell had been blown away by the impact of the lightning bolt. Not much point in spending the energy to bring it back.

His father's monitor talisman hung from his T-shirt, cracked to pieces, the spell it held inoperative. Good.

A luminescent glint caught his eye. He bent down and picked up a pearl button, then another, then the rest. They were from Kate's favorite shirt, the one with the lace collar. Blood roared in his ears, his fist clenching Kate's button tight in his grip.

Whoever had caused all this destruction was gone. With Kate

missing, it would take too long to do a forensic spell and piece together what had happened. A teleport trace would find her faster.
Casting the spell, he saw just enough magical residue to tell him that
someone had teleported out a few minutes ago. He snapped his
shield up, touched his teleportation talisman, and vanished.

Kate popped back into existence amid a thunderous rush of falling
water. Still in free fall, her descent paced the waterfall's flow, and
her stomach outpaced the rest of her. In an instant, her clothes were
drenched by the spray that surrounded her. Dylan, his form faint in
the mist, fell beside her, his arm holding hers. Through the water
drops, the pale-blue glow of a shield spell enveloped them both.

Dylan yelled over the sound of pounding water, "Feet first, arms
up straight behind you! Swim up—"

She barely got a breath in before they hit.

The force of the impact wrenched her away from Dylan. She
plunged straight down, deep into a churning, watery abyss. A flash
of cold shocked her system, still sweating from the tropical heat,
then the blue glow around her flickered and the cold moderated into
a pleasant coolness. As the roiling water pulled her down further she
reached an arm out, searching for Dylan.

She found only water.

The pressure in her lungs began to build. She could see nothing
but darkness, hear nothing but an oppressive silence. She spun,
searching. Still nothing.

Wait, above her… *Bubbles.*

She followed the wash of the bubbles, using the strong kicks she'd learned in swim class. She swam, stroke after stroke, her arms cutting through the water. It felt like it had been hours and still she hadn't reached the surface. Air escaped her lungs, bleeding out through her lips as carbon dioxide built up in her system.

I'm not going to make it. Oh God, I'm going to die down here, in this cold, watery blackness.

Then she burst through the surface, into the air, gulping fresh oxygen into her starved body. She bobbed at the top of a river, the roar of the falls behind her thundering in her aching head. The moon's light, shining across the ripples of the water, gleamed bright enough for her to see that the waves nearby held no trace of Dylan.

The blue glow had faded from her skin. She shook with the cold. She had to find him and get out of the water before they both froze.

Move. Have to move. It will keep me warm.

She struck out across the river. A bobbing form downstream caught her eye.

Dylan.

Let him be alive.

She swam over to him. His glasses were gone, lost somewhere, and he lay facedown in the water. Her heart thumped. She lifted him onto her shoulder, ignoring the twinge of pain, and scanned the river, looking for the shore, the current helping her along until she got her bearings.

Swimming kept her warm for the few minutes she needed to reach the embankment. She hauled him, arms first, as far as she could up onto the sand and rocks, her injured ribs protesting the effort.

Oh God. How do I do first aid for drowning? I should have paid attention during that required CPR class, instead of flirting with the cute blond guy behind me. Dammit. Mouth-to-mouth, that's it.

She tilted Dylan's head to the side to drain the water out, moved it back, sealed his lips to hers, and blew as hard as she could. She did it again and again, her mind racing ahead to what she would do if it didn't work. *Try chest compressions?*

Dylan coughed, his arms flailing. He sat up, brown hair plastered to his head, and spewed out a rush of water.

What should she do? Let him cough until he calmed down? She knelt beside him, laying a hand on his shoulder.

"Get away from me. What the bloody hell did you do?" He scrambled away, gaining the dubious shelter of a brush-covered boulder.

She backed away. "Okay, okay. It's just the twitchies. Chill out."

His breathing slowed as she retreated, and the wild look in his eye seemed to calm. She sat on the cold, muddy ground, her head in her hands.

The scent of something sweet, like honeysuckle or jasmine, wafted across the night air, along with a faint smell of a wood fire and the odor of diesel fuel. Brush swept up from the embankment and met a wide plain extending into the blackness beyond. A sand beetle toiled along in front of her. She didn't care where they were. Not really. As long as it was somewhere far away from Dmitri Makris.

The cold seeped into her. Her body shook, rattling her teeth. Pulling her knees up to her chin, she hugged them, trying to stay warm. But that hurt her ribs too much, so she curled up on her side, lying on the embankment. Her throbbing head joined the symphony of pain alongside the stabbing hurt in her ribs and the ache in her right arm. Then nausea rose up in her, so strong she couldn't hold it down. She barely got up before she heaved, over and over. Nothing came out but a thin thread of bile.

After a few more heaves, she thought she might be done. She wiped her mouth and tried to move. She looked up and saw Dylan kneeling next to her, his eyes sane again, and kind. Oh, God, he didn't see all that, did he?

"Casters react like soldiers do after combat," Dylan said. "The heaves, the shakes. It's normal. Take things slow and easy. You'll feel better if you can relax."

She tried to breathe the way Grayson had taught her. In and out, from her stomach. The nausea eased. Her pulse calmed. She realized that her shirt was still open, her bra visible. Blushing, she pulled the edges of her blouse together.

Dylan took off his jacket and handed it to her.

"It's wet, but at least it will—"

"Thanks." The jacket hung too large on her small frame, the wet fabric uncomfortable. She buttoned two of the wooden buttons. The row of silver talismans felt cold against her skin.

"Feel better? Any trouble with the paranoia?" His lip twitched. "Like me? Sorry about that."

"No problem. I handled the backlash."

She lied. Her spell back at the tree house hadn't caused any paranoia—none at all.

"I've got to get you back. Your father will be worried about you." He reached up to push his glasses back then paused, as if puzzled to find them gone.

"That's the understatement of the year. He's freaking out right now. He better not have given the stone away."

She stumbled to her feet, crushing several sand beetles beneath her. "Where are we, anyway?"

Dylan turned and pointed at the falls, its white spray barely visible through the darkness. "The Zambezi River, the Zimbabwe side, I think. That's Victoria Falls behind us, through the gorge. I came here once, looking for...something. It doesn't matter what. What does is that the best way to break a fall is in moving water. Victoria's the biggest waterfall I knew how to teleport to, once we fell far enough to be free of the teleport block."

"Well, I guess it worked." She started to shake again. "Can you get us home from here?"

"Sure, I—"

Across the plain, a flash of light glinted in the darkness. "Down!" She shoved Dylan as she dropped to the ground, her chest and arm both seizing in a spasm of pain as she hit.

A high-pitched whine sounded overhead as a lightning bolt sizzled and cracked above them, right where Dylan had been standing.

It took Kristof a moment to orient himself to his new location when the teleport trace landed him on a grassy plain by a wide river next to the largest waterfall he'd ever seen. He gave his senses time to adjust to the new location, trusting to his cloak and shield spells for protection, and after a moment he could ignore the rumble of the falls. Amid the high-pitched screech of insects and the small movements of animals in the bush, the zap of a lightning spell sizzled.

Kristof's head snapped to its source. *Dmitri.* Up the embankment and on the wide plain, striding toward the river. He hadn't even bothered to cloak himself. *Idiot.*

The lightning bolt barely missed Kate and a disheveled young man lying on the riverbank. He looked closer at the man. Dylan Pearce—Hamilton's primal magic specialist. Kate had a man's brown jacket wrapped around her—Dylan's?

Kristof needed to be careful. Although his monitor talisman had been destroyed, his father could still see through Dmitri's. He needed to make sure Kate got away from Dmitri and back to her family safe and sound, without his father knowing he had been here. And he had to find a way to keep the stone out of his father's hands.

Kate grabbed Dylan's arm and whispered something. Dylan's fingers twitched, the start of a spell. He stopped, and Kristof could barely hear him say, "We're blocked."

Dmitri didn't want them to teleport out again. Well, if Dylan could keep Dmitri busy for a few minutes, Kristof could take care of the teleport block.

He concentrated, searching with his magesight for the block. There, in Dmitri's hand, the silver horse talisman, sending its purple bands of power across the plain. Kristof didn't have a talisman to break the block. He'd have to do it the hard way and pay the price. He chanted, a quiet string of guttural words, and waited as the amber streams of magic wove their way through the bands of energy around the embankment and began to dissolve them.

Every shadow behind every tree took on a deeper meaning. *Who else is here? Did my father send someone else to help Dmitri? Anton maybe? Did I just expose my position?*

No. Calm down.

Dmitri flicked his hand toward Dylan, and three kinetic-energy blades cut through the air. Dylan grabbed Kate, fumbling in his jacket for a talisman. Probably trying to get a shield up before the blades hit.

He failed. Dmitri's ephemeral knives sliced into his chest, his blood spurting on the wet riverbank as Dylan toppled forward.

Only a few strands of magic remained in Dmitri's teleport block. Good. In a moment he could sweep up Kate and leave.

A gleam caught Kristof's eye, in the bushes beyond Kate. Shit. Someone else teleported in, someone cloaked like him.

The air rippled in front of Kristof. A force like a wrecking ball slammed into him and hurled him back onto the riverbank, laptop bag twisted around his chest. His shield took the brunt of the kinetic punch, flickering to a pale blue and winking out. His cloak spell dissolved in a shimmer as it was ripped away by the rampaging energy of the spell.

Damn, damn. How did anyone know I was here?

Kristof rolled down the bank, avoiding the lightning bolt that followed and hit precisely where he'd fallen. He searched with his magesight.

There. A slight glimmer in the darkness, behind Kate. He touched his last talisman, a silver lightning bolt, once, then again. The last charge in his talismans. Everything would have a cost from here on out.

The bolts hit where he'd aimed, tearing away his assailant's cloak spell and sending him stumbling back a few paces even through his glowing shield spell.

Kristof stared at the sandy-haired Hamilton security caster, whose clenched jaw showed grim determination. Well, no real surprise. He'd been wondering when Victor Cole would show up.

Kate cradled Dylan's head in her arms. *Oh God.* There was blood everywhere. But he was breathing. She had no idea how to do a healing spell—one of these talismans inside Dylan's jacket would probably do it, but which one? And even if she figured it out, casting from a talisman hadn't been covered in Grayson's last assignment.

Victor could help Dylan. Victor could get them out of here. But Victor was busy with the other caster who'd shown up, just a few seconds ago: Kristof Makris. In jeans and a T-shirt, a laptop bag slung across his chest, he traded spells with Victor faster than she could follow.

A few yards beyond them, Dmitri Makris glowered at her and raised his hand to cast a spell. There was no chance for her to cast a regular spell, even if she could remember the symbols and focus. Only one other option—cast the *other* way.

She descended to meet the dark ocean that lived in the center of her being. Stun, she willed at Dmitri with all her might. Nothing filled her mind except her intention, pure as a flame burning brightly in the sea of blackness. Diving down into the expanse of power within her, she touched its viscous energy and cast it forth.

She didn't see any symbols, any visible effects of a spell at all. One moment, Dmitri chanted, his arm outstretched, the next, he dropped to the ground like a marionette whose strings had been cut.

The mud around her went still and lifeless. All the beetles rolled over on their backs, mandibles open, their bodies curling up into small, dried corpses.

Kate stumbled to her feet, staring at the death-strewn sand.

The buzz of a lightning bolt snapped her attention back to Victor and Kristof. Kristof's spell had ripped away the last of Victor's shield, knocking him back a few steps. Kristof circled closer to her, keeping her between him and Victor. Kristof's own shield, renewed sometime during the battle, glowed with a mere wisp of sky blue.

Victor recovered and took a step toward her, his attention on Kristof. They were eyeing each other like two dogs about to fight over a bone. Kate got the uncomfortable impression that she was the bone.

Three Hamilton casters teleported in behind Victor—Missy, Gordon, and the guy who had hosted Brian's wake. Victor jerked his head toward Kristof, then spun a spell in the air, fingers flashing. They all moved to surround Kristof, the grim looks that twitched on their faces telling Kate everything she needed to know about the danger this guy posed.

Kristof didn't look scared or pressured. His eyes coolly assessed the situation, as if he was adding up the odds and calculating how to place his bet.

Then he moved.

"Kate, get out of the—" Victor said as Kristof darted over to her. He grabbed her, pulling her tight against him. His shield snapped up around them.

Her rib cage spasmed in pain. She pulled against his grip, trying to break free, but his strong arms held her so tight she could barely move.

No. He wasn't going to use her against Victor. She bit down hard on his bare arm, her teeth breaking his skin.

He flinched but never took his attention off Victor. But the scent of his skin, so clean, like the ocean air, brought the memories of dozens of intimate moments rushing back.

Kris. He smells just like Kris.

Kristof held Kate close against him. She flailed her elbow at him, and it connected against his ribs. He winced.

"Dammit, Kate, stop," he whispered. "I'm not going to hurt you. And neither are they."

She didn't answer, but she didn't stop struggling, either. He didn't have time for this. Not when the Hamilton team multiplied every second he delayed. Another glimmer shining in the bushes, against the dark sky, then another.

He blinked. Took one breath, then two.

No, no. There are enough Hamilton casters here as it is. Don't let the backlash make it seem worse. He ignored the phantoms his mind had created.

He had to break the teleport block Victor's team had put up on their arrival, and he had to do it now. A quick spell, the same one he'd used with Dmitri, and an amber glow appeared around his hand, shooting out to find the block and wear it down, strand by strand.

The fear came roaring back into his mind. A dozen new glimmers appeared around him. Hamilton casters, reinforcements.

His pulse raced. His muscles tensed. His eyes flicked from the

Hamilton casters, circling him, to Pearce, still and bleeding on the ground, to Dmitri, lying in a heap on the hill. The glimmers might have been artifacts of his paranoia. But maybe not.

Kate still struggled in his arms, trying to get free. He had to get her someplace safe. Someplace with security strong enough, with people who were loyal to him. Nothing else mattered.

Only one place he could go.

Kristof Makris couldn't be Kris Stevens. That was impossible.

Then Kate remembered the conch-shell key fob Kris had given her, glowing a bright purple in her purse right before she and Dylan were attacked. How Dmitri Makris managed to get through the security grid, how she couldn't call Victor on her phone.

Looking like someone else was child's play for a caster. A caster who could use his disguise to get close to her. Get her to confide in him about her family. Make her fall in love with him.

The last trusting place inside her started to fracture.

"Shouldn't have been so cautious," Kristof said to Victor as the amber glow around his hand spun off into the night. "Gave me a chance to get set up."

"Shit," Victor said. "Teleport block's down."

To Victor's left, a gleam of light shone from a talisman on Dmitri Makris's chest. He shimmered and disappeared. Victor cursed.

Gordon stretched his hands toward Kristof, prepping a kinetic punch. Victor yelled, "*Stop*. You'll hit Kate."

"Forget about me," she shouted at them. "Get *him*." She concentrated on a fire spell, tried to focus on its symbol. But while glowing flames flooded her mind, the symbol itself faded. Hell with it. She could do the other magic again—will the spell to life. She tried to concentrate, visualize the Old Bear, the long staircase. The images evaporated in the heat of her anger.

Screw it. She jabbed the heel of her shoe into Kris, Kristof, whatever his name was. He shuddered, but his fingers flicked out a new spell, weaving the complex symbol faster that she would have thought possible.

The Hamilton casters looked to Victor for orders, but Victor didn't move or speak. His eyes shifted from Kris to her, and something strange and unfamiliar flickered across those sharp features for a brief moment. *Fear.*

Then Victor's hand shot out, a spell forming around it. Which promptly died as Missy, a smirk flashing across her face for the briefest instant, jostled Victor's arm, disrupting his spell.

Kristof teleported them both out before Kate could do more than draw in a disbelieving breath.

Chapter Nineteen

Kate felt a cool breeze against her skin, a hint of moist sea air mixed with the scent of apple blossoms. The pain in her head had become even worse, crushing and throbbing as if her skull had shrunk two sizes too small.

Kristof still held onto her. His arms were wrapped around her, her back rubbing against his chest, her curves pressing oh-so-tight against him. *No.*

"Let go of me, you asshole." She jerked away.

He didn't try to stop her. She stumbled forward a few steps, catching herself before she fell. Rocks jutted beneath her feet, wet and slippery under her sandals. Seabirds cried as they dove for fish in the clear, blue ocean a few yards away.

She had no idea where Kristof had brought her.

Groves of fruit trees bloomed up a steep hill, and through their branches an imposing white estate house kept watch. Over the water, islands sparkled in the turquoise sea.

Kristof gazed at her with those deep-blue eyes of his, eyes so like and yet so unlike Kris's. It seemed he was fixing her face in his memory, like he didn't expect to see her again.

She took in his tanned skin, his wavy brown hair, his hard, closed face. The resemblance between Kristof Makris and Kris Stevens was superficial. Then she thought about how her memories of Kris came raging back when she'd breathed in the scent of his skin, how her heart sped up every time Kristof touched her.

Kris Stevens and Kristof Makris were definitely the same guy.

She studied him again. The corner of one eye twitched, an irregular, asynchronous beat. His mouth was tight. One hand struck his thigh repeatedly. She knew the signs. How many spells had he cast?

She took a step back, waiting a moment until the intensity in his eyes eased and his stance relaxed.

"Why? Why pretend to be Kris Stevens?" she asked. "I'm not important. I'm not...anyone."

His head jerked up. "You know—"

"Give me some credit." Did he think she was too dumb to figure out that he and Kris Stevens were the same person after he stood so close to her that she could feel his heart beat? Oh God. She *had* been an idiot. Her face burned. Too clueless to figure out she'd been played by a Makris spy. A spy who should never had targeted *her*.

"Why break the Rules?" she said. *Why break my heart?*

"Did you think your father's enemies wouldn't try to get to him through you? Are you really that naive?"

"I'm a *Null*. I'm supposed to be off-limits."

"You think that's going to protect you? From us?"

Oh God. What had she told him? About her father, about Grayson, Victor, Hayley, Brian...the stone? He'd seen her with it, how it had possessed her. He probably figured out that it had killed Brian. She had told him so much, more than she ever should have, about her training, about how her status had changed. She kicked the stones under her feet. Had he figured out she was a caster?

She had played right into his hands. Confiding in him, taking his damn conch-shell love token, giving him and his bastard cousin the opportunity to kidnap her and trade her for the stone, as if she were a piece of property. Was that what was in his laptop bag? Did he handle the trade-off while Dmitri...

"So whose plan was it to kidnap me? Yours?"

"I was in charge of the mission." His eye twitched.

"You let your cousin..." She jerked Dylan's jacket closed around her.

"No." Kristof's eyes travelled from her torn blouse to her face. His voice softened. "I told him not to touch you. He'll pay. I promise."

"Do you care about me at all? Did you ever? Or is this a game to you, a job? Sleep with Hamilton's daughter, spy on her for Papa, get a prize?"

"Kate," he said. "Kate..." His hand touched her cheek. He let it fall and stepped away from her. His voice went harsh. The operative was back. "I'm Kristof Makris. Not Kris Stevens. I did my job, a job I'm good at. Getting inside my enemies heads, finding out how they tick. You were just a mission." He smiled at her, a self-satisfied smile so unlike Kris's. "A really pleasant mission until the end, I have to say."

She slapped him, hard.

"Feel better?" he asked.

"I'll feel better when I'm home, I know the stone is safe, and I can focus on grinding your pathetic little family's empire into dust." *I should stop. Saying more is really bad idea. But I don't care.* "You think I'm naive? Maybe I was. But that's over. I'm done with sitting out. As of now, I'm in the Game."

His eyes widened, for a moment, then they closed like the shutter of a camera.

"Quite a speech. But you're on the Makris estate, inside our security grid. You aren't going home until we let you."

Her hand lashed out at him again. He stopped her before she'd swung halfway to his face. The shock jolted her already sore arm. Heat rushed through her body, burning her skin and making her muscles tremble.

She would not be his captive, held hostage against her father. There had to be some way out of this.

She didn't know how to teleport. Oh, she knew the theory. Visualize your destination, fix it in your mind and hold it steady, then merge the symbol for the spell over the picture of where you want to go and tap out the spell. Sounded simple enough. But according to her uncle, not so easy. Make a mistake and she could materialize inside a wall. Or deep in the earth.

But even if she could teleport, she didn't know how to break a teleport block. An operative learned to break a block, or a security specialist like Victor. Not a student like her.

But there might be another way.

Kate turned around, head down. Let him think she'd given up.

She walked a few steps forward on the rocky ground. The less Kristof saw her do, the better. She blocked out the sea, the cries of the gulls, the pain in her head, her rib cage, everything except the power deep inside her.

Running down the staircase in her mind, she threw open the doors that held the power back. The vastness inside lunged toward her. It promised her so many things, if only she would let it out.

Later. I'll deal with it later. Now, she wanted one thing. To leave.

She touched the dark power and sent her magic out. It searched the Makris's security grid for the teleport block. *There.* The violet strands of the block entwined themselves all around the island, from the rocky shores of the beach to the top of the lonely white estate that capped the hill. Break a few strands, squeeze through the hole she'd made, and she'd be home.

Break, she willed.

The strands snapped as if they were guitar strings plucked by a too-rough hand. Two seabirds, fish in their beaks, plunged from the air and hit the ground, their lifeless bodies breaking on the rocks. *Now. Quickly.* Before he saw his spell had broken and fixed it.

She searched out the remnants of the teleport spell he'd used to bring them here. There, glowing bright orange in her magesight, the last few motes of energy swirling listlessly against the rocks.

She dipped down into that well of darkness again and threw its power into the remains of the teleport spell.

Home. She envisioned the foyer at their Hamptons estate, the black-and-white checkerboard pattern for incoming teleports, the little Queen Anne table, always topped with fresh flowers, the smell of freshly baked cookies from the kitchen. Home.

The sky brightened with a flash of light. A figure darted into view just inside the range of Kate's vision. A rush of energy hit her, a burst of white light that surrounded her and caused her vision to blur and waves of dizziness to wash over her. Her teleport spell disintegrated, losing all her connection with the feel of home. The orange motes of the teleport spell fizzled and died.

Her head spun. A young woman only a few years older than Kate, with long brown hair trailing down the back of her green dress, strode toward her, light blazing from her outstretched hand. *Is that Melina Makris? Kristof's sister?*

Kristof said something in Greek to his sister, then took a step toward Kate.

The woman's eyes darkened, and she tapped out another spell. Before Kate could even think of willing a spell into existence, the pain in her head flared into an exquisite agony as a tight band of pressure flexed around her skull. The sky, the sea, the cries of the gulls, all faded into blackness. She fell to the ground and knew nothing more.

"Why? I had her under control. What made you—" Kristof rushed toward Kate.

"You had nothing under control," Melina said. "She was seconds away from teleporting out."

"She can't. She's a Null." He bent down to check Kate's pulse.

"I think she's a little more than that. Your girlfriend broke our teleport block, using a spell I've never seen before. The security grid alerted me. When I got here, she had prepped a teleport spell."

"That's impossible."

Melina regarded him with cool green eyes. "That's what happened." Her gaze flicked to the laptop bags. "I see you got the stone." Her tone went cold.

Damn. He'd blown off their plan to hijack the stone so that he could save Kate from Dmitri. A waste of time—he could have left the rescue to her own people. Then he'd wrecked his plans further by coming home instead of taking Kate and the stone someplace secure, like his mother's old house in Istanbul.

Returning home while under fire was a reflex drilled into him since childhood—the Makris estate had close to invincible shields. After casting so many spells, his paranoia about the Hamiltons had gotten the better of him. *Damn, damn.*

"We can still—" he began.

His father's voice, from behind him. "I see you carried out the mission, my son."

Kristof turned around slowly. His father stood on the beach, no bodyguards, only his ever-present shield protecting him, holding out his hand.

I could strike now. I have a chance, a small one.

He glanced at Melina. The brief shake of her head told him everything. He unslung the laptop bag from around his chest, handing it to his father. "Of course. That's my job."

I hope you choke on it, monster.

His father took the case containing the stone from the bag, then tossed the bag at Kristof's feet. "We'll discuss the mission later." He nodded toward Kate. "Lock her up, Melina. With caster bonds."

Kristof started. How did he know about Kate?

"Papa—"

His father stopped and turned his deep-pitted eyes on Kristof. "What?"

"We have the stone. We don't need Kate. You should return her—"

"If your brain wasn't so addled by the girl, you'd realize that she is far more than she appears. Perhaps the stone had something to do with making her a caster or perhaps Hamilton has been lying about her Null status all along. Until your sister figures out the answer, I'm not giving her back."

"Holding her is against the Rules. Hell, you're begging the Hamiltons to throw everything they have at us."

"You brought her here. Deal with them." His father turned and strode up the stone steps to the estate house.

When his father's form had disappeared over the rise, Kristof yanked the remains of the monitor talisman from his shirt and dashed its broken form against the rocks.

Melina looked up from Kate's unconscious body and frowned.

"We need to talk," he said.

"Yes," she replied. But her eyes said something more. They said he wouldn't enjoy that conversation.

Kristof trudged up the wooden steps set into the hillside to the stone courtyard behind his father's estate house. He didn't have much time before his father got tired of admiring the stone and summoned him for a report. Minutes, perhaps. Not enough time to consider all the implications of Kate being a caster.

But he had an eternity to consider his monumental screwups.

Bringing the stone with him instead of carrying out his and Melina's plan. Grabbing Kate and teleporting home, like a first-time operative too tweaked to consider a better alternative. A strategic retreat may have been his only option, but he'd picked the worse possible location.

And what had brought him into such a fucked-up situation? Ah, yes. There was more than time enough to consider what he'd found in the tree house and stashed in his pocket. He reached inside and fingered the smooth surface of the pearl buttons ripped from Kate's shirt.

He had business with Dmitri.

He rounded the courtyard and found his cousin lying on the floor of the columned portico at the rear of the house, where the automatic retrieval spell in his talisman had brought him as soon as Kristof had taken down Victor's teleport block. Still out cold. He bent down and gave Dmitri a hard slap.

Dmitri groaned and opened his eyes, blinking against the harsh sunlight.

"Wake up. We have things to discuss."

"Are they gone? Did you get the stone? What happened?"

Kristof grabbed Dmitri by the front of his shirt, jerking him to his feet. Dmitri's eyes still had a slight glaze to them—the aftereffects of the stun spell.

His hand tightened on Dmitri's shirt. "You're going to tell me exactly what you did. Leave nothing out."

Pulling a struggling Dmitri with him, he walked off the intricate green-and-blue mosaic tiles that mirrored the frescoed ceiling and threw Dmitri down on the stone courtyard.

Kristof circled around his cousin, his hands fingering the pearl buttons in his pocket.

"Tell me. How did you lose a Null in under an hour? She bash you over the head with a bottle? Or did she scratch you with her nails?"

Dmitri got to his feet and brushed the dirt off of his jeans. His eyes held his customary sharpness—the glazed look was gone.

"She had help."

"I told you she might. Was it too much for you to handle?"

"No. It wasn't a problem. Dylan Pearce was there when I took her. I knocked him out, but he must have traced the teleport."

Kristof stopped pacing. "That's impossible. No one can trace a teleport through that many blind routings."

"Pearce did."

"How?"

"How should I know? I was busy dealing with the girl." He leaned back against a stone column. "She put up quite a fight."

"I told you not to hurt her."

"Hey, I didn't do anything. I just asked her if she wanted to play." He smirked, then a frown settled on his face. "She wasn't so enthusiastic about it."

Kristof's hand clenched around the buttons in his pocket.

"Then she pulled a nasty little trick and burned me. It must have been an incendiary device of some kind." Dmitri shrugged. "Got me with my guard down. I wasn't expecting a Null to fight back."

"I bet you couldn't handle it when she did."

Dmitri's cheeks flushed a deep scarlet. Then he took a step toward Kristof, hands balled into fists. Kristof locked his gaze on

Dmitri, and Dmitri stopped. His cousin's arms were red and blistered, even after whatever healing spell he must have done. Incendiary device? Not likely.

"So you tried to assault her and she burned you? Good for her. What happened next?"

The smirk crept back on Dmitri's face. "I had to teach the little bitch a lesson, didn't I?"

"What did you do to her?" Kristof's fist spasmed.

"I gave her a taste of the latest version of my pain spell." He chuckled. "She took it for longer than anyone else has. I wonder if it'll leave permanent damage."

A red haze fell over Kristof's vision. His body moved of its own volition, his fist shooting forward and striking Dmitri in the face. He watched as Dmitri fell to the ground. Stepping forward, he grabbed his cousin's shirt, lifting him up. His fist smacked Dmitri—two, three times, each impact a loud *crack* that echoed across the courtyard. He was aware, somewhere in the back of his mind, of Dmitri's wildly flailing fists, his cries, his own bloody knuckles. He had no idea if any of Dmitri's punches landed. It didn't matter. What did matter was that the throbbing pain in his fist cleared his mind. The haze receded. He dropped Dmitri to the ground and backed away.

What the hell was he doing?

He stared down at Dmitri's bruised and bleeding face. Shit. Dmitri would retaliate. And the retaliation wouldn't stop. Unless Kristof made it clear, once and for all, who was fit to be heir.

"I gave you strict orders not to harm her. You disobeyed me."

"I don't care what you 'told' me to do. I don't report to you." Dmitri got up and wiped the blood from his mouth. A flicker of jade-and-silver energy crept around the edge of Dmitri's hand, the cloaked spell barely visible to Kristof's magesight. Kristof got his own spell ready, hiding it from Dmitri's view.

"When you're on a mission you do what you're told. If you can't follow orders, you're useless. You might as well be a Null."

Fire rose in Dmitri's eyes, a split second before Dmitri let loose his spell. A ball of green-and-silver lightning struck Kristof, arcing off the bright-blue glow of the special, reflective shield that sprang into place around him.

The ball boomeranged to its maker. Dmitri screamed as his own pain spell hit him, his back arching in agony, hands clutching his head as his fingers tore at his eyes in anguish.

How long should I let Dmitri enjoy a taste of his own spell? A smile flashed across Kristof's face. *A long time. Just like he did to Kate.*

A single pair of hands clapped three times, echoing through the walkways of the courtyard. Kristof spun around. His father, expressing his appreciation for Kristof's brutality, his two bodyguards flanking him.

"Very nice, my son. Turn off the spell while your cousin still has a brain cell left."

Kristof hesitated but a moment, then ended the spell with a snap of his fingers. Dmitri whimpered, a long, low sound.

"Now heal him."

"No."

"Perhaps you did not hear me, my son. Heal him. If you want your Hamilton girl healed."

Kristof closed his eyes for a moment. Then he stepped to Dmitri, knelt, and took his head in his hands.

I could cave his head in with a kinetic punch. Or slice his throat open with a kinetic knife spell. No one could stop me. Not my father, his bodyguards, and not Dmitri.

Then he thought about Kate, suffering the aftereffects of Dmitri's spell alone with Melina and whomever else his father had sent to watch her. He tapped out the healing spell. The warm, amber light flowed down from his hands into Dmitri's head, and slowly, the moaning grew softer. When his magesight showed that Dmitri's aura was in balance again, Kristof stopped.

"Leave him. Come and sit by me. We have much to talk about." His father motioned to a pair of hovering servants to take Dmitri away.

Kristof obeyed, following his father to the portico. *How much of my betrayal did he see through the talisman? Is he planning to have me killed, here, now? I should run while I can.*

All that might be true, but the paranoia creeping through his head from the two spells he'd cast was spreading lies as well as truth. Papa wouldn't kill him—yet. Not after he'd brought back the stone.

He sat across from his father on one side of a weathered cedar table. His fingers picked at its splintered edge, and he wondered how much the old man had seen through the monitor talisman, of Dmitri's little game with Kate. He certainly hadn't stopped it. Maybe he had even ordered it. His father could always let Dmitri take the fall for any charges the Hamiltons brought against them for the assault. But at the same time, his father had found a clever way to twist his knife even deeper into Kristof and watch him squirm.

His father tapped him sharply on the chest. "I'm disappointed in you. You risked the stone to go after the girl."

Kristof straightened, smoothing his clothes back into place. He needed to spin events for his father, keep him as far away from the truth as possible. "I still hadn't heard from Dmitri. The Hamiltons broke their word. They attacked me. I—"

"Yes, convenient how their attack shorted out my monitor talisman, wasn't it? It isn't like the Hamiltons to break a truce, especially when we have such a valuable hostage." His father drummed his fingers on his chair and regarded Kristof. "Why didn't you come straight here with the stone?"

"Dmitri missed his check-in. He hadn't delivered Kate to the rendezvous. Something had to be wrong. I needed to—"

"Don't try to convince me you were concerned for your cousin."

"Dmitri's recklessness could have sunk the entire mission."

"How? You'd already gotten the stone. The girl didn't matter after that, did she?"

Damn. He wasn't even convincing himself with these excuses. "I'd given Grayson Hamilton my word to return Kate in exchange for the stone. I wasn't going to let Dmitri break it for me."

"Dmitri, Dmitri. This is not about Dmitri." His father shook his head. "You led the mission. You were responsible. Ah, Kristof, you are learning, but not fast enough. What do I have to do to show you how to manage Dmitri? Look over there." He pointed to where an unconscious Dmitri was being tended to by two servants. "Now, after today, he may respect you. You punished him when he disobeyed you. You have shown him you are faster, more brutal, than he is. That is what it takes to be a leader."

Kristof stared down at the blood on his fist, then glanced over at Dmitri, still moaning in pain. How many times had it been Kristof laying on the stone floor, his father standing over him? No. Whatever that was, it wasn't leadership.

"Despite your other errors in judgment, I am proud of how you handled Dmitri's disobedience. You are finally understanding what it means to lead this family." His father smiled, a smile that spread darkness from the sharp points of his teeth to the red pinpricks of light deep in his eyes. "It mitigates some of my concerns about you."

He motioned to his servants. They swept in and set down a bottle of ouzo and two glasses, poured a splash of the clear liquid in each, and backed away. His father held up his glass.

"To success. May the Makris family always find it, and may the Hamiltons always lose it." He drank and slammed his glass on the table.

Kristof picked up his glass. He downed it all in one shot. The liquor burned his throat and he struggled not to cough. But it cleared the rage from his head. He could no longer afford it.

"Today you succeeded, my son. Despite yourself. You took unnecessary risks. One mistake, one, and we would have lost everything." His father slapped Kristof across the face, hard, the *smack* echoing across the portico.

Kristof took the hit, the pain stinging his cheek, and stared straight ahead, expressionless.

"You are too young to remember what it was like when your grandfather ruled. Chaos. Weakness. Failure. After he lost half our arsenal to the damned Americans, I gained the support of the Synedrion and overthrew him. Showed them what a strong hand at the wheel could do. But the damage was already done. The Delacroixes had taken half of Italy. The Adelekes seized the Sudan. Even the Guptas made incursions into Iran. It's taken years to regain what he lost, and even now we have yet to take back Rome."

This was hardly the first time Kristof had heard his father recount family history, but he had no choice but to listen. His father seemed to think he would learn something from the lesson.

"That is why—" his father leaned forward and poked Kristof's chest "—you must...not... risk...*the stone*. I won't let Hamilton get another artifact that should be ours. Especially not one as powerful as this." He stood. "Hamilton cares more about his daughter than the stone. Watch and learn. I will use the girl to force a retreat, and we will be able to wield the stone's powers without any hindrance from the Hamiltons."

Kristof frowned. "Won't they file charges? Gain allies against us? We kidnapped her against the Rules—"

"No. She's a caster. And they hid it, somehow. They have no cause to complain about us breaking the Rules."

"Then they'll protest what Dmitri did." Kristof remembered the pearl buttons, still in his pocket. "And the spell he used."

His father shrugged. "Let them. I don't care. It won't get them the girl back."

His father smiled, a dark look that froze Kristof's heart. "Don't concern yourself with her. You have more important things to worry about. The security of this estate, for one. Melina will be too busy with the stone to monitor the grid. Take over for her. Now."

Kristof obeyed, concentrating until he could feel the estate's security grid thrumming in his senses like the smooth hum of his

Ferrari's engine. The force boundary, the teleport blocks, the cloaking talismans, everything seemed to be fine.

A sudden flare against the boundary. His eyes shot open. A simple probe, nothing the grid couldn't handle. He relaxed.

"You feel it? The Hamiltons." His father grimaced. "They'll try something, in the next day or two, as soon as they realize they're getting nowhere at the negotiation table. Be prepared, and make sure our security forces are ready."

"I'll need backup. Anton—"

His father waved a negligent hand.

Kristof pushed the wooden chair back and stood.

"And Kristof, make that your only concern for the next few days. Leave Hamilton's daughter to Melina. If I hear that you've interfered... Well, you know how inhospitable this estate can be to the girl, if I so choose."

"Yes, Papa." *I will tear your heart out and grind your bones into dust, old man, if you put her in the Pit. I swear it.*

He watched his father walk into the old estate house, his bodyguards following.

Your bodyguards won't save you, the Synedrion won't save you. And if I have to kill you without the stone, I will.

Chapter Twenty

Kristof slammed open the doors to Melina's sitting room. "*Melina*. We have to talk. Now."

The room was quiet, just the bubbling of ever-present chemicals on a burner to provide a background harmony to the calls of birds outside her window. A lone cup stood on her desk, the aroma of freshly made coffee still in the air. She was here. He hadn't wasted the long and treacherous climb.

He stalked past the sitting room and her office, desk cluttered with a dozen unfinished projects, and made his way to her Sanctum. He put his palm on the door. It read him, and he felt it acknowledge his presence. Then nothing. It didn't open. She had locked him out.

Damn her. He swept a hand across her desk, scattering talismans, papers, her bone china cup, and the photo of the two of them with their mother on the beach at Mykonos across the expanse of her office. Melina had better tell him what she'd done with Kate. Had she healed her? Where was Dmitri? Far away from Kate, or he'd...

He paced in front of the Sanctum door. Was Melina in there right now with the stone?

A temper tantrum did him no good. He couldn't help Kate, or figure out what to do about the stone, if he was out of control. He slumped into Melina's desk chair. She'd come out when she was ready.

How did he screw up so badly? Kate should be at home with her family, and he and Melina should have the stone in their safe house while Papa thought the Hamiltons had the damn thing. Shit. He could blame Dmitri all day but he's not the only one who went off mission.

A *click*. The door opened. Melina. Her long brown hair fell over her face, and she motioned him inside the Sanctum. *About time.* He rose and went inside.

The Sanctum's hum coursed through his body as he crossed the threshold. He soaked in the magical power as he attuned himself to his sister's space, letting its energy permeate him as he closed the door.

Blue-green light glowed from the gems set in mosaic patterns along the floor, ceiling, and walls of the small room, bathing him in an ocean of color. Melina was already sitting inside the crystal circle, the stone open in its silver case in front of her.

Kristof watched as she picked it up carefully, her hands encased in silk gloves. It shone with a radiant green glow in the Sanctum's low light, the colors playing across his sister's face. Its dark depths drew Kristof in the longer he gazed at it. He snapped his eyes away.

"So. Here it is," Melina said. "Not that it will do you and me any good." She slid it back in its box. "Whatever possessed you to skip our rendezvous and chase after Kate? You've ruined everything." She slammed down the lid of the box.

He stumbled through his explanation, running a hand through his hair as he leaned, exhausted, against the wall of the Sanctum.

"You didn't need Dmitri." Melina rose to her feet and picked up the box. "I saw how you handled Hamilton in London. You went after Dmitri because of Kate."

He opened his mouth to protest, but nothing came out. She was right. That's exactly what he'd done. And he would do it again.

"You care more about Kate than you do about our goals. Do you want Papa to destroy this family?"

He looked at the silver box gripped tightly in her hand. When had his mission changed from overthrowing his father to protecting Kate? And why hadn't he realized the shift when it had happened?

He'd made the fatal mistake too many operatives made: letting his emotions control his actions. Damn, he knew better than that. But now that he was aware of it, he could fix the problem. It should be simple: just change his priorities.

"You're right. I wasn't thinking straight. I should have kept to the plan."

Melina gave him a long look. "Yes, you should have. But we can turn events to our advantage."

"Really?"

"Tell me how Kate became a caster."

He straightened. Everything he'd learned since Brian died began to make sense. The "accident" that killed Brian coinciding with her bringing home the stone. Her insistence that she stay and learn her father's "business." How her family seemed to be training her. Her miraculous escape from Dmitri, using what sounded to him suspiciously like a fire spell. He explained his theory to his sister and told her his conclusion.

"I think the stone changed her into a caster. When it killed her brother, it somehow transformed her."

She held a finger up to her mouth, and her eyes stared into nothingness. Then something sparked behind them, and a smile flashed across her face so quickly that he thought he might have imagined it in the dim light of the Sanctum.

"The stone is the key to everything. It always was," she said.

"So? We can't use it now. Papa—"

"Keep Papa busy and leave Kate and the stone to me. I'll make sure it does what I think it does."

"Which is?"

She studied his face. "You'll find out when I'm certain. But I have to know one thing: Are you going to leave me out in the cold again the next time your little girlfriend needs you? Or can I count on you?"

He met her gaze. Melina was the only real family he had left.

"You know you can." The decision settled on him like a shield spell.

"Good. Now go and deal with the Hamiltons. After all, every good war needs two sides. We have to have someone to blame for Papa's demise."

Kate came awake, her eyelids fluttering. The sheets and pillows of her bed were soft and white, sunshine streamed in from the window above. For a moment, she thought she had awoken back home, in her own bed, her own room. But this bed was much bigger, and the room... No striped wallpaper and old bookcases here. A carved, blue cabinet and a yellow armchair were propped against white-washed walls. Rich Turkish carpets covered the hardwood floors. The air smelled of perfume. Sandalwood?

On the other side of the room, a girl wearing a red-and-gold caftan, black ponytail trailing down her back, huddled on a wide bench, her head down. Seeing Kate stir, she leaped to her feet and ran from the room, closing the door behind her. Kate heard the *click* of a lock turning.

This must be the Makris estate.

She sat up. Memories rushed back and cleared the sleep from her mind. Kristof grabbing her, the ocean-clean scent of him exactly like Kris, their argument on the rocky shore, her aborted attempt to escape. *Kristof. Shit.*

Someone had undressed her, put her in a white gauze nightgown, gotten her into bed, and healed her wounds. No more pain in her head, no more broken arm. Instead, strips of silver covered her hands, winding from her wrists around her fingers like a bracelet gone wild. The silver strands joined together on the backs of her hands under a glowing, green stone. A peridot. Maybe a green tourmaline.

Her clothes sat on a wooden chair next to her bed, all folded in a neat bundle. No sign of Dylan's jacket with all his talismans. Or her earrings, or Brian's journal. No surprise there.

But it wasn't as if a bolted door could keep her here. She was a caster, right? She could teleport herself back home. If a regular spell didn't work then by willing herself there. It was risky, but she could do it. And the sooner the better. She kept feeling Dmitri's hands on her, could still hear the tearing sound her shirt made when he'd ripped it. Dmitri's home base was the last place she wanted to be. His home—and Kristof's.

No. She wasn't going to think about Kristof.

She had to concentrate now. Try to remember the spell she'd see cast a dozen times in the last few days and duplicate it, even without having had the official lesson. Hands under the covers, she tapped out the complex spirals that would teleport her home while she visualized the foyer of her house, its cool marble floor under her feet, the smell of fresh bread baking.

Burning pain shot up her arms and into her shoulders. A relentless agony that intensified until she stopped trying to cast and curled up in a ball, whimpering. Her hands felt like she'd dipped them into a lake of fire.

After a moment the burning subsided. Her hands throbbed, red and sore, but she could make a fist, move each finger. They didn't seem injured. She could use them for anything, apparently, except casting.

When her heart calmed down and the pain had dulled to an ache, she pulled at the wires binding her hands. They wound around every finger—too snug to slip off. She slid out of bed.

First things first. Clothes, then figure a way out.

But Dad must be trying to rescue her. Negotiating for her release, sending Victor and a team of operatives here. To get her and the stone back. She was probably supposed to sit tight.

She pulled her clothes on. Someone had washed them, gotten all the dirt, river water, and blood out. New buttons had been sewn onto her shirt, as well. Her fingers flashed as she got dressed, the silver filigree of her bonds catching the sunlight as she moved. Clearly they meant to keep her captive. At least until they got whatever it was they wanted. Some concession from Dad? After all, what could she give them? Kristof had already gotten the stone.

Kristof. How could she have been so stupid? Kris Stevens had seemed like the perfect guy when she'd met him at an audition at the beginning of spring semester. Funny, charming, cute, from a family of shopkeepers in Florida who never would have believed in casters or the Game. All that time he'd been milking her for information about her family, data he'd fed straight back to his father. The fire in his eyes when he kissed her, the heat burning in his touch, the words he whispered to her in the dark. All lies.

She couldn't stay in Kristof's house one moment more. She needed to find a way out of here and back home.

She sat on the bed and closed her eyes. Then she stepped down the staircase she'd constructed in her mind, down to where the magic lived. Opening the wide metal doors, she touched the sea of ebony that roiled and swirled around her, drawing up a swirl of power. The dark energy swarmed over her, sliding into her soul, permeating her being.

No teleport spell to reactivate here, as there had been at the shack and in Africa. She'd have to try it from scratch. *Home*, she willed.

The power washed over her like a tsunami. *What the hell? No, no...too much. Too...* She grasped for a handhold, a life preserver, anything, but the magic tumbled over her, its hunger ravenous. Finger by metaphorical finger gave way until she slid down and down into the vastness within her.

Light shone from high above the dark, rolling waves. Its cleansing rays burned the blackness from her like an ice cube melting in the sun. Inch by inch, the power crept back until she felt herself lifted high above its inky ocean, no longer its captive, free from its hunger. She basked in the warmth of the light.

She opened her eyes, and she slumped against the foot of the bed. The willowy brunette from the beach yesterday—Kristof's sister—crouched before her. White light poured forth from her upraised hands and played over Kate's body. As Kate's eyes focused on her, she clasped her hands and the light disappeared.

"Well." Melina arched an eyebrow. "You're a surprise a minute, aren't you?"

Chapter Twenty-One

Kristof gazed out the conference room's floor-to-ceiling windows at the Piazza del Popolo below. The sun shone down on the usual summer crowd of Rome's pasty-faced tourists toting cameras, local girls in oversized sunglasses, and businessmen stopping for a quick lunch at a sidewalk café. The day-to-day life of the Normals of this embattled city, fought over by so many families it might as well be considered neutral territory, wasn't that interesting. But staring outside gave him a moment to gather his thoughts before sitting down at the negotiating table with the Hamiltons.

He ran his hands along the lapel of his navy blazer. His father had been blunt last night. Melina needed time to examine the stone, to understand what it had done to Kate, before she could find out how to use it for him. Kristof had to get the Hamiltons to stop their attacks. The bombardments, the probes, were all too much of a strain on Melina, who managed the complex magical infrastructure of the Makrises' estate, despite all Kristof did to shore up the security grid.

He rubbed his eyes. The attacks had taken their toll on him, as well. Despite having Anton relieve him, responding to the Hamiltons' intermittent attacks had drained both his magical and physical energy.

His father had appointed Kristof lead negotiator—another one of his father's tests. Prove his worth by protecting the estate. Stay away from Kate. And win concessions from the Hamiltons. It wasn't like casters his age never handled the talking end of the Game, but they were generally more valuable throwing spells around than words. He glanced over at the long walnut table, the middle seat on one side reserved for him. Today would be one hell of an initiation.

His father would ensure he'd see Kristof's success himself—or his failure. Papa sat at the table, chair pushed back, a dark jacket trying and failing to hide his heavy middle. Behind him, Dmitri lounged against the marble-covered wall, his smirk already firmly in place.

The tall wooden doors of the large conference room opened. The Hamilton delegation was ushered in by their host, Stephano DiOrsini. The Independent, all dandied up in an Italian suit with a red pocket handkerchief way too loud for Kristof's taste, gave Kristof a nod. Maybe he'd keep his vow to witness the temporary truce. Maybe not. Kristof had never completely trusted Independents, but he'd rather rely on a powerful rogue like Stephano to make sure both sides kept their word than count on the Hamiltons to just keep it.

Grayson Hamilton took the main seat on the Hamiltons' side of the table.

So Grayson's going to lead the negotiation. Interesting.

Kristof hadn't reported Grayson's encroaching paranoia to his father, but the Hamiltons had to assume he knew about it and had passed the information along. Grayson's role as lead negotiator could be seen as either foolhardy or a show of confidence.

Kate's father, black hair slicked back, tie perfectly knotted, sat next to Grayson and studied Kristof's family. His sharp eyes seemed to miss nothing. When they landed on Dmitri, they went as intense as a hawk after his prey. Kristof felt Hamilton's eyes laser in on him, as well. Fair enough. He could take the heat.

Hamilton's reaction wasn't lost on Kristof's father, who watched from the other side of the table, toying with his pocket watch. His eyes took in the whole room in but always came back to Cooper Hamilton.

Hamilton acknowledged Kristof's father with a nod and a sharp "Nico." His greeting might sound polite, but the steel in his eyes said something else.

Victor stood like a soldier at parade rest behind Hamilton, his sharp-eyed gaze steady on Kristof. Kristof gave him a brief nod, one hunter to another.

Kate's rescuer, Dylan Pearce, stood against the wall, halfway between the door and window. He was wearing khakis and a button-down. Kristof had seen the arsenal of talismans that lined Pearce's jacket earlier—and he remembered the way Kate had clutched it tightly around her. If Kristof had had access to that kind of fire-power, he wouldn't have given it away to save a girl's modesty. Not even Kate's.

That arsenal sat secure in lockup now. Hopefully Pearce didn't have any backups.

Kristof came to the table and sat opposite Grayson.

Grayson raised an eyebrow. "So you're speaking for the Makris family. You have some nerve. You already broke your word once by keeping Kate."

"I did what the operation required."

"In my day, that was called being a faithless bastard."

He felt heat rise to his face. "I didn't—"

Stephano stepped up to the table. "Mr. Hamilton, Mr. Makris, are you ready to begin?"

Kristof nodded, redness fading from his face. A small smile played on Grayson's lips a moment before his answering nod.

"Before we consider any of your demands—" Kristof had reviewed the long list Grayson had sent in advance of this meeting "—you have to take the orders of execution on me and Dmitri off the table. You have no proof that we violated any of the Rules."

"Do you want to see the recording from the forensic reconstruction again?" Grayson said. "Dmitri's guilty of attempted rape, attempted murder, and kidnapping a Null—"

"Kate's no longer a Null, so let's cut the crap." Kristof pulled Kate's silver earrings out, his hand brushing her pearl buttons as his fingers left his pocket, and placed them on the table. "And since she isn't, then the attempted murder charge is void also. Casters are fair game." He swallowed. "As to the rape charge—"

"Dmitri tells me the girl led him on," his father broke in. Kristof's jaw clenched. Dmitri's smirk broadened.

Grayson didn't so much as twitch. "No. He assaulted her. She fought back. Regardless of whether she's a Null or a caster, rape is against the Rules. Since you won't—or can't—control your people, Nico, we have no choice but to retaliate." He glanced at Kristof. "Against Dmitri and Kristof. Running an operation on a noncombatant—Null or not—is illegal, as well. Not only the operation you just ran but the one you've been running for months. Isn't that right, Kristof? Or do you prefer Kris Stevens?"

Kristof fought to keep his expression cold and serious. It wasn't hard to figure out how the Hamiltons had ID'd him as Kris Stevens. The conch-shell key fob Dmitri had carelessly left at the scene had given him away. At least he had the satisfaction of seeing Victor's grimace at his failure to catch Kristof's deception for so long.

Grayson continued, "As you won't respond to our request to discipline your operatives, we use the only sanction we have available. Orders of execution. Two of them."

Kristof's father leaned forward. "Do you think holding your threats over my head is going to ensure I treat your little girl with respect? Ha! If you send your casters after my boys I will treat her like we treat our lambs: pull her insides out, roast them in the coals of my fire pit, and serve them with a nice bottle of tsikoudia."

"You son of a—" Grayson began.

Kate's father stirred from his seat and turned his focus on Kristof's father. "Don't. Touch. Her." His quiet words echoed in the marble hall.

"You got our demands. You know how to ensure her safety," Kristof said. His father had better not mistreat Kate. He might not be afraid of Kristof's retaliation, but surely he would be concerned by Cooper Hamilton's implied threat.

"We aren't willing to discuss a cease-fire until you return Kate,"

Grayson said.

"Then we're deadlocked. And so early," Kristof said.

"Do you want a war?"

"No more than you do. But Kate stays with us, as does the stone."

"You have a poor track record of holding onto your artifacts."

His father shifted in his chair.

"Perhaps the tide is turning," Kristof said. "The Hamiltons lost the stone. Not the Makrises. Maybe you should cut your losses."

"No. Some things are nonnegotiable. Return Kate to us. Unless you do, the attacks will keep coming. You know we'll find a way through your defenses sooner or later."

"Then I'm afraid Kate will have to remain our guest."

Grayson's lips narrowed into a tight line. He gripped the table hard, knuckles whitening.

DiOrsini broke in. "Perhaps now would be a good time for a break. There is wine on the sideboard, and antipasto."

All around the table the participants rose, eying each other rather than the food and drink. Before Kristof could take Grayson aside for a little one-on-one negotiation, his father pulled him into a corner.

"You need to press them. Force them to concede. Why aren't you—"

"It's barely started, Papa. They aren't going to give up anything until they've fought for a bit. That's what you taught me." *And with the restrictions you placed on me, I have almost nothing to negotiate with.* He'd love to give them Dmitri but his father wouldn't let him. Giving up himself wasn't an option, and Melina wouldn't let him give them Kate. The only thing they had all agreed on was keeping the stone. Melina needed time to figure it out.

"Bah." His father threw up his hands. "I'll do it my way."

Why did his father want him to run this negotiation only to take it over himself? Grayson spoke to DiOrsini over a glass of wine. His father walked past Kate's uncle, cornering Cooper Hamilton instead, and whispered furiously in his ear. Kristof stalked to the table and speared a piece of cheese. So much for his role as lead negotiator. He just had to hope his father wasn't giving away his life as a trade for the stone.

"So how'd you do it?" Victor was behind him, more than a little anger in his voice. Kristof didn't have to ask what he meant. Victor had been in charge of Kate's security—security Kristof had breached. He turned around.

"Why should I tell you?" He touched the ring he still wore on his right hand.

"You like to crow about it, don't you? How you pulled one over on me? This isn't the end of it."

"Maybe it is. Maybe Hamilton fires you for incompetence, and you end up a rogue again."

"Maybe I shove those words down your throat. Right after my people leave this useless excuse for a wine-and-cheese party, wipe that island of yours off the map, and bring Kate and the stone home."

"If you could have cracked our security grid, you wouldn't be here."

A hint of a smile flashed across Victor's face, so quickly that Kristof thought he might have imagined it. "What makes you think our operatives aren't getting Kate and the stone right now?"

Shit. He couldn't be telling the... No. None of the monitor spells he had set on the security grid had been tripped. Melina hadn't contacted him. Victor was yanking his chain.

"That look on your face was worth the price of standing here and listening to your crap, Kristof. Better check in with your people. Just to make sure."

"No need. I know when you're bluffing."

"What if I'm not?"

Then I'm screwed. But at least Kate is safe. And with the way this negotiation is going, that's better than what's likely to come out of this meeting.

"Gentlemen, if I can have your attention, the Makrises and the Hamiltons have come to an agreement," DiOrsini said.

Neat trick, considering the negotiator didn't know about it. Victor resumed his place behind Kate's father as Kristof took his seat at the table. The only two not in their places were Dylan and Dmitri, facing off by the door, the tension between them almost combustible.

Dylan lit the fuse by shoving Dmitri hard. "You aren't going to walk away from what you did to Kate."

"Keep your hands off me, *koproskilo*." Dmitri stepped toward Dylan. Dylan didn't flinch at the insult, but maybe he didn't know Dmitri had just called him dog shit.

"That's enough." Kate's father's voice cut through the tension. Dylan's head snapped to him, and his shoulders dropped.

Kristof's father stayed silent, his eyes on Kristof, not Dmitri.

Great. He expects me *to rein Dmitri in. Another stupid test.*

Kristof squared his shoulders. How had Kate's father gotten Dylan to stand down? "Dmitri. Let it be."

Dmitri paused, waited long enough to let Kristof think he'd dis-obey here, in front of the Hamiltons, where disobedience would reflect worse on Kristof than Dmitri. Then he sauntered back to the far wall, and Kristof read the word *later* on his lips as he passed by Dylan.

DiOrsini cleared his throat. "These are the terms of an interim agreement worked out between Mr. Hamilton and Mr. Makris. This agreement does not cover the issue of the return of Katherine Hamil-ton to her family or ownership of the stone.

"First agreement: a cease-fire of three days during which neither the Hamiltons nor the Makrises will engage in any hostile activities toward the other family. This includes..."

DiOrsini went into the usual list of family operations, and Kris-tof tuned him out. Instead, he watched his father—and Kate's. Their eyes were on each other, judging, Kristof guessed, their seriousness about keeping the cease-fire. He didn't know how either of them could tell. As DiOrsini recited the Makris concessions, Kate's father shifted his gaze to Kristof.

"...the Makrises will enforce the following sanctions against Dmitri Makris within the next twenty-four hours: five hours in the Makris torture Sanctum known as the Pit, two weeks of personal service, completely at their discretion, to the female Nulls of the Makris family."

"Are you kidding?" Dmitri voiced his protest loudly. "What kind of a stupid—"

One sharp look from Kristof's father silenced Dmitri's whining. Kristof had no idea why Dmitri bothered to complain. Kristof himself had done worse to Dmitri in the courtyard yesterday. And when he had the opportunity, he'd do more. Of course, being at the beck and call of the family's Nulls was a nice touch. Except for Dmitri's inevitable retaliation against women who could do nothing to stop him. Had Hamilton thought of that? But still, the punishment hardly fit the crime. Why had the Hamiltons agreed to—

"The Makrises will enforce the following sanctions against Kristof Makris within the next twenty-four hours: twelve hours in the torture Sanctum known as the Pit."

Kristof sat still against the back of his chair. So that explained his father's eagerness to broker a side deal. Kristof would never agree to let Dmitri off so easily and take the harsher punishment for himself.

The Hamilton delegation rose to leave. Kristof looked up at Kate's father.

"Why? Dmitri tried to *rape* her. I only— "

"Because, as horrific as your cousin's actions were, Kate will get over his assault. We'll bring her home, take care of her, make sure she understands nothing he did was her fault." His gray eyes were hard as iron. "You are a different story. We knew she had a boyfriend. Victor checked Kris Stevens out, but your real identity slipped past him. I know you meant something to her—that's why she tried to keep your relationship private. Your betrayal isn't something she'll get over with some counseling. Think about that while you're hanging upside down in the Pit."

Hamilton turned and stalked out, his delegation following.

Oh, he would think about it. He glanced over at his father. In between thinking about how soon Melina could complete her investigation of the stone so he could use it to kill the heartless bastard sitting next to him.

"You sacrificed me to the enemy for a tactical advantage?" His throat felt so tight he could hardly speak. He didn't understand the shock, the hurt. What had he expected?

His father slapped him on the back. "It's only twelve hours, Kristof. Be a man. At your age, your grandfather had me in there for days at a time. A small price to pay to give your sister the peace she needs to work on the stone."

Easy for him to say. He wasn't scheduled to be hanging in the Pit. *More's the pity.*

His father went off to talk to DiOrsini about monitoring the terms of the agreement—both sides would want to know the other kept their end. Normally talking to DiOrsini would be his job, but, well... He pushed his chair back.

Something else about the deal stank like week-old fish. The Hamiltons had made a fuss about not agreeing to a cease-fire until they got Kate back, then caved when they got him and Dmitri punished for breaking the Rules. That made no sense.

That wasn't it, not exactly.

I'm monitoring our security. They gave my father what he wanted in order to get me out of the way for twelve hours.

That must be why. Though something else nagged at the back of his mind. The Hamiltons shouldn't have negotiated at all. Kristof's family held all the cards except one—they wanted the Hamiltons to end their attacks. All the Hamiltons needed to do was refuse to cooperate, and eventually his father would have had to make concessions. Coming to the bargaining table now was preemptive.

So why had they done it?

And what else happened here that I missed?

Chapter Twenty-Two

Kate struggled to her knees at the foot of the bed. She studied the woman in front of her.

"Melina Makris?"

Melina nodded. She offered Kate a hand up.

"What happened to me?" Kate asked. "What did you do?"

A smile quivered at Melina's lips. "Isn't that obvious? I saved you from being eaten alive."

Kate stiffened. Melina tapped out a spell, chanting low guttural words in a language different from the one Kate's family used. But the chant seemed to work fine as they vanished from the bedroom and reappeared a second later on the patio of a windswept cottage set high on a cliff. Old stone tiles felt warm and solid under Kate's bare feet. The breeze brought in the smell of the sea, and for a moment, Kate remembered home. She blinked back tears—couldn't show weakness. Not to a Makris.

"Where are we?" she asked.

"You don't get to ask the questions here. I do."

Melina led Kate inside and through a sparsely furnished sitting room. They came to a large, metal door set with a palm lock—like the Sanctum at home. Melina put her hand up to it, and the door opened. She entered.

Kate hesitated at the door. The round room was smaller than Kate's family's Sanctum but lined with the same swirling patterns of glowing stone. Green, blue, lavender—cool washes of color flowed across the room. According to Grayson, the hues of the stones didn't matter. Green, blue, red, yellow—they all provided the same protection. But the energy felt different. Melina's room—her Sanctum—vibrated with a rapid, hyper thrumming that set Kate's teeth on edge. *How does she stand it? Working in here must be a pain in the butt. It would make me want to kill somebody.*

"Come inside. I want you in the circle stones." Melina walked to just outside the circle stones in the Sanctum's center—green instead of warm amber.

Do different colored circle stones work the same, as well? Grayson never said.

Kate didn't move. "What if I don't?"

Melina shrugged. "You already tested your spellcuffs." At Kate's look of surprise, a smug smile flashed across Melina's face. "Yes, I can tell from the talismans on the cuffs. You know how much pain they can pour into your body if you cast. But I can make them do more than that."

Melina's brow furrowed. Kate's hands tingled, then burned with a fiery pain.

"Stop, please stop. I didn't do anything." She stared down at her hands, wrapped in the silver bindings Melina called spellcuffs. The green stones glowed as the pain in Kate's hands went from a slow burn to an incessant, scorching agony. She clutched her hands, gasping.

"You asked me what would happen if you refused. Here's your answer. If you want to make this process difficult, it's your decision."

"Fine, fine. I'll do what you want." The pain in Kate's hands eased, then disappeared as Melina concentrated on the cuffs again. She stretched her fingers against the restraints, then walked into the Sanctum and into the center of the circle stones.

What had Grayson told her about Melina before the funeral? The oldest but not the heir. A whiz kid who became the Makrises' senior technician after her mother had lost it to paranoia. Kind of a junior Grayson but, in his words, *lacking my wisdom and experience.* Someone who manipulated from behind the scenes. So much for hoping Melina wasn't a monster like the rest of her family.

Melina's brow furrowed in concentration, and soon a soft hum came from the circle stones around Kate. A glow lit each stone from the center outward, and a shimmering barrier rose through the air. Just as Victor had done to her in her family's Sanctum the day after Brian died, Melina had activated the holding function as well as the protection function.

Melina went behind a blue glass wall set in the back of the Sanctum. Kate could see her silhouette, reaching onto a shelf and picking up a square object.

"Why do you need me in the circle?" Kate held up her hands. "You spellcuffed me."

"I'm not worried about you. I'm worried about what's inside you."

Kate shivered. "What…is it?"

Melina didn't answer.

Whatever's inside me has to be something the stone put there. If Melina knows, I have to find a way to make her tell me.

"Sit down," Melina said.

Kate sat. The slate floor was rough and cold even through her jeans. Melina came out from behind the wall with an old, tattered book and a small silver box. Kate hugged herself. She knew that box.

Melina sat cross-legged on a floor cushion, the book and silver box next to her. She opened the book and flipped to a well-used page.

"What do you know about the Pandora Stone?" Melina asked.

Kate started. That's what Dylan thought it was.

"Just the legends. It's supposed to bring the old magic back if it is ever completely lost. Other than that…"

Melina picked up the box. "Oh, I think you know a bit more. Your brother entrusted it to you. You managed to fend off an attack by a rogue who wanted it—"

"How do you know about the attack?"

"And it killed your brother, didn't it?" Melina walked around the circle stones, studying Kate as her dress trailed her. "Is that when it made you a caster?"

"Why don't you ask Kristof? Apparently he knows everything about me."

"You shouldn't have been so open with him. But then, you

thought he was your boyfriend. Not your enemy."

Kate crossed her arms.

"My brother believes he can have anything he wants," Melina said. "Anyone. Our father sends him on a mission to gain information from an enemy, and he thinks nothing of breaking the Rules to get it. Even if he breaks a girl's heart in the process. Typical. Makris men are like that, you know. Callous. Privileged. Out for themselves."

And you aren't? Please.

"You're angry at Kristof for his betrayal, at Dmitri for his attack. You want to get back at them for what they've done."

What kind of game was Melina playing? "Sure. Of course."

"Then help me figure out how the stone works. Help me understand the power inside you. How you broke the teleport block around the estate, why the power tried to consume you a moment ago."

She shifted on the cold stone tiles. "Why?"

"Simple. Whatever power you called up, you can't control. You need my help."

Kate's heart sank at Melina's words. She was right about the lack of control. If she tried to use the power again, anything might happen. Something awful. Something fatal.

"I don't need you. I have my own family. My uncle, my friend Dylan, they can—"

"They aren't here. I am. And they don't have this." She opened the silver box. The stone sat inside, a black disk lying against the pristine white of its silk cocoon. It drew in the blue-green light of the Sanctum's gems and wrapped the gems' glow around its obsidian darkness, as if taking the Sanctum's power as its rightful tribute.

She tried to avert her eyes, to look at something else, anything, even Melina's smug smile. But the stone drew her gaze back as surely as a swaying cobra held a mouse's attention.

It whispered to her. Sang to her, in a deep, dark voice, like a quiet echo of the power that spoke inside her. *Touch me, touch me. Pick me up, look into my depths. Then everything will be over.* She wrenched her attention back to Melina.

"I'm going to examine you," Melina said. "You have two choices. You can help me, or you can fight me. If you fight me, I'll win." Her eyes gleamed in the green light of the Sanctum. "If you help me, we might both benefit. Make the right choice."

No, there's a third choice. Pretend to cooperate, learn all I can, and use it to control this power inside me. And bring down its darkness on you, Dmitri, and Kristof.

I'll take option three, thanks.

She drew her knees in and hugged them close. "Okay. I'll cooperate. Just don't use the spellcuffs. Please." She sniffled. Playing the scared little Null wasn't much of a stretch.

Melina's smiled a knowing smile. "Good choice. Now stay quiet and don't resist."

Melina tapped out the points of the symbol, sang her chant—so like yet unlike the Hamiltons' language—and tendrils of green energy, smelling faintly of chlorine, shot from Melina's hands, penetrated the circle stone barrier, and wrapped themselves around Kate.

But the stone played its old games. Trying to entrance her, to get her to lose herself in its ebony depths. Trapped by the circle stones and the cuffs around her hands, fighting the pull of the Pandora Stone, she could no more stop Melina than she could hold back the summer sun.

Melina's spell sank into her body, and she felt it rummaging through her tissue, her bones, her blood, her muscles. A sharp, cold tingle ran through her spine. Then a ripple of pain crashed through her skull, a rush of warmth flushed her face, and the sharp, acidic scent of chlorine choked her nostrils.

Pure fear seized and shook her. *No. I can't afford to lose it. Not here, not now.* She visualized Melina: her eyes narrowed in concentration, her lips curved up in an arrogant smile. She wasn't going to let another Makris get the better of her. Dammit, she was a caster now, too. There had to be something she could do.

Two problems: Melina and the stone.

She'd better take one at a time.

The stone first. She took a breath. Another. Then she focused on the stone's voice in her head, calling to her. She pretended its words came from a brassy horn, calling in the distance and imagined the horn moving farther and farther away. As the stone's call faded, she pulled her gaze away from it, millimeter by millimeter. The pressure in her head eased the further away her gaze drifted.

She could still see the stone, in the corner of her vision, but its dark power no longer swamped her.

Melina didn't notice. Head thrown back, eyes unfocused, she seemed caught in the flow of her own spell.

Melina's spell poured through the circle-stone barrier, its green energy like a solid rush of water. Kate's body absorbed the energy with a sharp tingle. It felt like the spell Grayson had done after she'd been changed. Maybe it did what Grayson's spell had done—delved into the depths of her cells and into her DNA itself to see what she had become. But it felt like Melina's spell went further. Its green energy not only scanned Kate, but Kate could also see it flow between her and the stone. Did the spell watch the stone as it sang to Kate and assess the stone's function, as well?

If so, Melina would know what the stone had done to Kate as soon as her spell finished. She'd know how Kate had cast the spells that let her break the teleport block and burn Dmitri.

That would be more than Kate knew herself. Was there any way she could see what Melina saw? She scrutinized Melina's spell with her magesight. Then she looked at the stone. Nothing. She wasn't a master technician like Melina—only a newbie caster. Despair welled up in her.

What had Dylan told her? Lyndal, the stone's creator, had made the Pandora Stone to bring back primal magic—the kind that had existed in the First Era. Was primal magic the kind of power she'd called up in the tree house and in Africa? But according to legend, primal magic casters had no problem controlling their spells. They just had to pay for them in...

Shit. They paid for their spells in death.

The butterflies in the catalpa grove, the lizard in the tree house, the beetles, and the seagulls. All of them dying, even as she called up the blackness inside and cast her spells.

Oh God. That's what I am. A primal magic caster.

If Dylan was right, that meant the stone really *wasn't* finished with her. Its calls to her were attempts to complete its programming, interrupted by Brian's spell. Attempts to finish making her into a primal magic caster—one with control.

Was Kate supposed to touch the stone and complete its transformation? Maybe she'd gain the control over its power she now lacked. Or maybe she should find some way to undo what it had done. Being a Null again would suck, but being powerless was better than losing herself to...that *hunger* rising up from the dark ocean of what had to be primal magic inside her. The force that threatened to pull her down and consume her. Every time she used the power, it killed something. What would it do if she lost control again? Eat her alive? Kill someone else?

Melina's eyes opened, and the stream of green energy snapped off. Kate slumped to the floor, exhausted. Her body ached, her head hurt, and her mind spun.

"That's...very interesting." Melina shut the stone's silver box.

Kate relaxed as the stone's call muted. "I don't suppose you're going to tell me what you found out?"

"Why would I keep it from you? That wouldn't help anyone." Melina walked behind the blue glass wall and put the stone and book away. She came back around to face Kate. "The Pandora Stone is trying to possess you, permanently. Its creator, the First Era caster Lyndal, designed it to take a blank slate—a Null—and transform it into a tool to awaken primal magic from its long sleep. The stone planted a direct link to primal magic inside you, and primal magic plans to use you as a gateway back into the world."

No, no, no. She's lying. She must be. "How can primal magic 'plan' anything? It's not alive."

"Isn't it? You've felt the call from the stone, how primal magic speaks to you. You think it doesn't have intention?"

Oh, it did. It definitely had intention. If only she could figure that intention out.

"It wants to return, seeks what it views as its rightful place. That's primal magic's purpose, not any of these legends that you've heard. The stone is its agent. And after so long an absence, it's very hungry."

"What? You're... You've got to be kidding." Kate sat on the cold floor, silent. Melina's story could be true. It made sense in a weird way, as much sense as the explanation she'd come up with. The stone had possessed her before. Maybe its call to her served as the set-up for the final possession. She made her hands into fists before Melina could see them shaking.

Melina's a Makris. Just like Dmitri. And Kristof. They all lie, break the rules, and take what they want. So why is she bothering to tell me anything? What does she want from me that she can't take?

"How do I know you're telling the truth?"

Melina shrugged. "You don't. But why would I lie?"

Because you're a Makris? "How do I stop the stone from possessing me? Reverse what it's already done?" Kate asked.

"I don't know. Not yet. But I can find out. And when I do, I can use the stone to take away that dark void inside."

"Would I still be a caster?"

"I don't see how I could change that. I don't have the ability to remove anyone's magic."

I have no idea what you can or can't do. Kate glanced up. Melina presented the same half-arrogant smile, the same superior gaze as she flicked her hair back and looked down her long Makris nose at Kate. Like all the other caster girls, certain she's smarter, prettier, better than a poor little Null like Kate. *Well, if that's what Melina thought, maybe I should keep her thinking that.*

"What do you need to do to fix me?" She huddled in a tight ball on the floor. *Better sell it.*

Melina shrugged. "Work with the stone, and you. Understand the connection between the two of you so that I can reverse what it did."

"Why would you? You don't have any reason to help me."

"That's where you're wrong. Don't you understand what you did in the bedroom? What almost happened? Kate, there's a reason we stopped using primal magic. One that isn't in the history books. Primal magic takes what it wants. We can't control it for long. And when it slips the leash we try to put on it, thousands die. Makrises as well as Hamiltons."

Shit. Kate had felt the hunger of the power inside her, the insatiable appetite that lurked underneath that dark ocean. Melina could be telling the truth.

"Is that what you want? Having your soul eaten by ancient magic, being responsible for the deaths of thousands of people? Casters, Normals..."

"Of course not."

Melina smiled. "Then let's get started."

Chapter Twenty-Three

Kate sat, legs crossed, inside the circle stones. Melina rested on a floor cushion a few feet outside the circle. A stack of books, some older than Kate thought possible, lay beside her. The hum from the activated circle stones set Kate's teeth on edge.

After the examination, Melina had taken a break long enough to set the Sanctum up with the supplies she needed. Kate took the time to think. What Melina had told her was plausible. Too plausible. It tasted just true enough that Kate looked hard for the inevitable lie within.

All Kate had to go on was Grayson's teachings, what Dylan had told her, and instinct. All three said that the dark, hungry ocean inside her was indeed some kind of link with primal magic. Just as the spells she'd cast were that ancient form of death magic. More difficult to figure out was Melina's story that primal magic wanted to possess her and use her as a gateway. She felt primal magic's hunger every time she touched it, but Melina's explanation sounded a bit too self-serving. Make Kate afraid of primal magic, and she'd never learn to use it against Melina.

And then there was the stone. Its call to touch it didn't feel like destruction. It felt like completion.

Five containers sat inside the circle around Kate. A glass aquarium contained some plants and insects: ants, beetles, butterflies, and the largest cockroach she had ever seen, all buzzing with frantic activity. A second aquarium held a few lizards, tongues darting out to taste the air, and a large snake coiled in the sand. Rodents—a few mice, rats, a rabbit, and a guinea pig—scratched at the glass of another, their claws leaving long, thin marks. Inside a wire cage, a flock of small yellow birds chattered and swooped. A much larger cage held a beagle, a small piglet, and a feral cat. The beagle whined, a high, panicked sound. The piglet squealed a breathy oink and kicked it hooves against the reinforced glass of the terrarium. The cat huddled in a corner.

Kate reached inside the last cage and stroked the beagle's head. "Is this really necessary?"

Melina glanced up from her book. "Before I can change what the stone did, I have to understand it. Test the limits of what you can do."

Maybe. Or maybe she has another reason for this "testing."

"How am I supposed to cast with these things on?" Kate held up her hands, still encased in the silver spellcuffs.

"Don't worry. I'll free you long enough to cast each spell." A small smile lifted the corner of her mouth. "I've set up the circle to prevent you from teleporting out—or doing anything other than what I specifically ask you to do."

Kate remembered what had happened when she'd touched the screen the circle had thrown around her back at her Sanctum. Melina's countermeasures wouldn't be as relatively gentle as Victor's. "What if I don't do what you want?"

"You could say no. After all, I can't make you. All I can do is make it very painful for you to refuse. But then again, I also didn't have to pull you back from that dark place you went this morning, did I? Next time, I could just leave you there. And you will end up there again. Even if you don't use the power again, it will make sure it takes you back into that darkness and never lets you back up again."

Yeah, Melina was a Makris, just like her brother and her cousin. Melina just had a different twist to her nastiness.

That little smile had returned to Melina's face, the smile that said, *I was born a caster, and I'm so much better than a poor little Null.* Kate wanted to slap that smile off Melina's face.

But she couldn't. The situation called for a different tactic.

"I... You're right." She slumped over and sighed, putting a little pathos into it. Her acting teachers would be proud.

Melina flipped back a page in her book, read for a moment, then set it down. She concentrated, head back, and flicked her fingers. A purple band appeared around the circle, about halfway between the floor and ceiling. The strip hovered, a steady, unwavering light.

"What is—" Kate began.

"Don't ask questions, just do what I say. Cast a light spell, the way you were taught."

Mouth dry, Kate nodded. Melina's eyes fluttered, and the green stones in Kate's spellcuffs glowed for a moment.

Kate's hand shook a little as she traced the points out, the silver cuffs pinching her fingers. Melina better be right about freeing her from them long enough to complete the spell. She wasn't looking forward to feeling her hands burning in a bonfire again.

Thinking back to the lesson of a few days ago, she focused on the symbol for light. She murmured the short incantation and finished tapping out the symbol on her thigh. A small ball of light appeared in the air before her, burning steadily. No paranoia—normal for casting in a Sanctum. Whatever the purpose of the purple band, it didn't react to her spell. It hovered in the air around the circle, humming gently.

Melina scribbled a few notes in her notebook. "Now turn the spell off."

She obeyed. The light went out as quickly as it had turned on.

"Now comes the interesting part." Melina reached behind her. She lifted up a small red bag and reached inside, hand swathed in a piece of silk. She drew out a white bowl.

Kate's eyes locked on the bowl. She heard a faint whisper in her mind, not the brass horn of the stone's voice, more like a reedy piccolo. Just loud enough to set her teeth on edge. She squinted. The white material of the bowl looked just as the stone had before she'd touched it and the white had changed to black.

A primal magic artifact. It had to be.

"Do the spell again," Melina said. "Only, use the same method you did when you tried to break our teleport block. Cast it the way you did when you burned Dmitri."

Great. The last thing she wanted to do—dive down into that

hungry blackness again.

How the hell was she going to stop primal magic from pulling her in? No idea. But she'd better figure it out if she wanted to master the darkness and get the hell away from Melina.

She let her eyes go into soft focus, as she did when engaging her magesight. She inhaled. Then she walked down the steep steps and into the basement of her mind, opened the doors once again, and looked out at the ocean of blackness that confronted her.

The waves of ebony energy lapped at her feet as she searched its dark waters, looking for some clue that would let her understand the magic's intention. Nothing. She raised her eyes above the horizon and beheld the dark clouds, heavy with power. Torrents of jet-black-colored force streamed down like a rain of darkness as it struck the sea below, replenishing its black vitality.

The waters inched closer to her feet. The darkness pulled at her, tried to drag her into its tarry depths. Her stomach tightened.

Light, she willed. The dark force responded right away, reaching out beyond her and making something happen. She felt something else, as well—primal magic making a choice. *This* for *that*.

The darkness surrounding her brightened, a glow on the horizon. The light shone dimly, like a lamp seen through a veil. *Must be the light spell in the Sanctum.* She sharpened her focus on the light, and her contact with the force inside her fell away. She became aware of the Sanctum around her again, that she was still sitting in the circle stones, Melina sitting outside. The animals in the circle with her screeched in terror, the beagle howling, the rodents throwing them-selves at the cage walls in a panic. A new ball of light floated in front of her, looking no different than her previous casting.

Inside the aquarium, a large beetle dropped from the glass wall onto the sand. A flicker of purple shone along the border of the circle.

The bowl sitting in front of Melina had changed from white to black.

Melina got to her feet and paced around the circle, peering in at the cages.

"That was different, wasn't it?" Kate said.

"Did you concentrate on the symbol? I didn't see you trace it or hear you chant."

"No." She thought about what she had done, how she had contacted primal magic inside her. Its subtle threat to consume her until she cast the light spell. How could she explain how that felt? Words were inadequate. "It was different. I just willed it into being."

Melina didn't look all caster-haughty anymore as she stared intently at Kate. Instead, the gleam in Melina's eyes reminded Kate of the look one of her classmates had given her once when she came to school with a new designer handbag.

A look that said, *I want that, and I don't care what I have to do to get it.*

"What did I do? It's not regular casting."

"No, it doesn't seem to be. Let's see what another spell will do."

Melina wrapped the bowl back up and placed it behind her.

Bitch. She's doing something with that bowl, something she's not likely to tell me about. And she knows I'm a primal magic caster. The spell uses death as its price, not paranoia. And from what Dylan said, that's primal magic. Forbidden, death magic.

She rubbed the metal of her spellcuffs and thought about the alien power's cool regard when she cast the light spell. *This* for *that*.

"I...don't want to," she said.

"You don't *want* to? If you ignore this it won't go away. You'll use it, and when you do you won't know how to control it. Is that what you want? Do you want the darkness to take you over?"

She gulped down her fear. "What do you want me to do?"

"We'll try a bigger spell, something that requires a larger sacrifice." Melina paced in front of her. "Try a shield."

She didn't want to touch the void inside again. But what did Dad always say? *If you don't control the situation, the situation controls you.*

She focused and again dived into the blackness. First order of business—maintaining contact with the power inside her while still seeing her outside environment. She couldn't deal with Melina if she couldn't see her.

The principle must've been the same as with magesight. Like Grayson had said, *Maintain a soft, easy focus on your inner world, then let the outside world leak in through your peripheral senses.*

She tried it, watching the dark sea before her, eyes relaxed, then pictured the Sanctum around her, separated from her inner world by an imaginary white veil. Bit by bit, the outside world appeared just beyond the veil. First Melina, then the animals in their cages, the circle stones, and the rest of the Sanctum.

It worked. Hallelujah.

Before the force inside her could do more than lap its waves against her feet, she acted.

Shield, she willed.

The spell popped into being around her much quicker than a

normal shield spell would form. Then the power went out and chose. A squeak started up, then broke off suddenly. A mouse.

Poor thing.

The purple band flickered again. Melina peered into the cages, frowning, then scribbled in her notebook.

They tested every spell Kate had been taught. Each time the purple band flickered. Each time something in the cages died: a mouse, some fish, a trail of ants, a rabbit. As each animal died, the others became more frantic. What made the magic pick three mice one time and a flock of canaries the next? Kate had no idea.

But she thought Melina did. She wrote in her book after each spell, pacing in front of the circle stones. Her steps grew shorter, her strides faster. But Kate grew more tired. Tired and worried.

She didn't know what hidden consequence there might be to using so much primal magic. Every time she went down into that black well, did she lose a little bit of her own light? She had no way of knowing. But the hunger from the primal magic felt real. As real as her own dread.

Melina didn't heed Kate's pleas to stop. To eat something, get some sleep. Each spell needed to be measured, each sacrifice had to be noted. Finally there were only three animals left inside the circle with Kate. A mouse, rummaging around the floor of its cage, whiskers twitching; a king snake lying coiled in the corner of an aquarium; and the dog.

"I can't do this anymore. What if the spell I do is too powerful, and the magic doesn't want any of the animals?" *What if it wants me instead?*

Melina tossed her hair back. Beads of sweat ran down her face.

"Don't worry about that. Just try the stun spell."

That spell had killed all of the beetles on the riverbank in Africa when she'd used it on Dmitri. There were no beetles left to kill here. If the magic didn't consider the animals that were left a fair trade for hundreds of beetles, what would it do?

"We've done enough. Turn off the circle and let me out."

"Oh, we're not close to being done."

"I can't do this all day. There's not paranoia backlash, but it's...draining."

"How? Tell me."

All this note-taking... It didn't make sense if Melina was telling the truth. If the stone was trying to possess her, and all Melina wanted to do was sever its connection to her, why did Melina want to know how her power worked?

"Why do you care?" Kate could barely get the words out, sitting on the floor, with her head in hands.

Melina studied Kate's huddled form. Then something behind her eyes shifted.

"I know you're tired. Do this one spell, and we'll take a break. I promise. It's important."

"How? What will it tell you—"

"You'll have to trust me."

Like she'd ever do *that*.

"I want you to try something different with the stun spell. Stun the mouse. Make the magic take the dog as a sacrifice, not the snake. Do you understand?"

"You want me to *tell* it what to take? Not allow it to take whichever one it wants?"

"Yes."

That's it. Kate narrowed her eyes at Melina. *She's figuring out which spell requires what level of sacrifice, how much control I have over primal magic. But why?*

Shit. I don't want to go down into that blackness again. One slip, just one, and... I don't care what she'll do to me.

"I can't. It won't do what I say." She closed her eyes, weariness catching up with her.

"Try it, Kate." Melina tapped her pen against her notebook.

"No."

"Do it."

"I said—"

Fiery pain burned her hands from the inside out, then raced up her arms. She gasped and rolled onto her side, shaking. The pain intensified, turning her arms into burning brands. The agony roared in her chest, the pain transforming every muscle, every rib into a cauldron of torture.

No, no, I'm not giving in. I'm not...

The pain washed through her stomach like a torrent of acid. It ate into her middle, burning through her guts and down into her hips. She curled into a tight ball and bit her tongue. The blood dripped on the Sanctum floor.

"Stop, please stop."

"I don't want to hear you say no. Not ever again."

Kate tried to draw in a breath. All she felt was pain. She focused on the white mouse as it shuffled along in its glass cage a few inches from her trembling hands, oblivious both to her agony and its potential fate as it sniffed the wood shavings lining the floor of its terrarium.

"Are you going to do what I asked?"

"Yes." *Until I learn how to control this thing inside me and use it send you and the rest of your family to hell.*

The pain eased first in her hands and arms, and then slowly, far too slowly, in her chest and middle. She lay curled on the floor for a moment longer than she needed to, breathing. Watching the mouse wiggle its nose, the dog's paw twitch as it slept. Then she sat up and wiped the blood from her mouth.

The whole "I'm just your big sister trying to help you out" look had vanished from Melina's face, and only raw ambition remained. As Kate held her gaze, Melina's eyes filled with discomfort until she looked down at her notebook, pretending to read whatever she had written.

Huh. Maybe she has a conscience after all.

Kate gave Melina a sharp nod. Diving down into her internal abyss, she sought out and touched the primal magic lightly with her presence. It acknowledged her. She quivered, queasiness filling her with a kind of sick terror. She tried to set it aside and move on. She had work to do.

Keeping half an eye on the Sanctum, she sent her will into the heart of darkness within her.

Stun, she willed, thinking of the mouse in the cage next to her. As soon as she willed it, the air rippled and the mouse fell on its side. *The dog. I have to...*

She gasped at the slithering magic inside, trying to make it obey. The energy swirled past her as easy as a desert wind, swamping her with its darkness. It would consume her without thinking about it, as

317

if she were plankton scooped up in the mouth of a blue whale.

No. Oh no. It's going to pull me down again. I've got to make it obey me. Make it pick the dog.

She tried to grasp at it, twist it with her mind somehow. *Do what I say, dammit.*

The power loomed over her. It slammed into her with a tidal force, washing over her and rushing around her feet, her legs, her torso, pulling her down into the void.

Stop, stop... Forget about the damn dog and let me go.

It couldn't end like this. Eaten alive by what the stone had put into her. She willed it to *stop*, to *halt*, to *go away*. Anything, anything. Her feeble attempts at control failed. It kept coming, sliding up her chest, around her arms, entwining her in its ebony blankness.

She was lost.

A burst of white light shone down upon the darkness. *Melina.* The light dissolved the blackness that pulled Kate under like a flame melting a candle. The primal magic retreated, bit by bit, as the light intensified, freeing her arms, her stomach, her legs. Kate's fear eased a little as the darkness slinked back into wherever it hid inside her.

The light. Now that she'd seen it a second time, it seemed familiar. Someone, somewhere, before Melina, had used it. Either on her or near her. But who, and where?

Kate, sprawled on the floor, blinked to clear her eyes. The mouse lay stunned. The dog howled in its cage, terrified. She had no idea if the purple band had flashed or not, but she didn't need its evidence to see her complete failure. The snake lay dead, the price for the spell. The power had taken what it wanted.

Melina's eyes shone with a cold light. A smug smile hovered

around her lips.

"Well. Your attempt at control wasn't too successful, was it?"

That smile... She wanted me to fail. Why?

Melina picked up her notebook and make another notation, her hand flying across the page.

Oh God. Is she going to make me control the power again? She said I could take a break. When the hell will this end? What happens if the power goes after me again and she can't bring me back?

Kate noticed Melina watching her. She wiped the fear off her face.

Melina went behind the blue glass wall. She came back with another cage—this one holding a rat, two small ferrets, and a turtle.

"Again," Melina said.

Chapter Twenty-Four

Kristof leaned back in Melina's leather chair, staring out her picture window. Gulls circled in the blue sky, nothing on their tiny minds but when to dive into the deep, blue waters below for another fish. He wished his life were that simple.

Twelve hours in the Pit had taken its toll. The pressure of the chair made his thighs and back ache. The roughness of his linen shirt scratched his sensitive skin. The light, even filtered through his sunglasses, stabbed like daggers through his eyes. Every breath was agony. The long climb up hadn't helped, but Melina hadn't responded to his request to lift her teleport block.

Hamilton thought the punishment would teach him a lesson. He doubted the thoughts he'd had while hanging upside down in the dark, lashed with needle-thin whips of magical energy over and over again, met Hamilton's ideal of apologetic.

Kristof knew how much he had hurt Kate. It wasn't that he didn't regret it. But once he'd stayed with her long enough to realize the damage he'd done, the trap had snared them both.

No, he focused on something else while his father's enforcers sent spell after painful spell coursing through him. The stone. He needed the stone to make his father pay.

Melina's precious work had better show her how to use it. God knew it had cost him enough. They needed a plan, one they could execute quickly. Once his father got his hands around the stone they'd never be able to pry it out.

The door to Melina's Sanctum cracked open. He took his sunglasses off, hooking them onto his collar. Melina slipped out, a small silver box in her hand. The stone. Kristof caught a glimpse of Kate, lying like a broken doll in the center of the circle stones, her red hair gleaming in the light of the crystals.

He shot to his feet, overbalancing for a moment when the dizziness hit him, then steadied himself. "What have you been doing to her?"

"Nothing you need to be worried about."

"Really? Doesn't look that way. *What* have you been doing?"

Melina shut the door on Kate. "Finding out what the stone did to her. How she broke the teleport block when she tried to escape. Trying to understand how we can use the stone—" she caressed the box "—against Papa. Isn't that what you want?"

He slumped back into the chair. "Yes. What did you find out?"

"It's the Pandora Stone, exactly as we suspected. What we need to know is which of the legends around this thing is true." She set the box on the small wooden table in front of Kristof and sat facing him. "Now I know."

"Well?"

Melina studied Kristof for a long moment, her fingers running against the smooth arm of her chair. Then, "The stone transformed Kate into a primal magic caster. Like the ancients. Your girlfriend uses death magic, brother dear. Remember that the next time you want to get close to her."

"You're wrong. Only artifacts can channel primal magic."

"Until now. Remember the legend that the Pandora Stone will bring magic back into the world? Apparently it does, but the kind it brings back is the ancient's kind—death magic."

Shit. When she tried to break the teleport block yesterday, I could have paid the price. "Can she control this power? Choose what it kills in exchange for a spell?"

"No. The stone isn't finished changing her. I think her brother interrupted it, probably with a counterspell. It's locked on Kate until it completes its programming."

"And if it does?"

"Kate will be the world's only primal magic caster. *A Hamilton*, Kristof, not a Makris. Capable of feats of magic only the ancients could perform, just for the price of a few fish or the man who catches them. All that power, and she'll never be locked away, mind gone, trying to tear her skin off, screaming her agony until she dies." Melina stroked the arm of her chair. Her eyes wandered over to the picture of their mother, back in its place on the old oak cabinet against the wall. Melina had never told him why she'd chosen to be a technician instead of a combat mage, but he could guess. Being two years older than him, she'd witnessed more of their mother's descent into madness and death. Technicians have a gentler path into darkness than that of a combat mage.

"What are you thinking? You aren't going to let the stone complete its programming."

"No." She hesitated. "Kristof, what do you want? More than anything else?"

His hand slid into his pocket. *Why didn't I throw out Kate's buttons?*

"I want to run this family. I want our father gone," he said.

She smiled. "Good. I know how to use the stone. It creates primal magic casters from Nulls. We can use it to create our own primal magic caster, someone loyal to us, our own assassin whose magic can kill Papa straight through every shield and bodyguard he owns."

"How? And who do you plan to transform?"

"Leave the how to me. I'll use Aurelia, the Null I have tending to Kate. She's been well-treated—she'll be loyal to us."

He frowned. "So do it."

"I have to sever Kate's connection to the stone first." She paused, giving Kristof a long look. "Breaking the link will kill her."

"*No.* No, I won't let you—"

"Make up your mind, brother dear. What do you want? Some half-trained girl like Kate whose lack of control over her power will get you killed, or to sit in Papa's place? You can't have both." She stood. "I'm sick of your vacillating. Are you in or out?"

He stared at his sister, the hard gleam in her eyes. His pulse raced like he'd cast a dozen combat spells. *I can't let her kill Kate. I can't.*

Make up his mind, Melina had said. Time to do just that.

There had to be a way to win—save Kate and depose his father. He ran a dozen scenarios through his mind. None of them got him what he wanted.

He remembered the way Melina had touched the stone's silver box. *She's going after what she wants regardless of what I say.* He needed to buy himself some time.

"I'm in," he said.

Kate looked up as a *click* sounded. Melina, framed in the light beyond the open Sanctum door. No, no more of this hell. Not one more descent into the darkness within her.

Melina waved her hand. The Sanctum lights came up. Another quick pass of her hand and the circle stones dimmed, the shimmering barrier rising from them disappearing.

"Get up," Melina said. "That's all for now. I'll come for you when its time to resume."

Was she...dismissed? *Oh, thank God, thank...* She stumbled to her knees, then her feet. The room spun and stripes of green, blue, and purple light swirled around her head. No, she wouldn't fall, not in front of Melina. She planted her feet on the cold slate floor and steadied herself. She focused on the door, a few yards away, and the room stopped spinning.

After a few steps the dizziness faded, and she crossed the perimeter of the circle stones. A few more and she had reached the metal door, pausing a moment to lean against the doorjamb. A breath and she exited the Sanctum and left Melina behind, her gaze on the hardwood floor as the very effort to navigate the simple sitting room seemed like more than she could cope with.

A strong hand took her arm. "Here, let me help."

Kristof.

"I don't need—"

"Yes, you do. Unless you want to stay here. I'm taking you back to your room."

She looked up at him. White linen shirt tucked into tight-fitting jeans, sunglasses hanging off his collar, deep-blue eyes gazing down at her. He had the stone, his family had her. He probably didn't have a care in the world.

Asshole.

She yanked her arm away. Anger powered her steps as she strode past him and out the French doors onto Melina's porch. He followed her outside. The afternoon sun warmed her as the salty breeze blew through the cedar trees. A tray of food—figs, apples, fresh crusty bread, some kind of white cheese—sat on a table next to a jug of water. She devoured it in a quick minute, leaving nothing but crumbs. After downing a long drink of the cool water, energy rushed back into her body.

She blinked the strong sunlight from her eyes. Life bloomed all around her. From the large ants crawling across the terra-cotta tiles of the teleport pattern underneath her feet to the small dots of the fishermen on the boats out to sea, to Kristof, sunglasses on, leaning against the whitewashed wall of Melina's cottage and toying with something in his pocket. She felt each organism's life force, a faint shadow through her magical senses, like the beating of a drum. *Huh. A side effect of my connection with primal magic?*

A connection that gave her the power to take life, as well as feel it.

The anger drained from her. Dread rose up instead. She turned to Kristof.

"Take me back to my oh-so-cozy prison cell. Anywhere but here."

He joined her on the tiles and tapped out a teleport spell. She watched, trying to fix it in her memory, while she took his arm and the power seized them both. They were whisked back to her room.

As they materialized on the Turkish rug, Kristof pulled his arm away and backed up, his hand rubbing his bicep.

Kate's eyes narrowed. What was wrong with him? Twitchy, yeah, but the backlash wouldn't account for the way he kept his sunglasses on, his reaction to her hand on his.

He was hurt.

She sat on the bench against the wall. He joined her, sitting close enough that she could sense the tension in his taut back, his rigid shoulders. She scooted away. He slid his sunglasses off his face and leaned his head into his hands.

"Get in a fight?" she asked.

"Something like that."

A vicious satisfaction rose up in her. "Victor?"

"No."

"Don't they heal you—"

"Things will go much easier for you around here if you stop asking questions."

She flushed. "Just tell me when the hell I'm going home."

He started to reply, then paused, his eyes so lost, the way they had been back at the beach when he'd touched her face and said her name.

"Kristof…please. Tell me what your sister is doing."

He didn't reply.

Was there anything at all of the guy she'd loved inside him? Or was that man an illusion he'd cast, one as carefully crafted as his preppy Kris Stevens haircut? How could she get through to him?

He wasn't Kris. No matter how her pulse raced when he sat next to her, he wasn't her college boyfriend. He was her family's enemy.

But had she imagined how he sat a little nearer to her than he needed to? How he touched her more than he had to? The intensity when his eyes met hers?

She didn't think so. How much of Kris was in Kristof?

She remembered so many of the things they'd said to each other. Stories of their families, their lives growing up, their hopes and dreams. Had everything he'd said been a lie? Or had some or it, maybe the most important parts, been as true as the confidences she had told him? Only one way to tell.

"You once said you needed to stand up to your family. Learn where to draw the line. Was that true? Or just part of the Game?" She held her breath.

"No. That was true."

"Then maybe this is one of those times when you should."

His eyes held hers for a long moment. Then he tapped out a spell, one she'd come to know well. A cloak. After its purple iridescence covered them, his shoulders relaxed.

"Things are complicated—more complicated than you can imagine. But I'm trying to get you out of here. Away from my sister. From my father."

"Why would you—"

"Why do you think?" He reached out and brushed her hair away from her forehead.

"No, no, you don't really... You can't have done the things you did and feel anything for me. You—"

He leaned forward, and his lips on hers, warm and insistent, caused the very core of her to soften. He drew her into his arms and winced as her body met his.

Then he pulled her closer.

His hands were gentle where Dmitri's were rough, his lips asked instead of took. Heat rose through her, flushing her skin. When they broke apart she felt dizzy for a moment, like she had the very first time they'd kissed, outside her apartment on Linden Street. "Kris... *Kris...*"

No. It didn't matter how her body responded to his familiar touch. His name wasn't Kris, and she couldn't trust him. Not after what he'd done.

But no need to tell him that.

"What's your plan to get me out of here?"

"I'm working on it."

"Melina's not going to free me, is she? No matter what the Rules say."

Kristof's silence provided all the answer she needed.

"Why? You have the stone. You don't need me."

"You're much more valuable than you know."

"The primal magic stuff? I can't control it. She told you that, didn't she? What use is it? Kristof, please...just tell me what the hell's going on. You owe me that much, at least."

329

Kristof ran his fingers up and down the arm of his sunglasses. He set them on the bench. Then, "Melina needs to understand how your primal magic works in order to get the stone to create...a weaponized caster. Someone who can use death magic as a tool of untraceable assassination."

"What...the...*hell*?"

"Think about it. A primal magic caster, completely in control of what the power takes, could cast whatever spell he wanted—destroy a family's security grid, kill a bodyguard, assassinate a pawn. After, instead of spending days in a straightjacket, he could direct the magic to take an enemy's life instead."

Is he telling the truth? Is that the Makrises' plan for the stone? Use it to create a living weapon?

"I can't control the power. So what do you need me for?"

"That...depends."

"On?"

"What happens next. What your family does, if they keep the terms of the truce we negotiated long enough for me to—"

"My family?" She grabbed him. "Did you see them, talk to them? Are they—"

He rubbed his arm. "Your father sends his love. I—"

His eyes jerked up and got a faraway look in them, just as Victor's did whenever he checked the security grid. He launched himself to his feet and strode to the door. "Something's wrong. Sit tight. And no matter what happens, trust me." The door shut behind him, the purple traces of his cloak spell vanishing.

Trust him? Not likely.

She got up from the bench and ran to the door, testing it, hoping beyond hope he'd left it unlocked. No such luck. Dammit. She slammed it with the heel of her hand, then gasped when the metal from the cuff bit into her.

There had to be some way she could get out of here before Melina did whatever she had planned.

Kate paced in front of the door, the rug warm underneath her feet. Melina's story about the stone wanting to possess her was probably bull. A tale intended to convince Kate to cooperate long enough for Melina to achieve her goals. No, Kate had to be right about what the stone wanted—to finish making her into a primal magic caster. One who could control her power. That made sense with what Kristof had told her.

Or Melina's tale could contain enough truth that ignoring it might be lethal. The magic inside her felt hungry. It wanted her. That much she couldn't deny.

But Melina wanted the stone to make someone else into a primal magic caster. Would the stone have to finish making Kate one first? Or—the room felt so much colder all of a sudden—would Melina just kill her?

A *boom* rocked the air. The building shook, and plaster rained down from the ceiling, dotting her shirt with little white sprinkles. What the hell was going on? Had Dad sent a rescue operation?

If he had, the Makrises would send someone to guard her. And it wouldn't necessarily be Kristof.

She scanned the room, looking for something, anything, she could use to get the drop on a caster and run as fast and as far as she could. Maybe far enough to find the hypothetical Hamilton strike team.

There. On the bookshelf, tucked in the end of a row of books. A small brass figurine of some Greek god. Good enough for her needs if she hit her guard hard enough and in just the right place. She grabbed the figurine and hid behind the heavy curtains by the door.

Another *boom*. A streak of fire, barely visible through the high window by her bed. *Something* was happening.

After a minute, the door whirled and clicked, its heavy wood hiding her from the intruder's sight. She held her breath.

Dmitri. Soccer jersey hanging over cargo pants, neck swathed in silver chains, barely shaven. He stepped into the room, his head turned away from her. "Kate?"

She targeted the vulnerable point at the base of his neck and struck.

Chapter Twenty-Five

Kristof raced down the wide stone hallway toward the central plaza. He passed Dmitri and tried to flag him down, but he waved Kristof away. His phone buzzed, the estate's alarm system sounded, and the monitor spells he'd set on the security grid sent urgent alerts screaming in his ears like the high-pitched whine of a wake-up call he couldn't turn off.

He grabbed his phone. "What?"

Anton's voice. "We're under attack. Tracking spells show several operatives, unknown origin, at the west gate, the main house, and on approach to the dock to Melina's island."

Not unknown. Hamilton. How the hell did they breach security?

He'd have to worry about that later. They were after the stone, and Kate. The rest of the attacks were diversions.

"Where's Papa?"

"The main house. He's leading the defense there."

"Good. Concentrate your forces on the island. I'll meet you."

"Got it."

He hit Melina's number. Nothing. *Dammit*. She had to drop her teleport block, just for him. She couldn't stand up to a Hamilton strike force alone.

He stuck his phone back in his pocket as he burst out into the plaza.

Outside, the sky lit up with bursts of fire. The air rippled with trails of kinetic-punch spells. Kristof dodged right to avoid one of his father's bodyguards as the man slammed against the side of the main house, his chest torn open, blood pouring down the front of his shirt.

A blaze of green fire from one of his cousin's hands shot across the dimming sky. It hit its target and tore the enemy's cloaking spell off in an explosion of blue sparks. The impact sent the revealed operative flying across the plaza and into one of his father's prize cedar trees. Her wail of pain joined the rise and fall of the estate's alarms.

A sonic spell buzzed by his head, and a blue urn that had been in his family for generations shattered behind him. A shard spun by his ear to slice through his shirt and into his shoulder, the blood splattering his cheek.

He ran on.

He caught a glimpse now and then of the enemy when a hit from a Makris spell ripped their cloaks away. They were clad in form-fitting gray battle suits, almost invisible in the twilight, talismans lined up in a row on their chests, deadly in their efficiency. He recognized a Hamilton operative he'd fought in Paris last year as a lightning bolt tore the guy's cloak spell apart and sent him crashing into the garden wall. No question now—the Hamiltons.

He didn't have time to deal with this diversion. The Hamiltons were after the stone, and he couldn't let them get it. Besides, they might get lucky and take out his father. He could always hope.

Melina's island. The enemy attack would focus there, and so must he. The din behind him receded as he approached the docks that provided the one way in or out. The mist rising from the water gave his movements a natural cloak. The only sound besides the crickets chirping and the gentle creaking of the two boats tied to the dock was the quiet pad of someone else's footsteps in the sea grass. Then nothing.

Probably a Hamilton operative. Anton would have texted me if he'd made it here.

Kristof circled around the side of the dock, using it for extra cover. He had to assume the enemy knew how to get to Melina's cliff-top Sanctum—they'd be making straight for the skiffs. If he moved fast, he could cut them off.

He tapped out a quick cloak spell to keep him on even ground with the enemy, making his chant as quiet as possible. *Damn.* He needed a couple of talismans to take on a team of operatives, but his father had left him with nothing but his ring. He'd have to take the backlash and deal with it.

A deep breath, then another, seeing movement in every shadow until his mind quieted. He rose above the waving reeds and climbed up onto the wooden platform of the dock, its splinters scoring the still-tender skin of his hands. He crawled along the dock until he reached the first boat, a small skiff bobbing silently on the water. He slipped inside, crawled under a tarp that lay in the back, and prepared his spells. A shield spell, cast now. Then his attack spells, racking them up one by one in the back of his mind, ready to cast.

The boat wobbled—once, then again. Two operatives. If they took the boat and left, with him in tow, he would lose any chance of Anton and his men arriving in time to help. He needed to act.

He estimated the position of the operatives from the movement of the boat and rose from the tarp to strike.

Three kinetic knives rippled from his hands and sliced through the air. Sparks flew when they hit a Hamilton operative's cloak spell and tore it away, cutting into his glowing blue shield and knocking him back. The tall man toppled over the side of the boat, shock turning his face as gray as his battle suit. Kristof barely registered the splash of the man's impact before he let his next spell off, a lightning bolt aimed a few feet to the right, where the number two caster would likely stand.

A hit. The bolt sizzled away both the cloak and the shield spell, its charge eating up all the azure power of the shield spell in a blast that lit up the water. A girl, short-cropped hair mussed from the fight, eyes wide, stood revealed. Her hands reached for a talisman on her chest.

He had to get his next spell off before—

A kinetic punch slammed into Kristof, barreling through his defensive spells and throwing him half in, half out of the little skiff, his back slamming painfully against the boat. He got to his feet, the boat shifting under him. *Another operative. Damn, damn. Where...*

No time. The girl in front of him posed a bigger problem. He cast at her just as her fingers reached her talisman. A flash of light, and she flew against the dock, hand falling to her side, her head impacting the wooded railing with a sickening *crack*. She slid into the boat and lay still.

In the distance, footsteps pounded in the grass. *Anton. If Anton wants to take me out, make his own play for heir, now would be the perfect time. Blame the Hamiltons, go for Dmitri next...*

He got ready to cast. Got ready for Anton and anyone else he'd bring.

No. Calm the hell down. Breathe in, out. Anton's not the enemy. Focus.

He replenished his shield spell, its bright glow springing up around him. Let Anton find the last guy. His job was to guard the boats, make sure no one got past him to attack Melina. He stomped on the hands of the Hamilton operative trying to pull himself out of the water.

He grabbed his phone and texted Anton:

H op clkd loose by dock. 2 ops down.

A moment later he got a reply:

I c u. Wait.

Not long after, a purple mist swept out from the beach and rushed up the landing, swirling around the dock and into the boats. It surrounded a figure running down the dock and jumping into the second boat, and revealed him for a gray-suited Hamilton operative.

Anton hurried from the cedar trees, followed by two of Kristof's security team. They spread out and hit the operative in the back with three lightning bolts, rippling away his shield, his cloak, and sending him flying headfirst into the bottom of the boat with a thud. A moan of pain rose from his huddled form.

Kristof climbed out of his boat and into the other one. He turned the limp caster over.

Dylan Pearce, a row of talismans on his chest, wire-rimmed glasses bent from the impact with the boat. Pearce groaned and stirred.

Anton ran up. Kristof motioned to Pearce. "Secure him. Get him away from the boats. Get all of them away."

He jumped out of the boat. "Anybody seen Victor yet? He wouldn't sit this out."

Anton shook his head.

"Station a force here. Make sure Melina's safe." She'd wisely sat this out. Her mission was guarding the stone.

Dmitri sauntered up the dock, blue shirt torn, too late to be of any use.

"What took you so long?" Kristof asked. "And what were you doing by Kate's room?"

"Huh? I was at the west gate, polishing off the Americans."

Dmitri made no sense. The west gate lay on the other side of the estate from Kate's room. And when he'd seen Dmitri in the main corridor, a few minutes ago, he was wearing a red jersey, not a blue shirt.

Shit. He took off running, his hand on his phone.

The stone wasn't the real target. Kate was.

He knew something had bothered him about the summit meeting—now he knew what. The normally calm Dylan arguing with Dmitri, pushing him. For a technician as skilled as Dylan, one touch might be enough to do the type of spell a combat mage like Kristof had only dreamed of when he'd tried to breach the Hamiltons' security grid a few days ago. To read Dmitri's aura—his security signature for the Makris grid—well enough to clone it. Transfer that duplication to a talisman someone else could use. Someone who could bring the Hamilton team into the fully-guarded Makris estate undetected.

Someone who could take Kate outside it, as well.

Kate brought the brass figurine down hard on the back of Dmitri's neck. Right before it hit, he spun around. It landed with a crack on his shoulder instead. He winced, stumbling forward, then turned to her, arm forward to cast. She backed away, holding up the statue.

Then Dmitri's face twisted in a familiar look of annoyance.

"Damn it, princess, can't you figure out when you're being rescued?"

"Victor?" She lowered the little brass idol.

"Who else? Let's get the hell out of here."

Hearing Victor's words out of Dmitri's mouth sounded...weird. Weirder even than reconciling the idea that Kris was Kristof. She wanted to hug Victor and give him another whack with the figurine at the same time.

He rubbed his shoulder.

"Can you heal—" Kate began.

"No time. We have to leave."

She lifted up her cuffed hands. "How about getting me out of these?"

"I'll have to. They're keyed to keep you on the Makris estate. Dylan gave me something…"

He reached into his pocket and pulled out a small silver talisman shaped like a key. He placed it against the green stone on one spell-cuff. It glowed for a moment, then the cuff released with a *snap*. She pulled her hand out with a sigh and threw the silver cuff to the floor.

Footsteps pounded down the hall. "Hurry," she said. Victor repeated the process with the other cuff, and it released.

"Let's go," he said.

"Wait. Brian's journal. Dylan's talismans. I don't know where—"

"Journal? What haven't you told me… Never mind. We'll have to leave them." He opened the door a crack and peered outside, then grabbed her arm and pulled her out of the room and around the corner. He pushed her out of sight as a team of Makris enforcers marched down the hall.

"Come on," he said.

"Where are we going?"

"The east gate. If we're separated, head there—behind the house, past the apple grove. Grayson's waiting outside. If anyone stops us, follow my lead."

He led her down the tiled hall and out a side door that opened on a long staircase. Alarms filled the air, sirens rising and falling. They took the stairs at a run, Victor first, Kate following. The staircase ended at a small courtyard. She barely kept up as Victor tore across it, dodging the blue-tiled fountain set square in the middle and making for the portico at the far end.

They ducked into the covered walkway and ran across the terracotta tile floor. As they turned the corner they ran smack into a team of three red-clad Makris enforcers, who pulled up short at the sight of a young man who looked like Dmitri dragging Kate behind him.

The lead enforcer, mouth set in a grim line, said something to Victor. *Greek. Not good.*

Victor imitated Dmitri's smirk. Then replied. In Greek. Who would have guessed Victor spoke Greek?

Doubt flashed across the enforcer's face. Greek spilled from him, and he pointed at Kate. Kate didn't know the words but she could figure out the meaning. Victor yanked Kate closer, his hand roaming exactly where Dmitri's would.

Better help Victor sell it.

Kate tried to pull away from him, taking care to conceal her cuffless hands. "Please. Can't you help me?" she pleaded to the enforcer. All she needed to do was think about Dmitri and his hands on her in the tree house, and the revulsion and dread came back up in her. She imagined it must have shown in her eyes. Method acting.

The man glanced at Victor and grinned. He motioned his team to move on.

Kate drew in a breath, shuddering.

Victor let go, something approaching sympathy in his eyes. "Let's get you home."

She nodded. Victor took her hand, gently this time, and they were off again.

They burst through the end of the corridor and out into the deepening twilight. Victor dodged a prone form of a woman in a gray battle suit, her black hair limp across pale skin, her eyes staring open at the sky. Grayson's other assistant, the one who'd faced off against Dylan the other day.

She stumbled. *Shit, oh shit.* That girl died, rescuing her. Her. And she didn't even know the girl's name.

They ran across the wide swath of lawn to a small gate leading down to a large dock area, screened by a grove of apple trees. They ducked into the cover of the trees. A rabbit darted away from their path. Kate stared at the gate—the east gate? A pair of guards stood, one at each side, under trees infested by a flock of ravens.

Shouts from behind them, toward the house. Kate spun around. Guards, three of them, coming this way. The same three they'd run into before. The lead enforcer spotted them and ran faster.

Looks like Victor's Greek isn't exactly native-sounding, after all.

"Victor," she whispered, then jerked her thumb back to the guards running toward them.

"I see them. Come on."

Victor ran to the gate, straight up to the guards. They didn't move or react—nothing. Kate scrutinized the guards with her mage-sight. A small wavering of their auras gave them away. Illusions.

She ran up to Victor, glancing back at the guards gaining on them. "Grayson's on the other side?"

Victor gave her an annoyed glance, then pulled Dylan's key out of his pocket. "Yeah, about a quarter-mile back, out of range of the Makrises' trap spells. Can you cast a shield?"

She nodded.

"Do it. And stay out of the way."

She called up the symbol for the spell, tapped it out, and chanted as quietly as she could. A soft blue glow sprang up around her, paler than the one Victor was casting on himself. She glanced at Victor as he put the talisman against the gate's large lock, its purple stone glowing with swirling light. He looked so much like Dmitri. Exactly like Dmitri.

What if Dmitri's running an operation on me, getting me to believe he's Victor? What if he wants to get me someplace alone, to take revenge on me for burning him without anyone getting in the way? Maybe I should take him out now, before he can...

She shook her head to clear it. Paranoia was a bitch, but it was better than killing an innocent animal in order to keep herself safe.

The guards were in the trees now. She glanced back and saw them fanning out, beginning to cast. "Victor..."

He spun around, hand going for the pile of silver chains around his neck. He grabbed one and spoke a command. A flash of fire sprang from his hand and shot to the grove of trees like a flamethrower, spewing over the fragile branches and lighting them up as if they were kindling. Screams rose from the guards as the fire spread from the trees to the men, their casting forgotten.

Victor winced as he lowered his arm. "I'm right-handed. Couldn't you have whacked my other shoulder, prin—"

White light flashed and a loud *crackle* tore through the air. A bolt of lightning hit Victor, and he stumbled back into the gate, his shield spell flickering a much paler blue. The smell of ozone rose in the night.

Kate scanned the darkening lawn, squinting with her magesight to see into the shadows lining the concrete wall that framed the gate. Nothing. Wait. A flicker, there, by the curve of the wall. A flicker that moved.

Victor saw it, too. He pulled himself up from the wall and grabbed a chain from around his neck. A word of command and the wall exploded into chunks of stone and metal. Chunks that launched themselves toward the flicker, hitting their assailant's cloak spell and ripping it away, revealing Kristof, a bit more battered and worn than he'd been what seemed like hours ago in her room.

Kristof, who'd said he'd get her out of here. *So much for trust.*

A ball of green energy crashed against her shield, sending her staggering. The pale-blue glow of her shield flickered, then blinked out completely. The energy of the spell's attack shot through her body, sending her arms, her legs, her stomach into searing torment. She screamed and dropped to her knees. A crushing grip clasped her wrist as she was yanked to her feet.

Dmitri. Blue shirt half in, half out of white jeans, face twisted in a sneer that Victor couldn't begin to duplicate. "Where did you think you were going, little *kôta*?"

She had no idea what a *kôta* was, but nothing coming out of Dmitri's mouth would be a compliment.

Kristof and Victor traded spells, Victor's shield glowing paler and paler with each hit Kristof scored. Each time Victor tried to cast, his wounded arm interfered; Kristof scored two hits for every one of Victor's.

Dmitri pulled the cuffs they'd taken off her in her room from his back pocket. She tried to squirm away. He tightened his grasp.

"Stay still. The cuffs won't hurt. That will come later."

No, it wouldn't. The symbol for fire, so elusive the last time she faced him, came to mind at her call. She started the chant, tracing the symbol with her free hand.

He reached down, fast as a striking snake, and crushed her fingers together before she could finish.

She gasped. It felt like the bones in her fingers would crack from the pressure of his grip.

He slammed a cuff on her hand and chanted a quick command. The silver wrapped itself around her wrist, her hand, then her fingers.

Kristof had Victor trapped against the iron gate—down on one knee, arms raised to cast, his shield only the palest wisp of blue. Kristof tapped out a spell, and a branch cracked free of the tree above. It shot toward Victor and hit him like a spear falling from heaven. The impact slammed Victor against the gate, his shield shattering into nothingness. He blinked and tried to stumble to his feet.

Dmitri reached in his pocket and drew out the other cuff. *No, no, no.* She couldn't let him take her captive, even if she couldn't cast the normal way. She had to do something to help Victor.

She sank her consciousness inside her mind, into that place so deep and dark she had no idea where it lived within. She ran down the steps and opened the cast-iron door again, her hand hesitating just for a moment on the cold lever. Time seemed to stretch out, and everything around her slowed down. Dmitri moved so slowly as he inched the cuff toward her hand that it felt like she had all the time in the world to deal with primal magic.

There it lay—the endless black sea of power, stretching for an eternity uninterrupted. She needed to control the magic this time— teach it who was boss. If they didn't escape now, they might never get free.

She touched the writhing darkness. A jolt of fear shot through her, and she snatched her hand back.

No. Forget what Melina says. Forget my fear. I have to master

345

it.

She reached for the magic and let the fear wash over her as the dark liquid played upon her skin. Would it let her go this time? Or would it drag her down again into its black depths until she drowned in its oily embrace, without Melina here to save her?

She wouldn't let it. She pushed her fear down and commanded the power to punch. She willed the spell at Dmitri. No hesitation. No fear.

The primal magic responded, flexing out to send a rippling wave of force straight at the brute holding her so cruelly in his grip. The kinetic punch slammed into Dmitri and he tumbled across the grass, his head hitting hard against the ground. He let go of her as he fell, the remaining spellcuff dropping from his hand.

Yes. He so deserved that. Now all she had to do was—

She felt the icy intelligence lurking beneath the waves reach out. *Oh no. No.* She tried to make it choose the rabbit she'd seen in the grove, the flock of ravens in the trees above her. The rabbit should be about right...

The magic saw her feeble attempt at control. Instead of obeying her, it turned its regard to the casters fighting behind her. Victor and Kristof. And chose a sacrifice. A ball of black energy rose from Kate and rushed straight to Victor.

"No!"

The power wasn't supposed to act like this. The spell hadn't been powerful enough to demand a sacrifice that big. Not from what she'd seen in Melina's Sanctum.

She dove back into the darkness, determined to wrestle it into submission. She'd give it herself if need be. *Just don't let it take Vic-*

tor. Please, God, no.

The white light, Melina's white light—how did she do it? She had only seconds before...

The darkness swirled like tentacles around her, crawling up her legs, her torso, her arms. It dragged her step-by-step into its all-encompassing depths.

The darkness was around her neck now, then over her mouth. She choked on its foulness, tried to spit it out. She needed to fight it, to protect Victor from the black ball of destruction rushing across the grass to take him.

The spell, the white light, what was the spell, dammit...

The darkness swirled into her nostrils and leaked into her eyes, blinding her. Everything went away. Victor sending a burst of fire at Kristof. Dmitri lying prone on the ground. The ravens rising from the trees. Everything around her faded from her sight. She raised her hands, tried to claw the darkness from her eyes, but her hands fell back, no strength left in them. She sank to the ground as the darkness crept into her lungs and stopped her breath.

Was this how Brian felt when the stone killed him?

She fought for breath as the magic froze the blood in her veins, leeched the life from her cells, and reached for her heart.

Light flared around her, erasing the dark from her eyes. Thank God. Thank God, she could breath again, see again.

Victor stood above her, silhouetted by the rising moon. He chanted, his fingers tracing a circular pattern on his thigh, and the chant sounded so familiar. The light streamed from his hands and flowed over her, chasing the darkness from them both like the tide washing blood from a kill off a beach.

The spell. She knew the spell. Victor used the same words that Brian had chanted in the Sanctum, the same symbol he'd traced out. Now that she knew, maybe she could...

The magic fled, but not far. From the grove she heard a scream, then a thud. Primal magic taking its price.

"What the hell did you do?" Victor reached down a hand to lift her up, his face grim.

A shadow loomed over him. "Behind you—"

Kristof's hands twisted the chains tight around Victor's neck. Victor's eyes bulged, and his hands reached up and back, grasped for his assailant. Kate stumbled toward them, so weak one step felt like a marathon. Victor struggled, jabbing his elbow back into his opponent's midsection. Kristof grunted but held on. Victor's eyes flickered closed, and he slumped forward.

Kristof let him drop. He bent down and picked up the spellcuff from the ground. He grabbed Kate's arm and jammed it on her hand, giving the one-word command to activate it. She felt the cotton-wool feel settle in her mind again.

She glared up at Kristof. "You said you would—"

He put a finger to his lips. "Not now. Your family blew the plan."

They blew the plan. Seemed to her like she might have had a chance before he and Dmitri showed up. Unless his plan involved a lot more than setting her free.

Weakness kept her slumped on the ground, propped on her elbows. Whatever the dark power had done to her, its assault had taken a toll.

Kristof took out his cell phone. "I've got them. The east gate."

He glanced out at the grove, where the guards dragged out the lifeless form of one of their teammates. "One casualty."

Damn. All she'd accomplished was killing a Makris guard. Primal magic's price for her walloping Dmitri with a kinetic punch. Nausea rose from deep inside her gut. *Not* an accomplishment.

Dmitri stirred and groaned. Kristof prodded him with his foot. "Get up. We need to make sure they don't have any more surprises."

"I can search her."

"You do that. Touching her uninvited worked out so well for you last time." Kristof pulled the talisman chains off Victor's neck, then patted him down and found the lockpick talisman in his pocket. Kate watched the slight rise and fall of Victor's chest and let out the breath she hadn't realized she'd been holding.

A group of guards trotted up. One of them slapped a pair of spellcuffs on Victor.

Kristof addressed Dmitri. "Finish searching Victor, then take him to the plaza. I'll meet you there with Kate."

"Sure you don't need help?" Dmitri wiped the blood from his mouth, then gave Kate a look that promised he wasn't finished with her. Not by half.

"Just go."

Dmitri gave Kristof a smirk and turned the still-unconscious Victor onto his front. He rummaged through Victor's clothes.

Kristof bent down over Kate. He held out a hand. "Come on."

When he touched her the same electricity sparked between them, the same warmth as when they kissed not long ago in her room leaped from her to him. Or was it the other way around? His gaze shot to hers, and she saw the surprise in them—and the momentary wonder—then the mask shuttered down over his eyes again. Back to playing the operative.

She let him help her up, getting to her feet slowly. Her entire body ached.

Kristof motioned her back to the house and its large central plaza.

She marched forward. Time to face the music. The Hamiltons had gambled...and lost.

Chapter Twenty-Six

Kate knelt on the cold stone plaza of the Makris compound, between Victor and Dylan. A cold sea wind blew in from the beach below, hitting the wall of the estate behind her and raising goose bumps on her skin. She still felt the ache the primal magic's assault had left her with. Her hands, twisted behind her back, throbbed inside the spellcuffs. Her throat burned with the smell of smoke and salt and defeat.

A group of Makris enforcers loomed over the vanquished Hamiltons, Dmitri's smirking face leading the bunch as he walked up and down the line of prisoners. Kristof stood against the estate's wall where it bent to form an *L* shape and faced the line of Hamiltons, his face and neck spotted with blood. They were waiting but for what?

Victor looked like Victor now, dressed in the same gray uniform as the rest of the Hamilton strike team, an angry red welt around his neck. Dylan was missing his glasses, but neither of them looked half as beat up as the remaining Hamilton strike team. Broken limbs, bloody skin, torn uniforms—her father's best operatives lined up on either side of her, on their knees, hands spellcuffed behind their backs, heads bent down.

Then there were the dead.

Over by the still-burning stand of cedar trees, the corpses were laid out in a row. Two Hamiltons and one Makris. Grayson's assistant, looking almost peaceful with her hair pulled back and arms crossed over her chest, lay next to Gordon, all anger gone from his still face. Slightly apart from the Hamiltons, the Makris guard Kate's magic had taken lay stiff and cold on the green grass.

Kate swallowed down the tears that threatened to well up. She glanced at the still form of the Makris guard. *I killed him. I can blame primal magic all I want, but if I hadn't tried to cast a spell, that man would still be alive.*

Her gaze skipped over the Hamilton casters, settling on the hard ground in front of her.

But then, in a way, haven't I killed them all?

The Hamilton strike force came to rescue her and get the stone. And her stupid idea to call up her primal magic had blown the op. After she'd been captured the others had no choice but to surrender.

Still, there had to be a way out, right? Rules for when things went bad? No one had ever attacked her home before, but she'd heard stories of ops gone sideways. Well, maybe not as bad as this, but...the Game had Rules, and the Rules covered how to treat prisoners. Ransom them back, treat them with respect. If the Makrises wanted their prisoners to be cared for in the future, they'd have to follow the Rules.

She nudged Victor with her elbow. "Got a plan?" she whispered.

"Working on it. Keep quiet, and don't provoke anybody. Think you can manage that?"

"I—"

The Makris enforcers came to attention. Kristof pushed off the wall, and Dmitri's head whipped around to stare at the entrance to the Makris house. Kristof's father stalked out, bodyguards walking a few steps in front. His blue suit had a long, dark stain across the jacket. He took it off and handed it to a servant, who gave him an identical, clean one.

Melina followed him a step behind, in a short white dress. Her face seemed smooth, unlined by worries, untouched by the chaos.

They stopped in front of Victor. Dmitri reached down and grabbed the back of Victor's uniform, hauling him to his feet. Kate's heart began to pound.

"How did you break our security?" Nico Makris asked Victor.

Victor gave a half-smile, his version of name, rank, and serial number.

"You can tell me now or later. Later you will beg to tell me how you did it."

Victor said nothing. But Kristof glanced from Victor to Dylan. His hands ran through Victor's talisman chains. His gaze settled back on Victor, then he straightened and shoved the chains into his pocket. His eyes held that look of Kristof's—that calculating, "I'm plotting something" look.

He *knew*. Kristof knew how Victor had gotten through the grid. Or he thought he did. But why wasn't he saying anything to his father?

Victor still wasn't talking. Kristof's father gave a dramatic sigh.

"So be it. After a few hours in the Pit, perhaps you'll be more forthcoming. But we have a few other matters to settle." He held his hand out, and his servant gave him a cell phone, the connection already established.

"Ah, Cooper. Thought you should know I have your people. You aren't getting them back."

The bitter taste of adrenaline flooded Kate's mouth. She strained to make out her father's rapid-fire words across the phone line.

"You speak to me of Rules?" Makris said. "*Rules*? You broke the truce. You sent a strike team into my home. My home! And you have the audacity to talk to me about Rules. I make the Rules now."

More muffled words from her father. Nico Makris's face got redder, and his hand on the phone went rigid. Kristof stepped forward, mouth open to speak, hand reaching for his father's shoulder. But Melina leaned in, gently pushed the phone away from her father's ear, and whispered to him. The redness paled back to pink, a toothy smile curved his lips, and his eyes gleamed in the light of the still-burning fire.

He spoke into the phone. "Shut up. You broke the truce. You will pay the consequences. I don't care about the Rules, I don't give a fuck-all about DiOrsini and his so-called oversight. You will pay for this. You will pay."

The cold seeping into Kate's bones from the tile floor was nothing compared to the ice in Nico Makris's voice.

"Come here, tomorrow at noon, alone. I want you to witness the execution of two of your people, in exchange for the one of mine your daughter killed. Victor Cole and..." His eyes went down the line of Hamilton operatives. "Your primal magic specialist. Dylan

Pearce. You won't be needing him anymore."

Dylan went still beside her. He swallowed. Victor didn't react at all.

More words from her father. Then Nico Makris's response: "Well, of course, you would be a fool not to come. A fool with a dead daughter. Kate will join them if you don't show. Remember: noon, alone." He hung up.

Kristof opened the cell door and led Kate inside the small concrete room. The cell looked clean, but the smells hit her before she crossed the threshold: the stink of urine and vomit, the faint odor of dead animals and decaying vegetables. No amount of scrubbing could eradicate the stench of despair. Kristof stepped in with her and closed the door behind him, dismissing the guards who had accompanied them. He traced out a cloak spell, its violet mists settling around them.

Kate studied his face. Back at the plaza, Kristof had followed the interplay between his sister and his father, intent on what they said and did. His eyes had flared when his father pronounced his sentence of execution on Kate.

But Kristof hadn't stopped his sister from whispering her suggestions in their father's ear. Hadn't said a thing to stop his father from ordering Victor's and Dylan's executions. Hadn't said or done anything to save her.

Afterward, he'd followed his father's order to take her to a cell while Dmitri took Victor to the Pit. And the whole way here, he'd been in his own little world, silent and brooding.

Maybe Victor could break free. Maybe not. They'd have people guarding him—Dmitri, their enforcers. And they had so little time. Twelve hours, maybe less, before the deadline arrived and her father showed up…

Or not.

She'd have to try something. And with the primal magic determined to defy her control, Kristof was her only hope.

She sat on the spare cot against the wall, hands still secured behind her back. Kristof leaned against the cell wall, his eyes somewhere far away.

"Can you at least let me move my arms?" She shrugged her taut shoulders. "Where am I going to go?"

Kristof pushed off the wall and reached for her. The brush of his hand against her brought a shiver to her skin. Heat rose in her cheeks. She flinched back as he touched her cuffs. They disconnected from each other at a word from him.

"Better?" he asked.

"A little." She leaned forward and circled her shoulders, restoring some of the impeded circulation. Pins and needles rushed into her arms, and she winced.

"Sorry." He sat next to her. Close. Too close. The sea breeze scent of his skin mingling with the sharp, coppery tang of blood from the cut on his shoulder filled her senses. The solid presence of his body next to her felt comforting and familiar. But his eyes were shuttered behind his dark lashes, his mind analyzing, strategizing, playing the Game.

"Are you going to let your father kill me?"

He looked away from her.

"Are you? Is that the kind of man you are?"

He shot to his feet and stalked away. "Events are spinning out of control. Melina—"

"You're the heir, right? Doesn't your father listen to you?"

He laughed a bitter laugh and turned to her. "Maybe it works that way in your family. Not here."

She'd seen who had the influence in the Makris family. The one who whispered in her Papa's ear.

"You said you had a plan."

"Between my family and yours, it's pretty much shot to hell right now."

"Why didn't you let me go? You had the chance, you could have—"

"Yes. I could. But if I had, my father would have known I'd betrayed him. One betrayal too many. I would have been left without the means to fight him. I'd prefer a plan that leaves us both free, not one of us dead."

Kate peered up at him. She couldn't tell whether he was lying or not. But then, when had she ever known his thoughts? "So what now?"

"I...don't know yet. Either your father shows up tomorrow and my father executes Victor and Dylan or he doesn't, and..."

"And you're okay with that?"

He looked at her, his eyes a desolate wasteland. He turned and walked out the door, slamming it behind him. The lock clicked with a finality that almost stopped her heart.

Kristof opened the door to the Pit and stepped inside. He walked down the narrow staircase, watching his steps in the glow of the dusky gems lining the black walls. He felt like one of his father's fishing boats that had lost its moorings, rudderless and adrift. He fingered the long silver chains he'd taken from Victor. One of them provided the key to the Hamilton's ability to clone Dmitri's aura and slip through the grid. They might provide the key to much more. He shoved them in his pocket. What he needed was a plan.

Victor hung in midair, upside down from the center of the room, inside the circle stones. His eyes were half open, chest rising and falling slowly. A single drop of blood fell from his clenched hand to the black floor.

Dmitri leaned against the wall, arms crossed. Melina stood beside him, a hand on his shoulder. She let it trail down his arm and leaned in close to whisper something in his ear.

Melina and...Dmitri? A vague discomfort arose from the depths of Kristof's gut. He'd told Melina he'd back her. A lie, but she didn't know that.

"We need to talk," he said to Melina. "Now. Outside."

Melina let go of Dmitri and walked up the stairs to join Kristof. A brief flicker of her eyes in the dim light betrayed nothing of her intentions.

Dmitri posed another problem. Dmitri couldn't be allowed to find out how Victor had cracked the security grid. Not while Kristof might have his own uses for that information.

He knew just the words to achieve his goal. "Dmitri."

His cousin's head snapped up toward him. "What?"

"Go easy on Victor. I don't want your usual over...*enthusiasm* wrecking Papa's show tomorrow. We need him presentable."

"I know how to run the Pit. Aren't you still feeling the result?" He shot a hand out and green lightning hit Victor in the back, shaking his body back and forth until something cracked. Red spittle flew from Victor's mouth, and his eyes rolled back in his head. His limp body swung above the circle stones, around and around, until it gradually came to a stop.

"Shit. Out cold." Dmitri stalked to Victor and hit him, a sharp slap meant to wake him. Nothing.

Kristof hid a smile. With spells like those, Victor wouldn't be providing Dmitri with information anytime soon. It wasn't like Victor wouldn't have done the same thing, in his place. Besides, Victor could take the punishment. After all, Kristof had, time after time.

He opened the door for Melina and stepped outside. The night was quiet, with the sharp wind from the sea calming down to a gentle breeze that brought the scent of fig and apple blossoms wafting by. Cicadas buzzed as they walked up the stone path toward the courtyard behind the estate.

Kristof reached out to stop Melina before she walked through the vine-covered pergola. He pulled her over to a small wooden bench and sat her down hard, crushing the apple blossoms that lay on it. "So. What the hell are you doing?"

She turned to face him, her eyes hooded. She tapped out a cloak spell, and when its purple light had settled around them, she said, "What do you think?" She frowned, then smoothed her face out in an effort to control the backlash from the spell. "Going ahead with our plan."

"Tell me how executing Dylan, Victor, *and* Kate has anything to do with using the stone and overthrowing Papa."

"I told you to leave the stone to me. Your job is to deal with the Hamiltons and keep Papa's attention away from the stone. Focus on that."

"I can't if you keep interfering. What does luring Cooper Hamilton here have to do with our plan?"

"He won't come. No clan leader has ever come into another leader's stronghold. Alone. Unarmed. And when he doesn't show, we can kill Kate without Papa suspecting why."

The warm night air turned cold against his skin. "How do you plan to do that?"

"You'll have to trust me on that one, brother dear. Do you want to run this family or not?"

"Yes. You know that."

"What are you willing to sacrifice? Is sitting in Papa's chair worth a few Hamilton lives or not?"

He pictured Kate's hair lying on the pillow next to him, smelled the rose-petal scent of her perfume, remembered the soft feel of her skin.

Depends on the Hamilton.

If you want to save her, you need to concentrate, he told himself.

"How are you going to kill her?" he asked. "Are you going to use Victor's and Dylan's deaths to power the stone?"

She put a finger to his lips. "Be ready to move against Papa when I give the word and make sure the Hamiltons don't interfere. You'll leave the stone to me, yes?"

He nodded, watching her eyes. Where the hell was the sister he'd played with for hours on the beach as a child? The one who'd hidden him in her closet when his father had his rages, who'd held him tight when their mother passed? He didn't see that girl in Melina's eyes. The ambition that shone like a hard beacon he understood all too well. But when had the little girl in the pink jumper and the happy green eyes disappeared so completely?

"Good," she said. "I have a lot to do before tomorrow. So do you. Make your preparations, and stay away from the Hamilton girl." She rose, her dress swirling around her, and shut off the cloak spell.

He let her go. When she disappeared from sight over the crest of the hill, he pulled Victor's silver chains from his pocket. Kate's pearl buttons fell to the ground. He picked them up and smoothed them over in his hand. He tucked them back in his pocket where they would be safe.

He focused his magesight on Victor's silver chains. He peeled away and put back the lightning-bolt talisman, glowing with the green power of the spell, then the kinetic-punch chain, then the fire talisman, and the others he could identify until there was only one left. It shone with a purple iridescence that sparkled under the moonlight.

Piece by piece, a plan formed in his mind. He'd have to keep this one loose and limber. No battle plan survived contact with the enemy, and he had a lot of enemies.

Maybe he could level the playing field a bit.

He took out his phone and searched his contacts. Time to bring in an asset.

But first things first. He couldn't just walk his asset past Anton, who was watching the grid as his backup, or his father's eagle eyes.

He needed another way to sneak his ally through the grid in time for tomorrow's deadline.

He put the chain, still shimmering with a faint purple glow, in his pocket, next to Victor's lockpick. He got up and strode toward the prison cells.

Kate finished picking at the stewed greens and rice in the wooden bowl in her lap. If this was her last meal, it sucked.

She threw the spoon in the bowl and tossed it on the floor. The *clang* echoed across the small cell. What was the point of eating anything? In a few hours—best case—Victor and Dylan would be dead. Worst case, she would be joining them.

And everything would be her fault.

If she'd refused to take the stone from Brian, it wouldn't have possessed her. Brian would still be alive. She wouldn't have this horrible…power inside her. Wouldn't have sneaked out to seek comfort from Kris. Damn, from *Kristof.* Wouldn't have taken the conch shell from him, letting Dmitri through their security spells. She wouldn't be a prisoner. And Victor and Dylan wouldn't have to pay for her mistakes with their lives.

So what was she going to do about it?

She stared down at the spellcuffs around her hands, the wrappings so tight they raised red welts against the skin of her fingers. Even if she could get the damned things off again, the darkness inside her would only try to eat her up. Her heart sank.

Across the cell, a line of the red ants attacked the last remnants of greens and rice, marching in the bowl to efficiently devour the food. A black bug with huge pincers on its head darted in to rip a piece of spinach away, then another joined it, then another.

There was still a chance that Victor could escape and get her and the rest of the Hamilton team home. Yeah, right. She'd heard of the Pit—the torture Sanctum of the Makrises. She should be the one trying to free Victor, not the other way around.

And she couldn't count on Kristof for help. He'd said he had less power than she thought. Tears welled up and spilled down her cheeks to land in a wet puddle on the scratchy blanket of the cot. She wiped them away.

Screw him. He had his own agenda—one that had nothing to do with her. Kate curled up on the small cot, hands tucked into her sides. But there had been that deep yearning in his eyes right before he'd left her cell, the same connection their eyes made at the beach yesterday, the look that told her heart that there had been more between them than operational necessity.

But if he didn't act on his feelings, then his love might as well be ash.

The light glaring from the bare bulb would have made it difficult to sleep, even if the threat of death wasn't hanging over her head. But who was she kidding? Dad would get them all out. Dad always won. Always. He had to.

But what if he didn't?

Oh, he would come, sure. Or pull some other rabbit out of his hat. But what if Dad's scheme didn't succeed? What if his plan ended in the spectacular failure of the last one?

A column of ants broke off from the main line and swarmed the pincer bugs, pulling them from the greens. They tore the pincer bugs apart, piece by piece, until nothing was left but one twitching mandible.

She had to come up with an idea. Something that would give them an ace in the hole.

The spell. The white light Melina, and Victor, had cast. The same spell Brian had cast in the Sanctum when he'd tried to save himself. Dylan told her Brian had cast a counterspell—one aimed at stopping primal magic.

She stretched out her hand. The spellcuffs would prevent her from actually casting, but she could go over the spell in her mind—try to remember the symbol, the chant.

Better get started. It wasn't like she was going to get any sleep.

Chapter Twenty-Seven

Kate had seen the north side of the Makris estate once before, in grainy photos smuggled out by Hamilton agents. Grayson had shown her photos of the entire estate in his briefing, before Brian's funeral. She remembered the pictures. Craggy rocks set in a cliff above a narrow expanse of pebble-and-seaweed-strewn beach, a small quay for boats to tie up, a narrow staircase leading to the whitewashed estate house at the top, ringed with groves of apple and fig trees. Not very welcoming, but that wasn't the point.

The next day, as she knelt in a broad circle of turquoise stones on a rocky ledge just up from the beach, nothing about the place had the distant feel of a photograph anymore. The wind whipping the strands of her dirty hair around her face, the sand grinding into her cramped legs, and the stink of dead sea creatures rotting in one of the tide pools behind her told her that everything was real.

She was here. About to die.

Sunlight glinted off the water. The line of boats bobbed up and down on the quay, their sails flapping lightly in the breeze. Everything on the other side of the Makrises' security grid had a hazy, unreal look to it, as if Kate were viewing the scene from behind a painted veil. She blinked, and her vision cleared. Another sunny day on the Aegean.

Victor knelt beside her, hands cuffed behind his back like hers were. She couldn't see any open wounds, and the welt around his neck had been healed. Blood flecked his uniform—much more than yesterday. Deep lines carved tracks on his face—evidence of suffering so bad she shied away from thinking about it. His eyes were half shut, his jaw tight.

Victor didn't have a way out. Victor could hardly breathe.

Dylan knelt on her other side, eyes blinking against the sun, sweat dripping down into the collar of his sand-stained uniform. His foot tapped against the rocky ground, a nervous twitch of anticipation.

Kristof stood outside the circle, rigid as a tuning fork, eyes focused on the quay. Probably waiting on her dad.

Look at me, damn you. Look at me. Do *something.*

But he hadn't met her eyes since the guards had brought her out here a few minutes earlier. Hadn't spoken to her. Hadn't done anything more than exchange a few words with Dmitri, lounging on the rocks. He'd done nothing but stare at the quay and fiddle with something in his pocket. If he had a plan, she couldn't tell.

Melina had her hair pulled back in a twist and the sun reflected off her white linen suit as she stepped inside the circle stones. The servant girl from Kate's room trailed her, holding a small black bag.

Melina walked around Kate and set the bag down on a flat-topped rock tall enough to be used as a table. The bag pulled at Kate with a dark intensity, willing her to come closer.

The Pandora Stone.

Melina had brought the stone inside the circle.

Shit, oh shit.

Melina's eyes scrunched up, and the circle stones lit with an inner fire. A fine violet shimmer—the energy barrier—rose from the circle in a sphere that surrounded Kate, Victor, Dylan, Melina, and her servant.

So much for help from Kristof. Now nothing and no one could get in to interfere with whatever Melina had planned.

Melina took out the red silk bag Kate had seen in her Sanctum and set it on the rock next to the black one. Even through the fabric Kate felt the bowl inside reach out to her, a gentle tug of power.

The sun neared its zenith and still no sign of Dad. Sweat itched at the silver bindings of her hands and at the collar of her shirt. How much time remained?

Footsteps sounded from above. She peered behind her. Nico Makris lumbered down the walkway from the estate, one heavy leg at a time, his bodyguards hovering before and behind him. He sat in the stout wooden chair that had been set out for him on the beach, facing the quay. A servant poured him a glass of wine.

He sipped. And waited.

The sun rose higher. It gleamed into Kate's eyes from the water, causing her to squint in pain. Her knees hurt with a fierce ache now, as if all the weight of the world was driving down between her shoulder blades, straight down her body, and through her knees into the hot granite ground on which she knelt.

Come on. Come on. Where's Dad?

Victor shifted next to her. "How much time?"

"I don't—" Kate began.

"You have about seven more minutes of life, " Melina broke in. She opened the red silk bag and pulled out the bowl, black now like the stone from whatever Melina had done to activate it in the Sanctum.

The bowl whispered to Kate with a voice like a thousand rats chittering through a mile-deep cavern.

Dylan's eyes widened.

"What is that?" she whispered.

"The Chaos Bowl," Dylan said. "A primal magic artifact. I'd heard the Makrises had it."

She remembered what he'd told her about primal magic artifacts—using the spells contained in one required a sacrifice. Just like her magic. Making a primal magic artifact the perfect executioner's axe.

"Is that what she's going to use to…"

Dylan nodded. "It can drain the life force from a person. Using it is illegal. But so's their whole operation, and that isn't giving them pause."

Seven minutes. Just seven minutes and she would know Melina's intentions. But by then it would be too late.

Kate watched Kristof pace across the sand. If he had a plan, he'd better make it happen now. Forget pretending to be her boyfriend— did he really think she'd ever forgive him for letting Victor die? For murdering Dylan? Either he was the greatest actor in the world or there was a man inside trying hard to get out and stand up for himself. Which one was it?

Her eyes jerked back to Dylan. A subtle purple glow glinted at the corner of his spellcuffs. A tendril of purple light crept into the green gem with a tiny finger of power. His eyes scrunched up with pain.

Melina strode over to Dylan and seized his head in her grip. Red fire shot from her hands into the back of Dylan's head. The acrid smell of sulphur filled the air. He stiffened, then slumped.

"Don't try that again."

She returned to the rock outcropping.

Kate pulled against the spellcuffs, her hands slippery with sweat. The edges bit deeper into her already-tortured flesh, and she winced. How much time remained? Five minutes? Three? Oh God, what the hell could she do to free them?

She glanced back at the dark bowl sitting on top of the rock. Only one thing to do. Reach inside and dig up that dark power inside. Touch it once more. Ignore the inevitable backlash from the spellcuffs and tell it to free her, free Victor and Dylan.

Now. She needed to make her move right—

Melina put her hand above the black bowl. "Time's up. Too bad about your father, Kate. Apparently he's like everyone else: loves himself a little more than you."

Kate went still. Nico Makris rose, a gleam of anticipation in his eyes. Kristof, eyes intent on Kate, took a step toward the circle, then another. His hand reached into his pocket. Melina said a single harsh word, and black energy swirled inside the bowl like a gathering storm.

A flash of opaline light whitened out the sun. The light glistened off the ocean like a shockwave traveling along the horizon, exploding where it met the beach. At the center of the light, he was there, striding down the quay as if hovering on the surface of the calm ocean.

Dad.

Chapter Twenty-Eight

The sunlight haloed his black hair. His navy suit jacket swayed gently as he strode toward the beach, eyes glancing from Victor to Dylan and then settling on Kate. She read everything in those eyes, everything she'd wanted to see and know and hear for so long. *I'm here. Don't worry. I'll save you.*

Her hands shook, and her lips trembled. A tear spilled over from her eye. *Thank God, thank God.*

Behind her, Melina's hand stroked the top of the bowl, almost as if she were containing the black energy still swirling inside. Her eyes were dark and filled with tempests.

Her father stopped at the end of the quay—the barrier where the security grid hit the beach. Arms crossed, he waited. "You asked me to come alone and unarmed. I'm here. Give me my people back."

"Kate, perhaps. The others have forfeited their lives," Nico Makris said.

"We'll see."

Makris motioned to Kristof, who went to the barrier and tapped out a spell. A beam of purple light sailed through, scanning her dad from his windblown hair to his Italian leather shoes. Kristof squinted. He appeared to hesitate for a moment, then turned and nodded to his father.

"Let him through." Makris waved his acquiescence as if welcoming an enemy leader to the execution of his own people was routine.

Kristof passed his hand down the barrier, and the shimmer in the air grew lighter. Kate's father stepped across, his form wavering for a second as he passed through the security grid. He paused, his gaze remaining for a moment on Dmitri, standing with the guards surrounding the circle, then on Kristof. He walked with her father in the wet sand to where Makris stood waiting.

"You cut the timing close. I was beginning to think you did not love your daughter," Makris said, motioning her father to take the seat next to him.

Her father didn't move. "I told you not to hurt Kate." His eyes flicked to Dylan, then Victor, lingering on his neck and chest. "Or any of my people."

"You are in no position to make demands. You—"

"I'm here to make you an offer. Do you want to listen?"

Nico Makris stared into his rival's face. "I could kill you. You could do nothing to stop me."

"Perhaps. But remember the story of the last time one clan leader assassinated another? Nothing brings the families together like closing ranks against a rule-breaker of such magnitude."

"Hmm…point."

"Papa, the time for negotiation is over." Melina took a step out from behind her rock altar. "He has nothing to offer us. We need to proceed with the execution."

Kristof studied Melina, then turned to his father. "I think you should hear what Hamilton has to say."

"Why?"

"The Rules exist for a reason. You taught me that, a long time ago. We break them more than most, maybe, but a few of them have to stand. If they don't, like Hamilton says, what separates us from the rogues?"

Melina shot Kristof a glare.

Nico Makris looked from his daughter to his son and then said: "Very well, Cooper. What do you offer for your people?"

Her father sat next to his rival and began to talk. He started small. Noninterference in the matter of who ruled Rome. That wasn't large enough for Nico Makris. Then came bigger concessions. Handing over control of a small town, long fought over, in the Golan Heights. Makris salivated for a moment, then refused.

Dad leaned back and steepled his hands. "Why are you charging such a hard bargain? Victor and Dylan aren't worth anything to you."

"They came here. They broke through my security, wrecked my estate. They should pay."

"Don't you think they have? Look at Victor. What I did might have been illegal, sending them here, but what you did to him was worse."

"Perhaps." Makris shrugged. "The matter remains. What are they worth to you?"

Her father leaned forward. "London. Free and clear. No more fighting, no more backstabbing. You can have it."

Victor groaned. "I'm not worth that," he muttered.

Dylan's eyes closed. Kate could imagine how he felt about the Makrises getting his family's old territory to save his life.

"Tempting, but no. You have yet to offer me anything I can't take for myself. Eventually."

Kate started. He refused? Refused *London*? What kind of a game was Makris playing?

Her father didn't seem surprised. He studied Makris, then Melina, the wind whipping little strands of brown hair around her forehead. He held her gaze just long enough to make her lower her eyes, then turned back to Makris.

"All right. Let's change the terms of the negotiation. I want all my people back, unharmed. Dylan and Victor, unharmed. Kate, the same. And the Pandora Stone."

"Hah! You don't want much. And what will you give me for your people and this treasure?"

"Your arsenal back. All the artifacts my grandfather stole from your grandfather Arkady, those long years past. The Chronos Dagger, the Pearls of Remembrance, Xue's Dream Needles, all of them." He reached into his jacket, his hand moving slowly. Makris's bodyguards took a step toward him. He brought out the amulet Kate had seen hanging in his office all her life: Arkady Makris's amulet.

"In exchange for my people and the stone—the pride of the Makris Family, restored."

Kristof's head jerked up. Here it was. His opportunity.

His father stared at Hamilton, his eyes blank. Then, "You are serious? Everything, all our artifacts, for one little stone?"

"And my people."

"You know what I could do with those artifacts. What I *would* do."

"Maybe. But the Rules are still the Rules. Try it and every family will turn against you."

His father stood and paced. "It might not matter if they did."

"Papa—" Melina began.

"Shush."

"No. Papa, that's not what we discussed. I need the prisoners. I need—" Melina said.

His father cut her off with a sharp slash of his hand, then turned to Hamilton. "How do you propose making the trade?"

"The artifacts are packed and ready to go. Grayson is prepared to deliver them here on my command. Provided you hold up your end."

His father stroked his chin. He stared at Hamilton for a long moment, then Melina. He had to take to deal. Once Kate was free, Kristof could use his father's bad decision against him with the Synedrion. Undermine his authority, weaken his leadership. Secure his own position as heir and oust his father the old-fashioned way. Without the stone.

Which is why he had to speak against Hamilton's proposal, cement his position with the Synedrion. *Maybe we can all walk away from this standoff.*

"Papa," Kristof said. "This is a bad deal. If the Hamiltons have the stone, and Kate, our old arsenal doesn't matter. They can still—"

"No. I want my artifacts back. Melina, put away your weapon. Today there will be no killing."

Well, his opposition to the deal had its predictable effect on his father. Kristof's hand eased in his pocket. He slid it away from his cell phone.

Kate's shoulders relaxed. Victor's head slumped a bit, and the tension in Dylan's eyes lessened.

"No." Melina said the word with a finality that echoed off the cliffside rocks of his family home. "No, today is a perfect day to die."

She brought her hand off the top of the bowl, and its dark energy lashed out straight for Kate.

Chapter Twenty-Nine

The ancient energy of the bowl called to Kate—an awful, screeching sound that raced straight for her, trying to pull her down inside its deep, dark roundness where nothing, not even light, escaped.

The spell, the white light. I need to try the spell. If it worked on primal magic, it would work on the bowl.

She chanted the words, the same ones Brian had muttered in the dimness of the Sanctum last week, stumbling over the unfamiliar pronunciation. She traced the symbol—a triangle with an indentation halfway into the longest side, like a ginkgo leaf. But the image, the one in her mind...what should it be? She had no idea.

Light. She held on to light—a vast white sheet of it, filling her mind as she focused on the ginkgo-leaf pattern, chanted the words she'd heard Brian speak, and felt the burning pain of defiance begin in her spellcuffed hands.

This is going to hurt.

All around her chaos had busted loose.

"Kate!" Kristof faced the circle stones, hands glowing green, about to cast at the shimmering screen trapping her Then Dmitri barred his way, a lightning bolt launching from outstretched hands. The bolt hit Kristof with a crash, and he flew back onto the sand.

The energy barrier stayed up.

Victor struggled with his bonds, his fingers working the lockpick talisman he'd somehow gotten hold of, his face scrunched in pain. Purple energy pulsed through Dylan's spellcuffs, his body twisted in agony as Melina sent spell after spell into him.

Dad was surrounded by Makris's guards as Nico backed away, shield glowing blue around him. Her dad fought his way toward her, fingers crackling with crimson energy as he threw bolt after bolt at Nico's men.

Concentrate. Make the light brighter. Come on, come on.

The light flared, the darkness receded. And pain overwhelmed her. It ate into her hands, burning the nerve endings like acid. She screamed, over and over, her voice trailing into hoarseness.

Victor's spellcuffs clicked open. Kristof smashed Dmitri into the energy barrier with a crash of lightning. He focused on the circle stones, willing them to drop their barrier, and the glowing energy faded. Dylan tumbled out of the circle. Victor grabbed for Kate, only to be thrown back into the sand by the rippling energy of a kinetic punch cast by Melina. She focused for a moment, eyes going blank, and the energy barrier came back up.

Kate kept pouring light into the bowl's darkness. The pain tore into her hands until her eyes rolled back in her head. Finally the darkness crept away, searching inside the circle until it found new prey. Melina's servant gasped and fell to the ground.

No, oh no. That's not what I wanted to ...

"Who taught you how to cast that spell? My brother?" Melina said.

"No, *my* brother," Kate answered.

Melina had the stone, still in its silk covering, in her hand. The call went off full blast: *Touch me, touch me now.*

Kate stumbled to her feet. *If I can get the stone, touch it ... Melina's story about possession was a lie. She had me in the circle to kill me, the Null here to transform into a primal magic caster.* She reached for the stone.

"Oh no. The Pandora Stone's not for a Null like you." Melina removed the silk covering from the stone and clasped it between her bare hands.

A jolt like a killer earthquake went through Kate. Then a giant hand grabbed her heart and squeezed, hard. She gasped and fell to her knees, weak and shaking. The stone glowed green in Melina's hands, its call diminished to a whisper. The stone had found a new muse.

"You want the damn thing, take it," Kate said.

"It isn't that simple," Melina said. "Before I can use it, it needs to let go of you."

"*You* use it? You can't, you're not a Null."

Melina laughed. "I lied. It works much better on a caster than a Null."

Melina held her hand over the stone and muttered a harsh, guttural word, one Kate didn't recognize. Darkness rose up from the artifact and swirled around Melina's hands. The spells embedded in the stone swirled with viridescent energy. They rose, flickering. As Melina concentrated, the spells swirling around the stone went off, one by one, like bubbles bursting in the air. The magic reached for Melina and swathed her in a gleaming green glow. Melina fell to the rocky ground and screamed as the stone's energy cascaded around her and shot into her body. Exactly as it had Kate's, back home in her family's Sanctum.

No. This couldn't be happening. It had taken the stone hours, *days* to prepare Kate for the change. Melina hadn't gone through that whole programming thing...

But Melina wasn't a Null.

Kate knew what would happen as soon as the stone finished. It would reach out and find a sacrifice. And she was the only person left in the circle.

The stone's green-black energy crawled over Melina. Her body writhed in agony. Tendrils of dark emerald power shot through her skin and into her body as the magic changed her.

Outside the circle stones, Dylan had gotten free of his spellcuffs and smashed them into the bloody face of a Makris guard. Nico Makris lunged toward Kate's dad. Victor aimed a kinetic blast at Kristof's father, and a shower of sparks flew as Makris's personal shield dissolved. One of his bodyguards sent a cascade of ice into Victor's stomach, and he tumbled across the beach and slammed into the jagged rocks leading to the estate. And her father, blue shield blazing, dogged by a ring of Makris enforcers, strode across the sand toward Kate, step by slow step.

Kristof, standing at the circle stones, rose from Dmitri's groggy form. His eyes narrowed as he concentrated on the shimmering field shooting up from the circle stones. The barrier flickered but stayed up.

The stone's power sparkled rapidly across Melina's body then coalesced into a green-and-black ball of energy that blazed above her. Kate felt it search for its price. It considered her with a cool regard.

One way to stop it. Maybe.

The stone lay in Melina's hand, burning with green energy like the heart of a nuclear reactor. Lying there, waiting for her to touch it.

She struggled to her feet and threw herself toward Melina just as the stone's malevolence was poised to strike her.

It hit her with a whoosh of power. The energy sank into her body, trying to consume her soul, turn the light in her into darkness. Her sight dimmed, her hearing faded. The blood seemed to slow in her veins, shutting down like the rest of her body.

She stretched her hand out. An inch, maybe less, and she'd have the stone in her grasp. Almost there, *almost...*

Her hand fell. No energy left to fuel it.

Melina stumbled to her feet. Kate heard her laugh, a distant sound like a mockingbird.

Kate was dying, like Brian. Just like Brian...

"No!" Kristof yelled, and the subtle hum of the barrier ceased as it dropped. Footsteps rang on the rocky ground, then he bent down at her side, another spell already shimmering on his hands.

The energy let her go. Kate could see again, feel again. It lifted away from her and swirled to a target it liked even better. Kristof.

No, no... I have to do something. Stop it.

Kate felt the life returning to her body, but slowly, too slowly.

Melina closed her eyes. The stone's energy turned from Kristof and shot out of the circle stones to where she directed it. Under Melina's control the primal magic became a sharp, sleek hunter focused on the kill.

The energy cleaved through Kate's father's shield as if it were made of water. The dark energy whipped around his arms, his legs, his torso. As Kate watched, helpless, he tried the same counterspell she'd used, the same one Brian had tried. The light poured out of him, brightening his dark hair with the power of its magic.

Yes. That would do it. Even the stone couldn't hurt Dad. Even the...

Light and darkness met in a cataclysmic explosion that turned the sand into glass for a three-foot radius around her father. The sound echoed back to the circle in a whip of power, cracking against the stone held in Melina's hand and throwing her against the wind-worn cliffside.

When Kate's vision cleared, she slumped to the rocky ground, a wail rising from deep inside.

Her father lay still, eyes open and staring at the blue sky, the wind ruffling his hair.

Melina struggled to her feet, the powdered pieces of the Pandora Stone shifting through her fingers to fall to the ground. "Well, that was interesting."

Kristof took in the scene: the stone crushed to pieces, Hamilton's still body lying on the wet sand, Kate's devastated eyes, his sister's calculating gaze. His father hovered behind his bodyguards, one foot on the step leading to the estate house.

Alive.

He closed the few paces it took to reach Melina. "What the hell did you do? Hamilton wasn't the target."

"No. He was a harder one. We'd never get another chance at Hamilton. I can take down Papa anytime now." Her smile had a hard edge to it. "With or without your help."

"Now that you have Dmitri's?"

"If you won't cooperate, he will. Step away from Kate."

"Why? Don't you have what you want from her?"

"With the stone gone, she's the only person who can challenge my power. She can't be allowed to live."

Kate, head in hands, sat still behind him.

"No. Take out Papa. Leave Kate alone," he said.

"You seem to believe you're in charge here, brother dear. You're not." Melina's eyes went dark. She drew in a breath, and her arms stiffened. Her aura rippled, morphing from rainbow caster hues to a deep-green shot through with black. She turned to Kate and raised her hands.

He pulled out his cell phone and spoke. "Target Melina. Now."

At the top of the cliff, tucked behind an outcropping, Brooke stood, bangles glinting in the sun. Victor's silver chain glowed purple around her neck, Dylan's talisman-lined jacket gripped tight in her hand. She fired three blades of red kinetic energy down from her position. They hit Melina in the back, slicing through her white suit and splashing her blood across the hot rocky beach.

As Melina dropped to the ground, stunned, Kristof turned and scooped up Kate in his arms. Touching her spellcuffs, he spoke the word to release them. He leaped over the circle stones and onto the beach. Only a few minutes before Melina recovered from Brooke's attack, healed herself, and came after them. He had a only a few minutes to get Kate to safety.

Victor and Dylan were still fighting Dmitri and the remaining guards. Kristof was tapping out a teleport spell as the chant left his lips.

Kate's fist slammed against his jaw with a painful crunch. "Let me down. Now."

"I have to get you out of here—"

"I'll get myself out. Somehow."

The despair in her voice broke his heart. She squirmed out of his arms and dropped to the ground, stumbling as her feet hit the deep sand.

"No," his father's deep voice sounded. "You won't. You've done enough damage, all of you."

Kristof spun around. His father stood braced by his bodyguards, a deep cut across his chest, a frown creasing his square jaw. "You aren't taking Hamilton's little girl anywhere, my son. I have changed the codes on the security grid. Neither you nor your sister can teleport out. Hand the girl over. Your plan is finished."

Kristof glanced up the cliff at Brooke, scrambling down the steps, then at Victor and Dylan, fighting his father's guards. At Melina, slowly getting to her feet. Back at his father, his shield torn to shreds by Victor, his bodyguards tired and bloodied.

"Maybe not, Papa."

He aimed a kinetic dagger straight at his father's heart.

Kate got to her feet and ran across the sand. Dad. She had to get to Dad.

Dodging a guard running for Kristof's father, she reached her own. She fell to the ground, reaching out a hand to touch his face. *He's hurt, like when I blasted him at home. That's all. Victor can heal him.*

But he lay still, eyes sightless, skin starting to cool.

He was gone.

She could use primal magic—bring him back. The ancient casters could do it, the legends said. She pulled open the door inside her mind and ran down the staircase.

Then she stopped. If she brought him back, who would pay the price? Victor? Kristof?

Her whole body felt rigid and cold. The beach, the fight, everything looked unreal, as though she viewed it through a haze.

Can't let myself feel anything. Not now, not here. No time. Have to get my people and get out.

In front of the stone circle, Dmitri slashed his hand in a wide arc and three pulses of kinetic force caught Victor in the midsection. Victor doubled over and flew back onto the beach, landing with a thump.

Dylan fought two of the guards, one arm limp at his side, the other desperately trying to reinforce the pale-blue flicker of his shield spell. He took a step back, then another, the rocky cliff at his back. The guards closed in.

Brooke fought her way toward Victor and Dylan, her shield flaring with every attack it absorbed. She reached Dylan and tossed him his jacket. He caught it with a wince.

What the hell is Brooke doing here? Whose side is she on?

The security grid around the island hummed distantly with a tinny whine. Somehow Victor had broken through the first time; she doubted the Makrises would let him break them out, too.

Kristof fought his own battle now: he cast spell after spell at his father while Makris's bodyguards protected their master with glowing blue shield spells.

She shook off her haze. Their escape was up to her. And what did she have? Minimal caster training. Primal magic inside her, magic that threatened to eat her alive if she so much as touched it. Magic she had no chance of controlling now that the stone had crumbled into dust.

Great. No options. *Still, just because I'm down, doesn't mean I'm out.*

She touched Dad's blue-topaz cufflinks, the talismans that worked as his personal shield. Maybe they would give her some kind of protection. Turning the clasps let her slip the cool silver jewelry from their buttonholes, her fingers brushing the backs of his hands.

He'd said just the other day that I wouldn't have to worry about what artifacts did for a long, long time.

She choked back a sob and clutched the talismans in her hand, their sharp points stabbing into her palm. Feet unsteady in the shifting sand, she struggled to stand.

"Where do you think you're going?" Melina said.

Kate twisted around. Melina stood behind her, fists clenched, her white suit spattered with blood. The blue glow of a shield spell surrounded her. Her brown hair spun in disarray, pulled from its neat twist, her eyes snapping with the light of a thousand dark spells.

Melina. All through Kate's life, casters had told her she wasn't like them. Wasn't good enough. Strong enough. Magical enough to play in their Sanctum. Now, Melina stood sneering down at her, hands dripping with her father's blood.

I'll show you just how magical I am.

She'd seen enough casters use talismans by now to put the theory she'd read into practice. Kate sent the command for shield to her father's talisman with quick mental order. A strong blue glow sprang up around her, and for a moment, she felt his arms wrapped around her again.

Melina's black-and-green aura flared, just as it had when she'd killed Dad. Her spell had cut straight through Dad's shield. It would tear this one into pieces. *If I don't try something, I'll...*

Melina sent a swirling ball of dark primal magic straight at Kate. *Dive deep, now.*

She dove. Into the jet-black depths that swelled below the surface of her thoughts, into the deep, dark ocean that teemed with antilife. Her connection to primal magic hadn't changed with the stone's destruction. The hungry darkness that awaited her felt exactly the same.

She felt the power's connection to the bowl sitting on Melina's rock altar, and through it a link to the rest of Melina's artifacts on her cliff-top Sanctum on the neighboring island. Faintly, she felt a thin draw to every primal magic artifact, everywhere on the planet, including the ones in the Makris arsenal that waited in Lost River with Grayson, waited for the word from her father that would never come.

Kate slipped into the darkness, its viscous ink coating her body and soul. She dimly felt the shock as Melina's spell ripped her shield away. It grabbed her legs and pulled her under the sand. The rough grains abraded her skin with a scouring pain. A wet, smothering weight crushed her on all sides. She couldn't breathe, couldn't see.

Her lungs seized as she tried to take a breath. No air here, no air anywhere. Just pressure, crushing pressure. She couldn't move her arms, her hands, her fingers.

I'm going to die. Right here, next to Dad.

One chance. Primal magic. No spellcuffs now, nothing to stop her.

Out, she willed. She felt herself move, a few inches at first, then fast enough that the sand fell from her like rain. Then she burst from the ground like a rocket into the sky. Air filled her lungs, and she gasped in breath after breath. She landed hard on the sand, a few yards from Melina, every muscle aching. *God, oh God. Please, please give me a minute—*

Then the primal magic spiraled out and sought the price for its spell. It reached for Dylan.

No, not Dylan. Futile to try, but she had to. Touching the power, she told it, *Melina. Take Melina.*

The power paused, considered her request. Then swept on toward Dylan, who, seeming to sense the power rushing for him, turned from the guard he fought.

Now or never, no matter the cost, I have to control the magic. Kate plunged back into the darkness.

Chapter Thirty

Kristof rolled to avoid a cascade of rocks raining down from the cliff above. Doberman One, black suit covered in blood and muddy sand—stalked up to him, a snarl twisting his face.

"Missed me, *koproskilo*." Kristof got to his feet and fired off a kinetic punch. The spell took the man in the midsection, throwing his unshielded body across the beach and sending him crashing onto the jagged tide pools of the lower rocks. He lay still, legs twisted unnaturally.

Doberman One had been the last of his foes left standing. Slinging spell after spell, he had destroyed his father's battered shield and killed Doberman Two. Now all the remained was to dig his father out of his hiding place, and finish the job.

Got to move. Before Melina...

His head snapped around to search for his sister. *Melina lied to me. She planned to make herself a primal magic caster all along,*

maybe from the first time she'd heard of the stone. What other be-
trayals is she planning?

He breathed in, then out, letting his heart rate slow to clear the
effects of the spell. He didn't need the help of spell-tweaking to be
paranoid about Melina.

He walked to the little cave where his father had taken shelter
with the body of Doberman Two. Jacket muddy with blood, a large
red slice across his stomach, his father's chest heaved in and out like
an overworked bellows. Kristof scanned the area for anyone else,
any other dangers. Nothing. Just the drip of water leaking from the
rocks above and the scuttle of a few hermit crabs looking for their
next meal.

Shield up, he knelt at his father's side. He reached down and
loosened the man's shirt collar. His father's breathing eased.

"Get it over with, my son. Do me the favor of making it quick,
the way I did for your grandfather. That's the point of having family."

Make it quick. A kinetic knife across the throat. A spike of ice in
the back of the head. The feeble pinpricks of red light in his father's
eyes seemed to beg him to make a choice.

He thought about Kate. About lying next to her on the small bed
in her little apartment in Ithaca, her feeding him fresh apples and
crumbs of cheese, and her laugh as she rehearsed lines from her latest play with him. He thought about a thousand afternoons in the
future like that one, afternoons he would probably never have.

He remembered the lessons his father had tried to teach him—
strike fast, strike hard. The way he'd beaten Dmitri into a bloody
mess after their botched mission, then provoked him into an attack

that left his cousin half-dead.

Did he want to be the man his father had raised? The one who would plunge a dagger into his own father's heart to take his place? Did he want to belong to a family that invited Kate's father here under a flag of truce, then murdered him?

He hauled his father to his feet. "Come with me."

Kate struggled as the primal magic wrapped its inky tendrils around her. She opened her mouth to scream, and darkness filled her throat. She tried to take in another breath, and the blackness sank into her lungs. She pulled against the tarry ropes, and they snapped tighter. The more she resisted, the more she was engulfed by the primal magic's shadowy doom.

Her heart went pitter-patter, like a rabbit trying frantically to escape a snare. Her breath rasped in her throat. Her vision dimmed— the form of Melina standing over her, of Dylan reaching inside his jacket for a talisman, shielding himself from the power rushing toward him with the same white light she'd used. Then everything began to fade. The sound of the battle, the gulls overhead, the waves on the shore, all muted out. The feel of the grainy sand rubbing into her skin disappeared. She couldn't even taste the blood in her mouth anymore. Blackness filled everything inside her.

The white light, the counterspell. She had to try it. It had worked before. If she could just move her fingers a little. She tapped out the ginkgo-leaf pattern to the spell and chanted the words as best she could.

The light sprang into being around her, like the sun rising after the longest night. It swept across her stiff body, pushing against the blackness. *Maybe, just maybe...* Then the darkness washed over it like an oil spill, extinguishing it completely, and she felt the magic's cool contempt, as if to say, *Oh, that thing again.*

The last bit of hope deep inside her went out like the spark of a campfire on a stormy beach. She had nothing left to try.

Kristof marched his father down the beach to where Melina stood, hands on her hips, watching Kate as she lay on the sand. Kate was curled in ball on her side, eyes closed, fists clenched, shaking.

"What did you do to her?"

"Nothing. She did it to herself. Fighting the primal magic, trying to control it. She'll kill herself. I don't have to lift a damn finger."

Kristof took a step toward Kate. Melina's eyes went hot with anger. "Oh no. You've interfered quite enough." She glanced down at their father. "Do your job. Finish him, brother dear."

"What will you do if I don't? Make Dmitri your puppet instead?"

"Maybe. At least he'll shoot from the front."

He pushed his father down to kneel on the beach. A few yards away, Dylan rolled shaking to his feet, counterspell no longer needed. Victor stood braced against the cliff, Brooke at his side, fending off a pair of his father's enforcers. Dmitri moaned at Victor's feet, hands clutching his bleeding stomach.

"Let Kate go," Kristof said. "You don't need her."

"'You?' Don't you mean 'we'?"

He looked down at his father, crawling toward the amulet Cooper Hamilton had brought as a good faith gesture, blood coloring the dark sand an even darker black. "What do you think?"

"I think someone has to teach you what family means." Melina glanced down at Kate. His sister's aura lit up with a black-green fire.

Kate's breath left her body with a soft finality. Her lungs burned, aching for one more inhale, one more beautiful whiff of air. Her blood yearned for oxygen, for the vital pulse of life. More, just a little more.

There must be something she could do. The white light Brian had used in the Sanctum had been a clue. Maybe he'd left her another.

The journal. No, no, that hadn't meant a damn thing. But in his room, when she'd been looking for clues... She'd found that copy of the *Tao te Ching*, the last thing Brian had read.

Why was she thinking of it now? It was a stupid *book*, something Grayson would assign as a way to think about magic, about power.

Yes. Maybe it was exactly that.

The passage Brian had marked... What had it said?

When two great powers clash
the one that yields
will emerge triumphant.

Brian had known what the stone did all along.

She yielded. Stopped fighting the blackness that suffocated her. Relaxed into the power and gave up.

Its insatiable hunger responded. It reached in and dragged her completely under, its ebony liquid filling her with its essence. Her heart slowed. Her pulse wound down to almost nothing. Her entire body froze. Her thoughts flowed like the dark sea itself, a thick, viscous ooze through her mind. Primal magic flowed around her and through her.

And it welcomed her.

The sea of blackness sprung into glorious life before her as all the shades of darkness revealed themselves to be shades of gray. There were depths in the depths of which she had been unaware. As she looked around at her inner landscape, she realized the power held still and quiet. Its magic no longer flowed in an unending circle above her, its waves no longer crashing on her shore. The intention she'd felt became a presence—one that paid attention to her.

Looming before her like a dark torrent, it waited for her to negotiate. For her to offer it a price, instead of her life.

Melina. Take Melina.

No. A strong no.

Before it could lash back, she made another proposal.

Kate felt outside herself for all the life that roamed the rocky seashore of the Makris family's little island. From the thousands of life-forms crawling, running, and flying around her, she made an offer.

A hundred tuna, swimming in a school offshore. It considered, and she thought that somewhere in its vastness it calculated the worth of a hundred tuna versus the effort it had taken to release her from Melina's spell holding her under the sand.

No. Too small.

She thought about what else she needed to do, thought about how Dad had negotiated. Then she made another offer, for this spell and another.

A little short, the feeling came back.

Cut me a deal. This is a long-term relationship.

Primal magic brushed Kate with a light touch of its power. Just enough to acknowledge that the deal had been made.

Kate's lungs burst open and sweet, sweet air rushed in.

Kristof's counterspell flared white against Melina's black primal magic. Inch by inch, she pushed his shield back until it barely surrounded Kate and himself, their forms overshadowed by the power of her dark art.

He had to come up with another plan. And fast. Before...

Melina's veil of darkness wiped his counterspell away like ink spilled across virgin-white paper.

His veins were on fire. Every muscle in his body popped and twisted in an agony ten times worse than any he'd suffered in the Pit. His hands clawed at the sand, looking for anything he could grab, throw at her, anything.

"What happened to you, Kristof? Why didn't you trust me to know what was good for us both?"

Through a haze of pain, Kristof saw Melina standing over him, arms outstretched, green-black fire arching down into him. The pain increased, his blood boiling in his veins, his skin combusting. In a moment there would be nothing left of him but smoking bone on the shores of the warm sea, with his sister's burning hands bearing witness.

Then, from behind him, hair blazing in the noonday sun, Kate stood and reached into the stream of power. She pushed its greenish darkness back into Melina. The power welled up and imploded, filling Melina with a verdant miasma that permeated her skin, her eyes, her hair. She screamed and screamed again, her body convulsing. Her eyes rolled back in her head, and she dropped limp on the sand.

The pain racking him ended. He could breathe. He could swallow.

The magic left Melina, searching for its price. And found it. His father tumbled to the shore, a step away from Cooper Hamilton and the amulet he wanted back so very much.

Chapter Thirty-One

Kate sat on the warm sand next to her father. She held his stiffening hand in hers, her thumb tracing the lines of his palm. She should close his eyes or something. Wasn't that what people did?

"Kate." Kristof. He was standing behind her. She felt his life force, the trillions of cells in his body that made him *him*—a side effect, she supposed, of her deal with primal magic. Kate sensed Melina's life force, as well, along with Melina's own connection to primal magic. Her spell had suppressed that connection, not killed her. *What does it say about me that I wish it had?*

"We have to talk." Kristof's voice was gentle.

Victor knelt on the other side of her father's body. His face had a cut across it, and he reached up to wipe the blood away. "Go," he growled with a glare up at Kristof. "I'll take care of him."

She tucked her father's hand against his chest and stood.

The breeze from the sea had intensified, whipping Kristof's hair around his face, framing those deep-blue eyes. His shirt was ripped across the shoulder and stained with blood, dirt, and sand. Something inside him had loosened, broken. She didn't know what, only that the tension that had tightened his shoulders and chest had disappeared and his eyes were clear.

Well, good for him.

They walked down the beach until they were a little ways away from where Victor sat vigil over her father's body, from where Dylan stood guard over Melina's unconscious, spellcuffed form. Kristof tapped out a privacy spell, and they waited until the violet shimmer settled over both of them, watching the sun sparkle over the waves.

She glanced back at the beach. Brooke argued with Victor, waving her bangle-clad arms at him. He shook his head, crossed his arms, and turned away from her. She tugged at the sleeve of his uniform like a puppy, taking the silver chain from around her neck and offering it to him.

Some of the pieces of the puzzle fell into place. "Brooke thinks she works for us. Why?"

"Long story. Not important now." His eyes drifted to the boats far out to sea.

"Isn't it? Brooke works for you. You sent her after me, after the stone. You could have taken it from me, that night at my place. All you had to do was put it in your pocket and walk out the door and everything would have been over. Why didn't you?"

He sighed. "I asked myself that more times than you know. I made all kinds of excuses—operational needs, my father not finding out—but none of those reasons really mattered."

"What did?"

"You. I didn't want things to end. With you."

The waves crashed on the shore as she processed what he'd said.

Then, "I'm sorry. About Brooke, the stone, Dmitri, bringing you here, your father... I can't tell you how much." He fell silent, staring out at the sea. "If I could change what happened..."

A painful, dry chuckle erupted from deep inside her. "Who are you trying to fool? You wouldn't change anything. You have exactly what you want. Your father dead. Control of the Makris family. Your sister under your thumb."

"What if that's not what I want?" He brushed a strand of hair from her face. The touch of his hand on her cheek made her breath catch.

"Don't." She stepped back.

"What if I could throw all this away? Running the family, dealing with Melina, Dmitri, all of it? What if you and I could be together, no politics, no families...just us?"

She searched his face and recognized the deep yearning in his eyes for everything he'd said. The life they'd led at college, built on a foundation of lies—only this time it would be built on truth.

"Kristof..." She leaned into his arms and held him, her head resting on his bloody shirt. He bent down and kissed her, and he tasted like the ocean and lost nights in Ithaca. Her pulse jumped as he stroked the soft place under her ear.

"You can't walk away from your family. They'll come after you."

"Maybe. But after today they'll have other things to deal with. Melina. Choosing a leader. Chasing down the heir gone rogue won't be the highest priority."

She searched his face, looking for the cocky young operative, the secret agent who could run a hundred scenarios through his head in an instant. He had vanished in the flare of a teleport spell. Kristof's face had softened, and a touch of Kris's ease had entered his eyes.

"I can't make any promises," she said. "I don't know if..."

"Can we try? Just Kate and Kristof. No lies, no secrets, no families?"

She stood still for a long moment. So many dead, on both sides. So many betrayals. Then she thought about what he'd done on the beach—standing against his sister, providing Victor with the lockpick so he could free himself, using Brooke as a distraction. Protecting Kate from Melina long enough for her to make a deal with the primal magic insider her. Did those actions make up for his betrayals?

She wasn't sure. But she knew what her heart wanted.

She slipped her arm into his. They walked back down the beach, his hand on the small of her back, and as she leaned into him she felt like maybe, just maybe, something good would come from today.

Kristof held out his hand to bring them to a halt. Back at the cove, Dmitri faced off against Victor, who still guarded the body of Kate's father. Behind Dmitri were the three members of the Synedrion. Aunt Elena stood in the deep sand, crimson robes draped around her, arms crossed. Uncle Stavros's hand rested on a set of talismans pinned to his neat, red military uniform. Dmitri's father—Kristof's uncle Yannis—led a row of Makris guards to surround Dylan and the still-unconscious Melina. A troop of Makris enforcers lined the cliff above them.

"What—" Kate began.

"The Synedrion. Our ruling council, like your Council of Affili-ates. Let me handle this." Kristof let her go and strode toward his relatives. Kate hurried after, her bare feet pulling in the sand.

"—can't let Kate leave here alive. She used primal magic. That's a killing offense." Dmitri addressed his relatives, then turned to point at Kate. His face paled, customary smirk absent.

"She's not the only one who used primal magic." Kristof bowed to his aunt and uncles. "This is a complicated matter. It isn't some-thing that should be decided quickly." *Time. Got to buy enough time to get her away. Both of us, if at all possible.*

Victor grabbed Kate and pulled her away from him. Further from the Synedrion and the enforcers. Good.

"No, we should act now," Dmitri said. "I saw what she can do. Kill her now, or she'll destroy us all."

Uncle Yannis spoke. "Dmitri has a point. He told us what she is—a primal magic caster. And our enemy. Why shouldn't we act now, while she is here, in our territory?"

"Because if you try it she will destroy you, like she killed Papa. Let her go."

"We have our own primal magic caster." Aunt Elena pointed at Melina, still lying unconscious on the sand. "At least, so Dmitri says."

"Yeah, and she used primal magic to kill, too," Victor said. "She's just as guilty of breaking the law as Kate. Come after Kate and we'll go after Melina. Stalemate."

Dmitri smirked. "Not exactly. You're here, now." He pointed to the row of Makris enforcers on the cliff above them. "No matter how much primal magic she uses, one of their spells will cut you in half."

"No." Kate stepped up in front of the Synedrion. She shoved her hand into the pocket where Kristof had seen her put her father's shield talisman earlier. "There's been enough killing today." She looked at his aunt Elena, who drew herself up as if Kate was about to blast her into tiny pieces, then his two uncles. "I was always told there were Rules to this Game of yours. Nulls are off-limits. Normals can't know who we are or that they don't run things." She glanced over at her father's body, and the pain in her eyes caused his heart to ache. "That we don't assassinate each other. It seems like the Rules don't matter anymore. Maybe they should.

"I didn't want this power. Frankly, it sucks. I don't intend to use it. You leave me alone, I'll leave you alone." She turned and walked back to Victor.

"You can't trust—" Dmitri began.

"Shut up. You don't have any say in this," Kristof said.

"Oh and you do? Uncle Nico never officially named you heir."

Kristof rubbed his hand across his eyes. He wasn't going to fall into this trap. *Kate*. He wanted Kate.

"I don't see any reason we should let them go," his uncle Yannis said. "Dmitri is right. Take them out now, while they are weak. That's the only way."

The light that had blossomed within Kristof died. He turned and looked at Kate, a sad smile on his face that said good-bye in all the ways he couldn't say out loud.

"My cousin is an idiot and completely unfit to be heir," he said.

"Me? You're the one who helped the Hamiltons fight Melina."

His aunt drew herself up. "You did what? Explain." Kristof put a hand on his aunt's shoulder and walked down the beach a few steps with her and the rest of the Synedrion. He mixed just enough lies with the right amount of the truth—that Brooke appeared to be working for the Hamiltons made his case even simpler. He slowly won his aunt over, and she nodded her head when he told her he had to stop an out-of-control Melina from killing their father. Then Uncle Stavros was next to agree. Uncle Yannis was a lost cause. But it only took two to make a ruling.

When they returned, his aunt addressed Kate. "You are free to go, provided you agree to the following: No charges will be filed against Melina, should she recover, or any member of the Makris family for the use of primal magic or assassination. No vendettas will be pursued. All discussion of primal magic will be kept private, between our families only. This agreement will be sealed between you, as the presumptive Hamilton heir, and the Makris heir, Kristof."

Kate looked up at him, her eyes reflecting the loss in his. "The Makris heir?"

"Yes," he said.

She let out a breath, and with it, he felt their hopes and dreams evaporate.

His aunt continued. "And you will return the Makris arsenal to us in exchange for your freedom, as your father and Nico Makris agreed before the unfortunate…incident. Now. Before you leave."

"You've got to be kidding," Victor said. "There's no way—"

"Whatever," Kate said. "We don't need those toys, Victor. I just want to take Dad home."

Kristof called over a guard. "Get the Hamilton strike force from lockup. And bring me Kate's possessions. Now."

They walked down the thin strip of beach together one last time.

"I guess you had to make that deal," Kate said. She slipped her hand in his.

"Seemed like the only way to keep you safe."

"I don't need your protection."

"You do here. Unless you want to kill a lot more of my relatives."

She turned to him. "Kristof, I'm sorry. About your father."

"Don't be. Things can change here without him in charge. I can be a different kind of leader."

"Can you?"

"Yes." He looked down the beach at Dmitri gesturing wildly to his uncle Yannis, at Melina unconscious on the sand. At his aunt Elena taking his uncle Stavros aside. Somehow, he'd figure it out. "Take your people and go home."

He leaned down and brushed her forehead with his lips. She squeezed his hand, one tight pulse, then let go. He watched her walk back to the cove where his people had brought the rest of the Hamilton operatives to join Victor, Pearce, and Brooke. Grayson Hamilton appeared on the dock in a flash of green light, wooden crates piled at his feet, waiting for the Makrises to pass him through the security grid.

Kristof slid his hand into his pocket and drew out Kate's pearl buttons. He ran his thumb gently across their smooth surfaces. Then he let them fall, one by one, to the beach and strode through the shifting sands to join his family.

Chapter Thirty-Two

Get used to being the heir," Grayson said as he leaned against the doorway, his thick hair combed back. "Start playing with the tools of power. After the confirmation comes through from the Council, you'll have to sit in on meetings."

Kate sat back in the leather chair behind her father's large walnut desk in his—no, Grayson's—office. She should get up. Sit in the other chair, on the other side of the desk. The Council of Affiliates had confirmed her as a caster yesterday, after Grayson had shown them her test results and told them what happened in Greece. Well, most of it. Confirmation as the Hamilton heir would take longer. Politics, Grayson said. He had been confirmed as Regent, of course—she was way, way too inexperienced to run anything, much less a family, for years.

"Meetings—on top of training, classes, and what else?" she asked.

"We have a lot of work to do, training you, honing your new

powers. Despite everything...everything that happened, the one good thing that came out of this was you. You're a primal magic caster, Kate. Do you know what that means?" His eyes lit up with a fervor she'd never seen in him. Not when riding a horse to a steeple-chase victory or when teaching a student his first spell. "I'm proud of you, sweetheart." He stepped outside and closed the door.

He was proud. Okay, maybe she had single-handedly decimated the Makris family, become the modern world's first, and maybe only—no news on whether Melina would ever wake up—primal magic caster, and helped broker a deal that got her and their people away from the Makrises. But the cost? She ran her hand over her father's cigar box.

The cost was steep.

She picked up the scholarship letter sitting on the desk. Another price to pay. She stared at the words, the sentences, the ultimate confirmation that she could make a career of what she loved. Acting.

Maybe once. Before Brian and the Sanctum. Before Melina. Before Kristof. Now... She crumbled the paper and tossed it into the fireplace, locking that pain in her heart away for good.

She'd be transferring to Harvard—Brian's school, her father's school—splitting her time between the estate's caster academy and Cambridge. Like Victor had said, she needed to learn how to make the powerful people dance to her tune. *Oh joy.*

No room for theatre in her life any longer. No role for Cornell...or anything else from her past.

The next time she'd see Kristof they would most likely be trading kinetic punches. Like every Hamilton and Makris had for the last few hundred years. She drew in a deep breath, but the ache in her chest didn't lessen.

The door opened, and Victor stepped inside.

She shot to her feet. "I—"

"Sit down. It'll be your chair soon enough." Victor grabbed a beer from the fridge under the liquor cabinet—Dad's favorite, a local microbrew. *Asshole*. That was her father's beer—he shouldn't make so free with it, he shouldn't... Tears trickled down her cheek. She wiped them away with the back of her hand.

He pretended not to notice as he took a seat across from her and focused, his eyes going hard then distant as he engaged the room's security spells. "You know, we've never really gotten along. You're spoiled—"

Her head jerked up. "I'm not spoiled."

"Willful, headstrong, rebellious, and won't do a damn thing you're told."

"And you're not my father. You're not even my brother." Her voice caught. "You've no right to talk to me like you are."

"Maybe not. But you're Cooper Hamilton's daughter, and he's the man who took me in and gave me a chance when everyone else wanted to kill me on sight. I will *never* stop owing him." He paused and rubbed at something in his eye, then twisted the cap off the beer bottle and took a drink. "That means I owe you. There's only one problem."

You're an arrogant jerk with delusions of grandeur?

"You don't trust me," Victor said. "Why didn't you tell me about this power of yours? I can't protect you if I don't know the threat." He leaned back in his chair, hand around the beer bottle.

"Victor..." Why hadn't she told him? If she had, if she'd trusted him with the knowledge of how her magic was different, they could have...done what? Well, she wouldn't have gone around him to see Kristof, wouldn't have gotten kidnapped, and Dad would still be alive, sitting in this chair, instead of her.

The hard line of his mouth softened as he gazed at her. Behind him, her mother's portrait hung above the fireplace, reflecting the light from the big picture windows.

She sat back down. "Why did you take me to San Francisco, the night my mom died? Keep me there, not let me call, talk to her, anything?"

He sighed. "All this is about your mother."

"It's about you. You asked me why I don't trust you. So answer the question."

"Kate, she was trying to kill you. The mirror smashing, the paranoid break—it all came together when you came back from school that day. We took a knife away from her right before you hugged her at the front door. She'd figured out a way to get free of the spellcuffs. She was convinced that if she could sacrifice you to the ancient casters, they would leave her alone."

No. That can't be true.

She tried to remember that day, two years ago, when her mother had her last, and worst, paranoid break. The way her mother had run toward her, the hard gleam in her eyes, how she'd clutched at Kate and screamed. And the knife. The knife that had flashed once in her hand before Victor twisted it away.

Victor is telling me the truth. She wasn't trying to escape. She was after me.

"Why didn't you tell me? Every time I yelled at you about keeping me away from her, every time I... Why did you keep it a secret?"

"Because that's what your dad wanted, princess."

Well, shit. She buried her head in her hands.

"Can we start fresh?" She raised her head. "Pretend we're meeting for the first time today and start trusting each other?"

"Let's begin with this." He tossed Brian's journal on the desk, along with her grandfather's watch.

She sighed and told him about finding the journal and the watch in the catalpa grove. About using primal magic for the first time, no idea what she was doing, to extract the journal and watch from their hiding place. Combing through the journal, trying to figure out why Brian would hide a book filled with pointless facts behind a magical ward spell.

"He wouldn't hide something irrelevant." Victor picked up the journal and flipped through it. His eyes had gone soft, unfocused, as if he was using his magesight. "The book's spell-coded."

"What?"

"Someone encrypted it using a cipher spell. The spell makes the writing look like a bunch of meaningless crap, unless you have the original cipher spell. Or the key."

"Key? What would..." Her gaze fell on the watch. It couldn't be that simple, could it? She picked it up. "Is this it? I found it in the cache along with the journal."

"Stupid to hide both in the same place. Maybe he was in a hurry."

"Or he knew I was the only person who'd find anything in the catalpa grove, and he wanted me to find the journal and the key to decode it."

Victor raised an eyebrow. "You like your answers all wrapped up in little packages, don't you, princess?" He took the watch from her. "Let's see what happens when we put it alongside..." As he placed the watch directly on top of the first page of the journal it lit up with a bright-green glow. "Whoa. I'd say we found the key. Want to see what Brian wrote?"

"Yes."

"What do you think you're going to find in there?" he asked.

"The name of the person who sent Brian after the stone."

"Haven't you figured that out yet?"

She'd suspected some things when Dylan had told her his theories, when Melina had confirmed them, when she'd finally understood how to deal with primal magic. An understanding she gained from the book on Brian's bedside table. A book only one person would have given him.

"I think so," she said. "But the journal should confirm it."

He set the watch on the desk. "So let's decode it. You need to put up a shield. I wouldn't put it past Brian to booby-trap his precious tell-all."

She touched her father's cufflinks, still in her pocket, and sent the quick command for shield. A strong blue glow sprang up around her. Victor raised his own shield.

She watched as Victor sent a tiny purple tendril of energy into the journal. It scanned the pages of the book, first slowly, then faster until it spun on the desk like a firecracker about to burst. The watch glowed green and began to shake, moving closer and closer to the book. When they met, the glow flared in brilliance, then went dark.

"No bang," Kate said.

"Nope. Maybe Brian really did want you to find it."

Kate turned off the shield, picked up the journal, and opened to the first page. The gibberish about the tests Brian had aced and the girls he'd dated was gone. In its place was an account of the meeting where Grayson had sat Brian down and set about convincing him that becoming the world's first primal magic caster would be a great and wonderful thing.

Kate read, and read more, then handed the journal to Victor. As he paged through the book in the dying light of the summer sun, she took the cufflinks out and spun one on the table.

Then she leaned back and planned her first move.

Acknowledgements

I labored over this novel for a very long time, and many people have extended to me their time, expertise, support, and guidance. If you enjoyed this book, it is in a large part thanks to them. Any mistakes made are mine alone.

Many people deserve my thanks and acknowledgment, and given that I am quite scatterbrained at times, I am sure I will inadvertently leave someone off my list who was tremendously important to this book. If so, I humbly apologize and thank you for your assistance.

My editors—Mark Clements and Danielle Poiesz—gave me oodles and oodles of help making sure that my plot made sense, my characters were compelling, my facts were straight, and my grammar and spelling were top-notch.

I received invaluable help and support from my fellow writers while working on this book. Some critiqued individual chapters, some read the entire book and let me know what they thought, some gave me helpful advice on the industry, some offered a shoulder to cry on and a friend with whom to celebrate. I want to especially acknowledge the Gorilla Writers (Scott Barbour, Suad Campbell, Charlie Daly, Aron Diaz, Melanie Hooks, Rick Landin, Doug Lathrop, John Mullen, Cris Powell, Ely Rareshide, Kathy Paulek, and Indy Quillen), the Freedom Writers (Aron, Melanie, Doug, Cris, Ely, and Laura Perkins), and the Flying Pink Elephant Society (Marie Andreas, Shoshana Brown, Cassi Carver, Melissa Cutler, Rachael Davila, Lisa Kessler, Georgie Lee, and Tami Vahalik). I also want to give a shout-out to friends and family—John Rogers, Barbara Vivian Rogers, Sharon Arkin, Margaret Bloodgood, Stuart Dervish, Cat Gengler, Sue Glueck, Bree Kauzlaurich, and Cindy Leech—who read my book and gave me an unfiltered reader reaction.

I am fortunate to belong to several communities of writers. Each one was unstinting with their help and advice. My colleagues at the San Diego Chapter of the Romance Writers of America provide a supportive environment for learning, networking, connecting with publishing professionals, and sharing my triumphs and disappointments. The staff and attendees of the Southern California Writers Conference gave me editorial help, critiques, valuable information on the business, and endless camaraderie. My friends from Martha Beck's Writers' Retreat and San Diego Writers Ink have encouraged and supported me.

My writing teachers—Nancy Holder, Orson Scott Card, Stephen Potts, Mark Clements, and Judy Reeves—were instrumental in teaching me the nuts and bolts of the craft of writing. My work would be infinitely poorer without their lessons and advice.

Kim and Chris from A Butler's Manor B&B in Southampton,

NY graciously provided both hospitality and useful local info on my research trip to the Hamptons.

Finally, my family has supported me and sustained me when stinging rejections and creative frustrations made me want to pound my head against the wall until the gremlins of disappointment and despair flew out my ears. This book would not have been written, much less published, without the unfailing support of my husband, John Rogers. He guided me, comforted me, consoled me, and encouraged me every time I needed his love and friendship. I love you more than I could express in an acknowledgments section, or for that matter, if I had all the words and all the pages in the world.

ABOUT THE AUTHOR

Janet Tait has loved writing for as long as she can remember but tried IT administration, website development, market research, and product management before surrendering to her inevitable destiny. She lives in San Diego, California with her husband and, in her spare time, enjoys haunting the halls of comic and science fiction conventions, playing old-timey tabletop role-playing games with her friends, and binge-watching British TV shows on Netflix. You can reach her at www.janettait.com or via email at janet@janettait.com.

Dear Reader:

I hope you enjoyed *Cast into Darkness*. I am hard at work on the next book in the series. If you'd like to be notified when it comes out, get the see the cover before it is released, and find out about my other books, you can subscribe to my monthly newsletter at http://www.janettait.com/newsletter-signup.

If you liked this book, please consider leaving a review where you purchased it. I welcome your honest feedback.

In gratitude,
Janet Tait